AURORA TERMINUS

S.E. Fanetti

Aurora Terminus © 2017 S.E. Fanetti
All rights reserved

ISBN-13: 978-1986589116
ISBN-10: 1986589110

The song Helen sings at the beginning of Chapter Twenty-Five is "The Leaving of Liverpool," a traditional English folk song.

For Jim, who finally read one of my stories.

And who thus saved Buddy.

ilyf

AUTHOR'S NOTE

In July 2012, a huge solar flare—two massive explosions of plasma from the sun's surface—barely missed a collision with Earth.

The scientific name for such an explosion is a "coronal mass ejection," or CME. Events like these happen fairly often; they are the cause of the Northern Lights (aurora borealis) in the Northern Hemisphere and the Southern Lights (aurora australis) in the Southern Hemisphere. Normally, the power of these eruptions causes nothing more than a lovely spectrum of dancing color in the night sky near the Earth's poles.

But the solar storm in July 2012 was the most powerful in at least 150 years. Had those CMEs hit Earth's atmosphere, rather than being a near miss, they would have caused a global cataclysm, likely knocking us instantly back to the 18th century, in terms of technology. For an excellent discussion of the implications if the 2012 storm had hit Earth, see:

https://science.nasa.gov/science-news/science-at-nasa/2014/23jul_superstorm/

Reading about this near-miss storm *two years later*, when it was first publicized (note the date on the linked article), I found myself transfixed by the idea of something so lovely—we dwellers on the fat part of Earth book expensive vacations to Scandinavia specifically to see the Northern Lights in their full glory — destroying the modern world in a blink, and doing it simply by unplugging us. Reading that the 2012 storm was so powerful because the two flares on that night traveled a path cleared by a smaller flare a few days earlier, I took a bit of creative license and imagined what would have happened if the storm had been even bigger, if even more CMEs had occurred in succession, hurtling toward Earth in the same chute, creating a storm long enough to encompass the entire planet.

This is the premise of the cataclysm that ends the modern world in the story you're about to read: a beautiful, silent, natural, cosmic event.

Aurora Terminus.

Aurora Australis: The Southern Lights

Aurora Borealis: The Northern Lights

Aurora Terminus: The Lights at the End

Book One: Homesteader

Yet if anyone believes that the earth rotates,
surely he will hold that its motion is natural, not violent.

~Nicolaus Copernicus

One

The sun was bright and the air was warm, with just a light waft of cool in the breeze, like a memory of the winter not long past. Already, while the last of the snow still stretched thin fingers to cling to the ground, the wide field had gone green with soft new growth, and the air swelled fat with the rich smells of tender shoots and damp, warming earth. The returning birds sang to each other, lifting occasionally into dancing sweeps through the air before settling in the tops of the trees.

A lone doe raised her sleek head and went still, but for the alert twitching of her ears. Perched in a tree some distance away, the woman looked down at her dog, waiting on a damp drift of old needles at the base, who'd made the noise—just a snap of her jaws, probably at a flitting insect, but enough to alert the doe. Now the dog was quiet, and after a few more seconds of reassuring stillness in the spring morning, the doe dipped her head and returned to her breakfast, nibbling daintily at the fresh leaves of a bush.

The woman in the tree eased her body carefully, changing her seat so that she could draw her bow. She hadn't meant to shoot from the tree; she'd only climbed to get a good view of this field, but the doe was there, still winter-thin and alone, with no fawn to orphan, so she had to take this shot.

She'd learned over the years to hunt in the early morning, when the world was quiet and the animals were calm, and when she'd have the light of the whole day to butcher her kill and hang the meat and hide in her smokehouse.

Managing to move without alerting the doe again, once she felt stable enough on the thick bough of the ancient but dwindling fir, the woman pulled an arrow from her quiver — slowly, carefully, silently — and nocked it, then drew. A head shot was best, so the woman waited in readiness until the doe raised her head again, chewing.

The loosed arrow struck the doe just below her ear, and she fell into the grass with barely a sound. The dog, knowing her duty, leapt forward and ran to the kill. She stood over it as the woman worked her way back to the ground.

There had been a time, in a world growing thin in the woman's memory, when she would never have been able to climb a tree, much less shoot an arrow true. But that world was dead, and that woman was gone. This woman had made her body learn the things it needed to learn, do the things it needed to do. This woman lived in this world. Alone.

Landing softly in a crouch on the ground, the woman stood and slung her bow over her back. She crossed the field to her kill, and to her dog who watched over it.

"Good girl, Fee. Okay," she said, and the dog relaxed and trotted over to meet her, wagging her long, flagged black tail. The woman ruffled Fiona's wide head and, with a particular wave of her hand, released the dog to do dog things. Tail wagging, Fiona dropped her nose to the ground and went exploring.

The woman watched after her, smiling, and then, with a quick but careful scan of the field and a lingering look along the tree line, she set her bow aside, pulled three blades from the holster on her thigh, and got on with the work of dressing her kill.

Field dressing an animal was another thing she'd had to learn in this world—and butchering it and smoking it as well. The woman she'd been before had fed herself at fast-food restaurants or with microwave meals. But microwaves and restaurants were of the past, and the woman understood food in a new way now. It was nothing to take for granted. A meal was precious. Now, she took life from lives she'd taken, or lives she'd grown, and she cherished the relationship as well as the sustenance.

Before she started, the woman eased the arrow out of the doe's body and set it beside her bow. She was glad of the clean, quick kill, without suffering or fear. The death had been gentle, and the meat would be savory and would last for weeks. She stroked the warm body—such a beautiful animal. In this world, beauty abounded in every direction. The end had come, but quietly, even gracefully.

People had brought about the death and horror and destruction at the end of the world. Nature had simply carried on—and grown stronger.

When she closed her eyes, both hands on the soft shoulder of the doe, she didn't pray. As far as the woman knew or cared, God, any god, had died with the world before. She simply took a moment and felt gratitude for the life she'd claimed and how it would sustain her own. It reminded her that she had no special place in this world, was due no particular consideration.

Rolling the doe to her back, the woman picked up her guthook and opened the belly, starting low and cutting shallow, to avoid opening the stomach. Cutting all the way to the sternum, she then set the hook aside and emptied the abdominal cavity. She'd kept the stomach intact, so the smell was no more unpleasant than any smell of blood—sharp, metallic, but not foul. Still, Fiona caught the scent, and turned toward the woman, then sniffed her way close, crouching low, showing respect. To the dog, the woman was the pack alpha, and she hoped her turn for meat would come.

She worked carefully, but also quickly, knowing that Fiona might not be the only creature drawn to the bloodscent. Since the old world had died, bountiful wildlife had returned, and the woman understood that she was nothing more than a link in the food chain now.

After removing the stomach and entrails, the woman took a heavy knife and cut through the doe's sternum, making the way clear to take the heart and lungs. Then she used thick snips to cut through the pelvis and remove the bladder and remaining viscera.

When the doe was dressed, the woman gathered up the entrails and carried them away from the kill site, leaving an offering to the omnivorous and carnivorous creatures with whom she shared this mountain.

Hooking her arms under the doe's forelegs, she hoisted the body and stood, embracing the animal, as the rest of the blood drained out. Then she laid the carcass on the ground, gathered up her tools, hooked her bow across her lower back, and heaved the animal over her shoulders. The dressed doe weighed maybe a hundred pounds, and the hike back to her homestead was just more than two miles. There had been a time when such a trek would have been far beyond her, but now the woman was strong.

Pursing her lips and making a kissing sound—whistling was one thing she hadn't learned in this new world or in the old one—she called Fiona to her.

By the time the woman had the venison she meant to preserve salted and hanging in the smokehouse with the hide she would tan, the beautiful morning had aged into a beautiful evening. A glow rose up on the near horizon, courtesy of the pinking sun glinting off the lake nearby. A few early-rising spring peepers peeped at the shore, warming up for their evening chorus. The breeze's morning kiss of chill came back for an evening caress, stirring the woman's hair, which had sagged from its braid over the course of the day. Her hands still bloody, she used her wrist to push the tickling strands back and felt the smear of blood she left across her cheek.

No matter; she would wash after her meal, heating water while she fried her venison over open fire.

"We get tenderloin tonight, Fee. Sound good?"

Fiona had lain outside the smokehouse, her ears and eyes alert; now, she rose to her paws, swinging her tail happily back and forth. The woman crouched at her dog's side and gave her a hug. Fiona licked the blood from her face.

The woman closed up the smokehouse and headed to the garden, and the dog followed, as ever. She'd only sown the garden a few days earlier, but she walked through the rows, while Fiona sat on her haunches outside the rough fence, and did a quick check for signs of sprouts. Then, with Fiona as her shadow, the woman finished her evening chores: she turned over the compost, checked on her worms, closed up the chickens.

"Okay, let's get cookin'." As the woman and her dog turned back to the cabin, the breeze kicked up a stronger gust, and carried on it a scent that stopped Fiona in her tracks. The dog lifted her big head and took a deep breath.

The woman tried to scent the air as well, but her human nose was no match. All she smelled was spring evening near a mountain lake — and blood and smoke and salt. But she gave the dog her full attention. More than once, Fiona had alerted to trouble, and more than once, that alert had saved the woman this life she had built after the end of the world.

Her heart sped up, but only to ready her body for fight. Fear no longer ruled the woman. She'd experienced the depth of horror man and nature could visit upon her, and she knew what she could survive, and how she could survive it. She knew the lengths she would go to protect the life she'd made.

She still wore her holster of knives. Now, she pulled the heavy blade and gripped it. She had guns, too; in her years on the mountain, she'd foraged well, for all sorts of supplies to make a life alone, but she had learned early that guns were loud and could draw even more trouble. She preferred a bow for range and a blade when danger was close. She preferred stealth.

Fiona walked forward, her body tense, her attention focused on the path to the lake.

Casting a glance at the cabin, the woman wondered if she should go in for her axe. A Viking axe. Once, that axe had been a decorative piece, purchased at a Renaissance Faire, in a world that had had time for such things. But it was an authentic piece, made in the true style of the Vikings, its sharp blade Damascus steel. In this world, it had become a weapon.

Then Fiona's tail began to wag again, and the woman relaxed. Another minute later, she heard a gruff rumble she knew well, and a large, shaggy, dripping-wet black bear lumbered over the rise. Shrek. Fiona barked a greeting and bolted forward, meeting the bear halfway to the cabin. The large dog leapt at the larger bear, and they both rolled over, doing the wrestling routine that was their friendly hug.

Smiling now, the woman sheathed her knife and went into the cabin. She'd make dinner for three tonight.

"Here. Last bits."

The woman tossed the final hunks of cooked venison at the bear and the dog. Fiona caught hers, but Shrek missed, and his landed on the ground between his monstrous paws. Fiona tried to snag it before he could, but he knocked her ass-over-teakettle, with a grunt and a swing of a paw, and snapped the meat up.

Ass over teakettle. What a strange phrase. A favorite of her grandmother's, in the world before. The woman paused to wonder how it had come into being.

Fiona got up and shook off whatever pains Shrek had caused her. When she went back to him, he gave her a rough snuffle, making sure she was okay. She licked his snout. Then they both sat on their haunches and stared at the woman.

She laughed and stood up from her chair beside the fire pit, in the little yard behind the cabin. "I told you, that was it. Dinner's over. Unless you want to help me wash up, why don't you go play."

Shrek rose up on his haunches and paddled his forepaws before him. He flapped his lips.

"Nope." She waved her hand side to side, and the bear put his paws down. "Sorry, bud. All done. Go play, you two." She made the sign they both understood.

The animal friends got up and ambled off together. The woman knew they wouldn't go far. Fiona never left sight of the homestead unless the woman was with her, and Shrek never tried to lead her away.

That night, after Shrek had gone off to his sleeping place, wherever that was, and Fiona was settled on her pad beside the woman's bed, after the woman had washed in fire-heated water and put on fresh clothes, she sat in her cabin, in an upholstered chair that had once been her father's and, by the low, quietly hissing light of a Coleman kerosene lantern, scanned through her diaries, looking for the memory she wanted.

When she'd first come to the mountain, she'd been cavalier about her note-taking, writing pages a day, in the large, round handwriting that had been hers in the world before. She'd started out as if she'd had a correspondent, writing her entries like letters to a friend, signing her name to every one. But after the first year, she'd seen how quickly she was going through writing supplies, and by then, she'd foraged enough to understand how short her range was for a day's travel and to realize that someday there would be nothing left but what she could grow and craft. Someday, there would be no more paper, no more ink.

After that, she made her handwriting as small as she could and only took brief notes of each day's main events, and, when she had a memory she wanted to keep, she wrote only its skeleton, trusting her mind to be able to conjure it when prompted.

And she never signed her name now. Her name had become alien to her, disconnected from her self-awareness, a dead thing from a dead world.

She hadn't heard it spoken in five years.

Living all this time alone, with only her dog, and a bear, and her own thoughts, the woman feared losing her reason the same way she'd lost her name. Having done research in the world before about the psychology of isolation, she'd known to expect it, and to guard against it. She'd begun right away, keeping notes of her new life and writing down memories of her old to relive. But time worked its way, regardless, and the past had become another woman's life.

Still, of all the things she'd studied in the world before, all the ways that study had helped her in this world, the woman thought that single idea—to keep writing, to keep remembering—had been the best. She was no longer the woman she'd been, she barely felt that past as her own, but she was still human, and she was still rational, despite everything.

Despite what lay inside the earth at the bottom of the ravine.

At first, when she'd written those long, round letters, she'd kept track of the date as well, but over the years, she'd had occasions of lost time, and she could only make educated guesses now, based on the weather and the position of the sun, about the time of year.

In her current journal, she made her skeletal, microscopic notes for this day, fitting everything into two lines on the page: *Sunny, clear. Temp. ~70F. Took a doe, good kill. Good meat in smoker, good hide. No sprouts yet in garden. Chickens healthy, all 5 laid. Food: 2 eggs. Last of rabbit stew. Venison steak, fried. Bread. Green beans. Canned stores low but okay for now. Shrek was here.*

Finished with her notes, she picked up the old book and found the passage she'd sought earlier, written in the expansive narrative and space-and-ink-wasting handwriting of her previous self.

Wednesday, June 8th

3 months and 4 days since the end.

Someday, maybe I won't care anymore what the date is. Maybe calendars will be irrelevant someday. Maybe they already are. As the weeks stack up, it looks like everything I thought would be, is. This truly is the end of the world.

So far, no one has come this far up the mountain. I hiked down far yesterday – too far, and had to stay in one of the empty houses overnight. I didn't get much sleep, but not because I was afraid someone would hurt me. The opposite, actually – there was nobody around at all. I made it all the way down to Hatterville, that weird little town Dad always called Hippieville, but it was totally empty. I know for a fact that there were a lot of people there who lived off the grid, and they should have been fine, like me, but there was nobody.

There weren't even many bodies – they weren't piled up in the gutters like in Pinon Valley, for sure. There was a decomposing man in the back room of the organic market, and there was a couple in one of the houses with bullet holes in their heads. A murder-suicide, or a suicide pact, something like that. Can't be sure – no weapons around – so maybe somebody just up and killed them. They weren't badly decomposed yet. They smelled, but they'd been dead maybe a week only. Otherwise, the town was totally deserted. Like someone had rounded everybody up.

That scared me for a while, and I walked around for an hour with my axe cocked, until my shoulders were killing me. I really need to get stronger. But there wasn't anybody around. Whoever killed that couple, or at least took the gun that killed them, was gone, with the whole rest of the town. It wigged me out.

The town was pretty picked over, but I made a good haul, I think. Nobody ever takes books, and that's just stupid. At the bookstore, I found a book on curing meat. It even has instructions for building a smokehouse, though I don't know if I'm up to that kind of work. I guess I'd have to cut the wood *myself. Could I cut down a whole tree? And turn it into boards? I don't know. But I also found a little book on how to dress and butcher large game. (And learned that pulling out all its organs is called "dressing" it, and now Thanksgiving dinners and turkey dressing retroactively feel extremely weird to me. Not that I'll ever have another Thanksgiving dinner.)*

Anyway, found some very helpful books, and some novels that look good – all paperbacks, hallelujah – and a stack of blank journal books – Moleskines! – and boxes of pens. Plus a few canned goods and seasonings. Not a bad haul, though I wish I'd had something more than a couple of packs to carry things back up with. It's too long a hike for one day, especially on the way back up. I was useless when I got back tonight. I don't know when or if I'll get back there, and I left a lot of good stuff behind.

But the best part!! When I got home, OMG!! There was a little bear cub, just the tiniest little guy, on the front steps, trying to get into the cabin. I could hear Fiona on the other side of the door, trying to get out. At first I was scared, expecting a very angry mama bear to come charging at me, but it was almost dark, and he was crying so pathetically, and I didn't know what to do.

What I did was probably super stupid, but he's just such a baby I couldn't help it. It turned out okay when I found Fiona, right? Okay, yeah, she's a puppy, so apples and oranges and all that. But she's almost as big as a bear. No lie, young as she is, she's as big as the cub. Who I'm calling Shrek because obviously. They're sleeping together on her pad, side by side, nose to nose, and it's so cute I could die. I think I have a pet bear cub. Unless his mama shows up. Then I just hope she doesn't tear the wall off the cabin and kill me. But if he's an orphan, he's welcome to join this little orphan pack.

I hope he's weaned. I don't know how I'm going to give him milk if that's what he needs. Milk is the one problem I haven't figured out. Well, the one problem I know of so far. Everything else, I'm learning. Hell, maybe I'm even going to be able to smoke my own meat. Which would be great because I am already very sick of fish.

It's only been a few months, but being constantly alone is harder than I expected, even with all the stuff I read about it before. Lately, my mind gets wonky sometimes. I hoped that things would settle down after the panic, and the world would find its feet again, but I don't think that happened. Maybe it never will. Maybe I'm going to be up on this mountain alone until I die. That scares the hell out of me.

In these last couple of weeks, finding Fiona and now Shrek, it feels like the universe is trying to give me a family. That makes me a little less scared.

Okay. If I don't get eaten by an angry mama bear tonight, I'll write more tomorrow.

Diana Wolf
Formerly of Los Gatos, California.

Two

Although she'd long ago lost track of days of the week, and even months of the year, and although all the clocks had stopped, the woman still kept ways of time that mattered in this life. She had a sundial in the garden—it had only been a decorative thing, something her mother had picked up on a whim at Target, but it did its job well enough, and the woman could read it well enough to keep a sense of how long each time of daylight was, when days lengthened and when they grew shorter. She followed the night sky, too, and could judge the progress of the seasons well enough that way. So she'd learned to tell a freak winter thaw from true spring and to make a good guess about when an early frost might wreak havoc on her squashes before she could harvest them.

She'd become a pioneer woman, she supposed. Pioneering in reverse, going back in history to the days before California was a state. Staking a claim on the past.

Of all the ways she managed to track the progress of time, the most important way was her work. She was diligent in keeping to a specific cycle of jobs, making a week of days that made sense to her. In the spring, summer, and autumn, they were Forage Day, Clean Day, Hunt Day, Garden Day, Fish Day, Protect Day, when she'd check her fences and the weapons she had stashed around the perimeter, and Rest Day. Each day included more than simply the task she'd named it for—there was always some cleaning to do, always some light gardening—but the bulk of the day was spent on the work of its name.

In the late autumn and winter, when the lake froze and the snow eventually piled up to the roof of the cabin, she had different days: Preserve Day, Shovel Day, Wood Day, Clean Day, Protect Day. She got two Rest Days in winter. But in bad storm times, every day was Shovel Day.

Little upset her as much as falling out of that cycle. It had only happened a few times—among them, when she'd slipped off a wet rock at the lake and had badly sprained her ankle, and when she'd gotten sick with what she thought had probably been pneumonia—but when she missed a day, or more, she had trouble finding the tempo of her life again. It was as if Wednesday had fallen out of the calendar. Or a whole weekend. How would you know what to do if the day after Friday was suddenly Monday?

In the summer, her favorite work day was Fish Day. She didn't especially like fish — she hadn't liked it that much in the world before, and she'd quickly had her fill of it when she'd started this life, before she'd become adept at the bow or had learned how to butcher and preserve meat.

She didn't enjoy *eating* fish, but she loved *catching* them. Sitting on the lakeshore, among the reeds and grasses, with butterflies and dragonflies fluttering and flitting about, with crickets scratching their legs and water striders making tiny circles over the surface of the water, the fish rising up and leaving bubbles behind — all of it was a joy.

Often, Shrek came to the lake on Fish Day. He caught his own, of course, but he was a lazy, entitled slob, too, and if he could get fish tossed to him, he'd sit on the shore with his mouth open and catch them that way.

On this day, he'd dropped in only for a quick visit and a snack, then ambled off again to do bear things. Fiona sat forlornly and watched him go, letting loose a frustrated whine.

The woman called her over for a hug. "Sorry, baby girl. I guess it's you and me today."

Fiona sighed and drooped down to lie beside her on the grass on the shore of the little lake.

She was a huge dog. Not bear size, though she'd been cub size as a puppy, but bigger than any other dog the woman had known. The woman had found a dog encyclopedia in a house once. It had been big and hardbound, too heavy to take with her, but she'd flipped through it. She thought Fiona was a Newfoundland dog, or something like it. Her black and white coat was long and dense, and she drooled constantly. She was gentle with the woman, and with Shrek and even the chickens, but she was ferociously protective and wary when they left the homestead. The woman felt safe with her dog at her side. She loved, and she felt loved. She felt not alone.

The book had said that Newfoundlands had an average life span of eight years. Fiona was five years old, as old as this world. Though the dog was strong and sleek and lively, the woman felt the time passing whenever she thought of their bond, and she worried.

Those weren't thoughts she wanted to think right now, so the woman shunted them aside. She petted her dog and enjoyed her peaceful moment beside the lake.

It was barely a lake. Compared to the enormous crater that had made Lake Tahoe below, this was just a large puddle tucked into the mountain. But there was no one here but her and her dog, no dock but her own, no visible house but hers. Her lake, with no reminders that there had ever been other people in the world. She could set her rod and lay back among the reeds and close her eyes, feel the warm sun on her face and know this life, lonely as it was, was right.

Fish Day was one of the few times she felt consumed by recollections of the life she'd had before, and one of the only times those recollections weren't dangerous or disorienting. Here, she could remember her family, especially her father, and what this place had been in the world before.

Her father had taught her to fish when she was five years old and still an only child. In his floppy canvas hat with the orange band, his plain white t-shirt and his saggy-bottomed plaid shorts, his raggedy Keds sneakers, he'd stood beside her and shown her how to hold her first rod, a straight bamboo pole, how to dangle the bobber and make the nightcrawler dance under the surface, how to hook the fish when it took the bait.

The first time she'd pulled a fish—a young catfish, not eight inches long, but huge to her little hands—her father had cheered and hugged her and taken photos. She'd run back to the cabin with her rod, dangling the fish, to show her mother and grandparents, and they'd all cheered, too.

She'd wanted to keep it for a pet. She'd named it Lisa.

That was how she'd learned that catching fish was about killing them and eating them. She'd cried and begged her dad to save Lisa. He'd hugged her and promised to do everything he could.

He'd been a doctor, so she'd known he'd save Lisa.

For years, she'd believed he had. After she was grown, sitting around a Thanksgiving table, telling family stories at the end of a couple of bottles of Prosecco, her mother had let his secret out: he'd taken Lisa back to the lake and swished her around for ten minutes, trying to get the water through her lungs. But she'd been out of the lake for ten minutes before that, and it was hopeless. He'd finally buried her in the soft muck of the lakebed and set a rock on the spot to keep her from coming back up. Her mother had laughed about watching him, on his hands and knees in the lake, trying to raise the dead.

At first, the woman had been a little crushed, even as an adult who'd known that the fish could not possibly have lived. Her father had been her hero that day. But then, she'd seen that he still was. He'd gotten down on his hands and knees and tried to raise the dead for her. Because he hadn't wanted her to be sad.

Her parents had been in Europe on the day the world ended, visiting her sister. The woman had no idea if they lived. She never would know.

Any other place but this lake, any other day but Fish Day, the woman could never seek out these memories and relive them so completely. This was the only place they came so vividly, and the only place they were safe to come. She wrote them down when they came, to guard against the day when they would no longer be in her mind to be remembered.

The woman sighed, and she heard the rustle of reeds as Fiona came to her and stretched out at her side with a groan. She lifted her hand, and her dog set her head on her belly. They lay together, the woman letting memories have her while her fingers combed through her dog's long, soft fur. She thought she would write the story of Lisa down in her journal before bed.

Fiona loved Fish Day, too. She wasn't interested in fish at all, not to eat or catch or smell. But she adored the water, and she knew, if she sat quietly until the woman's keeper was full, she could swim. Often, the woman would strip and swim as well. The cold water felt sharp enough to slice her skin, but once that first brace of shock had passed, she liked the way the cold made every inch of her body feel alive.

She liked the way the water felt between her legs, too, the cold so heavy and thick it was like a touch. One that was not her own.

The little bell on her rod jingled, and she sat up. The line quivered tautly, so she picked up the rod and gave it a little play, let the fish get comfortable as it nibbled its meal. When she felt fight in the line, she gave the rod the light twitch that would set the hook and reeled it in.

A decent-size catfish. The woman liked catfish even less than she liked trout or bass, so she glanced into her creel, where four good fish already swam. She unhooked this one and tossed it back.

"You want to swim, Fee?"

The dog's tail wagged with excitement.

"Okay, go on." With a wave of her hand she ushered Fiona to the water. After she gathered up her gear, she stripped and went in as well, jumping in from the dock, where she knew it was deep enough to go under.

The water was just as frigid as she'd expected, and every cell in her body clenched at first, but then there was that liberating rush of adrenaline, and she broke the surface with a gasp. Fiona barked happily and paddled over, snapping at the splashes of water she made as she swam.

They swam and splashed and played for a while, then Fiona took off after a duck farther along the shore, and the woman turned onto her back and floated, letting the water move her, feeling her hair swirl around her head like a cloud. With her ears just under the surface, the world shrank to the dimensions of her own body. One of her favorite things in this world was the moment of peace she allowed herself when she swam. Weightless. Unburdened. Not lost in a vast, empty world.

But the slosh of the water against her got suddenly more violent, and the woman raised her head. Fiona was swimming fiercely for the farther shore, cutting at a slant across the lake, putting herself between the woman and the land. Over the sound of her swimming, the woman could hear the dog's growl, steady and threatening.

As Fiona reached land and climbed out of the water, the woman scanned the shoreline, trying to see what had the dog in guard mode. She saw nothing—no, there it was. A split in the tall grass, atop a low hill on that side: a mountain lion.

Naked in the lake, the woman eased as slowly as she could to water she could stand in, then went perfectly still.

These mountains were full of all kinds of wildlife: lions, bears, and even wolves jostling for position at the top of the heap. But both bears and lions, especially lions, preferred solitary lives, and steered clear of commotion. Lions preferred night hunts. She and Fiona had been playing loudly in broad daylight.

Maybe the lion had read their play as distress. Maybe it thought it would find an easy meal.

If they put the lake between them and the lion and ran like hell, they could get back to the cabin. But Fiona had gone *toward* the beast. Aggressively. Protectively.

"Fiona," she called, in a voice as calm as she could muster. "Come, girl."

The lion's head, its eyes, followed Fiona as the dog ignored the woman's command and stalked a few steps closer to the hill, her hackles raised like spikes, and her snout folded into a ferocious snarl. That steady, menacing growl hadn't stopped rumbling in her chest.

"Fiona!" The woman tried again, a little louder, but still without allowing distress into her tone. Her clothes, and her machete, were behind her; her dog and the mountain lion were before her. For a moment, she felt paralyzed, pulled in both directions. Then the lion stood up and made its sharp roar.

Fiona barked and snarled, setting her front paws. If the lion pounced, she was ready to do the same and meet the cat in midair.

But she was just a dog. No matter how big or strong, how capable, she wasn't a predator. She was a pet.

The woman went forward, to her dog.

Before she could get to the shore, the lion moved. It didn't pounce; it ran down the rise, and Fiona charged forward, snarling like a hound of hell, making sounds the woman had never heard her make before.

They met, and Fiona didn't flinch. She went right at the lion, setting her teeth into its neck. It roared again and batted her off, sending her flying. She landed and leapt up, charging again at the lion, though the white fur of her chest and leg was turning red already.

"Fee, no!" the woman shouted, coming up onto the shore, and the lion turned toward her.

Fiona vaulted forward and landed on the lion's back, biting down on the back of its neck. It screamed and tried to shake her loose, but she had her jaws locked.

The woman picked up a large rock at her feet. There was no way she could throw it and be sure not to hit her dog, so she ran up, holding the rock in both hands, and leapt into the fray, slamming her impromptu bludgeon on the lion's head. It shrieked again and caught Fiona with one of its — it was a female — talon-tipped paws.

Fiona yelped and fell back, and the woman raised her rock again, standing before a mountain lion, her bare skin still dripping icy lake water. She felt rivulets running from her hair down her spine.

The lion stared at her, its amber eyes wide, its mouth open. Blood streamed from its neck and back.

Letting instinct take over, the woman screamed and shook the rock over her head, and the lion spun and loped away.

It stopped at the tree line and looked back, as though it couldn't believe it had lost the fight, then gave up and ran into the woods.

Throwing the rock away, the woman ran to her dog. Fiona had struggled to her feet, but she rocked back and forth, whining, favoring her front leg, where blood from a long gash ran wet and red.

"You dumb broad," the woman cried. "You could have died, you dope!" She crouched low and pushed her head under Fiona's belly, lifting the big dog over her shoulders.

Abandoning her full creel, her clothes, her blade, and her fishing gear, the woman carried her wounded protector back to the cabin.

Fiona whimpered and licked the woman's hand, as she'd done with every pass of the needle through her skin.

The wound was about five inches long, but almost surgically straight. The woman had used a knife to shave fur away and then cleaned the wound and the area around it with rubbing alcohol. They'd run out of hydrogen peroxide and Betadine months ago and hadn't found more, and it had been a long time since there'd been antibiotics around. Alcohol was as good as it got, and someday, that would be gone, too.

"Sorry, baby girl. I have to do this. If you're brave and tough enough to scare off a mountain lion, I think you can suck it up for a few stitches." She pulled the needle through and tied off a stitch. "One more should do it. Then you can have one of the biscuits with some rhubarb jam. And maybe one of the bones from the last deer. How's that sound?"

Again, Fiona whimpered and licked her hand—long, slow licks, each one like a plea for mercy. But she didn't move otherwise. She let the woman hurt her over and over, closing up the wound, and then, when the last stitch was done, she scooted around so she could set her head in the woman's lap.

The woman bent over and laid her head on the dog's. "Thank you, baby girl. You saved me today. But if that lion had killed you, that would kill me, too, I think. We have to be more careful. It looks like we have a cranky new neighbor this summer. So be careful. Okay?"

Now that they were safe, and Fiona was cared for, now that the danger was behind them, the woman indulged herself with a moment of delayed fear and anguish. She buried her face in her dog's fur and cried.

Three

The woman crept around the full perimeter of the house, looking for signs that anyone was around. When everything seemed quiet, she patted her thigh quietly, calling Fiona right to heel, and eased up the steps to the back deck. Her axe at the ready, she slid open the glass door and stepped into a vast, stone-floored room.

This wasn't her first time in this house; it was one of her favorites. By now, she had a good sense of what all of the houses in this neighborhood offered—and the problems they presented. She knew where the bodies lay, and she preferred to avoid those places as much as she could. Not because she was afraid, not anymore, but because she felt a strange twinge of dislocation when confronted with the physical presence of other humans, in life or death. When she looked upon a dead body—they were by now nothing but skeletons—they seemed alien to her, unknowable. She couldn't reconcile those bones with the photos displayed in the houses of smiling people.

The only, the few, living humans she'd seen in all the years of this new world had meant her harm. They were the monsters that lurked at the edges of her knowing. She couldn't reconcile them with the smiling photos, either.

But perhaps worst of all were the now rare occasions in which she'd come upon a body still decomposing. Recently dead. Proof of the predatory monstrousness the old world had left behind, and that it still fed.

In her mind, she was the only person left in the world, and it made her thoughts stumble when she found signs that that might not be true. So she preferred the houses where the past was intact, like time capsules.

She hadn't foraged every single building in reach of her cabin, not yet, but those areas she hadn't searched yet were more dangerous, and she only made new searches once a year, when she was strongest and the daylight hours were at their peak. A new search meant any number of unpleasant risks, and sometimes the reward was paltry.

She liked to stay as close to her homestead as she could. Every trip away from it was an abandonment of sorts. If there were strangers that far up the mountain, they could take what she'd worked so hard to build. It had happened once. Only once, years earlier, and the woman had survived. She'd prevailed. Since then, no one had come upon her little home. But still, each time she walked away, she wondered what she'd find when she returned. She stayed as close as she could as much as she could, returning to the same areas again and again.

In nearer, fully explored areas like this, she'd come to think of these houses as storage. She'd taken all the food long before, all the paper and writing implements, and most of the weapons and ammunition, too. What was left of use were things like clothing, bedding, housewares, tools — things she had which would wear out and need to be replaced. And things she might not know she needed until she needed them. And, of course, things of the old world that she'd never need again.

This trip today was a replacement errand: she needed new bedding, new boots, new underwear, new jeans, among other things. A woman had lived in this house who was near to her own size. The size she was now, in this life. A walk-in closet and two bureaus in a large bedroom were full of clothes she could wear. Shoes and boots, too.

Despite her familiarity with the area and its buildings, the woman was careful as she moved through the opulent, chalet-style house. She kept an eye on Fiona, looking for signs of her wariness. But the dog, fully healed from her prize fight with a mountain lion, simply trotted around the rooms, sniffing her way about, not seeming to find anything out of the ordinary.

In the first year, whenever the woman had gone off to forage for supplies, she'd often seen evidence of other people, but she'd rarely come upon actual people, and when she had, the encounters had been hostile. She'd wondered about that a lot, at first. Her own cabin, which had been her parents', was fairly remote, far up the mountain and nearly a mile from the nearest paved road, but the mountain range had been internationally famous for year-round vacationing, and farther down were so many vacation homes they were like subdivisions. She had expected more people to be around.

Maybe it was that the world had ended on a weekday, in an early spring at the end of a dry winter, with little natural snow for skiing. Maybe no one had been vacationing. Or maybe the people who'd been on the mountain had done the opposite of the woman's strategy.

She had gone away from populated areas, not toward them. All of her study had shown that human beings were the most dangerous factors in a cataclysm. As soon as she'd understood what had happened, knowing what it meant, she'd packed up what she could carry and walked away from her little bungalow in her little town.

She'd walked three hundred miles, almost half of it up a mountain, in ten days. She'd fought for her life more than once. She'd been badly hurt, and more exhausted than she could acknowledge, but she'd kept walking while chaos churned around her.

Those memories seemed burned eternally into her psyche. She didn't need a diary to remember that journey.

Then, from her family's little mountain cabin, which they'd once called 'rustic' and 'quaint' and 'charming,' she'd begun to build a new life.

A few weeks had passed before she'd begun to forage through abandoned houses. Her first trips downward had been simply to see if she'd been right, and the world was over. She'd hoped to find people calming down and dealing with the new reality.

But the only people she'd found had been dead. Murders and suicides, mostly. People were the greatest threat, to themselves and each other.

So she'd begun to go through the houses and barns and shops and restaurants left behind. She thought of it as foraging, not looting, because she didn't think anyone who'd owned any of the buildings she went through or the things she took was alive. If they were, they'd given up their claim. These were simply resources to be gathered and used.

Once she was sure that the house was clear, she holstered the axe on her back and went to work. From an expansive hall closet, the woman pulled down two blankets and two sets of sheets. From a bed in a room nearby, she took two pillows. She wrapped the bedding in another sheet and bound the bundle with bungee cords.

From a bureau, she collected several fresh pairs of underwear and socks. The woman who'd lived here had been much bigger in the chest than she was, so she left the lacy bras in the drawer. The family of this house had had a daughter who looked, in the photos on the walls, liked she'd been about thirteen. She was smaller than the woman in every respect, but her stretchy beater tanks worked well enough as sport bras.

In the walk-in closet, the woman rooted through the shoe racks and shelves of boxes. Strappy sandals and stiletto pumps were of no use. She'd worn through a pair of Timberlands and three pairs of running shoes. There was another pair of hiking boots. They were lined with wool and would be hot when summer peaked, but they were waterproof and from L.L. Bean, so they'd hold up for a while. It was probably time to start looking for clothes in another house, but this woman had had lots of clothes, lots jeans and flannels and t-shirts, lots of activewear. Things the woman could really use. That fit.

As she yanked the second Bean boot from behind a shoe rack, she knocked something over, and it made a heavy, plastic kind of rattling thump. She bent down and pushed the hanging dresses out of her way.

A tube of tennis balls. The woman dropped the boots and picked up the tube, pushing the black plastic lid up with her thumbs. Still vacuum sealed. She pulled the tab, and when the tube made that familiar *pop*, she breathed deeply of the synthetic aroma of rubber, wool, and gas.

I used to take tennis lessons, she remembered. *Then Mom would take me to the club dining room for lunch. Just a salad. No dressing. And sparkling water with lemon.*

I used to shoplift Hostess cherry pies at the market and eat them at night, after everyone was asleep.

Her throat swelled, and her eyes burned. The sudden burst of emotion, as if she, too, had been vacuum sealed, surprised the woman, and she slammed the plastic lid back on the tube, trapping the past, and that fat, sad girl, inside it.

Just then, while the woman crouched on the floor of the large closet, Fiona pushed her head through the open doorway, and the woman forgot the memory and smiled at her best friend.

"Hey, Fee. Look what I found." She opened the tube again and took a ball from it. "Fetch!" she said and bounced the ball into the bedroom. Fiona spun, her big paws scrabbling for purchase on the hardwood floor, and chased after the ball. She brought it back and dropped it, drenched in slobber, onto the woman's legs. When the woman picked it up, Fiona hunkered down, ears perked and tail wagging, ready to fetch again. They had a tube of new toys.

"Okay, baby girl." She tossed the ball. "I think we've got everything we need. Let's go home."

The return trip, up the mountain as the light aged, was much harder, but the woman was strong now. She'd made the journey many times, and her body had shaped itself to its work.

She stayed on paved roads as much as she could, and kept her eyes sharpened and aimed into the dark forest at her side. As she climbed, she got high enough that one side of the road dropped steeply away, and the other rose steeply above, and then she relaxed a little, knowing that she had more than an hour of walking when the road was the only good passage, and she'd see any trouble as it came for her.

It had been more than a year, she guessed, since she'd seen another living human face, but her body still remembered its wounds, as did her mind, and she knew better than to assume her safety. That lesson had been well learned.

Fiona ambled at her side, pausing occasionally to do her business, or when a scent caught her notice. She, too, had made the trek down the mountain many times, and she knew her job, so her olfactory detours were infrequent, and the woman always paused and tautened her awareness.

They had gone over the pass, crossing a bridge far above the earth below, and left the safer span of the trek behind. The bridge was, like much of the paved road, showing age and neglect, and the woman assumed that, if she lived long enough, someday she'd be trapped on one side or the other. She hoped it would fall while she was on her side, where her cabin was.

As they rounded a bend and came to a turnout off the side of the road, Fiona trotted toward it, headed, the woman knew, for the gently sloping path beyond. In the world before, this had been a popular scenic vista site, and tourists had flocked to it, parking their big cars and trucks on the narrow shoulder, lining the road for at least a mile. Now, it was the spot where the woman and her dog paused for a rest and a light meal before they finished the last, hardest leg of the hike.

She followed her dog down the path to a cluster of smooth boulders that served well as a comfortable resting place, and cover if needed. The woman shed her load — her axe and a hiking pack and the bundle fixed to it — and sighed, rolling her shoulders.

"You hungry, FeeFee?"

The dog sat primly, watching and waiting while the woman pulled food from the pack: rabbit and venison jerky, hard rolls, a small jar of blackberry preserves. And the last two water bags.

She opened a water bag first. "Here, baby."

Fiona stood and opened her mouth, and the woman poured water onto her tongue. They had perfected the technique, and the dog barely lost a drop. The woman gave her about half the bottle, and then closed it back up.

Dog and woman sat together against the rocks and looked out over the world — the mountain range, carpeted with forest, the vast sky of radiant, gradient blues, the sparkling river rolling through the pass below. A hawk circled above, coasting on air currents. Summer had arrived, the woman thought as she shed her jacket and flannel shirt and let the sun warm the skin her snug beater exposed. She and her dog shared jerky and rolls dipped in wild blackberry jam, and the woman sipped at her water bag and leaned back, closing her eyes.

Fiona lay her head on the woman's outstretched legs. Stroking Fiona's ears, the woman allowed her mind to wander. The memory of tennis lessons had left a print of itself behind, and a life she'd thought dead had taken in a creaky breath. She remembered a mother, and a father. A little sister. Grandparents. She remembered a house with a wide arc of black driveway. She remembered school uniforms — blue and grey plaid skirts and blue blazers with white shirts. Horse-riding lessons as well as tennis lessons.

Summers on the mountain, in a cabin they'd called 'rustic' and 'quaint.'

Though she recognized them as her own memories, they were as real to her as the stories in the novels that lined the shelves of the cabin's bookcases. They were no longer part of her; she could barely believe that they ever had been. Only at the lake did memories feel real.

A cool breeze pushed up from the pass before them, lifting the fringy ends of Fiona's coat and fluttering strands of the woman's hair across her face. The cool foretold an end to the day's sun, and the woman patted Fiona's shoulder.

"Time to get going, girl. Want another drink before we go?" She offered the water bag, and Fiona took another drink. Not all of it; the woman felt superstitious about drinking all of their water before they had sight of the homestead. "Okay, baby girl. Do your business while I pack up." She gave the proper signal, and Fiona turned and headed into the brush, nose down.

The woman knew there was trouble before she could see the homestead.

The light was low and golden, making long shadows, and the cool breeze roused the leaves in the forest into a hushed moan. The woman stopped and stared at a tree near the dirt drive that led to the cabin. Against the base, shimmying softly in the wafts of wind, was a bandana. Yellow and faded. Creased with dark lines.

The woman had never had a yellow bandana.

As she stared at the strange thing on the ground, Fiona alerted as well, lifting her nose, taking great whiffs. Her hackles came up, and the woman picked up the alien artifact and got off the path, retreating into the cover of the trees. With a quiet cluck of her tongue, she called her dog to her.

Opening her senses as much as she could, she eased the heavy pack from her shoulders and set it aside, sheltered by bushes and deadfall. She pulled the axe from the holster she'd crafted for it and popped off the leather blade cover.

She was not afraid. Wary and alert, yes. Her heart knocked against her ribs, but steadily. Fear bred panic, and panic would get her hurt. So she was not afraid.

"Okay, Fee," she murmured on a breath. "Easy, girl." With a pat of the air before her dog's face, she crouched low and crept forward. They were nearly a mile from the cabin, but she didn't know where the monster who'd dropped the yellow bandana might be.

These woods, the woman knew in every detail. Every tree, every branch, every burrow and ditch. She moved swiftly, almost silently, snaking her path through the quiet. Fiona followed her, just as quietly, her hackles still up like gossamer spikes across her shoulders.

When she had sight of her home, the woman crouched behind a fallen tree. The dog came up beside her, lowering her body until her belly skimmed the ground.

Three men—no, two men and a woman. They seemed to think they were safe. The woman made that deduction on the evidence of their cavalier chatter and laughter, and the way they barreled around and through her home, crowing about their great find. She heard the rattle and thump and crash of her things being thrown about, broken.

They had to know that someone lived there. There was food and water, supplies. The chickens, the garden. Her life. They had to know that they trampled over a person's life.

The only person left.

Staying in her crouch, the woman crabbed over to an old oak tree and reached into the gap in its wide, fractured trunk. She pulled out her spare bow and strung it, then tested the string. She made a careful habit of maintaining all the weapons she had stashed in the woods, but the cycle of her routine had almost come around again, and it had been about as long as it ever was since she'd checked this bow. Yet the string seemed taut and supple enough, and the bow still had give. With the raiders' laughter stabbing her ears, the woman decided that the risk was acceptable. She pulled a small quiver from the trunk and hooked its strap over her shoulder. Then she sheathed her axe on her back and returned to the log to study her enemies.

The invading woman came out of the cabin and held up a china teapot shaped like … the woman sought the word for the big grey animal with the long nose … an elephant. Its nose—no, *trunk*—was the spout, its tail the handle. An heirloom from the woman's family of the world before, it had sat on the mantel longer than she could remember. It had no important use in this world, and yet when the invader held that teapot over her head, the woman's breath caught.

"Look at this shit!" the invading woman shouted at one of the men. "Bitch is havin' high tea like she ain't got a care in the world!"

An explosion cracked the air, and the teapot burst into shards. The invading woman shrieked and cowered. Male laughter rolled up over the fading report of the gunshot.

The invading woman stood straight and slammed her hands on her hips. Her clothes were filthy but seemed sturdy enough. She was skinny, and her long, dark hair hung in matted segments. "Fuck you, Mel!" she yelled at the man who'd shot a pistol and destroyed the teapot. "Coulda killed me!"

"Only if I wanted to, Sally baby. Only if I wanted to. You know I don't miss," the man called Mel jeered. He blew her a kiss, then turned and went back into the smokehouse. Sally flipped his back off with both middle fingers.

"You think she's young?" the other man called.

"You think you care?" Sally asked him. "If she's got a hole, ain't that good enough?"

"If she's young, I think I'll keep her. Be good to have a woman for keeps." He went into the garden and started pulling up lettuces.

Sally strode his way. "Maybe she's already got a man. Ever think about that?"

"Uh-uh. Mel said all the signs say she's alone." As if he'd heard something, the man stood up and peered into the woods, facing the woman and Fiona.

The woman ducked even lower and signaled Fiona to put her head on the ground. Her heart beat mercilessly, and now there was something like fear in her pulse. She knew what these men wanted. It was what men always wanted. She knew she could survive that; she had already done so more than once.

She also knew that she could do what she needed to do to fight, and to win—or to die. One way or another, she would not leave this homestead. Her homestead.

So she kept her head low and her ears open, and she considered her options. One of the men should be her first target. Mel was the leader, obviously. She should go for him first, and that would disorient the others and give her a chance to attack the other man before they'd figured her out. Sally would likely be no match in any kind of fight. That was the best plan.

She didn't know if the bow was sound or its aim true, and Mel was farthest away, ducking in and out of the smokehouse, stacking up the meat she'd worked so hard to preserve. Sally and the other man were closer, in the open, standing in the woman's lettuce patch. She had to be as sure as she could be of taking one of these foes out of the equation. Maybe, if she were lucky, she could get two.

The woman and the other man were the better targets. Then it would be just Mel and his pistol against the woman and her axe.

Nocking an arrow, she rose to her knees and aimed for the other man, the one standing on her lettuces.

At her side, Fiona growled and leapt to her feet, spinning in place. The woman looked over her shoulder.

A man and a woman stood about twenty feet away. The man bore a rifle; the woman with him brandished a machete.

The rifle was pointed right at her. Beside her, Fiona's rumbling growl became a roar, and she pushed off from her haunches. Before the woman could call her back, her dog was in the air, soaring with gnashing teeth toward the man with the rifle.

He shifted his aim and shot her dog in midair. Fiona fell to the soft earth. She lay there, her sides heaving, her front paws paddling the dead leaves as if in slow motion.

Her dog was dying. Her friend. Her family.

Grief tore through the woman like a thunderclap. She yelled and loosed the arrow still nocked in her bow. It struck the woman with the machete in the chest, and she sank to her knees, then fell forward, landing on Fiona. As she landed, the arrow pushed through her back. Blood flowered at once; it was a true shot, through the heart. A kill shot.

"Rach!" the man shouted. "No!"

The woman nocked another arrow while his attention was diverted, but before she could draw, he aimed his rifle again, at her head. "You *bitch!*"

"Don't shoot her!!" A man's voice blasted from behind her—the man in her garden. "Wait, Rod! I want her!" A hand grabbed her braid, and another her throat. She tried to send her elbow back to dislodge him, but he evaded her and clamped his fingers over her trachea and carotid artery. Stars glittered in the darkening edges of her vision.

She heard Fiona whine pitiably, but she couldn't turn her head to see. *Let go, baby girl,* the woman thought. *It's okay. Go on. I'll be okay.*

"Bitch killed Rachel," the man with the rifle snarled. He'd come close and now loomed over her, huffing foul breath into her face.

The woman glared up at him, refusing to close her eyes. She would face these monsters. She would know them. She would not fear them.

"Please, man. I ain't had a woman of my own all this time. Just half-dead leavin's is all. This one's strong, and shit, she's pretty. Lookit this hair." He yanked again on her braid.

"Now I don't got a woman, either," the man called Rod snarled. He scanned her up and down. "I'll split her with you."

"Yeah, okay," the man holding her said. "That's fair."

"But I got some payback to take first." Rod raised his rifle, flipped it around, and slammed the butt into her face.

Four

The woman woke to voices nearby. She remembered, and knew to keep her eyes closed as she fought for consciousness and recollection. Her home had been invaded. Her friend had been killed. Now, the monsters wanted to keep her as their hostage. Give her to one of the men. More than one of them.

That would not happen. She would kill them, or they would kill her, but they would not take her from this place, or take it from her.

Once before, monsters had tried to take her home from her, but they had not been so well armed or strong. Two men and a woman. They'd been vicious, and had hurt her, but not like this. She'd been far more skilled than they, and she'd known her home. She'd taken them one by one.

These monsters had guns. They had, no doubt, found her stock of arms as well. And they were strong. The men were obviously well fed. Their woman was skinny, but the men were muscular. The one who wanted her as his own was even overweight. None of them had washed in months, likely, but they ate regularly.

The woman understood that the odds were not in her favor.

A strange sentence, something like a memory, curled through her mind like smoke: *May the odds be ever in your favor.* She didn't know what they meant or where they'd come from. A song, maybe? She hadn't heard music since the end of the world.

Trying to make her mind work to form a plan, the woman catalogued her injuries. She would need all her strength to take these monsters down.

Pain throbbed through her body. Her shoulders were made of shards of it, digging deeper with each heavy thump of her heart. Her wrists were bound behind her back, tightly. She couldn't feel her arms or hands, but her shoulders screamed for relief.

Her head ached badly, filling her head with noise, and she felt the skittering creep of insects feasting on the bloody wound between her eyes. From the butt of a rifle. The man who'd hit her was named Rod. She killed his woman. Rachel.

Insects fed on blood between her thighs, too. She was naked below her waist. She'd woken once before, to the pain made there, the one called Rod shoving himself into her. Hurting and disoriented, she'd let herself fall back into the safety of black ignorance.

Her throat was constrained, and that was new. Without moving her body, the woman tried to understand that strange feeling. She swallowed. She tensed and released those muscles. She swallowed again.

There was rope around her neck. Unless she moved, she wouldn't be able to understand why, and she wasn't ready to let the monsters know she'd woken. So she lay where she was and opened her eyes, carefully, about halfway.

Rod and the others — what were their names? Mel. Sally. And the one who wanted her ... he was ... Greg. They lounged by the fire pit. Mel and Sally sat in the chairs, like king and queen. Rod and Greg stretched out on the grass. They ate the woman's cured meat. Several Mason jars lay about, half-emptied; they'd gone through her stores of canned vegetables and fruits.

Once she had a sense of their positions and activities, the woman closed her eyes again and listened. They seemed to be arguing lazily.

One of the men: "It's too far up, Greg. Come winter, snow's got to get ten-fifteen feet this high up. I don't know how the bitch's been doin' it."

The woman, Sally: "She's been doing it good, though, baby. I told you it'd be good to go up for once. Lookit all this shit. Like everything down there never happened. If she could do it, we could. Finally stay put, after all this time."

Another man. The woman recognized his voice as Rod: "Sally's got a point, Mel. We keep the cunt alive, she could show us how to live up here."

Mel: "She killed your woman. Now you want to ask her for lessons? We should kill her."

The third man, Greg: "Mel, man. She's so pretty. I ain't had a real woman since before. If we stay up here, we need more'n one woman."

"Neither of you's touchin' me anymore," Sally cut in. "That's for sure. Right, Mel?" Her voice quavered.

"Yeah, baby. That's right. You're mine." Mel was obviously their leader. The man with the pistol. A revolver, the woman thought, searching her mind for the image.

"I'll get what I need for Rach out of her, Mel. I'll break her."

"Not too much, though," Greg said. "Keep her pretty."

The woman heard rustling; someone was moving, possibly standing. She cracked open her eyes, just enough to see the sunset-washed fire pit, and the people around it. Sally had risen to her feet.

Rod was looking right at her. She closed her eyes at once, but it was too late.

"She's awake. Might's well get back to the breakin'." More rustling as all the monsters moved in some way or another, and the woman sensed heavy feet approaching. "I know you're here, little bitch. No good fakin."

Rod grabbed her bound wrists and lifted her up. Her shoulders exploded with pain, and she couldn't stop the squealing grunt that left her dry lips. He dropped her to her knees, and the woman understood the rope around her neck. She was leashed, tied to something. A tree, she thought. Yes. She knew which one: the little willow tree her father had planted as a sapling, two years before the end. In memory of her grandmother.

Rod was on his knees behind her, opening his pants. He held her head down, grinding her face into the dirt. As he shoved himself into her, she saw the others, watching avidly. The face of the monster called Sally twisted in a feral, rapacious grin.

When the monsters went into the woman's cabin for the night, they tied her up in the woodshed. Built in the world before to withstand harsh elements, the shed was enclosed, four slat walls and a barn-style double door, but, without a blanket, wearing only the beater she'd put on that morning, the woman shivered painfully. Even in summer, nights were cold at this altitude, sometimes close to freezing. She huddled against a slat wall in the half-full shed and stared at the logs she'd split. They could be weapons, if she could make her hands free, and if they would work again.

She tried to move her bruised, blood-caked body and crawl to the logs, seeking a sharp edge she might fray the rope on, but the leash around her neck had been tied too tightly to a ring in the opposite wall. The slats and posts of the walls were sanded smooth and treated; she'd get no good friction there. She sat and thought, keeping her mind busy, its attention away from her pain and the cold.

As the night wore and the cold deepened, the woman could not make her thoughts focus. Every idea petered out and wafted away. Finally, she gave up and tried to sleep. There would be strength in rest.

She dreamt of bright sun on her arms and warm sand between her toes, of the rich scent of sunscreen and salty sea breeze, of crashing surf and the rustle of palm trees. The cry of gulls. Loud, like a door creaking on stiff hinges. Like a door …

The woman woke before he touched her. He'd left the door open behind him, and moonlight flooded the shed in washes of blue. Greg. The one who wanted to keep her. The reason they hadn't already killed her, and the reason they held her captive.

"Hey, pretty lady," he said, his voice low. "I brung you a blanket. And some meat and water."

They hadn't brought her anything to eat or drink yet. She was inclined to refuse, as she'd refused to speak, but food and water were strength.

When he held out a piece of jerky, she leaned forward and snatched it from him with her teeth. Like a dog. Fiona ...

She blinked the thought away. Not now. When she was strong, she would remember Fiona, but not now, when it would make her weaker.

She drank when he offered her water from a coffee cup. Coffee was something she'd run out of years before, even foraging through as many places as she could.

"Good girl. My name's Greg." He fed her more jerky and let her drink again. "Will you tell me your name?"

She stared. She hadn't spoken to these monsters, but even if she might have answered this one, she didn't know what she'd say. Her name? She'd had one, once. It shimmered along the borders of her mind, but didn't move close enough to remember.

"Is it that you *can't* talk? I know you ain't deaf."

She stared, and he sighed.

"I know things are hard for you just now, but they'll get better. I won't let Rod hurt you too bad. You just gotta pay for what you did to Rachel. But then I'm gonna take good care of you, I promise." His eyes sank from her face, down to her thighs, lingered on her nakedness, crusted in blood. "What d'you say to a wash? You like that?"

She stared.

He got up and left the shed. He'd left the doors open, and the woman watched as he went to the pump, picked up the bucket, and filled it. He fished in the pockets of his pants but didn't find what he sought. He came back, lugging the bucket. The moon glinted off his shiny scalp and the breeze tossed the scant wisps of his hair around.

Crouching before her, he set the half-full bucket down with a quiet rattle. "Don't got nothin' to wipe you with, so I'm gonna use my hand." He plunged his hands into the water.

This one, the woman understood, was the weak link. He was, right now, unarmed, as far as she could tell. He was not being aggressive toward her. He wanted something from her—wanted her to *give* it to him, rather than to take it from her. She could use that. If she could stand him for a while, long enough to make a plan, she could use it.

So when he reached for her with hands dripping with ice-cold mountain well water, the woman didn't shrink back. When he wiped the blood from her forehead, his hands too rough over the open wound, she didn't flinch. When he put his hands between her legs to wash her there, she kept her thighs soft. Even when he pushed his fingers into her, opening tears and making them bleed again, she was calm and made her breath easy. When he licked his lips and brushed his fingers over her clit, she didn't cry out in pained revulsion. When his dripping hands pushed under her scant top and cupped her breast, she stayed loose.

"You're so damn pretty. When I first seen you, so clean, all this hair so neat and shiny, these pretty titties pushing out this shirt … I ain't seen a woman like you in so long, I could hardly believe it. I think you're the prettiest thing I ever seen, even before the light show."

His breath came out in shallow huffs, and the woman could see his arousal straining at his pants. She wondered if she could withstand that weapon right now. Could she take that, after everything, and not show pain?

But he shook himself free of his reverie and smiled at her. Most of the teeth on the left side of his mouth were gone; those that were left in his mouth were mottled brown. "I'm gonna talk to Rod, see if I can get him to ease up on you." He offered her the water again, and she finished it. "Hey—I bet you need to get some relief. They won't let you in the house, but I could take you out in the woods. You like that?"

She didn't think her body was capable of evacuating yet, after the abuse it had suffered, but it didn't matter. This was her chance. If he untied her and took her into the woods, she might be able to handle him, away from the cabin. How, with her hands behind her back, she didn't know. But it was the best chance she had.

She nodded.

He grinned. "That's good. Yeah, see? I'm gonna take good care of you. I know how to treat a woman, you'll see."

Said the man who'd just finger-fucked a woman who'd been repeatedly raped only hours before.

He stood and pulled a blade—a large pocket knife, with a dark wood handle—from a front pocket of his pants. The woman couldn't help but flinch as he opened it.

"Easy, pretty lady. I'm just gonna cut the rope back here. I can't let you loose, not until I know you see how things gotta be, but I can take you out and give you a minute to see to your needs."

He cut the rope from the ring and held it in his fist as he closed the knife. She truly was on a leash. "Okay, let's go. Quiet, though. It's my watch, and they're all sleepin'. Mel don't know 'bout this, and he'd take it outta me if he did."

As if it were his property and she the interloper, he led her around the woodshed and back, past the tree line. The woman still wore nothing but her beater, but her body

66

had forgotten the cold. The rocks and pinecones on the forest floor dug into her feet, sometimes broke through the skin, but she walked as steadily as she could, collecting these new pains into all the others.

He stopped at the wide trunk of an old live oak. "There. Go 'head."

This was the moment. She had to divert his attention somehow. And figure out how to hurt him without her hands.

Or get him to release her hands. She was leashed. Was there a way he might unbind her wrists, if he thought he still had her under control?

Acting as the plan formed in her head, she crouched low, as if to relieve herself. It hurt, tore more wounds inside her back open, but she did it—and then made herself fall backward, onto her dead arms. She cried out in pain, and got the notice from him she wanted.

"Shit! You okay? What happened?" He bent down to help her up, and she saw a new chance and took it. She kicked up with both her feet, as hard as she could, aiming for his chin. She connected, and his head snapped sharply back with a crack as loud as a branch breaking in storm. He fell backward onto the forest floor with an earthshaking thud.

The woman shifted to her knees and waited to see if he would get up immediately, only dazed. When he didn't, she got moving, rising to her feet and running to him. For a second, she considered putting her back to him and trying to dig his knife from his pocket. But if he woke while she did, her chance would be lost — and she'd be in worse trouble.

All she had was her bare feet, then. So she used them. She stomped on his head until her thighs shook and her knees ached, until the bones in her feet felt like loose stones rolling. Until his head had caved in.

Then she put her back to him and dug the knife out of his pocket.

It took her a long time to get to the knife, and a long time to work the blade through the rope around her wrists. She cut herself several times, and blood dripped from her fingers, but none of the cuts was deep or dangerous, unless they might get infected later. That wasn't a worry — before infection could set in, either the woman would be dead, or she would be able to give herself first aid.

When she was free of all her bindings, she considered taking his clothes, at least his boots, but decided against it. His clothes were rank, and the boots were much too big for her feet, so she wouldn't be able to control her footfalls well enough for stealth. She was better off naked and cold.

Before she left the forest, she went to her nearest stash point, where she kept a machete.

Armed and unsuspected, she crept back out of the woods. In the cabin, *her* cabin, her *home*, were three more monsters. Two large men and a small woman. Greg had said they were sleeping.

She hoped that was true.

Easing the back door open, lifting it over the squeaky point, she sneaked into her own home. It was dark, only the waning moonlight offering any sense of the space. She knew it well, but she didn't know what they had done to it.

Though her family had been wealthy, or at least affluent, this cabin was modest, only a large room and a loft above. Her father had wanted to 'rough it,' to 'get away from it all' and 'get down to the nut of the thing.'

She'd never quite understood that last one, but it had meant no electronics, a composting toilet, an outdoor shower, and a pump sink.

All things she'd hated as a child. All things that had saved her after the end of the world.

Since she'd arrived here at the end of the world, she'd rarely gone up the ladder into the loft. She used the main space, with a daybed and a foldout sofa.

Like the story about the bears, only in reverse, the woman found both taken by sleeping monsters, invaders in her home. The man called Rod snored on the daybed. Where she slept. Mel and Sally slept on the opened sofa.

The woman crept to the daybed, maneuvering around any creaky floorboards, and slid the machete through Rod's neck. He woke, his eyes glowing in the moonlight, and died gurgling quietly as his blood pulsed over her linens and mattress. In his final moment, he flailed out and clamped a hand around her arm, but it went slack before she could wrench away.

Then she crossed the room to the sofa sleeper and opened Sally's throat. Her dying throes woke Mel before the woman could kill him, and he sat up. She plunged the blade into his chest, feeling the metal grate against his ribs. He coughed once, then again, spewing blood in her face, and then he fell over his dying woman.

All five. She'd killed all five monsters. They were dead, and she was alive.

But they'd killed Fiona. Her family. Her constant companion since the end of the world.

She was alone.

The machete clattered to the floor, and the woman sank down with it.

Five

A woodpecker drilling at a nearby tree brought the woman back to the world, its rapid *rat-tat-tat, rat-tat-tat* breaking the numb rhythm of her heartbeat. She blinked and came back to awareness, the sensation one of rolling up the shades at the start of a new day. Bright sunlight slanted into the cabin. She'd been sitting in its beam and had become warm. Motes danced before her eyes like floating glitter. Her sight locked there, entranced, and saw nothing else around her.

She hadn't slept, as far as she was aware. She'd simply sat and turned inward, stared into a void in the center of her mind. But now, she heard the life beyond the walls, the birds and insects, the creatures of the forest, all their songs and sounds and movements adding a fullness to the air.

In this bright space, though, death lived. The air was rank with blood and befoulment. When she tried to rise, her body reminded her of all she had withstood, all she had wrought, in the past day. Again, she tried, and this time, she came up to her feet. They sent up spears of pain in protest, but they took her weight.

On her bed, the monster called Rod lay, wax-colored and stiff, his head off the bed and his throat gaping. His eyes had rolled up and showed only the whites, yellowed by the sun. On her sofa sleeper, Mel lay face down over Sally as if he'd tried to protect her.

In the forest was the one called Greg. She wondered if the animals had gotten to him since she'd stomped his brains out.

Somewhere, she didn't know where, was the other woman. The one … whose name she couldn't recall.

And Fiona. Where was Fiona?

Returned to reality, the woman focused her eyes and made them see everything. All around her was destruction. They'd torn books from the shelves and torn the pages from the spines. They'd broken cherished mementos from a life she barely remembered and left the shards in heaps on the hearth. They'd ransacked her stores of food.

She stood in the middle of it all, wearing only a beater so filthy and torn it was hardly more than a rag.

She had things to do. Her mind latched hard on that: there were things to be done.

First, she tore off the ragged beater and pulled on a baggy sweatshirt from her bureau. She started a fire in her woodstove and filled her biggest pot with water from the pump at her kitchen sink. She would need to wash and tend to her wounds before she could do anything more, or she would end up too ill to do anything.

While the water heated, she stripped all the bedding she could from the beds and stuffed it into a big reed basket she'd made, not very well, in the early days when she'd been teaching herself skills to live in this world. When she was strong enough, she'd take the linens to the lake for a wash. She left only what was under the bodies. She'd have to wash all that as well, but she'd have to deal with the bodies first, and that chore was for later.

She swept up the shards and dumped them in a pail. She might find some use for them. She picked up her ruined books and their pages and set them back on the shelves. She would find the pages' proper places.

They'd left her journals alone; perhaps they'd gotten bored before those shelves.

When the water was near boiling, she carried her pot to her bathroom and poured it in her washtub, then pumped cold water in until it was a temperature in which she could bathe. She did so, staying until the water was cool, washing everything again and again and again, ignoring the sting and the ache of her wounds.

A thought tried to push into her knowing, like a worm boring a hole to invade her consciousness, but she fought back against it at once, each time it poked its poisonous head up. What if the monster had left himself inside her? What would she do then?

No. No. No. She hardly ever had a ... thing ... a ... a *period*. For the past few years, only two or three a year, and months since her last. She tried to remember if that meant she was less fertile. Her father had been a doctor, and she remembered studying it, too. It was something she'd known.

She thought it was true. She wasn't fertile, or at least not very. It wasn't a worry she had to face. *Go away, little worm.* It went away, and her heartbeat found a calmer tempo.

Eventually, the water became unpleasantly cold on her body, which had been chilled to the bone out in the woodshed, and she pulled the stopper. The water drained from the bottom, into the earth below the cabin, and the woman set to the work of tending her wounds.

Studying herself in her mirror above her bathroom sink, she saw that the cut on her forehead was a gash, and already its ragged edges had a puffy, angry look. She soaked a clean rag in rubbing alcohol and wrung it out over her forehead, tipping her head in the sink. The extreme sting made her eyes water and the tendons in her neck go rigid, but she did it again, and again. And then, peering into her mirror, she stitched the gash closed, breathing deeply in and out as she pushed the needle into her flesh and pulled the sutures tight. Her forehead was already on fire, so the new pain of the suturing wasn't unbearable.

Her other wounds were less serious, sufficiently tended with alcohol and gauze and tape. Even the most traumatic of her wounds could be healed with cleanliness and care. The wounds of her body, at any rate.

Feeling shaky from the efforts of bathing and healing, the woman made her way to her bureau and dressed in clean but tattered clothes. She didn't know where her boots were, and the pair she'd foraged the day before were likely still a mile away, at the head of her lane, where she'd stashed her pack. So she put on a pair of sneakers. She braided her hair. And moved on to her next task. Her hardest.

The bodies were not yet in full rigor—just their heads and necks were stiff—so she got to work as quickly as she could. First, she carried the woman, Sally, out. She was skinny and small, and the woman had little trouble carrying her over her shoulder to the ravine and throwing her in.

The men posed more trouble, but, through sheer will and all the strength she could muster, she was able to drag them out of the cabin on the blood-soaked sheets, and there, on the ground, she used her butchering tools. She carried them in parts to the ravine. Those sheets, she would burn, with the clothes she had on. She'd chosen her most worn top and pants because she'd known it would be their last wearing.

Once before, she'd been attacked at her home. Before, she'd buried bodies in the bottom of this ravine. Now, she left the bodies mounded where they fell and went on to her next task. She didn't have time for burying now.

She butchered Greg in the woods and dropped his parts with the rest. The woman, the first she'd killed, she couldn't find.

But she found Fiona, lying where she'd died, flies already laying their eggs in her eyes. She brushed them away and sat for a moment on the forest floor, lifting her dog's, her friend's, head onto her lap and scratching her under her ears, in the special place she liked best.

She remembered the tube of tennis balls she'd foraged, only the day before. Meant to be toys for Fiona. She remembered her friend's puppyish enthusiasm as she'd tossed the ball, and slobbery mess that Fee had returned to her lap. Eventually, she hadn't come back with it; it must have rolled into a nook somewhere. They hadn't been able to find it, but they still had two more.

She bent low and laid her head on Fiona's.

76

Then the woman carried her dead dog down to the homestead and buried her beneath the little willow tree.

When she was done, she stretched out over the mounded earth of the new grave and wept.

The woman carried all the linens she could salvage down to the lake. Among the reeds and cattails, in company with ducks and dragonflies, she knelt on the pebbly shore and washed her bedding, dragging rocks over every stain to release the blood in the cold water. Her hands went numb in the chill water of her mountain lake, and her skin paled and puckered, but she scrubbed and wrung, scrubbed and wrung, over and over until the water ran clear from the twists of cloth.

A doe and two fawns, their spots nearly faded away, eased up along the side of the lake. The doe watched the woman warily, her ears flicking. The woman stopped beating a blanket with a rock and took the moment to catch her breath. Reassured by the fresh quiet, the doe nudged her babies forward, and the little family drank.

She remembered finding Fiona, just a little puppy, alone in an abandoned house, left in a crate. She'd been starving and dehydrated. Only a few weeks after the end of the world. The woman had picked up the pup, weak and whining, caked in feces and urine, and offered her water and a protein bar. She'd promised her that everything would be okay now.

After that, neither of them had been alone.

The woman kicked that memory away before it could break her. There were things yet to be done. She wrung out the blanket and added it to the mountain of twists in her flimsy reed basket. Unhappy with the new flurry of activity, the doe took her fawns and ran back into the woods.

Back at the homestead, the woman hung the linens to dry. Then she went into the cabin and pulled the mattresses out into the afternoon sun and scrubbed them, using a stiff brush. She'd leave them to dry in the sun that was left. Tonight, she'd have to make a pallet on the floor to sleep.

All the bedding was stained now, she'd never be fully rid of the blood that had washed over them, but she'd made everything clean enough to use again. It had to be; she'd never be able to carry another mattress up from another house, so she'd turn these over and try to forget.

While she knelt on the ground beside the mattress of the daybed, *her* bed, scrubbing away the blood of the one called Rod, Shrek ambled out of the woods. He stopped, and she stopped. She opened her mouth, meaning to speak to him, but there were no words near her tongue. She closed her mouth again.

Shrek lifted his snout and took a deep sniff. Another. He rose up on his hind legs and took another. Then he roared. The sound wasn't angry. It was a lament.

The woman understood. He smelled Fiona's death.

Dropping back onto his forelegs, he lumbered toward her. He sniffed at the mattress and pulled back with a grunt, batting a paw at his nose. He whined.

The woman set aside the scrub brush and held out her arms, and the big bear lay before her and set his head on her lap. She bent low, setting her cheek on his forehead, and scratched at his thick ears. Together, they mourned their friend.

But the smell of blood and death upset the bear. He covered his snout again and again with his paws and finally threw his head back, only missing a collision with the woman's chin because she'd sat up straight during his distress. He stood and grunted at her, swinging his head to and fro, but she had no answer for his confusion.

Finally, he turned and walked back into the woods. When she could no longer see his wide rear end swaying, she picked up the scrub brush and went on with her work.

There were things to be done. Her mind held to that like a vise.

By the time she had her cabin as right as she could, and had washed herself again and put on fresh clothes, a bloody sun rested on the horizon, and she could scarcely lift her arms or legs. The bodies were still piled in the bottom of the ravine, but she had nothing left inside her with which to bury them. They would have to wait until her strength returned.

It was dangerous, the scent of blood and meat would draw predators in the night, but she had no choice. There was no one but her, and she wasn't enough.

Too tired and spent to build a fire, too sore and stunned, the woman sat before the cold pit, where the monsters had sat the sunset before. She ate jerky and drank water. She waited for Shrek, leaving out a large chunk of his favorite cut of smoked venison, but he didn't come back.

In her heart, she knew he wouldn't come back again. He'd scented the death of his friend here. This was no longer a safe place.

Now, and always, she would be alone here.

When the sun set completely, the woman went into her cabin.

Her day of hard work had wearied her all the way to her marrow. Her head ached fiercely, her arms and legs and back and neck felt made of molten steel, and an angry throb between her legs kept time with her heartbeat. Her hands had swollen, and the skin cracked. Her feet felt full of rusty nails.

But her cabin looked almost like her own again. Things were missing, important things, and important things were broken. The mattresses leaned against the outside wall, drying, and the mantel was bare. But the reek of death was gone. The signs of invasion were gone.

Tomorrow, she would bury the bodies and burn their packs. She would put the mattresses where they belonged and make up her bed. If her feet were well enough, she would hike to the end of her lane and reclaim the things she'd last foraged.

There were things yet to be done, and then this horror would be over.

Already, the events of the past day and a half had taken on a shade of unreality, like a vivid dream remembered on waking and then forgotten in slivers throughout the day. She knew this working of her mind, the way it had, since the end of the world, sloughed off parts that didn't fit this new place. She kept her diaries to hold her memories, when flashes of the past flared, or when something noteworthy happened in the present.

These happenings, however—these she would let fall away. These she wouldn't write down.

She curled up on Fiona's pad and closed her eyes.

Book Two: Wanderer

For I am not so enamored of my own opinions
that I disregard what others may think of them.

~Nicolaus Copernicus

Six

"It's a bad idea. I say we kill her. Make it quick and gentle. It's better for her, too."

Gus took the jug, filled his cup, and passed it on to Mara. Then he turned his attention to Carver. "That's who we are now? Killing innocent women?"

"She's blind and deaf, Gus. And *pregnant*. She'll slow us all down. That's dangerous for the whole group."

Uncomfortable agreement rumbled around the fire, and Gus scanned the flickering faces of this group. "She's pregnant because she was raped. She's been kicked out of three substakes. This world has been hard enough on her, I say."

"That's why it would be a kindness to kill her." That was Talia, Carver's woman. Gus had been traveling with this group for only a few months, but it hadn't taken him more than a few hours to understand that Talia was the brains and Carver the brawn of this duo, the leaders. Carver was sharp, but oriented always toward action. Talia looked toward the future and saw long-term consequences. "Leaving her behind would be crueler. This world doesn't have room for people who can't take care of themselves."

"*You* say she was raped. *You* say she was kicked out of the subs," Jarod challenged. "You're the only one that can talk to her. I don't like having somebody around only one of us can get to know. I like you, Gus, but you're still new with us yourself, and I don't think I trust you enough for that yet."

"Gus saved your life, Jarod," Mara's voice was typically soft, and she kept her eyes fixed on the fire. She rarely spoke in group meetings. She'd been with them since the beginning, but she had three children, the youngest of them barely older than the Sunstorm, and she tried hard not to make waves and to pull more than the weight of her family.

The Sunstorm, the Light Show, the Last Dance, the Breaking Waves. Gus had heard the event that had ended the modern world called all those names and many more. What it had been was a massive wave of solar flares, the sun flinging out its energy like a whip, frying everything that had a motor, any electric or electronic mechanism, any circuitry, in one long crack. As a parting gift, the sky had been filled with beautiful, wildly dancing lights in the full spectrum of visible color, lasting for hours. They'd all stood still, looked up, and oohed and aahed at their own destruction.

Gus had watched it, too, standing on the wide balcony off the penthouse of a Manhattan hotel, dressed in a tuxedo, drinking a martini he'd lifted from a silver tray as a server had walked by, seconds before the end. The power had gone off below, like a giant master switch had been pulled, but above, the sky had swirled and pirouetted with color and light. The most beautiful thing he'd ever seen.

The world hadn't recovered and, to his eyes, showed few signs yet that it ever would. At first, like most everybody else, he'd thought it would be just a bump in the road, that the world merely needed a pit stop, and all the engineers and scientists and geniuses would get everything back up and running in a few weeks, a few months at the most. But vast stores of knowledge had been archived only digitally and instantly erased. Most engineers and scientists had learned their work in a digital world. And information all but stopped, with no way to share it except physically, from person to person.

Whole generations had been raised entirely dependent on electricity. People used it every second of their lives. People needed it to learn, to work, to live. Some people needed it to breathe.

The first deaths had been the direct result of the storm — when cars and trucks had lost power at speed, when trains had derailed, when airplanes and helicopters had fallen from the sky. People who'd been in surgery at the time, cut wide open, had expired on operating tables. People who'd needed machines to keep their bodies going — pacemakers, ventilators, dialysis — lost their lifelines in a blink. All the emergency backup generators in place to prevent such things had been fried, too.

The able-bodied and healthy had been yet too stunned to panic in those first hours. But then the medicines, in vials that needed to be refrigerated, went off. As did perishable food.

Nuclear reactors lost their cooling capacity and released radiation into the air.

And then the die-off really began. That was when the panic set in — and made the die-off ever so much worse.

The reactors were probably the worst, long term. Almost all of country's active reactors had been located on the East Coast. By now, everything east of Indiana had gone full Chernobyl. And anything that still lived east of the Appalachians was nightmare shit. Everybody who could move had moved west — but how much that would save them, or anybody, was a blind guess. Radiation was airborne, and even with the tendency of air currents to move from west to east, everybody knew that they were breathing some concentration of it in with each inhale. They'd probably all die of cancer, if they didn't die of something worse first.

Five years later, people were still in panic, living daily in states of fight-or-flight. Having serious discussions about killing people in greater need than themselves. If people were trying to make things better, word hadn't spread. Gus figured even geniuses were still too focused on day-to-day survival to see farther ahead than their next meal.

They'd been knocked back to the eighteenth century, and it looked like they were going to make progress from there at the same pace as the first time.

If progress was made at all. Information moved slowly in this world, mostly mouth to ear, and it was hard to distinguish rumor from fact, or to know how wrung out the truth was by the time it made your ear. From what Gus could see with his own eyes, though, nobody was trying to fix the world yet. Everybody was just trying to make it to the next day.

Knowing Mara wouldn't meet his eyes right now, Gus reached over and patted her hand in thanks. She'd been brave to challenge Jarod in support of him.

"I know, and I'm grateful," Jarod answered. "Like I said, I like you, Gus. You've got a good head, a steady heart, and a strong back, and I'm not sorry you're here. But it's a lot to ask, for us to trust somebody only you can communicate with."

"I can teach you to sign. And Erin can speak. When she feels safe with us, she will."

Gus had had a sister, born later in their parents' lives and far too early in her own, with profound challenges, blindness and deafness among them. He and his family had learned American Sign Language, and they'd learned how to fingerspell in Michaela's hands, so she could understand. She, in turn, had learn to speak.

She'd needed electricity to live, and she hadn't survived the Sunstorm. Gus wasn't sure exactly how long she'd lived, but he knew it couldn't have been more than a few hours. By the time he'd found his way from Manhattan to Philadelphia, there was a grave in the back yard of his parents' home. He'd found his parents dead in their own bed, holding hands. They hadn't left a note for him, but he hadn't needed any answers.

Since then, he'd been on his feet, looking for he didn't know what, and not finding it.

But he knew he wouldn't find it with people who could kill without provocation, kill an innocent woman who needed help. He'd thought this group was solid, more good eggs than bad, with reasonable leadership that kept the bad eggs in check. But if this meeting went the wrong way, he'd go, and he'd take Erin with him.

He looked over his shoulder at the woman, sitting in perfect stillness on a crumbling retaining wall, her back straight and her hands lightly clasped atop her belly. Beyond the warm light of the fire, her dark skin glowed blue where the moon touched it.

What must it be like, to live in this world of chaos in absolute darkness and silence? How strong and brave she was to have survived this long, subject to who knew what kinds of horrors and abasements.

At least one kind, he knew. She carried the evidence of it inside her. Infertility was rampant in this world, where the radiation of every failed reactor had, by now, spread globally. Rape was rampant as well, in this world where the protections of law were nil and basic human decency was a situational privilege. Pregnancy was rare, but Erin had won that bitter lottery.

She could speak, as Michaela had, with the slow cadence and thick diction of someone who'd never heard her own voice or any other. Like his sister had been, she was ashamed of her voice and didn't like to use it when she didn't know or trust her audience. Gus had gained her trust by signing into her hand, but still, she'd only spoken a few hesitant words to him. He knew that she wasn't sad about the baby. She considered it a godsent balm for her suffering. One of the things she'd spoken aloud to him had been *Love my baby.*

To find love in this world was brave in itself. To find love where she had was positively heroic.

He turned back and faced Carver. "I don't know what I can do to make you trust me if you don't, but I'll take responsibility for her. If she's too much of a draw on our resources, I'll give up some of my own share. If she puts the group too much at risk, I'll take her and go."

Alan, who'd had little to say so far, laughed. "You sweet on her, man?"

Carver waved him off before Gus could reply. "We need you, Gus. You're one of the strongest of us."

A smile pushed its way up Gus's cheeks. There'd been a time, before everything had gone to hell, that the idea of him being physically strong would have made just about everyone he'd known laugh, and even now he still found humor in the thought. He'd been a concert violinist, for fuck's sake. He'd been in decent shape, running three to five miles a day to keep up his endurance, and his hands had been strong and nimble as hell, but he'd guarded those hands like the precious commodities they'd been. He'd done no strength training, nothing that would have required him to lift or punch or in any way put his hands at risk.

In this world, though, a man who couldn't lift, and punch, and daily put his hands at risk in any number of ways, didn't live long.

"I don't intend to go, Carver. I don't think she's a risk, and I'll absorb her draw. If we start killing people because they need us, then we're not much different from the Ferals."

"We should vote," Talia said.

"Yeah." Carver nodded. "Raise your hand if you want Erin to stay with us."

Carver, Talia, Mara, Gus, Alan, Liz, Orion, and Dodge raised their hands. Jarod and Loni didn't.

"Okay. She stays. Gus..."

Gus stood. "I got her. Thanks."

"Just make sure this doesn't hurt us. We got kids to think about."

With a nod, he turned and left the circle, walking away from the fire. Erin sat as she'd been, her back still a primer for perfect posture. She faced the horizon and the moon, and looked like someone enjoying a peaceful view of a lovely night sky, one wild with stars.

That had been a revelation as well, the number of stars in the sky. Before the Sunstorm, there had been so much light on the ground that few stars could break through the ambient glow. Now, any clear night, like tonight, from anywhere, like here, you could look up and see not only millions, billions of stars scattered like diamonds across deep-blue velvet, but the swirl and streak of actual galaxies.

Erin couldn't see that. Gus wondered if she could feel their cool light, though.

Despite Alan's acerbic question, he wasn't 'sweet' on Erin. She was beautiful, with dark, smooth skin and a wild, wide halo of black hair. Her eyes were milky and almost entirely white, but the play and shine of sunlight gave them an iridescent sheen, like opals.

She thought she was seven months pregnant, but it only showed in her belly, like she had a playground ball under her tattered t-shirt. Her limbs and neck had the pencil thinness of many women in this world, especially the wanderers, like them, without the protection and relative comfort of a substake.

Most striking of all was her smile. She smiled easily, and in this world, people rarely did — and strangers, never.

He wasn't sweet on her, but he did feel protective of her. Despite the extravagant lights with which the world had died, there wasn't much light left, and he didn't want Erin to lose hers.

He came up to her and tapped her left shoulder — three light, quick taps. Every time he came up to her, he did the same thing to get her attention. It would be the way she'd know it was him.

She held out her hand, and he put his against her palm, fingerspelling, *Hi. All done.*

Nodding, she signed, *Can I stay?* In addition to learning to speak words she couldn't hear, she'd also learned ASL completely, more than fingerspelling. Michaela had struggled with that, but she hadn't had the control over her body that Erin had.

Yes, he spelled. *Keep with me, you'll be okay.*

"Baby," she said.

And your baby, too, he spelled in her hands. He didn't know how true that really was. There were few young children in this world. From the rare pregnancies that took and made it to term, he'd seen babies born all kinds of wrong since the storm, and he'd seen women die bloody trying to have them. He'd seen it happen, and he'd come across grisly scenes long after, too. But he wanted it to be true. It seemed to Gus that if the world ever would get better, the first thing it had to do was figure out how to make a new generation. And how to stop killing the generations it already had.

"Thank you, Gus." She hit the G hard, and nearly yelled his name. Then she signed, *I think you saved us.*

He hoped he had.

Gus tied the strap of the sheath to his thigh and snapped the band over the hilt of his bone-handled hunting knife. He checked for the length of chain, forged rigid, that he'd traded for a few years back. It made a fair approximation of brass knuckles and had saved his ass a couple of times. He strapped a band of throwing knives, three slots empty now, across his chest. After he pulled on his flannel-lined barn coat, tied his hair back with a length of twine, and wrapped a warm red scarf around his neck, he slung the crossbow and quiver on his back.

Erin sat quietly, knitting. She was a swift and talented needlecrafter and had made herself valuable over the past two months, as winter neared, by whipping up sweaters, mittens, gloves, scarves, and blankets in a flurry, spending whole days at the work. She even made lovely patterns, trusting others to find the yarn and Gus to describe their colors to her. Like his sister, though she had no idea what 'blue' or 'red' meant, Erin had learned to associate some colors with concepts, like blue for sky and red for roses, and she'd learned what colors complemented each other. She kept all that as abstract concepts in her mind, without any concrete image to ground them. And she knitted by keeping perfect count of her stitches, even when people interrupted her work.

They'd scavenged a surprising quantity of skeins of new yarns, but Mara's oldest children, thirteen-year-old Tiffany and nine-year-old Clark, earned their keep by unraveling tattered clothing and spinning the threads into recycled yarns. The whole group would be kept warm through this Great Plains winter by Erin's agile hands.

He tapped her lightly on her left shoulder, three times, and she smiled and stopped her work, setting her needles carefully in her lap and holding up her hands.

Time for me to go, he spelled between her palms.

She shook her head. "Dangerous."

Every day dangerous. Baby coming soon. Winter too. Need to find a place.

She lifted her hands away from his, toward his face. He crouched low so she could reach, and he closed his eyes as her fingertips traced over his features.

You're worried, too, she signed when she was done. He'd tried to smooth his cares away before she'd touched him, but he never quite managed to hide his feelings from those sensitive fingers.

Yes, he was worried. They were in Kansas, near Wichita, and the Great Plains region was notorious for Ferals—bands of men and women who'd abandoned everything remotely like civilization or society or morals early on, who'd taken the apocalypse as an invitation to act out in every conceivable way, as if the Sunstorm had been the dawning of an eternal Purge, like those old horror movies where there was no law for one day a year.

Every year, it seemed like there were more Ferals and fewer people trying to get by like human beings. Gus didn't know if that was because the Ferals were killing the human beings at that kind of rate, or if more and more humans were going Feral.

Trying to get find a good place to hole up before the winter sank in, they'd fought their way this far west and hadn't lost anyone yet and had only one bad injury. They'd been savvy and conservative, and avoided wide highways, where Ferals feasted on wanderers.

Feasted in the literal sense. At some point in the past couple of years, Ferals had seemed to decide they preferred human meat to animal.

Food wasn't horribly scarce, not yet, not for the resourceful and the allied, but there were no wide fields of crops anymore. Just small community gardens in substakes, with yields compromised by the waft of radiation in the air. Livestock had mostly been eaten or died off. Even horses, which had been common transportation in the first years after the Sunstorm, had become rare in the past year or two. Wildlife teemed, so hunters did okay. Some substakes put up stands outside their walls, or ventured out to one of the crossroads bazaars that sprang up out of nowhere, and offered wanderers vegetables for trade. Some wanderers were lucky enough to have things worth trading. Otherwise, they foraged for what greens they could.

Another help Erin had been to them, knitting away her days while her belly grew — they had valuable goods for trade.

Since they'd left the comparative safety of the Ozarks, they'd only been set upon once. They'd prevailed, but the attack had slowed them down since. Now, the weather was turning, and Erin's baby was due at any time. That morning, they'd woken to snow on the ground. It had been gone by noon, but the group had decided at breakfast that they needed to stop now, find a place they could fortify and settle into. If they got caught out in a Plains snowstorm, they could all die in a single night.

Hunkering down in land overrun with Ferals was fucking stupid, but Dodge's leg had been broken in the Feral attack, and at their pace since, the risk was too great to try to get to warmth before winter set in. They had the Rockies coming up. Winter was not the time to try to get through there. They couldn't go south; Texas had had its own reactor meltdown, wasting the bottom half of the state. The top half was guarded at the border, and they shot on sight anyone without papers to cross. It had become its own country, and it wasn't interested in immigrants.

West was the direction they had to go, and they'd gone as far as they could. Now, they needed to stop, so they'd have time to fortify whatever shelter they found.

Gus took Erin's hand and signed, *Yes. Worried. Want you safe.*

Close to Wichita?

Not too close.

Cities were the most dangerous places of all. Bands of Ferals could be avoided, outrun, or, if a group was strong enough, fought off. Substakes kept to themselves. Wanderers generally either cooperated or kept respectful space between groups, like an unwritten, unvoiced code. But cities were traps, every one of them run by some kind of megalomaniac on a power high, with roving bands of military-type 'enforcers' trained to shoot first, kill later.

In Manhattan, Gus had been at ground zero for what had happened to the cities. People had flocked into them in huge waves, thinking that cities, with lots of people, and schools, and hospitals, and government offices, and whole structures of civilization, were the safest places to be. He'd thought that himself.

The opposite had been true. When the panic set in, millions of people crushed together had simply killed each other, on purpose and by accident, in fear and desperation. Then bodies had lain everywhere, decomposing. People had gotten ill from the pervasive rot, and more death had come. Radiation had floated in above them, and brought still more death and disease

Gus had fought his way out of Manhattan before the onset of the worst panic, wanting to get home to his family. By the time he'd made it to Philadelphia, well more than half of the residents of his hometown were dead.

The people who'd survived all that and stayed were either too ill or poor or otherwise disadvantaged to leave the cities, or privileged enough to avoid the worst of the carnage even in the apocalypse. The privileged cleaned up the bodies and restored order, and from there rose the new kings and their subjects.

Best to stay away from those kingdoms. Once you went in, you were likely to end up dead, indentured, or outright enslaved. So they kept a decent distance from Wichita and sought shelter in the wild.

Gus, Orion, and Jarod had scouted a warehouse that had most of its tall chain-link fence still intact and topped with concertina wire. What was broken had fallen in and might be reparable. The few windows of the building seemed intact and imbedded with chicken wire or something like it. If the warehouse was abandoned, and they had a safe way to heat it, they could protect it with a two-man watch and make a decent stake there. Not long term, but through the winter. Well away from the borderlands of Wichita, surrounded by fallow fields and with woods in sight, they could hunt for food in the day and hunker down in the night, protect themselves from Ferals and make a go. Erin could have the baby somewhere warm and dry and safe, Dodge could get off his leg and let it heal, and they could all rest and recover in some kind of peace.

In the spring, they could head west again. Everyone said it was better on the west coast. People talked about San Francisco as a safe place, a good city. Gus hoped it was true.

This could be a good place. We need it.

"I don't want you hurt," Erin said, clasping his hands.

He lifted one of hers to his mouth and kissed her long, expressive fingers. What had once been a simple instinct to protect a woman in need had grown in the past two months. He was definitely sweet on her now. And she on him.

He opened her hand and spelled, *I'll be careful. Want safe place for Baby Michael.*

She grinned and signed in the air, *You mean Baby Angela.*

"Gus! You good to go?" Carver called from across the camp.

"Yeah! One sec!" He saw Tiffany headed toward them, and he caught Erin's hand and signed, *Got to go. Mara and Loni staying. Dodge here. Tiff right here.* Tiffany had learned ASL better than anyone else. She served as Erin's interpreter when Gus had to be away.

Tiffany rubbed a circle on Erin's right forearm, her sign of greeting, and Gus let Erin's hands go.

"Gus!" she cried and threw her arms up. He bent down and wrapped his arms around her, pressing his lips to hers. In front of a thirteen-year-old, he didn't want to go past a PG rating. But before he let her go, he signed *I love you* in her hand and left a kiss in the center of her palm.

She held up the sign for *I love you* as he backed away.

Seven

Overgrown prairie surrounded the warehouse. That was one of its assets as a stronghold: no one could sneak up on it; even from the forest, unless attackers slithered like snakes through the grass, they'd been seen from hundreds of yards away. But as the group sought to reconnoiter the place, they couldn't sneak up on it, either. The scouting team had used Carver's binoculars to check it out from a distance. Now, though, before they moved children and a pregnant woman in, a clearing team had to get in and go through.

All seven of them on the job—Carver, Talia, Jarod, Alan, Orion, Liz, and Gus—stood on the broken asphalt of an old state road, a half-mile or more from the warehouse, and watched, seeking any sign of life. Carver peered through his binocs, chewing on the corner of his lip.

"We're clear," he finally said, dropping the binoculars from his eyes. Carver rarely made a qualified or equivocal statement. He made assertions. "We stick together until we hit that fence. Stay sharp. Then we split up, go around the building in opposite directions, meet up in back. We'll break into search teams there. Clear?"

Everyone nodded or indicated understanding in some other way, and they armed themselves and set forth toward the warehouse. Crossbow nocked and at the ready, Gus walked side by side with Orion, following the rest of the group, watching their back. They didn't talk; everyone kept their full attention on the world around them. By now, their movements when they were out on what Carver, a career Army guy, called a 'mission,' were well rehearsed and practically choreographed.

Six months now, Gus had been traveling with this group. It was the longest he'd stuck with one group in all the time since the Sunstorm, and he was beginning to feel a sense of kinship. Even those he didn't much like, like Jarod and Loni, he felt protective of, and a grudging affection for, like he'd felt for his Uncle Sean, the family's token political wing nut—who'd gotten loudly drunk at every family function and started some kind of political fight that half the time ended up in a brawl.

Scanning the treeline of the forest about a mile off, Gus felt the corner of his mouth lift. So strange, and almost nostalgic, to think of 'Republicans' and 'Democrats' and all the screaming and hating everybody had done back then, both sides sure the other side was going to bring about the end of the world. Maybe they would have, but the universe got there first and shut them all the hell up.

A fairly decent argument for the existence of God, if your mind was of that bent. Gus's wasn't.

Now, Washington D.C., surrounded by reactors, was just a toxic mutant death soup, and nobody was a Republican or a Democrat, or a Green, or a Libertarian, anymore.

Still had Nazis running around, though. Those skinhead bastards were like cockroaches, and they swarmed together. He'd seen a lot of Ferals with faded swastikas inked on their skin.

It was definitely safer to stick to a group, but Gus had never been much of a joiner. His career had provided all the socializing he'd needed. More than he'd wanted, in fact. As first chair, second violinist of the Philadelphia Orchestra, he'd spent a lot of time surrounded by a lot of people, and when his time was his own, he'd generally spent it alone, watching television or playing video games in his apartment, or with his family. He hadn't dated much, hadn't hung out much with friends. Hadn't had many friends.

The truth was, he'd been pretty fucking awkward with people, unless he'd been wearing his Philadelphia Orchestra persona. He'd thought of it that way — acting as a representative of the Orchestra, he could be witty and charming, even debonair, if the situation called for it. He'd been a leader among the strings, and he'd done his job well. But take off the tux, and his smile died and his tongue rolled up.

But that was before. 'Social' was a very different thing in the after. After he'd left his family's dead house, he'd tried to go it alone for a while. Three days into his Gunslinger routine, he'd been savagely beaten and robbed of everything he had, including his shoes and coat. And his violin.

He'd have died right there, off the side of westbound I-76, if someone hadn't come along and helped him. Back in those days, people were more likely to offer a hand to the needy without a big conversation about the pros and cons first.

For a week or so, he'd traveled with that man and his ten-year-old son, until they'd come upon the first substake Gus had seen.

That one had been a gated community before the Sunstorm, and the residents had simply hunkered down and added armed guards to their ivy-covered brick walls and wrought-iron gates. Maybe all the first substakes had been communities where people had already lived afraid of the world beyond their walls. By now, though, he'd seen everything from trailer parks to apartment complexes turned into subs.

Gus hadn't yet heard them called anything but substakes. Across more than half the country, everybody seemed to call them the same thing, which was unusual; most new things of this world had regional names. He didn't know for sure how the term had happened, but he'd guessed it was some mashed-up version of 'subdivision' and 'stake.' Whatever its origin, it meant a heavily guarded compound, inside the brick walls or makeshift fences of which was a community trying its damnedest to pretend that the world hadn't ended.

At that first one, they'd let the man and the boy in, but they'd refused Gus. They hadn't wanted single men. The Good Samaritan who'd scraped him off the road had taken his son and gone into safety. Gus, turned away from the sub at gunpoint, had limped off alone.

Since then, he'd forged an existence moving from group to group, never finding a community he could settle with. Either they'd wanted to go a direction he hadn't wanted to go, or they'd had an ethos he couldn't live with, or he'd had some kind of personal tension with individuals in the group.

He'd even tried a substake once, in northern Illinois, but that had been some kind of Children of the Corn craziness in there. People who closed themselves off from what the world had become were losing their grip almost as fast as the Ferals.

This group, though, was solid and sane. After six months, he thought he could safely believe that. Maybe it was Erin, and the baby, and his need to feather them a nest, but for the first time in more than five years, Gus thought he might be able to let his guard down an inch or so.

Ironically, that scared the ever-loving fuck out of him.

They'd come upon the fence. It wasn't the fence that was down, but the gate, spanning a wide gravel drive. A dip in the lane had camouflaged the source of break from their previous distance.

Carver crouched down at the side of the lane and studied the downed gate.

"That's good, though, right?" Alan asked. "Easier to fix?"

"Weaker, too," Orion answered. He sounded distracted, and Gus considered him. Orion had been a civil engineer before the storm. A lot of what Gus and the others understood about the apocalypse had come from him.

Orion scratched his head, pushing his finger between his hanks of coarse hair, and crouched beside Carver. Just before the Sunstorm, Orion had done his hair in braids. He'd let time and life have their way with the style since, and now had a head full of thick, snake-like dreadlocks.

"I think this gate is a problem we need to solve. It's too wide to be secure, even after we get it back up. If Ferals come with one of those tree spears, they'll go right through it.

Somehow, as if the Ferals had a back-channel communication system, big groups of them all over the country seemed to have similar tools and weapons. Like tree spears—a whole felled tree, one end sharpened to a point so fine you could sign your name with it. It served well as a ramrod and spike both.

It was the big groups you really had to worry about. Like every other group of people, when they gathered in enough numbers, a sense of hierarchy developed. Somebody became a leader, and that somebody generally started planning. Ferals planned mayhem. They made weapons like tree spears and coordinated attacks on substakes, primarily. They'd lost their sense of humanity, but not their sense of purpose. They liked to have a boss and a goal.

"What's your solution, then, O?" Carver asked. "You got one?"

"I could have one. Need to think on it, jot out some ideas. It'll take some construction, though. A smaller gate will hold better. We don't need to drive a fuckin' semi through, anyway."

"How long?"

"Day, maybe two. Depends on how many people I can get working with me."

Carver stood. "That depends on what else we've got to do. Let's keep moving." He gestured at Alan and Liz to follow him and Talia to the right, and Orion, Jarod, and Gus to go left. They separated and checked the perimeter of the building. Nothing much to see: Cinderblock building, no visible signage. Double front doors, chained. Overgrown gravel lot around three sides, thigh-high grass on the fourth. Narrow windows, about five feet tall and one foot wide, along the front and back, intact glass with wire grating. No graffiti or trash or other signs of squatting. In fact, it was eerily bare.

"Place gives me the creeps, man," Jarod mumbled. Gus ignored him. Orion did, too.

At the solid metal back door, also chained, the group reconvened.

Carver waved his hand at his woman. "Okay, Tallie. Do your thing, babe."

Talia slid her machete into its sheath and climbed the short set of concrete steps to the back door. She pulled a pin from the side of her head. A thick, dark tress came loose and draped at her temple. She bent at the waist, peering closely at the large Master lock, and slid the pin into the keyhole.

Gus noted that the lock had no rust at all. In fact, it was almost shiny. The chain, on the other hand, was rusted bright orange. That seemed odd to him, but Talia had the lock open before he could mention it.

Talia pulled the chain free of the door. She put chain and lock in her pack as Carver came up and stood beside her.

"Okay. Talia and Liz with me — Team One. O and Gus, Team Two. Jarod and Alan, Team Three. Mission is to do a clear check. Just that and regroup. *Do not* split up from your partner. Right?" Nods and murmurs of assent. "Let's see what we see."

Once inside, they found themselves at the junction of a wide corridor, with a door leading somewhere forward. Carver sent Gus and Orion to the right and Alan and Jarod to the left. He took the women through that forward door.

The hall was lined with doors, on one side, one about every ten feet. On the count of three, Orion opened the first, and Gus ducked in, crossbow aimed. The room was musty and dark, with only one of those narrow, tall windows offering the muted light of the overcast day outside, but besides dust, it was clean. It was equipped like a dorm, with four narrow metal cots all in a row. Bare mattresses — the rubber-coated kind. They seemed discolored, but stained, not dirty.

Damn. Beds with mattresses? Even on metal cots, that was some luxury living in this world.

Four more rooms exactly the same—clean, four bare cots.

"Was this a hospital?" Gus asked at the last one. "Something like that?" Maybe someone had tried to build something after the Sunstorm, make a place to heal the sick?

But Orion shook his head. "Look at the head and foot of all the frames, man."

Gus looked. The cots were all painted a color that looked, in the poor light, like that pale, industrial green everyone had seen at some time or other. But sections had been rubbed to bare metal. Two sections, fairly even spaced, on each head and each foot.

He narrowed his focus, trying to understand. "People were tied to these beds?"

"Yeah. I know what this place was. J was right. It's creepy as fuck."

"Clear!" Alan yelled from the other side of the hallway.

Orion didn't elaborate on why it was creepy; he simply turned and left the room. "Clear!"

They were at the end of the hall, so they headed back the way they'd come, and met Jarod and Alan.

"Just rooms with beds on our side. What you find?" Alan asked.

"Same," Gus answered, putting the crossbow on his back. "Orion says he knows what it is."

"Yeah," Orion agreed. "I told you about these places, but y'all wouldn't believe me."

Jarod frowned. "Wait. You think …?"

Orion nodded, and Alan whistled in low shock. Gus had no fucking idea what they were all talking about.

"What the fuck, guys?"

Just then, Carver whistled sharply, calling them through the forward door. Nobody answered Gus's question.

But they didn't need to. Once in the space into which they crossed, he understood—or, at least, began to understand.

This forward room had obviously been the warehouse part—vast and dim, the concrete floor still marked with the pattern of the shelving that must have filled the room in long strips. Industrial fluorescent fixtures hung uselessly from a high ceiling mazed with pipes and ducts.

One wall was lined with metal desks, eight of them, placed perpendicular to the wall. Cobwebs made perfect lace drapes over the three desks closest to the windows. At the opposite side of the room, a crowd of wheelchairs was pushed together, their seats thick with dust.

But it wasn't a makeshift hospital, not to heal the sick. In the center of the space, arrayed in six rows of four, were two dozen examining tables. The kind with stirrups.

Each one was positioned under a one-foot-square skylight in the ceiling.

Around these tables, the floor was marked with more than the footprints of vanished storage units. It was dyed a darker color, its pattern an erratic hodgepodge of swirls and blobs.

It was blood. Old blood, badly wiped up and left to dye the concrete.

"No fucking way," Gus grunted as comprehension flowered fully. "No fucking way."

"Breeding farm," Orion finally explained, now that he didn't have to. His tone screamed *told you so*. "I *told you* I heard about these places. Cities round up young women and try to make 'em have babies."

"But we're like twenty miles from Wichita," Liz said. Her eyes had gone so wide they seemed to glow.

"Nowhere to run, nobody to hear," Orion countered.

"Brad!" Talia called. She was the only one who called Carver by his first name.

She'd gone over to the crowd of wheelchairs. Carver crossed to her. "What is it, Tal?"

"There's something back here."

Everybody armed up, and the eerie room crackled with the sound of weapons being readied again.

Gus went up to give him cover, and Carver pulled wheelchairs away, making a path to the wall. They found a body curled in the corner, almost entirely decomposed, long past the point of stench, just bones and hair covered with a filthy hospital gown, tiny swatches of blue cotton showing through the stains of death and decay. The hair was long and blonde. A woman.

When Carver went to the skeleton and nudged it, one of its arms dropped away, and a tumble of tiny bones fell with it. Baby bones. Something about them didn't seem … normal.

Gus staggered back to the middle of the room, framed by those horrible tables. "This is insane."

Jarod scoffed. "You're the one who says it's the next generation that'll fix shit. Seems like you'd get this. Gotta make babies to get a next generation, right?"

Wheeling on him, Gus snarled, "This is not what I mean, asshole, and you know it."

"Alright, alright," Carver said. "Enough. Doesn't matter what this place *was*. What it *is* is clear. It's dry and solid. We can defend it. We clean it up, we shore up the fence and vent out one or two of these skylights for a smokestack, and we can make this work."

"Why'd they pack up and leave it, I wonder?" Jarod asked.

"Don't know, don't care," said Talia. She looked as disgusted and freaked out as Gus felt.

Not ready to let it go, Jarod elbowed Gus. "Place is all set up for Erin, though, man. Time comes, you can drop her on one of these tables, throw her legs in the stirrups, and just play catcher." He chuckled at his own joke.

Orion put his hand on Gus's arm, anticipating his intent to punch Jarod in his smart mouth. No way in hell was Erin delivering their kid on one of these godforsaken things. "Let it go, bruh. J's J. You know that."

Yep. Just like Uncle Sean. Big mouth, small brain. Gus shook Orion off. "Whatever." He looked to Carver. "We can't stay here. The baby can't be born in this place."

"We don't have a choice, Gus. We're not going to find another place this secure. You know that. It *does not matter* what it was. We'll clean it up. We'll make it something better. Erin will be safe here. We all will."

Gus turned in an unsteady circle, reeling against the horrors that his imagination filled in as he fixed on every feature of this macabre place. Who did this? Who *would* do this?

It wasn't the Ferals who made this world terrible. It was the same people who'd made the old world terrible. People who thought they knew better than anybody what was good for everybody. People who didn't have to live their own consequences.

But Carver was right. They couldn't walk away from this shelter.

"She can't ever know what they did here." He met the eyes of everyone in the room. "Please."

"She won't," Talia said. "And the kids, either. It's just a warehouse. Before we go back, let's bury this woman and her child."

When they went out to bury the bodies, they found the worst thing yet: a mass grave. The disturbed earth, a patch of chokeweed growing over it in a near-perfect rectangle of about ten feet by fifteen feet in the middle of a barley field, would have been evidence enough of what it was, but animals had been at the grave and dug up a few patches — enough to uncover bone.

If Gus were of a more spiritual mind, he might worry about the ghosts of abused young women haunting the place. Even from its pragmatic place, his heart groaned under the weight of what had happened here.

After they buried the bones of the woman and child, they left Orion, Liz, and Loni on guard and cleanup duty and went back for the rest of the group. The sun hung low in the sky, drooping on its way to evening, by the time they were all together again inside the warehouse. Mara and Loni took Tiffany, Clark, and Mara's youngest, Melissa, around the whole place, so they could orient themselves. After the long walk on one leg and mismatched crutches, Dodge just wanted to lie down, so Carver helped him to one of the rooms.

With ten rooms and forty beds, there was more than enough for everyone. The way people had grouped up among themselves—Carver and Talia, Gus and Erin, Orion and Liz, Mara and her kids—there were enough rooms for something like privacy, at least until it got too cold to split up like that. Eventually, they'd all have to move to the main room and keep together, because they'd never risk building more than one fire.

For wanderers in this world, fire was a difficult thing, both necessary and dangerous. It was the only source of light and heat besides the sun itself. But, especially on the prairie, with horizons miles away in almost every direction and little to obstruct the view, fire, and its smoke, served as a pin on the map of the world: *People here. Attack at will.*

Out in the world, the group had managed that risk by judicious use of the element—burning the kind of wood that made the least smoke, keeping night fires small and brief, forgoing fire entirely on windless nights when the smoke would simply rise in a column over their heads, using the moon and stars as much as they could for light, and keeping warm by keeping close, using their own bodies and the layers of their clothing and blankets.

Gus hadn't been with the group in the last winter, but he knew they'd spent it, and those before it, as he had—wandering, finding shelter as they could every night, moving on every morning. There were plenty of abandoned houses around to take that kind of itinerant shelter, but they were abandoned because it was mortally dangerous to stay in one place unless you were fortified by membership in a large group. Nobody lived in single houses outside of subs anymore. Lots of people had died in them, though.

Taking shelter where you found it and moving on was a hard way to survive the cold, but it did offer one kind of protection: if you were leaving at first light, you could burn a small fire and have a solid chance of being gone before anyone who wished you harm had made their way to you, unless they'd already been right on top of you.

This winter, they weren't moving on. They were staying put in heavy Feral territory until the weather broke for spring. So they had to devise a way to use fire and obscure it.

Orion thought he could, and he'd already started tearing apart those fucking examining tables for parts.

Except for Orion's work, the evening had been quiet. All the adults except Erin had seen and understood what this place had been, and the knowledge had cast a pall. They'd sat and eaten a cold meal together, then agreed on rules and procedures and figured a work schedule for the next day. Then, before the sun set entirely and darkened the building, they'd claimed their rooms.

Gus led Erin into a room at the far end of the corridor, the last room he and Orion had checked. She'd been quiet, too, in her way, not signing much, not speaking at all, wanting him to stay within touching proximity.

Inside the room, he closed the door and dropped their packs. He lifted her hand from his arm and signed, *Beds and mattresses. Closed door. Just us.*

This side of the building faced east, away from the pale sunset, so the final dregs of daylight through that slot of a window barely showed her response—which was only a vague smile and a nod, anyway. Erin hadn't seen the big room; she hadn't heard their talk. But she was eerily perceptive, tuned into biowaves or something, and she rarely missed the mood of her environment. She knew something was off kilter. He didn't know how to explain it if she asked, though.

He led her around the room, and she touched everything, learning the shapes and boundaries of the space. Then he patted her hand to let her know he was moving away for a second, and went to shove two cots together. They weren't bolted to the floor and moved easily. He moved them into a far corner of the room, under the slot window, so they'd get as much ambient light from the outdoors as possible. The moon would only be a sliver tonight, and clouds had mostly covered the sky all day, so the light would be minimal at best.

They'd have to scavenge for candles and lanterns if they were spending months here. Both of which were precious commodities in a world without electricity. Or they'd have to learn to make tallow. And candles.

After he let her feel the new arrangement of the beds, he spread out their soft, knitted blankets and turned the top two back. They stripped down to their bottom layers. Nobody got naked anymore. Not wanderers, anyway. When the luxury to have a good wash occurred, people stripped and washed one part at a time. Even having sex, you exposed the important parts and kept the rest covered. A naked wanderer was asking for trouble.

They lay together, spooning, Gus behind Erin, his hand on her huge belly. The rest of her was skinny as ever, but she was carrying a beach ball these days, not a playground ball. She signed in the air, but the room had grown too dark, and he could only see the faint impression of her hands moving.

He caught one and spelled, *Too dark. Can't see your hands*.

She chuckled. Her laughter sounded almost like any woman's — light and airy, unforced. A sound that didn't need to be heard to be made. She took his hand in both of hers and brought it to her mouth. As he so often did to her, she kissed his palm. Then, slowly, so he could feel the shapes, she spelled against his hand, *Like me now*.

He laughed and kissed her neck, just below her ear. It was a spot she particularly loved to be touched, so he lingered there, letting his tongue taste the saltysweet of her, feel the vibration of her quiet moan.

What did you say? he asked.

A deep sigh preceded her words. *Here feels …* she paused for a long time *… heavy. A bad smell, too. Death but different. Something wrong here.*

He very much did not want to tell her. Not now, in her condition, made that way as she'd been. She loved this baby. He did, too. They would be a family of three. But she didn't need to know that women had been tied to the very beds they lay on and — what? Had they been raped here? Made pregnant that way? Or had they rounded up all the pregnant women in Wichita and imprisoned them here?

Forty beds. In five and a half years and thousands of miles of walking, Gus hadn't seen or heard of that many pregnant women altogether. No, already-pregnant women hadn't been rounded up. Young women had been captured, bound, and raped until they'd made babies. Or until they hadn't. What had happened to them then? How had they died?

If there was a god, he or she hadn't gone far enough in ending the world.

Gus was absolutely not going to tell his impregnated-by-rape woman about this place. But he couldn't lie to her, either.

Some dead animals. Weird feeling is probably nerves. Everyone nervous to stay in one place.

Erin didn't do the thing sighted people did when someone said something they didn't believe. Most sighted people did a double-take or something like it—a harder look at the speaker. But a gesture like that was meaningless to her. Instead, she showed it in her hands. They pulled from his and stretched out stiffly, like a rejection of the words he'd made on them. Her equivalent to a side-eye.

He fed his fingers through hers, meaning he was doing the best he could. After a second, she relaxed and closed her fingers around his, resting their hands on her belly.

The baby kicked at the weight, then did a series of gymnastic moves, making Erin's belly warp and roll. They both laughed, and Gus let go of her hand so he could spread his palm and fingers over the gyrating swell. The baby moved a lot, every day. That had to mean he was strong and healthy. Lying on a mattress for the first time in months, his arms around a woman he loved, waiting for a healthy baby to join the world, it was difficult, even in this polluted place, for Gus not to be hopeful.

That feeling was so old and strange to him it seemed more like pain than anything else.

Erin slid her hand under his and signed, *Am happy.*

Yeah. He was that, too.

Scared the fuck out of him.

Eight

The group was silent, crouched low in the bushes as Carver drew his bow and sighted on the buck. Nosing puffs of fluffy snow out of its way, the animal nibbled at near-dead leaves, still crisped from the night's frost.

It was the first large animal they'd seen in the forest near their winter stronghold. Fully grown or close to it, it was small for a buck, and its antlers swelled with bulbous eruptions. Not lesions — more like mutations, Gus guessed. Science wasn't his strong suit — he'd been an arts and letters guy, with a Master's from Julliard — but he'd bet the buck had been conceived around the time of peak radiation concentration for this area.

Didn't matter. It was meat, and they'd all been breathing the same air, anyway.

Carver took the shot, and the buck fell, its body making little sound as it landed on a cloud of snow.

Carver, Alan, and Gus rose from their cover and headed to it. As Gus and Carver laid out the dressing tools, Alan whistled, signaling to the rest of the foraging party that they'd taken down something substantial. In the space of a few seconds, acknowledging whistles rose up.

Loni and Liz were checking the snares for small game. Jarod, Talia, and Orion were out on water and fish detail. The others had stayed at the base, taking care of homebound chores, and seeing to the children.

And to Erin, who was still pregnant, two weeks after they'd moved into the warehouse. The baby had barely moved in almost two days. Mara said that was normal and meant he was feeling crowded and about ready to be born. As the mother of three children and a veteran of home births, she was the closest thing the group had to a doctor, nurse, midwife, doula, anything. So they trusted that she was right. But Erin was anxious, and so was Gus.

Crouching beside the buck, Carver lifted its head and studied the growths. "Seein' this more and more. Just looks like antler, though." He touched one, testing it between his fingers. "Feels like antler. I think it's okay."

"Yeah," Gus agreed and then added what he'd been thinking while they'd watched the animal feed. "Doesn't matter much. If we're gonna get sick, I don't think eating an animal living in the same world we are is the thing that'll make it happen."

Carver answered that with a sigh. "Sometimes I wonder what this fight we do every damn day is for."

"It's gotta get better eventually," Gus answered, and even he recognized that he sounded like he was reading a platitude scrawled on a bathroom stall wall.

It wasn't getting better. The real apocalypse wasn't the destruction of technology. It wasn't the radiation. It wasn't the loss of the modern world. It was the loss of humanity. The Sunstorm had torn off the fragile veneer of decency and shown most people to be, at best, insular and suspicious, and at worst, bestial and cruel. Whatever bond of humanity still pulled anyone was only strong enough, and elastic enough, to reach the limits of a small group. At best.

Their own group was just the same. These people had become his family. He'd found calm and happiness here he hadn't known still existed. Everyone in this group was a decent human being at heart, especially when weighed on the scale of this new world. But they'd sat around a fire not three months before and voted on whether to kill Erin or to welcome her.

And Gus, he'd sat there with them and voted, as if it had been a reasonable question for discussion.

Carver heard his lack of conviction and responded in kind. "Yeah."

"Christ, it's too early in the day to get philosophical," Alan complained, his voice wry. "Just gut the damn deer. You can kill yourself tonight, if you want. Me, I'm hungry."

Gus flipped him off, but the acerbic remark had served to break the existential angst off their mood.

While Alan kept watch, Carver and Gus dressed the deer. They tried to use as much as they could of any kill, but no one would eat the organ meat. One of the few luxuries they had left—food wasn't scarce enough, yet, to override all food preferences and assertions of taste, so they could turn their noses up at the strong taste and unsettling texture of organ meat.

They emptied most of the carcass. They kept the head and left the brain inside it for now, because Jarod knew how to tan skins using the brain, and even these strange antlers might be useful for tool-making.

When they'd drained the body of most of its blood, Carver handed Gus his bow and quiver and hoisted the buck over his shoulders. Alan whistled again, and two whistles answered. It was time to meet up and head back to base.

Loni had a keeper draped over her shoulder, with two rabbits, a squirrel, and another small animal Gus didn't recognize dangling from the hooks. Not a bad take for a dozen snares. Liz's pack looked full; she must have found berries or greens worth eating. That would be a treat. They hadn't had much but meat and hard barley bread for a while. Gus hoped she'd found acorns. Mara made a really good fried flatbread with acorns.

The water and fish team had done well, too. There was a freshwater creek in these woods—small, but with a lively current. A couple of times, Talia had taken fat young trout from it. Mostly, it was other kinds of fish, none of which Gus knew much about. On this day, she had a motley assortment of half dozen small fish on her keeper.

Orion and Jarod each carried two five-gallon collapsible water jugs, the vinyl still dotted with dewy spots of fresh stream water, on their backs. Those jugs had been one of their best scavenges ever, so good the whole group had been giddy. Shoved in the back of a rusting metal cabinet in the garage of a house that had been crushed under a fallen oak tree: five flattened vinyl water jugs, the kind people used for camping. One of them had leaked, but the other four were tough and watertight. The ability to keep twenty gallons of water at a go was a goddamn miracle.

Carver surveyed the results of their forage. "Good work. This is good. Meat for at least a week, and it's cold enough that it'll keep. What'd you come up with, Liz?"

Liz unzipped her pack and pulled the top open, showing it around. "Chickweed, sorrel, wild onion. A little faded and ice-burnt, but it'll do. And about five pounds of acorns." She smirked at Gus. "Just for you, hon."

Gus grinned and rubbed his hands together. Fried up in venison fat, Mara's acorn flatbread was just about good enough to serve at the swankiest restaurant in Manhattan. He could eat his weight in the stuff.

As Liz zipped her pack up, gunfire rang through the air. A single report. As one, the foraging team turned toward their base. They couldn't see the warehouse from here, they were too deep in the forest, but they all stared anyway.

Erin was in that warehouse. Blind, deaf, and so pregnant she could barely walk. She couldn't protect herself.

"Let's move!" Carver shouted, and they all ran forward. There was no wondering, no doubt. Gunfire meant trouble. Bad trouble. When two more shots rang out, they knew it was a crisis.

It was rare to hear shots fired. Ammunition had grown increasingly scarce, and everybody knew to use it prudently. Hunters used bows and arrows or crossbows and bolts, or knives and spears. More than simply the limit of the resource, firing a gun announced your presence, to a wide audience, and said you had something valuable to steal. Not smart. Guns were for emergency use only.

It was most likely—so much more likely than anything else it was basically assured—that those shots had been fired as an alarm. Gus pictured Mara firing one of the revolvers into the air. Or Dodge, still limping on his lame leg, firing at a first attacker, using the bullet for two purposes, as defense and call for help. Whatever it was, Gus was sure those shots had been fired by one of their own.

Because Ferals didn't use guns at all. In the early days they had, firing barrages of bullets into the air like firecrackers, shooting holes in anything, or anyone, they'd come across. But even they had run low on bullets, apparently. Or gotten too stupid to remember how to load their guns. Now, they used rusty blades of all kinds, and they used spears. They used discarded tools. They used handmade weapons, especially a kind of hammer they fashioned from a rock, a stick, and a strip of rope or leather. Or they used their hands and feet. They used their teeth. But they didn't use guns.

As the team ran, they shed the burdens of their forage. Carver threw the buck down. Orion and Jarod dropped the water. Liz unshouldered her pack, and Loni and Talia tossed their keepers into the melting snow. Moving faster, they left the forest and chugged across the field. Without breaking his stride, Gus tossed Carver his bow and quiver, and pulled his own crossbow forward, snagging a bolt as he ran. Orion unsheathed his katana. Liz and Loni pulled their hatchets from their belts. Jarod had a rifle, and Alan a machete.

By the time they were close enough to hear the first sounds of the trouble, all of the party was armed and ready. Gus's heart stormed against his eardrums, but he heard the sound clearly: the metallic rattle and grate of the chain link fence. Were Ferals trying to ram it down?

Orion had rebuilt the gate and fortified the entire fence line. Would it hold? Coming from the back, Gus saw nothing amiss, no sign of trouble but that grating sound. Then he realized that the fence was shaking.

Closer still, they heard the screams and shouts.

"SPLIT UP!" Carver yelled. "Half to the right, half to the left!"

Gus veered off with Orion, Liz, and Jarod and turned to the right. With the crossbow up, ready to shoot, he ran ahead. As he came around the first corner, he saw what the rattling was. The Ferals were going over the fence, trying to climb over the savage spiral of concertina wire.

Some were making it, too. Sliced up and bleeding, they dropped onto the gravel below and ran for the building. Gus aimed through the chain link at a half-bald woman scrambling away from the fence and fired a bolt. It went through the back of her neck; she ran several more yards, flailing wildly, flinging blood from the gashes in her arms, then fell face-first on the bloodstained gravel.

He was already nocked and firing at another when she fell.

A shriek pierced the air, and from the side of his vision, he caught movement. Reaching for another bolt, he turned and faced a Feral, heavy tangle of beard and greasy dark hair, dressed in a ragged work coverall. Brandishing a vicious hunting knife, he was too close for Gus to aim the crossbow.

In the same blink in which he readied himself to die, an explosion at the side of his head turned his eardrum to mush, and the Feral's head blew out, dousing him with blood and brains. The guy fell, skidding into Gus's legs and almost taking him down, but a hand grabbed him before he lost his feet.

Jarod, his rifle still smoking in the cold. He'd saved Gus's life.

There wasn't time to deal with that, but Jarod nodded as if Gus had thanked him, and they charged for the Ferals.

Nobody really knew what was up with the Ferals. Sometimes they looked wrong, somehow, like sick or mutated or just inbred, but for the most part, they looked normal. Dirtier, generally, fewer teeth, usually, a lot more scars, always, but it wasn't like they'd been made into monsters by the radiation or anything else. It was like they'd been assholes before the storm, really embraced their asshole nature after it, when law and social pressure died off, and they'd warped themselves into animals as they'd forgotten what it was like to be human. After almost six years of living their ids, they'd become genuinely monstrous.

It was rumored that they killed the few babies born to their women, and Gus had never seen a Feral child. But the groups kept getting bigger, so they were being made somehow.

This was a big group, twenty at least on their feet, outnumbering their own group of able fighters by more than double. Four big Ferals had a tree spear going at the smaller gate, the only way in or out of the compound besides over the fence. Most of the rest were trying to climb and push their way through the razors atop it. Five lay dead or disabled at the base of the fence. Mara and Dodge were fighting them off, Mara with her hunting knife and Dodge with the butt of his rifle. He must have gotten the shots off.

But the Ferals had blades and bludgeons, too, and they were getting their licks in through the fence. Dodge and Mara bled freely, and Mara looked ready to go down.

Roaring in unison, Carver and Orion charged at the Ferals attacking the gate.

From what Gus could see, it looked like only a few had made it over alive — three, no four, were moving on the warehouse. He focused on them with his crossbow and let the rest of the foraging party deal with the Ferals on this side. He could not let one of these psychos get into the building, where Erin and the children were.

He nocked another bolt and aimed through the fence again, firing and striking true. His bolt went through the back of a male at the warehouse door. The Feral dropped to his knees and then sagged forward against the door.

Movement again at his flank; this time he turned in time to face a male swinging one of their stone hammers. With no bolt nocked, and no time to pull his knife, he used the crossbow as a bludgeon and beat the Feral back, driving him to the ground, caving in his skull, unable to stop.

Something leapt onto him, grabbed his ponytail and yanked his head back, and a screaming face came at him, He felt rough metal sink into the side of his neck. Again, he slammed the bow against the Feral until she let go and fell away, but the blade slid through as she fell, and hot blood gushed over his shoulder and down his chest.

He got off one more bolt, killing another male Feral who'd reached the warehouse door, this one getting it open, and then his knees buckled, and his sight stuttered and went out.

Gus woke to the sensation of crowding, and opened his eyes to a blurry mob of figures looming over him. He tensed at once and tried to reach for the knife on his thigh, but his hand was bound.

No, not bound. Held. By a soft hand and long, slender, strong fingers. Erin. Then his hand moved, and he felt her lips on his knuckles. She was okay. She was okay.

"We're okay?" he asked, with his voice and his fingers at the same time.

Carver answered. The voice came from near his feet. "We killed them all."

There was a tone in Carver's voice Gus didn't like. He blinked to clear his vision and tried to lift his head, but vivid pain speared through his neck, and his head swam. Hands pushed on his shoulders and made him lie flat again.

"Be still," Mara said at his side. "You lost a lot of blood, and I'm still working over here." As a demonstration, she stuck something sharp in the side of his neck, and he remembered that he'd been cut by a Feral.

"What's wrong?" he asked and signed. He'd made a habit of signing and speaking, so that Erin could be a full part of every discussion; it had become so ingrained that often he signed his speech when she wasn't around.

No one answered him at first. Even Erin's hands were still. But they might not have told her details. The others still tended to forget her until she made a fuss.

As the silence persisted, he felt Erin's fingers on his hand, spelling, *Think one of us is dead.*

"Who'd they get?" he asked.

"Liz." Carver grunted. "O tried to save her. They got him bad, but he's hangin' on."

"Oh shit." *Liz*, he signed to Erin. *And Orion's hurt.*

Her hand clenched hard around his before she signed in the air, *Oh no. He loves her so much.*

Orion and Liz had been together for a couple of years. *Yeah.*

"Is he gonna make it?"

Carver glanced at Mara, who made a vague shrug. "It's too early to tell. He took one of their rusty knives in the belly."

"Shit."

"I'm doing all I can for him. And for you." Mara turned away and then back, bringing with her a thick length of gauze coated in reeking goo.

"Not that crap," he complained.

"Yes, this crap." She laid it on his neck, and it burned like fire. "The blades those freaks use are disgusting. Who knows what's growing on them. This crap works. It *works*."

In the desperation biting down on her words, Gus heard that the smelly concoction setting fire to his neck was supposed to save Orion, too.

At the last crossroads bazaar they'd come across, there had been a woman trading homemade healing ointments and potions, as well as the recipes to make them. Mara had made good trades with Erin's knitting. Good trades, as long as she hadn't bought a bunch of poison. But they'd had cause to use most of it by now, in small doses—minor work injuries and illnesses—and she was right. The stuff worked.

They'd lost Liz, and Orion had lost his love. But Erin wouldn't lose hers.

He gave her hand a squeeze. *I'll be okay.* He could feel that it was true. He was weak, and he hurt, but he wasn't dying. He'd be here for Erin and the baby. With them, he'd found a reason in this bleak world. A home. The thing he'd been looking for and never finding. *We'll be okay.*

She offered him a beautiful smile. *I know. Now I can take care of you for once.*

You take care of me every day.

He didn't speak those words as he signed. They were only for Erin.

Four days later, Erin shook him awake into a night of perfect darkness and heavy cold. When she knew she had his attention, she signed into his hands, *It's time. Baby coming.*

He sat up at once and blinked, trying to make light happen. There was nothing. Jesus, it was dark. Then he heard it—*tick tick tick* on the narrow window. Sleet.

It had been almost a week since their little tumbler had a good workout inside her belly, but he hadn't been completely still. Erin still felt taps and kicks, nothing like before, but enough to assure them that he was okay. Just snug, and not in a big hurry. And Erin kept growing, which was a good sign, if uncomfortable for her. Her belly was so big now that she honestly had trouble keeping her balance on her skinny, long legs.

Finally! he signed. *How do you feel? How close?*

Hurts. I think five minutes. I count in my head.

Five minutes is close. I'll get Mara.

She grunted and grabbed his hands before he could get up. *No! Don't leave me.*

Honey, Mara is going to help us.

I know. I don't want to do it in here. Lonely.

You want to have a baby in the big room? A memory of the way that room had been when he'd first seen it flashed through his mind. God, he didn't want her to be in there for this.

Warmer. Not lonely. Fam – an *oof* left her lips. She stopped signing and grabbed her belly, and a moan, quiet but strained, rolled out of her. In the dark, he could only sense the motion, but he reached out and found her hands and laid his over them. Her belly was hard as marble. He

140

counted seconds and got to fifty-six when she relaxed and her belly softened a bit. Minute-long contractions five minutes apart. From what Mara had explained, that meant labor was pretty far along.

Erin had been sitting beside him for a long time, having labor alone.

She grabbed his hands and signed, *Family. Be with family.*

He couldn't argue with that.

Everyone got up with them, in the middle of a dark, cold night. They burned some of the ill-formed tallow candles Tiffany, Clark, and Loni had made, and Carver started a fire in their makeshift wood stove. Even Orion came out, when Talia pushed him out on one of the wheelchairs they'd kept for seating. He'd been torn open, and his recovery was slow. But it was a recovery.

Alan and Jarod had already been on watch, but they took turns ducking in for hot barley tea and a status check.

Gus's attention was entirely on Erin, but he felt the ambiance around them, and knew she felt it as well: cozy and companionable. Family.

Erin went about her labor with dogged determination. She never wanted to stop moving, so Gus walked her around the perimeter of the room, over and over. Whenever they passed one of the group, that person would often reach out and make their sign on her, letting her know they were with her.

Each time a contraction took her, she stopped and folded over. Acting on instinct, Gus had taken to sweeping his arms under hers and embracing her, rubbing her back, letting her lean on him through the pain. Each time he asked how she was doing, she smiled and nodded, but her smiles got more strained each time.

By dawn, they'd stopped walking. Her contractions were ninety seconds apart and more than a minute long, practically on top of each other, and there were no more smiles. She screamed through each one and sagged against him, weeping, in the tiny spaces between. But each time he, or Mara, asked if she needed to push, she shook her head—and then moaned in despair when a fresh pain clamped around her.

"Mara!" Gus yelled for the hundredth time as Erin's fingers dug into his shoulders.

"I don't know what to do!" she yelled back. "I've never been on this side of things!"

"Shouldn't you check her or something?" Talia asked. "When my sister had her baby, she said the nurses were always putting their hands up inside her."

Mara wheeled on her and flailed frantic hands. "They do, but I don't know what to look for. I don't know what a cervix is supposed to feel like."

The latest agony passed, and Gus signed in Erin's hands what had been said.

She clapped her hands, meaning that she wanted their attention, and signed, *Please, Mara. Help me.*

Mara grabbed her hand and signed *Okay.* She scanned the room then stared at Gus. "I need her to be on a table, so I can see what I'm doing."

There were still three tables intact. They'd been shoved into a far corner of the room, waiting to be dismantled for parts. "Absolutely not."

"Gus." Carver's voice rose over the challenge Mara had begun to make. "I get it, I do. But that table's just a table. It'll help her. That's what it is. Nothing more."

Erin screamed again and said, in her strange and beautiful voice, thick with pain, "Gus! I can't do it!"

Tears that had been clawing their way up his throat since her first agonized scream finally made their target and ran down his face. *You can.* he signed. *I'm here. Your family is here. We'll do this together.*

Carver and Dodge dragged a table into the middle of the room, under one of the skylights, over the bloodstained floor. Gus swept his suffering woman into his arms and carried her to the cursed thing.

Erin wore a sagging pair of men's black sweatpants and two sweaters she'd knitted. Once she was on the table, Mara helped her strip off the pants and get her bare legs on the stirrups, and Talia spread a blanket over her legs. Gus let them do what they needed to do. He couldn't look at her legs in those metal contraptions. He focused on her face, beautiful even wrenched by pain and worry.

Another pain took hold, and she screamed yet again. Her voice had gone hoarse, and all that came out now was cracked torment. No longer able to let her hang on him, he leaned over her and caught her head in his hands, and set his forehead on hers, taking deep breaths and blowing them on her face, trying to get her to follow his rhythm. He didn't know why that seemed important, but it helped. She began to breathe with him, and she calmed. The pain passed again, and she relaxed with a whimper.

Into the moment of quiet, Mara said, "Gus, she's bleeding. I don't know if that's normal or not. I'm going to try to check her, but I don't know if I'll be able to tell."

There was something wrong. He knew it, and Erin knew it, but he wouldn't let the thought stick.

He nodded, keeping his focus on Erin, feathering soft kisses over her hot, soaked brow. Then he caught her hand and signed, *Mara's going to check inside you. I'm right here.*

She nodded and let her head droop against his arm.

144

Gus knew when Mara began, because Erin tensed, but with a different kind of pain. He stayed with her, kissing and caressing.

"Oh God," Mara said. It was just a whisper, but Gus heard, and knew. He turned and looked down to the end of the table. All he could see was the blanket, tented over Erin's knees. A blue and green pattern, like ocean waves.

"Get my kids out of here," Mara called into the room. Everyone stood up and came close. Loni went into action, herding the kids together. None of the three resisted; they all were wide-eyed with fear and confusion.

Oh God. Gus swallowed hard and made himself ask. "Mara," he said, afraid for her answer.

She looked around the blanket. She was pale, and her eyes were so wide they were perfect circles. "There's … I don't know what it is, but the baby … its head … something's wrong, Gus." Her voice shook with tears. "It's behind the cervix, and it isn't smooth. I think it should feel smooth, like a round head pushing. I feel a sharp edge. I think he's stuck."

Another contraction, and this scream was the worst. It cut out in the middle, and Erin coughed blood into Gus's face. She'd screamed so hard she'd torn her throat.

"Mara!" He just wanted Erin to be okay. He needed her to be okay. They had to help her, whatever happened to the baby.

"Okay." Mara shook herself hard. "She's got to push. I'm going to go back in there and try to help. It's going to hurt so bad, but I can't think of anything else to do. We can't give her a C-section. It'll kill her for sure."

"Just help her." He caught Erin's hands and signed. *You have to push now. Hard as you can.*

She shook her head. "Can't!" Her voice was gone; all that came was a croak.

You can. I'll help. He slid his arm under her and folded her up in his hold as well as he could.

And she did it. She pushed hard through five torturous contractions, collapsing into semi-consciousness between each one. The whole room had gone quiet, and the table was closed in a ring of their friends, their family, standing a sober, frightened watch. The sleet storm was over and the sun was up; the day outside was clear. Bright stripes of sunlight washed over the room, and the skylight above the table cast Erin in a soft glow.

Please. Please. The word thumped in his head with every beat of his heart.

On the sixth contraction, something happened. Erin tensed, her back arching from Gus's arm, and a gush of blood splashed on the floor under her legs. Mara gasped — and then so did Talia, at her side, assisting.

"Jesus," Carver muttered, loud enough for Gus to hear.

Erin had gone limp. Gus held her and turned to Mara. "What! What's wrong?"

Tears coursed down Mara's cheeks. "It's a boy, Gus. He's alive. But … I'm so sorry."

Talia took the baby. She turned to Gus. She was crying, too.

In her arms was Erin's son. *His* son. Fat little arms and legs wiggling. Pale. Paler even than Gus's coloring.

The baby's head stopped about half an inch above his eyes. It just stopped. All there was of his exposed brain was a small lump of bruised-looking tissue.

But he made his first cry, like a kitten mewing, and his arms reached out into the world, seeking comfort. He was alive and aware enough to reach out. To feel. How could that be?

"Gus!" Erin croaked weakly from her ruined throat. "Baby!"

He had to tell her. With a shaking hand, he signed, *He's sick. His head didn't finish. He won't live, but he's here now.*

Her hands yanked from his and went rigid, the fingers stretched out and hooked at the ends like claws. She shook her head wildly and then began to sign so fast Gus could barely keep up.

No! My gift! God gave him to me to make it better! I live for him! He won't die! No!

Gus grabbed her hands and tried to calm her. Between her legs, Mara was still working, now frantically. He glanced down at the floor and saw blood dripping into a deepening, widening pool.

She was bleeding out. He had to get her calm.

He's alive right now. This is your time to know him. Stay here and love him.

All at once, she calmed and held out her hands. Her opalescent eyes flooded tears. Talia handed Gus the baby, and he set him in his mother's arms.

She touched him everywhere, starting at his feet, counting all his perfect toes, his chubby legs and dimpled knees, finding his little package, his soft belly, still connected to the cord, his chest, arms, perfect hands and fingers. His face, with round cheeks and a serious little mouth, a tiny nose, closed eyes. He cried weakly, and she sensed it somehow and laid her hand on his chest, feeling the sound.

Then she touched his head, and she wailed in near silence, her mouth wide open and warped with her pain, as she touched the exposed edge of his skull and the small, unformed beginning of the brain he should have had. She lifted him from the cradle of her arms and set him on her shoulder and chest, and she sobbed against his small back.

The back of his head, just the inch or so that had formed, was covered with a thick stretch of black waves of hair. He would have had Erin's hair.

His little hand twisted into his mother's hair and clenched, and that was the thing that broke Gus. He laid his head on Erin's other shoulder, set his hand on their son's back, and cried with her.

Erin's hands dropped away from the baby, and Gus barely caught him before he fell to the floor. He scooped him up and cradled him to his chest.

He knew as soon as he looked into her face. Her skin had gone ashy grey, and her mouth was slack. Her eyes were open. Holding the baby tightly, he bent and kissed her throat, at the pulse point. Nothing moved against his lips.

She was gone.

This terrible world had killed her. No god, no love, no family had been enough to save her. Nothing was strong enough to survive this place.

Mara still worked between her legs. The floor was slick with blood, an ocean of it spilled over the stains from the room's awful past.

"Mara, stop," Gus sighed. "She's gone."

"I'm sorry," she cried. "Oh God, I'm so *sorry!*"

The baby squirmed in his arms. Gus picked up a tiny hand, and the fingers curled around his thumb and held on tight. There was a new life in his arms, but already the boy was fading. Each cry was weaker than the one before it. He was staying just long enough to know love.

Just long enough to break the hearts that held that love.

They had meant to name a girl Angela, for Erin's mother. And a boy Michael, for his sister.

He kissed Erin's cooling, still damp forehead, and then he walked away from her death, and Mara's tears, and the stunned, useless silence of the rest of them.

Tucking Michael under his shirt, against his chest, he walked out into the cold day and waited for his son to die.

Nine

Sleep had only just begun to relax his joints and pull his mind into quiet when Gus heard it. It wasn't a sound so much as an impression, a change in the way the air moved in the world outside.

He'd taken shelter for the night in one of the abandoned cars that filled the interstates. Normally, he tried to avoid highways as much as possible because Ferals prowled them looking for easy kills, but this stretch of Utah was nothing but a flat wasteland as far as he could see, and if he got too far from the fixed path of I-70, he got disoriented and started to lose his way—and his mind, a little.

Beyond sharing an occasional fire with a wandering group, or making a trade at a crossroads, he'd been alone now for ... months, anyway. The fangs of winter had receded, and spring was rising up. He'd gone through the goddamn Rockies in the thick of the winter, probably around January. While the snow was as tall as he was, he'd holed up in an old Park Service lodge, subsisting on what animals came close enough to the lodge that he could hunt them. For a while, he'd thought he might just stay there, for about a minute he'd even started to make a plan for it, but he couldn't stay still. He thought too much, remembered too much, when he wasn't moving, and by the time the snow melted enough that he could pass, he was halfway crazy and churning with rage and pain.

So he'd started walking again as soon as he could. Eventually, he would hit ocean and have to stop; he didn't know what he'd do then. In the meantime, walking was something to do. Better than sitting alone with his thoughts.

Not that he wanted company. He was done with company, done with letting his guard down, done with thinking that there was a way to fashion a life in this wasted world. There was no life to be had here. He'd sat long nights in the lodge and imagined killing himself, but never managed to get it done, sadly. He'd gotten all the way to the edge of the act, had the point of the knife pressing into the skin of his chest, or the blade at his throat, and he simply could not exert the next ounce of energy to get it done.

It wasn't fear that stopped him. It was like his body had a fail-safe in it somewhere and just froze up. A dead man's switch that prevented him from making himself a dead man.

So he kept walking.

Now he was in the wasteland of Utah, taking a few hours' shelter on the interstate. When he'd found this car, a Hyundai sedan with after-market blacked-out windows, he'd felt fortunate—those windows, despite the poor application of the film, would provide some cover.

He'd see how much cover any minute now, because a band of Ferals was walking up the road. He could hear the rumble of their feet, the occasional bark of their talk and laughter. The creaks and bangs of car doors being opened on rusting hinges and slammed shut again.

The back of this Hyundai's back seat had been torn out, exposing a trunk about half full with random crap. Keeping his body as flat as he could, below the window level, and moving as carefully as he could so the car wouldn't shake, he eased himself back, into the trunk, and pulled the trash and papers forward, for camouflage.

His pack was on the floor behind the driver's seat, and Orion's katana was under the front passenger seat. Everything he had in the world, besides the clothes on his back, the boots on his feet, and the knife in his hand. His water, his snares, his tools. Even if they didn't find him, he'd die for sure if they took all that.

Oddly, he discovered that he didn't want it to happen. He didn't want to die.

This is fucking stupid, Gus. Carver's voice rolled through his head. *It's suicide. You need space, I get it. You got shit to work out. We'll leave you be as much as you need. But goin' out there on your own, now? Don't be an asshole.*

He'd known it was stupid. He'd known it was suicide. He'd known he was an asshole. But it hadn't mattered. He could not have spent another night in that warehouse, with Erin's blood stained into the concrete on top of all the other women's blood. With Erin and the baby buried in sight of that fucking mass grave.

Mara's voice joined Carver's. *You have to stay, Gus. This is where she is.*

And that had been the problem, right? Erin haunting the place, everywhere his eyes landed reminding him what he'd had, what he'd lost, what he hadn't been able to protect.

Not what. *Who.*

Gus heard the heavy, hollow thump of boots jumping on a vehicle nearby. He thought it was the SUV right next to this Hyundai. He shrank farther back in the trunk and held his breath. At the same moment, the front passenger door of the Hyundai screeched open, and a bald Feral with a tribal tattoo crawling up his neck and over his scalp leaned in, searching. The full moon reflected off his smooth skull, so brightly that Gus could see the nicks in his scalp from the recent shave.

It was over. All he had to do was look between the front seats, and he'd get an eyeful.

Gus tightened his grip on his knife. He could kill this one, but he couldn't take on a whole band of Ferals himself. They'd kill him, and they'd get as much enjoyment out of the deed as they could. He'd be better off sticking the blade in his own throat. If he could get it done. Maybe imminent threat of torture would override the fail-safe.

"Rusty!" one of them bellowed outside. "Over there!"

The bald one pushed back, out of the Hyundai, and looked. "Smoke! Got a live one! Move!" another one shouted, and Baldy slammed the door shut and thundered off with the rest.

Gus lay where he was, breathless and trembling, while the road shook with their stomping feet. He didn't move, took barely a breath, until long after the night had gone quiet again.

Hours later, in the deeper dark of the predawn, he climbed out of the Hyundai. He took a piss, ate one of the last pieces of the rabbit he'd cooked to blackness before he'd left the lodge, and sipped his morning ration of water. Then he hooked his pack over his shoulders and sheathed the katana under it.

I get it, man, Orion had said when he'd handed Gus his sword. *Watch your back. Maybe we'll meet up again someday.*

Probably not. He turned west and started walking. He tried not to think about what was happening, or had happened, to whoever had started that fire.

"Here, fella." Gus held out a strip of raw meat. Conflict raging in his dark eyes, the dog stared, licking his chops. He whined and ducked his head, then turned and skittered back a few feet, turned again, and stared at the meat.

In his lengthening list of 'who the fuck cares anyway' stupid moves, hailing a wild dog was the latest entry. He didn't think he'd seen a pet dog—or any kind of pet animal—since a year or two after the Sunstorm. Dogs and cats were just more wildlife now, and avoided humans as much as they could. But Gus hadn't seen another living soul, not counting the small animals he'd killed to eat, in maybe weeks. No Ferals, no wanderers, nothing. The words he'd spoken to this dog were the first out of his mouth in longer than he could remember. He wouldn't mind convincing the dog to hang out with him a while. Maybe stay with him long term.

The dog was emaciated and filthy, with sores on his rear and a coat made of mats and burs, but Gus thought he might be a purebred. A Golden Retriever, if he had to make a guess. Somebody's beloved family member, once upon a time and long ago.

Gus had had a beloved dog, in the long ago. For his seventh birthday, when it had become clear to his parents that he would be an only child, and that he was not the kind of child who had friends, they'd given him a puppy so he wouldn't be lonely anymore. A purebred Newfoundland dog, solid black. He'd named him Mudge, after a dog in a book series he'd been reading. Mudge had been a roly-poly puppy, clumsy and cute, but he'd grown to be almost two hundred pounds and had looked like a bear. People on walks or at the dog park had often been afraid of him, on first meeting, but Mudge had been one-hundred-percent teddy bear and had been sure he was a lap dog.

Gus hadn't been lonely after that; he'd had a best friend.

But dogs that big didn't have long lives, and Mudge had died when Gus was fourteen. He'd returned from a shitty day in ninth grade—they'd all been shitty days; in his personal experience and the anecdotal evidence he'd acquired during a life surrounded by orchestral musicians, boys who played violin four hours a day didn't tend to get along that well in the social Hunger

Games of high school—and found Mudge, his face white with age, sleeping on his memory-foam pad in the kitchen by the back door, where he spent most of his time while Gus was gone at school or lessons. Just like always.

Except he hadn't been sleeping.

That day was the worst day of his childhood. The grief was carved so deep into Gus's psyche that even now, twenty years later, to remember it was to live it.

His mom had been pregnant with Michaela at the time, their miracle baby, and his sister had been born twelve weeks early less than a week after Mudge's death. Gus remembered thinking, though he'd been plenty old enough to know better, that Michaela had come early so he wouldn't be lonely.

He pushed away all those dangerous thoughts and tossed the meat toward the dog. "There ya go. More where that came from, but you gotta come closer."

Taking his attention away from the dog, Gus tore into the rabbit for a bite of his own. He ate his kills raw on the road. Even as he spent weeks in a row without seeing another human being, he avoided fire, just in case, and hadn't risked one since the lodge. Raw meat, water straight from streams—he'd had a few rough days at first, as his digestion got used to it, and every now and then, he still had a rough day.

His taste buds had never gotten used to it. But it was meat, and it kept him going.

Now that spring was almost summer, he'd had a chance to find other things to eat, and sometimes he found something that tasted actually good. Today was not one of those times.

He was, he thought, about halfway through Nevada now. Five hundred or so miles to the coast. He'd expected to find more wanderers moving in the same direction, but he'd been mostly alone through Utah and Nevada. Even Ferals were scarce. Since the close call at the Hyundai, he'd only seen three more bands, small ones, and he'd had plenty of time to stay out of their way.

Of course, he'd moved off the interstate once he'd gotten into terrain with some visual markers that kept him oriented, so maybe that was why the world seemed empty. Still, though. He didn't know what it meant that there were so few people. Only a year ago, every crossroads bazaar and multi-group fire had buzzed with talk about the west coast. Eighty percent of the wanderers had been headed in the same direction. The other twenty percent had been hoping to find a sub that would take them in.

Were they all dead now? Or had they all made it? Was he walking toward salvation or destruction?

Didn't really matter.

He chewed his raw rabbit and watched from the corner of his eye as the dog sidled up to the meat, whining all the way, his belly dragging the ground. When he finally got there, he sniffed it carefully and whined some more, then backed away an inch or two.

Eventually, he couldn't stand it, and he gobbled up the offering, then lay there, cowering, like he waited to see what terrible thing would happen next.

Gus pulled more meat off a leg and held it out. "It's okay, buddy. I'm not gonna hurt you."

The dog wouldn't come close enough to take it from his hand, but he inched a bit closer, and Gus tossed it a few feet away. Again, the dog did his Dance of Hungry Uncertainty, cowering, inching, whining, turning in circles, and finally taking the meat and waiting for pain.

This time, when the pain didn't come, he rose up and sat on his haunches. When Gus looked his way, he cocked his head, as if saying *Is there more?*

Gus chuckled. The unfamiliar sound felt rough in his chest. "There *is* more, in fact. There's water, too. This time, though, you gotta come all the way." He pulled off another hunk—the dog was getting more of this rabbit than he was—and held it out. "Right here, buddy. Come and get it."

It took about five minutes of sitting there with his arm out, but at long last the dog made it all the way to him and took the meat out of his hand. He snatched it in his teeth and ran about ten feet away to eat it, but when it was done, he came close again and sat, his front paws primly before him, and waited for another morsel. He sat like Mudge had when Gus had told him to 'be a gentleman.'

"Good boy." He offered him another piece of the dwindling rabbit. The dog took it from his fingers, and this time he stayed where he was while he chewed. Gus slowly reached to scratch behind the dog's ear. He pulled his head away, but didn't move otherwise, and when Gus followed that motion and reached him, he allowed the touch. "I'm Gus. Nice to meet you."

Gus leaned back against the boulder cluster that would serve as his shelter for the night and looked up through the canopy of leaves and needles to the vast sky. Full of stars, as always. Stars and planets and galaxies. Maybe there was a world up there that was better than this. A kind of people who were better than humans.

The dog finished chewing on his ass and flopped his head on Gus's leg, then shoved his nose under his arm in an achingly familiar request for petting. Gus scratched behind his ear, and the dog's foot beat the ground lightly.

"If you're sticking around, I'm gonna try to find a metal comb or something and try to get these mats out of your fur. Some of these things are tight as hell. That's got to hurt. I'd cut them out, but I'm afraid I'd get skin, too."

The dog rolled and showed his belly, and Gus gave it a good scratch. The dog groaned with pleasure and licked his arm. "You're a good boy, buddy."

The need for sleep rolled up his spine, and he hunkered down on the ground, against the rocks, and pulled one of Erin's knitted blankets over his shoulders. The dog curled up beside him, in the crook of his arm, and draped his head over Gus's elbow. He sighed heavily, ending it on an expressive canine groan, and Gus laughed quietly.

"Good night, Buddy."

Buddy worked as well as anything else for a name.

About two weeks later, on a route to skirt the probable horrors of Reno to the north, Gus and Buddy were camped for the night in the empty woodshed of a cabin that had been flattened by a fallen redwood. They weren't as far off the beaten path as he'd have liked, in fact they'd passed a heavily guarded and decidedly unwelcoming substake only a few miles before he'd stopped, but it was pouring rain, and the Sierra wind had him and Buddy both shivering hard. When he'd seen something like shelter, he'd had to take it and hope that the flattened cabin would suggest abandonment to anybody who might happen by.

The woodshed was only a lean-to, just three walls and a slant tin roof, but tucked in the corner, they were out of the storm, and that felt like a gift. They ate a scant meal left over from the day before, and they huddled up together to rest.

Buddy didn't like the clatter of the storm on the roof; he kept his tail tucked tightly against his tense body and whined softly at every change in sound or wind-driven splash of water across the concrete woodshed floor. Gus smoothed his hands over his fur—soaking wet after their trek in the rain, but mostly smooth, after two weeks of daily attention to the mats—and whispered soothing nonsense until his dog relaxed and finally slept. Then Gus closed his eyes as well.

Gus woke when the storm ended; the sudden quiet after hours of rain beating down on the corrugated metal was a rousing shock.

He was alone; Buddy wasn't in the woodshed at all. He opened his mouth to call him, and heard the sound just before he made one of his own: Ferals.

They weren't far, but not right on him, either. He listened hard, trying to pinpoint the scope and direction of their movement. How many of them? Which direction were they headed?

It was a big group, making a lot of noise tromping over the gravel road about half a mile south of the woodshed. They sounded like they were marching — toward that sub he'd passed the day before.

Gus stood and peered around the side of the shed. It was dark, and the storm had left heavy cloud cover, so he couldn't see much of the world around him. He didn't see Buddy. But the Ferals had torches, so he saw them fine. They weren't marching, but close to it. They carried a tree spear. Definitely headed for the sub.

That sub had been guarded with men in military armor and automatic weapons. Jesus, there was going to be a war a few miles away.

"Buddy," he whisper-yelled. The Ferals were making so much noise that he didn't think they'd hear him, but he didn't dare yell louder. "Buddy!"

He heard the dog before he saw him, a low pitch under the distant thunder of the Feral march. Buddy skimmed on his belly, back to the woodshed from the direction of the destroyed cabin, casting troubled glances toward the Ferals, uttering an odd sound, like a growl and a whine fighting for the territory of his throat.

Buddy was trying to be brave, but he was terrified. He knew the Ferals enough to fear them, but he wanted to protect Gus from them, too. He was caught between fight or flight.

Pulling him deeper into the shelter of the shed, Gus sat on the floor beside him. "It's okay, Bud. We'll keep watch together."

The next morning broke with bright sun shining through a world washed sparkling clean and fragrant, and noisy with animal life. Gus and Buddy did their morning business, shared a breakfast, and repacked their gear. They stood outside the shed, and Buddy peered expectantly up at Gus, ready to get moving.

But where to go? The Ferals had come from the west, and that band was the biggest he'd ever seen. They'd taken down a fortress of a sub, and then gone back west a few hours later, hooting and roaring in celebration. Though he'd love to get his hands on them individually, he didn't want to face them as a group. There were only a couple routes straight through the Sierras; he had no doubt at all that a group that big would own them both.

Should he turn and go back the way he'd come? To what? He'd left anything worth living for, or dying for, or going back for, in the ground in Kansas. Thousands of miles and half a year ago. There was nothing backward.

He stood with his pack on his back, his weapons sheathed, his dog at his side, and looked up at the mountains.

Up and around was the only way to go. It was almost summer; the way would be hard, but if he could get through the Rockies in winter, he could get through the Sierras in summer.

"Come on, Buddy. Let's climb a mountain."

Ten

Scooting on his belly, staying in full contact with the ground, Gus inched up the rise and peered over the narrow shoulder of the mountain road. Buddy breathed a tiny whine and inched up alongside him, but he didn't try to see. He cowered at Gus's side and waited.

A guard dog, he wasn't. But that was okay. He was good company and a warm sleeping partner, and he had a good nose for trouble. Gus preferred him cautious. Better chance for survival—for both of them.

After all the losses he'd already suffered, he'd tried to keep some distance in his heart, to see Buddy as a hiking partner and nothing more. Just the other member of this tiny group. But the dog slept every night tucked as closely as he could get to Gus, walked at his side all day long, laid his head on his lap every time they took a rest stop, and even seemed to listen when Gus talked. It hadn't taken long for him to love the beast. So yeah—he preferred him cautious and not running out to face down every threat.

This threat especially. A small band of Ferals, maybe a scouting group, was up ahead, twenty yards away, if that. From the looks of things, they'd come upon a smaller group of wanderers and had, as always, attacked. But the wanderers were fighting back hard.

They'd lose—they were outnumbered, and so far, it didn't look like anyone had been neutralized. Six Ferals, four wanderers. One of the wanderers was huge, head and shoulders taller and twice as wide as all the others, and he was likely the reason his people hadn't been obliterated.

If they had help, maybe they could take the Ferals out. Another fighter could tip the scales the right way.

But it wasn't his fight. Right? Right. Not his fight.

"Fuck," Gus grumbled and shed his pack. He wrapped his hand around the hilt of the katana. He'd left the crossbow back in Kansas, with the group. They'd needed the range weapon; Carver's recurve bow wouldn't be enough in a Feral fight, and their ammunition for the guns was low. A few times in the long months since he'd walked away, he'd missed the fuck out of that crossbow. Including right now.

"Buddy, stay," he muttered, firmly. The dog whined and set his head on his paws. "Good boy. I'll be back. Promise."

Drawing the katana, he leapt onto the road and ran toward the scuffle.

No one saw him coming, and he used the sword like a spear first, driving the point into the back of a male Feral, whose head swiveled and showed a rotten-toothed mouth gaping with shock. Blood surged up and spilled over his cracked lips and filthy beard. He tried to turn his body, and Gus yanked the sword out of his back and drove it into his neck.

The first one down was a Feral; that boded well.

When the Feral fell, Gus was face to face with an older woman, tall and skinny, her pale grey hair twisted into a braid that circled her head. Her face had the old-leather look that came with a life lived out of doors. A familiar look for wanderers of a certain age. So was the blood that washed over her cheek from an open gash below her left eye.

She gave him a one-second squint, then a single bob of a nod and turned to swing a claw hammer—just a regular hammer, the kind people had once used to pound nails in drywall so they could hang their family photos—at the head of the next nearest Feral, a brawny woman with a shaved head.

The old woman had swung the hammer with the claw end out front, and it sank into the Feral's temple. When she pulled back, the woman came, too—at least until the claw broke free and brought a chunk of scalp and skull with it.

With her temporal lobe drooping out of her skull, the woman stayed on her feet, and charged wildly at the old wanderer, knocking her to the ground. Gus lunged forward, swinging the katana in a wide arc, and hit the Feral sidelong, slicing off most of the meat on her back and left shoulder. She shrieked and tried to turn to him, but stumbled at last and fell to her knees. Gus swung again and relieved her of her broken head. It rolled past his feet, down the incline of the road, toward the spot where he'd left Buddy.

Two Ferals down—then the big wanderer pile drove one of the Ferals on him, slamming him headfirst so hard into the cracked asphalt that his head and neck appeared to simply disintegrate. The three remaining Ferals started to back off and turn away, but there was no room for mercy in a fight like this, and Gus and the battered wanderers chased them down and slaughtered them all.

Blood ran down the road, filling in the cracks and painting an abstract memorial to the carnage.

"What's the damage?" the old woman asked. Gus would have pegged The Mountain as the leader, but once the crisis was over, it was clear that the oldster was in charge.

"One of the bastards took a fucking bite out of my arm," another man complained as he wrapped a bandana around his forearm. "Otherwise, I'm good."

"Just scratches and bruises for me," said The Mountain.

A young woman, her shape surprisingly robust, clutched her side. "I took a blade. Just glanced off, but it hurts like hell."

The old woman went to her and lifted her shirt. Her side gaped open like a smile. "We have to get you back and clean that up." She took off her own sweater and stuffed it under the younger woman's shirt. "Howard, I want you to carry Chloe back."

The Mountain—Gus wouldn't have pegged him for a Howard—stepped up and swung the young woman into his huge arms. "Your carriage, milady."

Gus stood at the edge of the group, feeling awkward and out of place in a way he hadn't since before the Sunstorm. He'd just about decided to walk away, and had turned toward Buddy when the old woman addressed him.

"We owe you thanks, stranger. We've got a hold a few miles up the road. I can offer you a good, hot meal and a rest, and, if you're inclined to sit and tell us about yourself, the promise to bring it to a vote if you'd like a place with us."

"A hold?"

The smaller man — normal-sized, in other words — said, "Just a little … town, I guess. Such as things are these days. Used to be a rental cabin place, but we put a good fence up around it."

They weren't wanderers, then. They were substakers. Offering him a chance at a place with them. The chance to stop walking.

The regular guy came forward and offered his hand. "I'm Danny."

Gus blinked at it for a second, feeling unsure what he was supposed to do. Then he remembered and shook hands with the man. "Gus."

The old woman offered her hand next. "Sarah. Nice to meet you, Gus."

Blood soaked their clothes and ran over their shoes. Bodies lay about them, some in pieces. In the midst of all that and in the aftershock of the horror they'd fought off, they stood there making each other's acquaintance, following the old rules of civility. Shaking Sarah's hand, and nodding at Howard and Chloe, Gus felt nauseated and unsteady. Wildly disoriented. The world made no sense at all to him anymore.

He wasn't suited to life in a sub, or maybe with people at all. But a good meal wasn't something a wanderer passed up, if he trusted the one making the offer. These people, he thought he could trust, at least for the duration of a meal.

"I'll respectfully decline the offer of a place, but thank you. I'm on my way to the coast. I wouldn't mind a good meal, if it's not too much trouble."

A smile moved up one side of Sarah's face. "We're glad for the chance to repay your kindness. We need to get moving, though. The hold's just up the road."

Getting his bearings again, Gus remembered Buddy. "Uh — I have a dog. He welcome, too?"

"Sure!" Danny answered, scanning the road. "Got a few dogs. We even have a couple cats."

"No shit?" Housecats had almost entirely disappeared. Once out in the wild, they'd left people behind immediately. Very rarely, a wanderer might see the glow of small eyes, but in general, cats stayed far away from humans. You were about as likely to see an actual tiger as you were to see a tabby.

Gus went back for his pack. "Come on, Bud. It's okay."

The dog stayed where he was, whining, even after Gus started walking. He turned and whistled sharply, and Buddy raised his head from his hiding place. Another whistle, and the dog jumped onto the shoulder and trotted up. He made a wide, leery arc around the dead Ferals and the live substakers.

"Oh, he's beautiful," Chloe said. Her voice had taken on a breathy, weak tone. They needed to get her tended to.

"It's okay, Buddy. Come." He patted his thigh. Buddy stayed where he was, eyeing the new people with trepidation. Until now, the only people Buddy had seen since Gus had met him had been Ferals, and Feral stench was all over this road.

Normally, Gus would take Buddy's caution as good advice. But this scene was probably as confusing to the dog as it was to him. Maybe even more. "Bud. Here, boy."

The dog whined, but he put his paws on the road. That was as far as he'd go. He whined again and barked.

"Looks like we'll have to pass on the meal, too," Gus said, turning back to the group.

"Tell you what," Sarah said. "We have to turn back to take Chloe back, anyway, and it looks like you're headed up, too. Why don't you walk with us, follow with your dog. If we get to the hold and he still won't come in, then we'll bring you out some provisions and say our goodbyes. But it'd probably be us smeared all over the road if you hadn't come along, so I'd hate for you to go without some thanks."

That sounded reasonable. Gus accepted with a tip of his head and crossed the road to his nervous pooch.

Buddy calmed down once they got clear of the carnage of Ferals. Then he seemed interested in these new, not-horrible people, and walked ahead of Gus with his ears perked up, listening to their talk.

Gus listened, too. They discussed the likelihood of a retaliation attack once the rest of that band of Ferals found their bodies. Ferals weren't much for the social niceties and were almost as likely to kill each other as anyone else, but they were big on revenge.

"I'll go on the wall tonight," Howard said. "I'll get Trevor and Vince, and we'll pull up the catapult. That worked like a charm last time."

"Catapult?" Gus asked from behind them, forgetting that he'd been eavesdropping.

Danny grinned over his shoulder at him. "Yeah. We're pretty well set up." He held his hand back, toward Buddy, and the dog picked up his pace and gave it a sniff. He let him pat his head.

"Hey, big guy," Danny said to the dog. To Gus, he said, "You'll see what I mean."

The fence around the sub had been made like an Old West fort—posts made of tree trunks, bark left on, the tops sharpened to a point—like tree spears driven into the ground, about ten feet high. The gate was the same, a narrow assemblage of the same spikes, on heavy, polished wood hinges.

By the time they'd arrived, Buddy had made some new friends, so he trotted contently through the gate ahead of Gus. And then they both stopped dead.

Danny had said that this had once been a rental cabin place, and that was obvious. About two dozen log cabins of varying sizes circled a long, low cabin and followed a gravel road that trailed off behind it. A faded sign reading 'OFFICE' hung above the door of the central cabin. Tall trees, densely packed, made a canopy that kept most of the property in dappled shadow.

It smelled fucking amazing—pine and eucalyptus and fertile earth. God bless the mountains. He was getting up high enough to escape the sour reek of the toxic decay below.

The place was beautiful, and that was a rare thing—but it wasn't what had pulled Gus up short.

It was the people. And their … their everything. Weapons, clothes, all of it. What the hell?

Life in this world was a time warp anywhere. When the power grid had failed and destroyed everything that used it, it had snuffed out the modern world. Since then, they'd been living an eighteenth-century life on the bones of the twenty-first century. But this place? These people had literally returned to the eighteenth century.

Maybe the seventeenth. He'd stepped into a country village from Stuart-era England.

Proving his point, a heavyset man in cotton breeches, a loose tunic, and suede boots walked by, carrying a yoke with two wooden buckets full of water. He nodded at Gus and said, in a broad British accent, "Good morrow, sir."

Gus couldn't have answered under any compulsion. His jaw had dropped too far to make words.

Danny laughed. "Yeah, that's Doug. He's gone full native. We're not all that far gone. He's a good guy, though — Howard's brother. They're blacksmiths. I'll take you by their shop later."

Doug was not the only person in the place who looked like a feudal serf. Wait — blacksmiths? "What the hell?" Gus asked. Not the most cordial question, but relevant.

Again, Danny laughed. He had, apparently, been tasked to be Gus's guide. Sarah had gone with Howard to take Chloe for medical attention and get some herself, and they'd left Danny standing beside him.

"Okay. Promise it's not as weird as it looks. Before the Last Dance, we were ... well, you know about Renaissance Faires?"

Feeling not entirely phased into this timeline, he nodded. He'd never been to one, but he'd heard of them. "Turkey legs and jousting?"

"Yeah, right. Lots more to it than that, but yeah. Anyway, pretty much all of us here? We're Rennies. We worked the faires, traveling around the country, pretty much together. A lot of us are craftsmen—I'm a leatherworker, Howard and Doug are blacksmiths, Sarah's a weaver. There used to be a big faire up here every spring. Everything went dark a couple of weeks before it was set to open. A bunch of us came up early, for a little R and R, and when it all happened, we just … well, we hung out together and kept each other safe, and when it turned out that the world really had gone tits-up, we set up a stronghold here." He made a little flourish. "Welcome to the Shire."

The Shire. Of course.

Gus let his eyes move all around the area, stopping and taking in oddities where he found them. Women in full-skirted cotton gowns. Men in breeches and boots. Not everyone was dressed like an extra in *Excalibur*, most were dressed in normal clothes, or mostly normal, but a fair number were in breeches and tunics and those old-fashioned peasant dresses.

After awhile, it began to make sense. Who better to survive the end of the modern world than people who spent the great bulk of their lives living in the distant past? A pretty young redhead in a blue peasant dress, her noteworthy chest mounded over the top, strolled by and gave him a little dip of a curtsy. She had a basket of bread in her arms. She could have stepped straight out of a Rembrandt.

Then he heard the bleats of goats. Turning to that marvel of a sound, he saw a teenage boy herd a small group of goats, *including babies*—what were they called? Kids?—toward the back of the compound.

They had goats. Which meant milk. And oh shit! Maybe cheese and butter? "You have goats?"

"Yeah. Bob and Helen—that's their boy, Aidan, herding—had a little petting zoo, let kids feed the babies and learn how to milk, like that. They had a couple of sheep, too, and a burro, but they didn't make it. The goats are sturdy as hell, though, and doing fine. Even had a couple of breeding seasons now."

Gus found himself grinning. "Jesus. You guys are fucking brilliant."

"Come on." Danny clapped his hand on Gus's shoulder. "Let's get you off your feet and put some grub in you. We're fresh out of turkey legs, though," he added with a smirk.

Danny led him and Buddy to a lean-to behind the central cabin. There was a large fire ring back here as well, but the fire was banked, and no meal was in preparation. The lean-to was outfitted like an outdoor kitchen, complete with iron pots and pans and wooden utensils, as well as bins and shelves of foodstuffs. Danny rooted through a couple of wooden bins and brought out a handful of aromatic jerky and a couple of hard rolls. "This'll get you started. We eat supper before dark, but that's a bit later these days, while the light is long." He held out a piece of jerky to Buddy. "Hungry, boy?"

Buddy sat, his front paws primly together, and stared longingly at the meat. He glanced at Gus as if asking for approval. Gus nodded. When Danny tossed it to him, he snapped it out of the air.

Gus tore into his own ration of the jerky. He'd been eating raw meat for so long now that he nearly wept at the taste. And God! "Is that sage?" he asked around his watering mouth.

"Yeah. Darlene found a little stash of seeds in a garage, and she's cultivated a pretty good garden. We got tomatoes and everything. And herbs, too. Not many of those, but we got sage and peppermint, and dandelion, too. Elsie makes medicine from that. And a little wine, too."

"Wine?" Gus's head ached with the constant blows to his apocalypse paradigm. This little circle of cabins held the whole world out of time, like an hourglass.

"Well, we *will* have some. Eventually. It's a process. Come on. Sarah wants you to have a thank-you gift, since you won't think about staying."

Their next stop was the blacksmith's. By now, Buddy had decided that these people were all okay, and he occupied himself by huffing great whiffs of the whole compound. Danny had said there were other dogs, but Gus hadn't seen one yet. Still, considering Buddy's devoted attention to every rock, tree, and post he could find and his suddenly limitless supply of urine, other dogs were around.

Howard was at the blacksmith's shop, with his eccentric brother, Doug. Howard grinned as Gus and Danny approached. "Hey, man. Good to see you over here."

"Aye," said his brother and offered a hand, which Gus shook. "There's word we owe you thanks for your aid to our folk against the brigands."

That peasant affect was bizarre. "Uh, yeah. Well, glad I was there."

Doug bent forward in a short bow and turned back to the anvil.

Howard gave Gus a wry smirk. "Doug was Method back in the day, too. Some folks even back then stayed in character whenever they were with other Rennies. You get used to it."

"Not you?"

He lifted a huge shoulder. "I wasn't a lifer like Doug. I only did a couple of faires a year. I'm a farrier. Doug's the artist, though I've gotten a crash course the past few years. Anyway," he opened his hands and spread them apart, displaying his wares. "See anything you like?"

Gus peered into the rough-hewn shop, and his mouth dropped open again. Jesus, it was an armory. Swords and axes, spears and flails. Fucking shields!

He pointed toward a high shelf. "Are those *helms*?"

Still grinning — Gus hadn't seen as many smiling people in six years altogether as he'd seen in his half-hour in 'The Shire' — Howard crossed to that shelf and took down a burnished metal helmet with a nose guard. He handed it to Gus.

It was heavy. Dense. Well made. "How do you get the metal for all this?"

"Like everybody gets everything. We scavenge. Strip cars and trucks, appliances, useless tools, like that, and melt it all down. The Fiends come at us every few weeks, but we fend them off."

"Fiends? What we fought on the road?"

Howard's eyebrow went up. "Yeah. What d'you call 'em?"

"Ferals. Everywhere I've been until now, everybody's called them Ferals. And places like this are substakes."

He shrugged and took the helm back. "Never heard anybody else call 'em anything. We don't see many normal people. Just us and the Fiends out here. Everybody else seems to've done what you're doin': walk. Don't know what you're walking to."

Gus opened his mouth to explain, then closed it again. He wasn't all that sure, either.

As Howard walked away from the shelf of helms, Gus saw something else that shocked him. "Hey—can I see that?" He pointed, and Howard picked it up and brought it over. Gus's palms began to sweat with anticipation, and he almost snatched it out of Howard's hands.

"These things take a bit to learn. You ever shot one?"

"Crossbow is my weapon of choice." The one he'd had before had been a modern model, but after a few seconds studying this old-fashioned version, he understood it. "You got bolts for it?"

With a tip of his head, Howard fetched a quiver of bolts and brought it over. "There's targets at the side of the shed here." He led Gus around the building, where three thick logs, stood on end, were covered with concentric circles of colored cloth.

Gus nocked a bolt, aimed and fired. He missed the bullseye but hit the center of the next ring out. Nocking another bolt, he adjusted his aim and, this time, made the eye.

"Yeah, that's your weapon, alright." Howard nodded at the crossbow. "That one there. It's yours. If you want it. For helping us out today."

In civil society, he would have asked if Howard was sure, or said that he couldn't accept a gift so precious. But Gus simply smiled and said, "Thank you."

The whole group came together at the fire ring for dinner, as the last of the sunset washed the air in red glow. By the time people lined up to filled their plates and bowls and cups, the fire in that ring crackled with life. There were tables arrayed in this town center area—old picnic tables with peeling green paint, and plain, hand-sawn tables as well—but they all sat around the fire on this night, on hunks of tree stumps and long logs, or on wooden stools or leather puffs they'd carried to the fire with them.

The food was the best Gus had eaten in six years. Fat tomatoes—not red and round like he remembered from the supermarket or stunted and greyish like those grown in substakes down where the radiation had hit, but bulbous and multicolored, and mouthwateringly savory. Crunchy lettuce and crisp beans. A hearty stew with tender strips of meat and rich sauce. Soft brown rolls which tasted almost like pumpernickel. And butter. Cool goat's butter, chilled in the stream behind the compound.

A bit more tang than the cow variety, but an absolutely extravagant delight on Gus's tongue.

Gus was finishing his second bowl of stew and his third warm roll when the teenage boy, Aidan, who'd been herding the goats earlier, left the fire. Gus noted it because there was a general rumble of talk when he left. He came back in a minute or two, carrying something under a piece of linen.

As he sat down again between his parents, Bob and Helen, Trevor called across the fire, "It works?"

Blushing and grinning, Aidan nodded. "I think so. The test worked."

"Well, damn, boy," Howard boomed from his seat beside Gus. "Let's see!"

Aidan pulled the linen away. On his lap sat a wooden and metal contraption with a small crank on one side and a glass ball on top. Gus squinted at it, trying to understand what he saw.

The kid had the full attention of every person in the compound. The place had gone so quiet that the crackle of the fire seemed loud as fireworks.

Then he turned the crank, and a metallic whirr filled the air. He got it really going, holding the contraption steady with his other hand.

The glass ball began to glow, and a cheer exploded around him. The ball glowed brighter and brighter, until

Aidan stopped turning the crank. As its spin wound down, so did the light.

"Look what my boy did!" Bob crowed. Helen hugged her son. Sarah went over to talk to him. As he watched their leader approach, pride beamed from Aidan's face brighter than any light bulb.

"Jesus," Gus muttered. "He just invented the light bulb again?"

"Yep," Howard laughed. "Told you we weren't all living in the past. Aidan was some kind of science prodigy before the end. He's been trying to make power for the past few years. Supplies are hard, though. He got the crank piece and base pretty quick—Doug and me forged the metal—but figuring out the bulb was harder, I guess. It needs the old-fashioned kind of bulbs ... the ones they outlawed back in the day?"

"Incandescents."

"Yeah. Those just aren't around anymore. We've never found one, anyway. But it looks like he figured out how to make one."

"That's fucking amazing." There had been a time, early on, when Gus had expected a new, better world to rise up from the apocalypse. He'd expected people to rebuild what had been destroyed, to reinvent what had been lost, to reconceive and remember and remake. Early on, he'd expected that.

Somewhere along the line, in the years of endless end, he'd forgotten even to imagine that there might be someone in some place, possibly more than one, in more than one place, who would try to make life better.

But here he sat, in a seventeenth-century Shire, watching the next world's Thomas Edison demonstrate his invention.

A boy. The next generation.

"You'll stay the night, of course," Sarah said. The flicker of firelight in the dusk softened the creases of her face, and Gus could see that she'd been a beautiful young woman. She was still beautiful, in a wise, long-lived way.

Buddy trotted over from his play with a collie named Eddie and flopped at his side with a sigh. The dog had had a good day. A hunting party had returned from the woods and brought two dogs back with them. After his usual panic attack, he'd warmed up well to some canine company, especially this collie. But he hadn't gone far from Gus even so.

Gus patted his head. "We'd appreciate that, yeah. We'll head out at dawn."

"You sure you don't want us to talk about you stayin'?" Howard asked. "We could always use good fighters." He looked over his shoulder at the wooden catapult he and a few other men had rolled to the front of the compound, aimed at the gate.

Gus shook his head. "I'll fight with you tonight, if the Ferals come. But Buddy and I're headed to the coast."

The thought of leaving had a tinge of melancholy. He'd had a good day, too. The Rennies were decent people. He hadn't been so rested, so calm, or so full, in six years.

But as welcoming as these folks had been, he'd never felt so much like an outsider before. They'd holed themselves up in their 'Shire' and made a life they'd already known how to live. They'd been a community before the Sunstorm. The old-timey accents and the occasional corset aside, these people weren't weird like that sub in northern Illinois, but they weren't his people, either.

He didn't have any people. Not anymore. He'd walked away from the only people he'd had in this world. He'd lost the only one who'd truly mattered.

Then he heard the notes of a pipe being played, and he glanced around the fire to find the source. Before he found the piper, someone began beating a drum. His breath caught as a few people began singing—the old folk music you'd expect Faire people to know.

"Is there a violin?" he asked anyone who might hear the question. "Or a lute?" Anything stringed at this moment would do. Just to hear that sound again. If there was a violin, though … he might stay for that.

A man whose name he didn't know answered. "No. We had a luthier back in the day, but he wasn't up here yet when the lights went out."

"Ah." His chest ached as that old loss renewed. "Okay." He set his empty tin bowl aside and stretched out his legs. Buddy scooted over and licked up the crumbs and smears from his hearty stew and soft brown bread with butter.

They'd stay the night, help the Rennies defend the place if they had to, and get a good rest otherwise. And then they'd keep walking.

Eleven

With his katana unsheathed and at the ready, and his new crossbow on his back, Gus slid open the glass door and stepped into the house. Buddy came in right behind him, his ears pricked warily.

Leaf-filtered afternoon sun streamed through the dusty glass and showed a vast, stone-floored room, appointed with the expensive furniture that Gus had quickly come to recognize as rich Californians' idea of rustic—heavy wooden frames, leather upholstery, Native-American-style textiles. Usually, there was a cutesy carved-wood black bear standing in the front hall. It was all covered with dust, but not as thick a layer as Gus might have expected. These huge rooms—he assumed the owners, when they'd had owners, called them 'great rooms' — seemed not to collect dust as quickly as more humble rooms did.

All the way up the mountain, he'd found these little enclaves of wealthy leisure, wide lanes suddenly climbing up or down from the road, digging into a natural terrace in the mountainside, and a small neighborhood springing up out of nowhere. The houses were alpine style, like chalets, or cabin style, like log cabins, but hardly so humble as their inspiration. They were practically mansions.

Every here and there, he'd come across a humble cabin, a shack in comparison, usually right at the side of the stream that meandered through the area. But for the most part, this mountain had obviously been the playground of the rich and famous. Seeing as it loomed over Lake Tahoe, he wasn't all that surprised.

Rich or humble, chalet or shack, all the houses were deserted. He'd gone through a lot of them, looking for food and supplies. He'd encountered a couple of tiny ghost towns as well. Gus had seen no other human being, friend or foe, since he'd left the Shire.

He had, on the other hand, seen a lot of skeletons. Hundreds. Most of them outside, on the road or in the woods. It looked to Gus like everyone had come down the mountain en masse, and someone or something had gone through the migrating herd and slaughtered them all.

That couldn't be right, only Ferals would do something like that, and they couldn't have been that kind of homicidal threat so soon after the storm, but he could think of no other reason for so many empty houses and so many skeletons in the open. He'd seen nothing like it in all the six years of this world.

But as he and Buddy had followed the road up, evidence of people had fallen away. There were still little enclave neighborhoods with swanky houses, but there were few human remains around. Gus got the sense that he had climbed above the human world when he'd topped the cloud line. Like he'd reached Mt. Olympus, where only the gods dwelt.

This cluster of alpine McMansions was considerably more picked over than most others he'd come across in the past couple of days. There was not a single canned good in a single cabinet or pantry, not a spice jar, no salt, nothing. Food was the first thing that had gone, of course, but usually there was something left behind — canned clams or Spam, or something like that, something that even people living in the end times weren't desperate enough to take. Not here. The kitchens on this graceful circle drive were entirely stripped bare of food. Far stranger than that: the cabinets under the kitchen sinks, and the laundry-room shelves, were bare, too. All the cleaning products were gone.

Gus couldn't image a wanderer using room in his pack for bleach or dish soap. Would Sarah's group have come this far up to scavenge? Several days' walk each way? He supposed it had to be that. No one else was around but skeletons.

This house at the back of the circle lane was no different from its neighbors, except that it seemed strangely more *used* than the others. He couldn't put his finger on the how of the difference, but he could sense it. Buddy could, too. He was doubly careful here, peering around open door frames and taking slow, considered sniffs before he'd risk entry. Like he expected there to be someone in the house with them.

There wasn't. Gus had gone through each room, his katana cocked, to be sure they were alone. Then he went through again to check for supplies — and pick a bunk for the night. Since he'd started his climb up, he'd taken to spending a night in the shelter of a house, and the sun had dropped low enough, making long, dusky blue shadows across the road, that it was time to find his night's bed.

Each night on a comfortable bed made leaving it the next morning harder. If his plan was still to get to the coast, he needed to get over the mountain and back down, and after a week of walking, he was still going up. His pace had been cut in half by the thin air and steep incline. The same thing had happened in the Rockies, and there, he'd stopped and waited out the winter.

But that had been winter. This was the end of summer, and the days were still warm and long. He didn't know how early the snows hit in the Sierras, but it was too early to give up for the winter; he knew that. He was sure he had time to get out of the mountains before snowfall, even if it came early. And yet, he felt a push to make a decision now: either keep moving or stay put.

The compulsion to get to the coast was gone. He didn't believe he'd find anything better there.

If he stopped now, he wouldn't be making a winter holdout. He'd be stopping for good and making a home. That thought had planted itself in his head after he'd helped Sarah's group, and since then, as he'd climbed past human life, it had sprouted and flowered. He could stay up here. He knew how to hunt. There was a freshwater stream less than a mile away, running clear and sweet, probably gushing wildly during spring melts. There was plenty of vegetation to forage. Maybe this high up, he didn't need a sub. Maybe he was really alone and he could be safe here, away from the danger and degradation and desperation of the world below. The endless fucking despair.

Buddy trotted into the kitchen with a tennis ball in his mouth. His tail wagged so hard he had trouble keeping his back legs on the floor.

"What d'you got there, Bud?" He held out his hand, and Buddy dropped the ball into it. Gus gave it a toss down the hallway, and the dog scampered after it, his claws scrabbling on the expensive tile.

They played fetch for a while, and then Gus stuck the slobbery ball in a pocket and continued his scavenge of the house. All evidence suggested that he'd find nothing of value here, but there was something about it, a vibe in the air, that made him want to hang out. At the least, he'd spend the night.

The king-size bed in the master bedroom was stripped of blankets but had its pillows and sheets. This room was messier than the others—clothes were tossed on the closet floor, and several dresser drawers were open, showing dainty women's lingerie. Tossing Buddy's ball again, he went out in search of blankets, but found none in any bedroom or the wide hall closet.

On the other hand, in a small room furnished like a gaming room, with a large, dead-eyed television on the wall, pretty much all the final generations of gaming consoles shelved under it, and a wall of shelves full of video games, he dug into a closet and found two things: a faux-fur blanket, still in its wrapping, and something else, something that took Gus's breath from his lungs and his legs from his body. He sat down hard, knocking his shoulder painfully against the frame of the closet door.

Shaking, he stretched out his arm and wrapped his hand around the handle. He pulled the black case from the back of the closet and set it on his legs.

"Jesus," he muttered.

Buddy, standing at the doorway, picked up the change in Gus's mood. He dropped his fancy new tennis ball and whined.

"It's okay, Bud. I'm okay." He flipped the metal clasps on the case. Even that sound, such a trivial part of the soundtrack of his life before, so often repeated it had been like white noise, made Gus's heart cramp and flutter.

For a few seconds, he wasn't sure he could open the case. Danger lurked here. That most dangerous thing: hope.

With a deep, slow, breath, Gus lifted the lid. It opened smoothly, with no creak in its hinges. It was a good case, with thick, crushed-velvet lining, in a deep shade of red.

In that crimson bed lay a violin, the first Gus had seen since his own had been stolen from him. Two bows were seated inside the lid. His heart thumped heavily.

It was only a student violin, nothing like the one he'd lost, or any he'd had in the world that was, but it was a Knilling—a quality piece. The kind wealthy parents might buy for a child they didn't expect to stick with his lessons.

He ran a finger over the hair of one bow, and then the other. Both were surprisingly supple. He plucked one from its bed and tested it. Yes, it seemed sturdy, even after all these years of neglect.

Setting the bow aside, he finally lifted the violin from the case, using both hands as if it were a Stradivarius and not a five-hundred-dollar student fiddle.

He plucked at the strings. They'd been loosened, which was good; tense strings might well have broken the instrument after all this time. He tightened and tuned the strings. And then ...

Sitting on the floor of a closet, in the dim shadow of a day in its last gasp of gloaming, Gus set his chin in the rest, held his arms in a position his body remembered almost instantly, and struck the first note he'd played in six years.

With a painful blast of memory, he saw the last concert he'd played — at Carnegie Hall, the night before the storm. The Orchestra had made a guest appearance, and Gus had soloed. He'd meant to frame the program from that night and present it to his parents: *Violin Sonata No. 9, Beethoven. Angus Tolliver, soloist.* At Carnegie Fucking Hall.

Did he remember the piece? He struck the first note, and the next. And played Beethoven while tears ran down his face and over the polished wood of his new instrument.

The violin had been a sign, he decided. Gus made his home in that big chalet of a house. Maybe after the winter, he'd want to rejoin the world, or maybe not. He had a sense that he'd found a place he could be okay in. He and his dog.

After a few days of quiet, good catches in his snares, and decent forage for nuts and berries, he was sure of it. He'd had to go through all but one of the houses on the lane before he found a decent snow shovel or fishing gear, but he had them now, and he'd even found a washboard hanging up in a kitchen, decorated with hand-painted flowers and butterflies and bloomers on a line.

He was at the stream now, making use of that washboard, cleaning his clothes for the first time in months. He'd found some jeans to fit, and some underwear, even socks, so he could have burned the filthy clothes, but they were in okay shape, and discarding anything that had use in it felt insanely wrong.

Besides, Erin had knitted the sweater he was washing now. He'd keep that even if he had to ball up the unraveled yarn of it

The day was warm and sunny. Buddy splashed in the stream, chasing minnows. He'd filled out in the weeks they'd been together. His rear had healed, his coat was smooth and fairly clean, and he was happy. That terrified sack of bones Gus had coaxed to share a rabbit with him had remembered how to be a dog.

Gus smoothed the sweater over a rock, then stripped off his t-shirt, too, and scrubbed that. As the sun warmed his bare back, he stopped and closed his eyes, breathing in the fresh, sweet air and the noisy peace of the world around him. Just him and his dog.

The air was truly better here. Maybe not toxic at all. He'd gotten away from the end of the world and found a place where everything was okay.

The water ran over his hands. It was cold, but not painfully so. A thought that would have been crazy at any other point in the past six years entered his head, and he let it stay. He could get naked. He could wash his whole body at once in this stream and truly get the blood and filth off of him. Wash the apocalypse away.

He spread the t-shirt out on the grass and sat beside it to pull off his boots and socks. His toes spread out of their own volition and twiddled in the cool grass. God, that felt good.

When he stood and went for his belt, he couldn't quite get that done. Too accustomed to caution, he couldn't get fully naked. But he could cuff up his pants and put his feet in that water. He could splash and scrub his face and head, his armpits, his chest. At least he could do that. He'd scrub the rest in the house, with water heated in the fireplace. But he was going to get all the way clean today.

He stepped into the briskly rushing water and sighed at the cool relief on his hard, cracked wanderer's feet. The smooth rocks and pebbles of the streambed shifted under his weight and massaged his arches. Shit, they could have made a spa out of this place.

Buddy, elated to have a playmate in the water, rushed up with a sodden stick in his teeth. Gus took it and threw it upstream, and Buddy clambered after it, digging for purchase in the shifting stones. He snatched it from the water as it floated back, and then came back for another round.

The fourth time Gus threw the stick, it got hung up in brambles on the edge of the stream, and Buddy couldn't get to it. He tried, but failed, and stood there barking at his stick and his man, back and forth. Gus laughed and headed up the stream to help.

He stepped on a bigger rock, slimed with algae, and his foot slipped off and landed oddly. Gus heard the crack, over the sound of the water, a full second before he felt the pain.

But the pain came and forced a shout from his mouth. He looked down and saw his foot, at almost a perfect right angle to his leg. And then he fell into the stream.

It took him almost three hours to make the long trek back to the house on his hands and knees, get himself as treated as he could be, and crawl into bed. He'd managed to collect his clothes and get one boot on, but he hadn't bothered to put the rest of his clothes on.

There wasn't so much as an Ace bandage in the house, or in any of the houses around the circle, but he'd torn the top sheet of the master bed up and bound his ankle that way.

No question that his ankle was broken. It was swollen to at least three times its proper size, and the skin was almost black with bruising. Not a compound fracture, small mercy there, but it almost didn't matter. Gus had no earthly idea how to set his own ankle, and if — when — it healed wrong, he'd be lame for the rest of his life.

Which would make it a short damn life. Even here, even if he'd managed to get clear of the end of the world below, he had to hunt and forage to eat. He had to chop wood to stay warm. He could not survive without two healthy legs.

He sank back on the pillows and stared up at the ceiling. Goddammit. Every time he thought he had something to hang onto, Fate snatched it away. What was the fucking point?

Lying at his side, Buddy whined and set his head on Gus's bare belly. His big brown eyes stared steadily, full of concern. And also trust.

He *did* still have something to hang onto.

"Okay, Bud, okay. We'll figure it out."

By the next morning, Gus was fairly sure there was no figuring this problem out. His ankle had swollen even more over that first night and was so huge that Gus honestly worried that the skin might split. He'd had to unwrap it before he went mad from the pain. It was black and mottled all around, and the skin around it was an angry, alarming shade of red. His toes looked like weird German sausages gone bad.

And holy shit, the pain. Living as a wanderer, he'd been hurt plenty of times, sometimes badly. He'd been beaten, stabbed, sliced, and bludgeoned. He'd had mishaps, including a few sprained ankles and wrists. He'd wrenched a knee once, stepping off a broken concrete curb that he'd misjudged the height of.

He'd also been ill with a variety of bacterial or viral cruds that would have been minor before the storm. In this world, though, a fever, any fever, could be lethal. So he'd been in pain before. Lots of it.

This, though? This was a maddening, throbbing demon eating its way up his leg. The slightest touch, even of a sheet, even air, even the thought of a touch, made a scream rush up and nearly burst from his mouth. He'd bitten most of them back because Buddy freaked out when he yelled, but if it was possible to die of pain, Gus thought that might be an upcoming event.

It had him all but trapped on the bed, too. Though he didn't put any weight on it—at all—the effort of moving got his blood flowing, which made his ankle throb. He'd managed to hop his way to the toilet twice—it was, of course, dry and unflushable, but there was no chance he'd make it outside to piss, so the toilet would have to do—and by the time he'd fallen back on the bed, he'd been sweating buckets, shaking so hard his teeth rattled, and sobbing with pain.

Yeah. He was going to die on this bed. Of a broken fucking ankle. All he'd survived, and that was going to do him in. Brilliant.

Buddy lay with his head on his belly, staring up at him with worry. Gus scratched behind his ear.

"We're fucked, Bud. I'm really sorry."

Gus opened his eyes in an afternoon-bright room, and the first thing he did was flinch as pain surged back to the front of his consciousness. He lay in a slushy pool of sweat-soaked sheets. His head felt cloudy and his thoughts wouldn't line up straight.

But that wasn't what had woken him from his half-delirious nap. Buddy stood at the end of the big bed, his tail tucked so tightly between his legs it had disappeared. His whole body shook and made the mattress shimmy.

He was growling. A long, low, continuous rumble. All the fur across his back stood on end.

"Buddy, what is it?" Gus tried to sit up and clear his slipping mind, but the move shifted his ankle on the bed, and he nearly passed out. His thoughts scattered again. The dog kept growling.

He flailed for a weapon and found nothing. Shit! He'd dropped everything when he'd finally made it to the room, and it all lay scattered by the chair where his stream-washed clothes were wadded. All he had nearby was the violin, resting in its open case on the nightstand. Fuck, fuck, shit.

He made himself sit up. Prepared this time for the pain, he managed it without yelling. Or passing out. And he grabbed hold of his mind and made it focus at least halfway. Something bad was coming. But he couldn't swing his legs to the side of the bed. His injured one had overridden his brain's commands, and he sat there, staring at the black lump at the bottom of his leg.

Buddy's growl got suddenly more emphatic, and he hunched down over his front paws, ready to pounce. His chickenshit dog, still trembling, tail still tucked, meant to fight whatever he sensed coming.

He meant to protect Gus, despite his fear. He knew his person was disabled and couldn't do it himself.

"Buddy, no. Don't."

The door was half open, and Gus saw the shadow coming. Unable to fight or fly, his jumbled mind disconnected from his body and sat back, waiting to see what would happen.

A woman came into the room, brandishing a large axe, already cocking it back to swing. Buddy's growl became a roar, but he didn't leave the bed.

The woman froze, axe cocked, blinking, her wild eyes fixed on Buddy.

Adrenaline surged and straightened out Gus's head. "Please," he gasped. "Please don't hurt my dog."

Her eyes lifted from Buddy to him, and she gaped at him, no understanding at all in her aspect. She looked at him like she'd never seen his species before. She was obviously a Feral, and far gone. Ferals ran in packs, always. If she was here, others were close.

But *was* she a Feral? She was clean. As in shower fresh. Her clothes, her hair, her skin, everything. And the blade of that axe shone in the streaks of sunlight slanting through the room. Not a speck of rust, not a drop of dried blood.

Buddy growled again, almost a bark, and the woman's attention returned to him. She blinked again, repeatedly.

"Please don't hurt my dog. Please. Take whatever you want, but please leave him be."

The woman swung her axe and stepped forward. Buddy's courage broke. He yelped and spun, crawling to Gus's side and trying to shove his head under Gus's back.

The woman, however, hadn't been attacking. The swing had been her dropping the blade, letting it dangle over the floor. She frowned at Buddy, and Gus would have sworn in a court of law, if such a thing still existed, that her eyes had blurred with tears.

Yeah, she was most definitely not a Feral.

"Hi," he tried, with no better options than to attempt to make a connection. "I'm Gus. This is Buddy."

She stared at him, her eyes teary but otherwise blank. Obviously, she could hear. Maybe she couldn't speak? He tried something else, though his crazily pounding heart didn't appreciate the new ache of memory. He said, "If you can't speak, do you sign? I know ASL." For proof, he signed the words as he spoke them.

She glanced at his hands but didn't linger. No, she didn't sign. Her eyes had fixed at some point below his face, and suddenly she lunged for him. He flinched back hard, slamming his head on the headboard, as her free hand shot out at him. Buddy yelped and tried to dig his way into the mattress.

The woman only laid her hand on his chest. He looked down and watched her rough finger trace over the tattoo on his left pectoral. A portrait of Mudge, his childhood dog.

Dogs. She was reacting to his dogs. "That's Mudge. I had him when I was a kid. Do you have a dog?"

Her eyes flashed up at his, and he saw a glimmer of cognition in there. She could understand at least a little. He set his hand next to hers on his chest, and she yanked hers back and flipped the axe up, ready to chop him into pieces.

He put his hands up. "I'm not going to hurt you. I promise. I'm in some trouble, actually." He nodded at his leg and tried out a friendly chuckle. "I don't suppose you know how to set a broken ankle?"

She looked down his leg and frowned sharply at his ankle. When she bent closer, he clenched every muscle in his body, waiting for the agony if she jabbed at it or something. But she only studied it, carefully. She studied the rest of his foot. She studied his other foot. She pushed up his jeans leg — *oh shit ow* — and considered his shin and calf. Then turned and left the room.

He didn't know what to think.

In a few minutes, she was back, carrying a big hiking pack, the kind that had room for tent and cooking gear as well as bedroll and other essentials. She opened a side pocket and pulled out a long hunting knife in a leather sheath. She came at him.

Well, fuck.

"Hey, you don't have to—"

She stuck the knife, sheath and all, crossways in his mouth, and he understood. He wasn't sure this was so very much better, but he bit down on the leather anyway.

The woman went to the end of the bed, grabbed his ankle, and pulled.

There was no word or sound that could convey the electric agony as the bones shifted in his horror of an ankle. Gus clamped his teeth down into that sheath as every cell and sinew in his body lit bright and seized up.

Then it all stopped, and his own lights went out.

Book Three: Caretaker

At rest, however, in the middle of everything is the sun.

~Nicolaus Copernicus

Twelve

As the man passed out, the knife slid from his mouth and dropped to the wood floor with a *thunk*. She set his injured leg down and then simply stared at the bed. The man, dressed only in jeans, his long, dark hair sweat-plastered to his head, lay unconscious, his mouth open and showing strong teeth. At his side, hunched into a golden ball at his armpit, was his dog, its fearful whimpers muffled by the man's body.

Please don't hurt my dog, the man had said in a voice graveled and soft with pain and weariness. *Please don't hurt my dog.*

The woman didn't know what to do. She'd not laid eyes on another human being in more than a year, not since the monsters who'd taken Fiona from her. She'd not encountered one who didn't mean her harm since the world before. Her mind scrambled inside her skull, trying to put these strange new pieces of the world in place. There were no more good people, that was what she knew. Only her and the monsters.

So this one was a monster, too. He would hurt her if he could. But passed out and broken as he was, it didn't matter. He couldn't hurt her.

The dog shifted and eased his snout out of his huddle. One big brown eye peered out into the room and locked on her. She settled her own gaze on him and felt a little more centered. A dog, she could trust. But why was it here? Where had these two come from? Were there others?

She went to the window and peered out at the sun-dappled road. The world was quiet and empty beyond the glass.

This was *her* house; this was *her* room, *her* closet. It was Forage Day, and she'd come down to collect some of the few remaining winter supplies this house and its neighbors still offered. Always careful before she entered even this house, she'd seen signs of unfamiliar occupants right away.

And then she'd found this: someone lying in her bed. Badly injured. With a dog.

Such a pretty dog. Healthy and fit, with a clean coat of long, golden fur. That fur was a little bit tangled at the ends, and not as fluffy on his rear, but in good shape nonetheless. He was well cared for. He was loved.

Please don't hurt my dog.

Her eyes went to the man's chest and the tattoo of a big black dog, rendered with all the detail of a photograph, its face and head so much like Fiona's they had to be the same breed.

Memories of Fiona pummeled her, and her chest ached sharply, squeezing her lungs. Her vision muddied again, and she blinked it clear. She opened her mouth to speak soothingly to this dog, to promise she meant him no harm, but there were no words she could say.

She couldn't remember the last time she'd spoken. Maybe she'd forgotten how. Instead, she held out her hand. He growled quietly, and she let her arm drop to her side.

He was terrified of her, and the knowledge of his fear sliced through her gut.

She didn't know what to do.

Leaving the dog alone, she focused on the ankle she'd just set. It was horribly injured, with extensive tissue damage. The bones had moved fairly smoothly back into place, though, so the injury couldn't have happened much more than a day ago, two at the outside. There was a chance it would heal well enough, if it was tended now. The man would probably limp, but he wouldn't be lame.

She could splint it. She knew how, and she carried the supplies with her on Forage Days and Hunt Days. The question was: should she? Did she want this man alive, so close to her homestead? Wouldn't that be welcoming the monster? Like inviting a vampire across the threshold? Wouldn't she do better to use her axe and end his misery and her turmoil? She could bring the dog with her, if he would come to trust her.

He might never trust her if she killed his man.

Again she moved to the side of the bed and studied that tattoo on the man's chest. He had others—his left arm was sleeved with ink from his wrist to above his elbow, flowers, trees, snakes, and musical notes, all twisted together in a rainbow of faded color—but the image of that beautiful dog drew her eyes. She saw not the man's dog but her own. Fiona. She had no photos of her, no drawings. All this time, she'd had only her memory to keep the dog alive in her mind and heart.

Her hand trembling, she reached out and touched the tattoo again.

The dog lifted his head and growled more loudly, his nose pleating with menace. He was afraid, but he wasn't going to let her hurt his man. She backed off.

A man who loved dogs couldn't be a monster. More than that, no dog would love a monster like this dog loved his man.

She was deeply confused, pulled sharply in more directions than she could track. Kill him? Heal him? Leave this house and them to their fate?

The dog. She needed the dog to trust her. That was the only thing that really mattered. She didn't want to be the monster in this room.

She picked up her sheathed hunting knife and strapped it to her leg, then went to her pack and pulled out a bundle of venison jerky. When she turned back to the bed, the dog's head was up high. He watched her with suspicion, but some interest, too.

Breaking a piece into smaller bits, she spread them on the bed, making a line toward the dog. He let her get about a foot away before his low warning rumble of a growl sharpened into threat, and she backed off again.

He stared at the bits of dried meat, licking his chops. In obvious conflict, he swung his head to his man and whined, licking the man's beard. When he didn't rouse, the dog turned back and fixed those sweet eyes on her. She tried to make a smile, but it felt strange and wrong, and she wasn't sure she'd managed it. She might have only bared her teeth. The last time she'd smiled had probably been the last time she'd spoken, too.

The dog licked his chops and whined again. How long had he been at his man's side on this bed? How long since he'd eaten? Since either of them had?

With a last look at his man, the dog stretched forward and snapped up the nearest piece of jerky. He swallowed it in two bites and went for the next. When he got to the end of the bed, the woman held out her hand,

and he gave it a hesitant sniff. She tried to touch him, but he reared back, out of her reach.

At least he wasn't growling anymore. Or whining. He curled against the man's thigh and watched her, licking the last taste of venison from his lips.

She tried again to speak to him, and failed again.

She didn't know what to do.

Her glance caught the blackened ankle of the still-unconscious man. If she helped him, would the dog see her as a good person? Deciding it was worth it to try, she went back to her pack and pulled out a roll of bright pink duct tape and an old wooden ruler she'd split in half, longwise.

The top sheet for this bed was wadded on the floor, showing a tattered edge, and there was a sad bundle of yellow cotton strips straggling on the floor as well. The man must have tried to treat himself. And failed. She grabbed the sheet and tore the rest of it into wider strips.

When she put her hands on the man's leg, the dog growled again. Instead of backing away, she stroked the leg, showing the dog she meant to be gentle. He quieted, but kept his eyes on her.

The legs of the man's jeans had been cuffed high, as if he'd been wading in shallow water, but not quite high enough for the woman to work. Slowly and carefully, she folded up the denim as far as she could on his injured leg. Above the swelling, the leg was strong and muscular, covered in dark hair. She'd have to be careful with the tape.

First, she wrapped the ankle in a layer of torn sheet, not tightly — for protection, not support. Then she set the two lengths of ruler on either side of the bulging ankle and wrapped almost all of his foot and half his lower leg in more sheet, binding this firmly but not so tight it constricted blood flow.

The man slept on. When she had his ankle splinted and bound, she pulled the seat cushions from the striped chair by the window. Stacking one atop the other, she propped his leg on them, arranging it so it bent at the knee and the cushions supported him from there. Then she went to the head of the bed — the dog's concerned eyes followed her — and checked the man's pulse. Too fast, but steady. His skin was warm, too warm; she laid her hand over his forehead. He was feverish, but that might have been his body contending with pain, rather than infection. She'd seen no open wound.

As her hand rested on his brow, his eyes fluttered for a moment, and he mumbled "Erin," or "Aaron," then fell back into unconsciousness. She didn't try to rouse him. He was better off in oblivion.

Back at his foot, she picked up the roll of duct tape. Like books, it was one of the things that people had stupidly left behind all over the mountain, and she had amassed scores of rolls, in every color and even some

217

patterns, in her years of foraging. It was the most useful, versatile tool she had.

When she tore off the first strip, the dog jumped and yelped at the sound. But nothing bad happened, and he settled again. She wrapped the whole splint in duct tape. In the end, she'd made a respectable facsimile of a cast. Whether it would save the man his leg, she didn't know, but he had a better chance than he'd had when she'd come into the room and found him on her bed.

The task completed, the woman once again didn't know what to do.

Since the monsters had taken Fiona from her, she'd gone through every day from one task to the next. There were things to be done, there were always things to be done, and she kept doing them, every day. Today, she'd meant to pick up the wide snow shovel from the house across the street, a man's heavy, fur-lined parka from next door, and the last stack of towels from the third bathroom in this house, as well as gather the last of the wild blueberries from the patch behind the circle lane.

Instead, she had this. She had no day for this work.

Her mind clawed at its walls, trying to make sense of this day, but there was no sense in it. She lived in the world alone. Her world was alone. Only monsters and her. There were no men who loved sweet dogs in her world. There were only monsters who killed them.

She had to get back to Forage Day and what she understood.

But there were still things to be done here. Remembering his hot forehead, she took out her water bag, picked up one of the last strips of sheet, went into the bathroom, and poured cool water over the cloth. She wrung it out and folded it, then returned to the bedroom and laid it over his forehead. He sighed. The dog watched her.

Out in the kitchen, she took a fancy crystal bowl from a dusty glass cabinet, and the big copper pasta pot from the floor of the pantry. She took them back to the bedroom and filled the crystal bowl with the rest of the water from that water bag. The pasta pot, she left sitting on the floor beside the bed. She could think of several uses he might have for it as he convalesced.

From her pack she pulled one of her last two full water bags and all of her venison jerky. She set the bowl of water on the far nightstand, for the dog, and the water bag and pouch of jerky on the nightstand by the man's head.

Still lying at his man's side, the dog watched everything she did. He took a few loud sniffs and licked his chops again when she set the jerky down.

Now. Now there was nothing else to be done. Not here.

She packed up her pack, picked up her axe, and left the room. Before she turned down the hallway, she glanced back at the dog. His head was up and his ears at attention. He lay with his man and watched her go.

Buddy, the man had called him. That was a good name for him.

The woman bolted up from deep in the dream. A scream had crabbed into her throat and lodged there, blocking her airway. She tried to take a breath and failed, tried again and failed, tried again, frantic now, and finally felt a trickle of air move into her lungs.

The night was still dark, and the imprint of the last moments of the dream warped her vision, overlaid the dream on reality and deepened her sense of displacement.

What did you expect? Her mother's voice, full of disappointment and censure. *You should have taken better care. Always so careless. You'll not get another one, I can tell you that. Well, go clean up your mess. Bury her deep. I don't want bones popping up in my peonies.*

Her hands ached, and she stared down at them. They were fists, the quilt packed tightly in their grip. But over the quilt, she saw soil. Loose, dark soil. Grave dirt.

Fiona's grave.

As she watched, the soil faded away and there was only the quilt, twisting in her shaking fists. Then the dream broke apart, and she couldn't quite remember what it had been about.

But oh, how she missed her dog. That sorrow pressed on the back of her neck, wrapped around her throat, and sagged over her chest.

She curled on her side, clutching a pillow in her arms, and tried to sleep the pain away.

Eventually, she did.

Since she'd left the storage house the day before, the woman's mind had churned with conflict and confusion. Memories and feelings she'd locked away had broken free and lurched across her brain, tearing long tracks of new pain and fresh loss across her psyche. Digging into her dreams and her waking thoughts and setting her careful world on its head.

It was Clean Day. She wrapped her mind's hands around that thought and held on. There were things to be done.

Routine had become the most important thing in the woman's world. The *only* thing. It was how she kept time, how she ensured that her stores were full, how she knew things were as they should be, how she knew she was safe, how she knew to keep going. There were things to be done, and as long as that was true, there was life to be lived and purpose to be found.

The first part of every day was the same, no matter what the main work would be. The woman rose and took care of her own hygiene and bodily needs. She ate a hearty breakfast, today of strawberries, eggs, and smoked rabbit. She cleaned up her breakfast dishes. She checked the snares; finding them all empty today, she made sure they were properly set and camouflaged for the next day.

Then she went to the coop and released the chickens into their yard. There were eight hens now, and the rooster, whom she'd named Mac. She'd collected the rooster and three hens years before, finding them roaming the woods on Forage Days. Their first coop had been little more than a box, but she'd found a book on chicken keeping, and now they had a secure little home. In the time since she'd brought the first few home, she'd lost some to weather and predators, but the rooster had survived. He did his job, and she'd been gaining chickens slowly.

Thus far, she'd kept them for their eggs. It seemed a terrible waste to kill a bird for a meal or two when she might produce eggs daily for years. The woman butchered only the cockerels. Mac didn't like other men in his harem, not even his own offspring. He doted on the girls and attacked the boys. So the boys, she butchered when they got mature enough to be meat — and for Mac to be hostile.

The chickens loved to get her leftovers and were particular fans of strawberries, so she tossed the leafy tops — when she was a girl, she'd called them 'hats' — and the heavily bruised fruits from her breakfast. They clucked happily and strutted over for their treat.

While the chickens nibbled, the woman collected the day's eggs — only four today — and cleaned up the coop. Leaving the reed basket of still-warm eggs on the picnic table, she checked on her nightcrawlers, which she used for fishing bait. They didn't need much care, but the woman took no chances she could avoid. Every day, she checked the soil in the large bin, digging her hands in until she found a few fat worms and made sure they were healthy.

Then she turned over her compost and added ash from the fire pit.

Her next chore was her garden. It was late in the season, and most of her plantings had finished or were waning. Beans were yet going strong, and lettuces seemed content to grow until frost, but her few ripe tomatoes were small now, her carrots and potatoes were frail, and she had no more radishes or turnips. It would be time for Garden Day to become Preserve Day soon.

But for now, some things yet grew. She'd planted her squash and pumpkin seeds several Garden Days ago; young sprouts lined their mounded rows of dark earth, just beginning to vine. When the fruits grew and ripened, she'd can their meats and have good soups all winter.

When her daily chores were completed, it was time for Clean Day to start. At the outdoor pump, the woman filled her biggest galvanized steel bucket with water and lugged it to the cabin. With the clean well water and bath towels too tattered for their intended use, she wiped the outsides of all the windows. With a stiff-bristled scrub brush, she scrubbed the picnic table and the chairs at the fire pit. She dumped the murky water and refilled the bucket, then carried it indoors.

Every Clean Day, she wiped down all the shelves and organized all her supplies. Each pot and pan had a hook of its own. The Mason jars of preserved fruits and vegetables had an order, arranged alphabetically by their contents. Since she'd been alone, it had become crucial to take all the jars down, polish the glass to gleaming, scrub the shelves she'd made to hold them, and arrange them again.

Since the monsters had tried to take everything from her, it had been crucial to clean everything they had touched, everything she thought they might have. Every Clean Day. She couldn't be sure that she'd cleansed them from her home. She knew she hadn't. There was a mound under the willow tree in back, covered in the white petals of sandwort, that reminded her every day that she couldn't wash away what the monsters had done. But she couldn't stop trying.

Clutching the brush, she scrubbed the wooden worktop in the kitchen. She scrubbed the sink pump and the sink. She gave the bathroom the same attention, then switched out her water again. She wiped the insides of all the windows.

She scrubbed the walls, moving from the kitchen to the living area. With another old towel, she polished the furniture and the few mementos she had left. She stripped the bed and stuffed her big reed basket with her washing, then pulled all the cushions and mattresses out into the sun and beat them with an old tennis racket until she could see no motes jump into the sunbeams. The mattresses had been stained once; now, the pattern of the mattress covers had been worn off and the fabric had grown filmy there, but there were no stains.

As the sun stretched to the top of the sky, the woman made herself lunch: three eggs fried on the woodstove, raw green beans, and two chunks of rabbit jerky. As at breakfast, she drank clear water. She rarely drank anything else except in the evening, when she brewed olive or barley tea, or, if she was feeling under the weather, eucalyptus tea.

After lunch, she brought the mattresses and cushions in, remade the beds, and arranged the furniture, she got on her hands and knees and scrubbed the floor, from kitchen to living room to bathroom.

When all that was done, she emptied her bookshelves, carefully stacking all her books that the monsters had torn up. It had taken her days to find the places for all the loose pages. She polished the shelves and wiped each book, rubbing away the monsters' touch, making sure the pages were neatly aligned. She put each one back in its place, arranged alphabetically, first by genre, then by author, and then by title.

The journals that filled the bottom shelves, she didn't touch.

The sun cast diamonds the across the surface of the lake. The woman stood at the side and stared until her eyes were dazzled. The afternoon was heavy with late-summer warmth, slowing the bees as they buzzed from one wildflower to another, glittering their legs with pollen. A fragrant breeze stirred the reeds and grasses and filled the air with whispers.

A fish popped from the surface and swallowed a strider who'd been skimming his way across. She watched the ripples from its hungry kiss make the diamonds shimmer and dance.

Ignored at her feet sat her reed basket full of washing, with her washboard balanced on top. She had to get the wash done soon, or there wouldn't be enough good light and warm sun to dry the wash before dark. But she couldn't seem to move. A dream she barely remembered had grabbed hold. It dragged on her head and upended her thinking. She'd paused in her work, and now was lost.

Standing at the lake, remembering Fee's joy in the water, the way she snapped at the drops she flung with her paws, the great gouts of water that would fly from her coat when she shook herself on the shore, her bounding excitement when Shrek would amble out of the woods to play, the woman felt ill and sad, trapped in a past she'd lost. She barely remembered what had been before Fiona, but she remembered every moment of life with that dog.

She hadn't seen Shrek since the day she'd buried Fiona. She'd been entirely alone.

In the house down the mountain, a man sat with his dog. Broken, but not alone. In need, but not alone. He had a dog. Buddy. Could he protect him, hurt as he was? Were they in danger of monsters?

There were things to be done.

There were things to be done.

There were things to be done.

The thought beat against the back of her head until she heard it and remembered. It was Clean Day, and her washing sat at her feet. She finally picked up the basket and went to the water.

There were things yet to be done today.

Thirteen

The next day was Hunt Day. After her daily chores, the woman twisted her hair into a tight braid and dressed for the woods, in heavy jeans and socks, her good L.L. Bean boots, a old t-shirt, worn to sensual softness, and a canvas coat. It was a good, late-summer day, warm sun and blue skies, but when she left the homestead, she dressed for the chance she might spend a night outdoors and always wore a coat. Besides, it was better to keep as much skin as possible covered to guard against poison vegetation or venomous creatures.

She packed her smaller pack with four water bags and enough food for two small meals, a large pouch of assorted jerkies and a plastic container of fresh vegetables, another of four hardboiled eggs, her first aid supplies, and her field dressing kit and a spare knife. She strapped her favorite hunting knife, in its tooled leather sheath, to her thigh and sheathed another at the small of her back. She strapped her quiver and bow on her back and holstered her hatchet on her hip. On Hunt Days, loaded up with other weapons, she left her axe behind.

Before she turned down the lane and headed away from the homestead, she looked back, pausing, as she always did now, to see it all as it was, in case someone took it from her while she was away.

By the time she got down to the storage house, the woman hadn't taken her bow from her back even once. She'd kept alert and quiet, travelling as much as possible through the dense woods, telling herself she could check on the dog and hunt, too, but she'd seen no game as she walked, and she hadn't stopped to set up a blind to wait at any likely spots, either.

Some Hunt Days, she came home empty-handed, without even a squirrel. Just like the occasionally empty snares, some hunts weren't successful. As the season aged, though, and threatened cold, it was important to cure as much meat as she could. Though she had snowshoes, when the snow topped the roof of the cabin, there was little hunting she could do.

Maybe she'd find a deer on the way up — though by then it would be too late to take the time to dress it before the light gave out.

She'd given up a Hunt Day for this. Work she hadn't done. The woman stood at the edge of the forest and chewed on her lip, trying to settled her confused mind. If she turned back now, she had time to hunt.

She wanted to see the dog. She wanted to make sure he was okay. He was too sweet and afraid for this world.

So she went forward.

When she got to the storage house, she set her bow and quiver in its hiding place. She unholstered her hatchet and held it aloft. The man was injured, but two days had passed, and if he was on his feet and meant her harm after all, she would be ready.

Then she'd take Buddy to the homestead and take care of him. She'd stay here until he trusted her.

Creeping through the house, ready for anything, she went straight for the bedroom. As she peered around the hallway corner, she saw the man, standing in the bedroom doorway, his injured leg bent at the knee. He held the doorframe with one hand, and in the other, he held a long, thin sword. A katana, she recalled from the lingering shadows of the world before. It seemed a strange weapon for him to wield.

Then again, her favorite weapon was a reproduction Viking axe.

They stood at opposite ends of the hallway and stared at each other. The woman could see Buddy hiding behind him, poking his nose between the man's good leg and the doorframe.

"It's you," the man said and let the sword drop until its point sagged toward the floor. "Hi."

She didn't lower her hatchet. The man looked weak, his hair lank and his complexion pale, with dark smudges under his eyes. But he was conscious now, and mobile enough to have moved that much. What if he could put weight on his ankle now? It didn't seem likely, but she couldn't think of him as anything but a monster. What else could he be?

He swung his hurt leg forward, showing the bright-pink cast she'd made. He was coming for her. She leapt forward and charged down the hall, gripping the hatchet in both hands.

The man dropped the katana and threw his hands up. "Wait, wait, wait!" No longer holding onto the doorframe, he lost his balance and fell backward, landing hard on the floor. "Ow! Wait!" he gasped again, "Please!"

She drew up short, her arms tense and ready, her heart racing, her breath heaving. But he lay on the floor, gasping. Buddy crouched at his head, showing that same conflict she'd seen in him before: the instincts of fear and defense struggling with each other, and fear winning.

Hating to see his fear, she lowered her hatchet and turned her attention to the man.

"Shit," he said. "Ow. I'm not going to hurt you. I want to *thank* you. I think you saved my life." He held out his hand. "I don't suppose you'd help me up before you sink that axe in my head?"

She stared at his offered hand and didn't know what to do.

This was a bad mistake. She should have had Hunt Day. She should never have come back to this house again. It wasn't hers anymore. He'd taken it from her and made it his. He'd taken her house and her dog, and if she stayed he'd take more. He'd take everything. That was what monsters did.

Buddy whined and licked the man's face.

Not her dog. Not hers. Fiona was her dog.

Her head spinning, thoughts and memories and fears and losses roaring, twisting their claws together and slashing, the woman dropped the hatchet and slammed her hands against the sides of her head. She didn't understand, she didn't understand, she didn't *understand*.

When her knees hit the floor, she doubled over, trying to squeeze her head quiet.

"Hey, hey," the man said. "It's okay." His voice was close. Too close.

And then he touched her. She felt his hands on her hands. She screamed and knocked them away, pushing herself back as far as she could until her pack, still on her back, hit the wall. The hatchet was by her foot; she lunged for it and slammed back to the wall, holding the weapon before her.

The man stared at her, his mouth and eyes open wide. "Oh, honey. They got at you, didn't they? Ferals? Or Fiends? You know who I mean?"

She didn't. She stared at him, clutching the hatchet. Her head still screamed at her, exhorting her to run, run now, right now. Or fight, right now. But she couldn't move.

He sighed and scooted around until he could lean with his back against the end of the bed. "Look, I *promise* I don't mean to hurt you. I'm grateful for what you did for my leg, and the food and water you left, and … you took care of me and Buddy. Thank you."

She shifted her attention to Buddy, who sat at his man's side, regarding her with wary interest. As she focused on his big brown eyes, and his soft golden fur, her head began to calm. If he would come to her, she would welcome that touch.

But he wasn't hers.

"Can you speak?" The man asked.

Reluctantly, she returned her gaze to him. She didn't answer his question or even try; she knew there weren't any words to be said.

He moved his hands and fingers in a quick, intentional way. She understood he was using sign language, a way to communicate with deaf people, but she didn't know how to sign.

He gave that up. "But you can hear. How long've you been alone?" he asked, and the woman saw something soft in his eyes. Something not monstrous. Something human. His eyes weren't brown, like Buddy's. They were light. They were hazel, like her father's had been.

She didn't know how long she'd been alone. Since Fiona. Since forever.

She managed to lift her shoulder and remember that that was a shrug. It meant she didn't know.

He responded with a smile, and that wasn't monstrous, either. No greed or lust or cruelty in it. She didn't remember the words for other kinds of feelings, but it was those other kinds of feelings she saw.

"I'm Gus. This is Buddy." He patted the dog's head, and Buddy leaned into it, his eyes drooping with pleasure. "I don't know what to call you. You can't tell me your name?"

Her name. She'd had a name. In the world before. She gave him a slow shake of her head, though she wasn't sure what she was denying. That she had a name? Or that she remembered it?

"Okay, that's okay." He tipped his head toward her. "You think you can put that down now?"

The hatchet in her hands. He wanted her to put her weapon down. Her protection. She turned it in her hand, so that the blade was parallel between them. She looked around the blade to Buddy, sitting beside the man.

Her arms tense, ready to shift course instantly if this turned out to be a monstrous ruse, she lowered the hatchet and rested it on her thigh.

"Thank you. We're not a threat, I promise." He scratched behind the dog's ear.

A thread of belief unspooled inside her, and her chaotic mind grabbed it. A word came up to her tongue suddenly, and she opened her mouth to let it free. "Buddy." Each syllable creaked from her lips.

His smile widened. "Hey, yeah! Buddy. And I'm Gus. What's your name?"

Her name. Digging deep, she searched for it, but it wasn't there, not on her tongue or anywhere else. She stared.

"It's okay. You don't have to tell me. Or say anything you don't want to." He shifted on the floor and tried to stand without using his hurt leg, but when he tried to move it out of the way, he hissed in pain and sat back down. Again, he reached out to her. "Can you help me get up?"

His hands hovered between them. The thought of touching him made her skin crawl and turned her heart into a clenched fist. She could not. There was so much risk. So very much risk.

But she could help him stand. The idea struck her like a slap. She could help him, and that was something to be done. There were things to be done.

She stood up, and the man smiled and lifted his hands more. But she wasn't going to touch him, not let him grab her with those hands. She turned and hurried from the room.

"Wait!" she heard behind her.

Though the house the man and Buddy were in was her house, she thought of all the houses on this circular road, and all the supplies in them, as hers. During all her time in this world, she'd foraged in every direction that she could travel, as far as she could go and return in the space of a day, but she'd relied most heavily on what she found here, in this near place, with so much bounty and so few bones.

In the world before, people had lived in these houses mostly in the winter, playing in the snow, and the garages here were filled with skis and sleds and snowshoes. She'd taken all that she could use, but there were many that she couldn't—because they couldn't be made to fit, or because they weren't right for her needs. She had little use for downhill skis, but snowshoes and cross-country skis helped her stay alive in the heavy mountain winters. And toboggans and sleds made for good carts over snow. When something wore out or broke, she found another.

Someday, in this world, she'd have to repair the things that broke, and she was mindful of that and careful of her discards, but that day hadn't come yet. Alone on the mountain, its offerings were hers.

In the garage of her house, high in the rafters, was the last of the winter sports gear, the things here she hadn't thought she'd need. She set up the aluminum step ladder, climbed up, and pulled a pair of old wooden cross-country ski poles from the cobwebby ceiling.

She tested the poles. They were a little tall for her, but the man was, she thought, taller than she. He hadn't stood straight before her, but he wasn't small, she could see that. The first time she'd seen him, he'd been stretched out on the large bed, and he'd taken up most of the vertical space.

With the poles in one arm, she collapsed the ladder and put it back in its place between two exposed studs in the garage wall.

When she returned to the bedroom, the man had crawled to the chair by the window and gripped the armrests, trying to use his upper-body strength to get his good foot under him. His arms bulged inside a raggedy sweater he wore, and he almost had it.

She attempted to speak again, but didn't know what word to say. An odd, rusty noise came out of her mouth, and the man looked over his shoulder. He was sweating heavily, and his face shone bright red.

"Hey," he panted. "Thought you'd ghosted again."

Afraid to make that strange noise if she tried to speak, she held out the poles.

"Oh, yeah. That could work." He rested on the knee of his good leg, holding his injured ankle oddly, trying to keep it in midair.

She brought the poles to him, careful to keep her hands away from his. He took the poles, sliding each hand through a strap and gripping the handles firmly. Again using the strength of his arms and core, he heaved himself onto his good foot. Taking a moment to be sure of his balance, he set the poles a foot or so before him and hopped forward. The poles wobbled, but he kept his balance. Buddy watched him anxiously, then wagged his tail when the man was steady.

"I don't think I'll be walking far with these, but they're a big help." He grinned broadly at her. "Saving me again. Thank you. I don't know how I'm going to make good on all this debt I owe you."

The emotions on his face seemed alien and unknowable to her, but they weren't threatening. She tried a smile back. Her cheeks felt odd, and she raised her hands to touch them.

"That's a nice thing to see," the man said. "You have a pretty smile." His voice had gone soft, and she considered him again, looking for signs of a trap. Something greedy in his eyes. There was nothing. Only that softness.

Balancing carefully, the man took two more hopping steps and returned to the armchair. He maneuvered around and sat on it. "Sorry. Got a little lightheaded."

She remembered what she'd brought in her pack. It was still on her back, so she pulled her shoulders out of the straps and set it on the floor, keeping out of reach of the man's hands. She opened the compartment where she always kept her food and water, pulled out two water bags, the pouch of jerky, and the plastic containers of vegetables and eggs. In her crouch, she moved back to the man and held out the food and water.

When he took the offering, his fingers grazed hers. The touch seemed to burn her, and she snatched her hands away. The container of eggs dropped to the floor, and the lid popped open.

The man stared, then lifted shocked eyes to her. "Those are eggs. Chicken eggs. You have chickens?"

As she gathered the eggs back up, he tossed Buddy a big piece of jerky, then tore open the lid on the vegetable container and popped a tomato in his mouth. His eyes fluttered shut. "Jesus fucking Christ, first the Rennies, and now this. Going up is the best thing I ever did. Everything's okay here."

He smiled at her again, and she smiled back without thinking. His words didn't make much sense, but he was happy, and the woman discovered that she liked that he was.

Still, fear made its own pulse at the bottom of her heart. She needed a thing to do.

The bright pink of the duct tape around his ankle caught her eye, and she fixed there. The cast was intact and showed no wear on the bottom; he seemed not to have tried to put weight on it at all. She wondered how he'd gotten around to meet his needs and Buddy's during the two days she'd been gone.

The swelling had decreased. His toes were still puffy, but they looked like toes again. He was healing.

"You did a good job," he said, and she looked up from his foot and found him watching her. "I'm trying not to fuck it up." He took a bite of carrot. Chewing, he added,

"Were you a doctor or nurse or something before the storm?"

The storm? The lights, he meant. The solar flares and beautiful lights that had gone on and on and on until the world was dead.

Had she been a doctor then? No. Her father had been. A heart surgeon. He'd wanted her to be a doctor, too. A door of memory opened, and she recalled studying science in school. But she hadn't been a doctor. What had she done instead? She reached back, seeking the answer.

All your father's done for you, and he asks one thing. One thing! Instead you want to make those stupid games? Your ingratitude is appalling, Diana.

Her stomach rolled as the memories spun through her. She'd made games. Video games, like the ones in the little room in this house. She'd been working on a game when the world before ended.

She couldn't say any of that; it barely made sense to her. But one other thing had emerged in the torrent of recollection, and she tried it out. "Di ... Diana," she said. The sound of that name in the air had no resonance or relevance. It might have been the first time she'd ever heard it. She wasn't sure she *was* Diana.

But she once had been.

The man—Gus—stopped chewing and set the nearly-empty container on his thighs. "Diana. That's you?"

Although she wasn't sure it still was, she nodded.

"That's beautiful. Diana, goddess of the hunt. Seems fitting. It's nice to meet you, Diana."

He didn't hold his hand out, and she was glad.

But when she took a piece of jerky from her own meal and held it out to Buddy, the dog scooted warily closer and eventually took it from her. She left her hand outstretched, and after he'd eaten her offering, he licked the jerky taste from her fingers. When he was done, she leaned forward, reaching out to stroke the top of his head. His expressive eyes watched her closely, and his body was tense with ready flight, but he let her touch him.

When he scooted closer, seeking more of her touch, her vision blurred.

"Buddy," she whispered.

Fourteen

The woman slept well that night and rose early, before her rooster, and did her daily chores in the low light of a birthing dawn. It was Garden Day, and she was glad that the gardening season waned. She had the pumpkin and squash vines tended, the few ripe vegetables picked, and fresh compost turned into the soil well before midday. She added the last of the tomatoes — there were no more buds, so she was sure they were the last — and beans to the basket on the kitchen worktop, so they would ripen more and be ready for canning.

She packed the last batch of hard rolls, two jars of fruit preserves, a half dozen hardboiled eggs, and an empty collapsible water jug. She added two threadbare towels and a full roll of duct tape, this roll plain silver.

Then she packed her own provisions and zipped up the pack.

She was going down to see Buddy and Gus. To *check* on them, not to visit. Just to check on them.

Since she'd missed a Hunt Day, she took her hunting gear with her as well, so that she'd be prepared if she crossed paths with game. If she took a deer, she'd carry it to the storage house, butcher it there, and share it with Buddy and Gus.

For a long time, she stood near the door, ready to go. She stared into the corner of the room, near the fireplace.

Once, she'd badly sprained her ankle, and her world up here had tumbled just as she had. She hadn't been prepared for such an injury or the limited movement it had caused. She'd had only her father's old walking stick to help her get around.

After her ankle had healed, she'd worked to prevent such trouble again. She tried always to be prepared for every trouble she could think of. So she'd made herself a pair of crutches. She'd cut a young tree down and used its trunk, splitting it at the top and inserting a wedge, then binding the top with pieces of a worn comforter.

She'd never had to use them, but that didn't mean she'd never have use of them. If she gave them to Gus, she'd have to make another pair for herself. To be prepared.

She could do that. She knew how.

Just shy of an hour into her hike down, the woman saw fresh fox scat—so fresh that the scent was still strong. She crouched down and looked for signs that the fox was still around.

Foxes were night hunters, but in this new world, without human intervention, animals seemed to have loosened some of their long habits. It wouldn't be the first time she'd taken an animal when it should have been cozy in its den.

If it was a female with kits, she'd leave it be, she never orphaned babies, but if it was a male or a female who didn't have young at the teat, then she'd be grateful to be able to take a fox to Buddy and Gus. A fox would make a good meal for them, one without waste.

It would be enough to make up for Hunt Day. She had enough cured meat already for the winter. Almost as much as she ever had at the end of a season, and she'd always had meat left over when the snow melted.

But did she have enough for three?

As that question rose up, the woman sat back on her heels. Gus wouldn't need her help for more than a few weeks. She had no need to store extra winter provisions.

But Buddy. She didn't want Buddy to leave.

Those thoughts fell off a cliff and into a tangle of thorns. Too painful and dangerous to follow.

At her side she heard a light rustle, so she left her strange thoughts to die and turned, slowly, on her heels. The fox was there, about fifty yards away. It dug in the earth below a large growth of mountain heather. It had dug in well already, and its rear end was up, its tail high, showing quite clearly that it was a male.

Crouched out of cover, in clear view of the fox, should he bother to turn and look, the woman stayed still and watched. He was making a burrow for the winter, a warm place to take his rest.

She looked up through the leaves and pine boughs that swayed slightly in a gentle breeze. The day was warm and summery, and the sky was clear. There'd been a heavy fog in the morning, though. And that breeze had a northerly nip to it.

But there had been no clearer sign yet that summer had reached its end than a fox digging his den.

He still hadn't noticed her, or lifted his head from his work. Watching him carefully and moving slowly, she brought her bow forward, lifted an arrow from her quiver, nocked, and aimed. She made a soft sound, clicking her tongue against her teeth, and the fox flinched and pulled back to see the intrusion.

She loosed the arrow as soon as she sighted his head.

When she came to the storage house, she approached the area as always: with stealth, checking for trouble in every direction. But then she heard a whistle — three clear, bright notes, a short tune she suddenly recognized as the sound of someone calling a dog.

She stayed in stealth mode, creeping along the shingled side of the house, until she heard Buddy barking. A loud rustle of years-old dead leaves followed, and then he was there before her, yellow butt wiggling with his wagging tail. He dropped something to the ground at her feet and barked again.

Crouching to run her fingers through the soft fur around his ears, the woman saw what he'd dropped: a tennis ball. Yellow under a lot of dirt and slobber.

A memory rammed into the back of her head: Fiona's last day. They'd come to this house for supplies, and the woman had found tennis balls in the far recesses of a closet. They'd played with one, and it had gone missing before they'd left.

They'd played with this one. This ball, in her hand. The last time she'd played with Fiona.

Tears filled her eyes, and loss clenched her chest. She couldn't see, she couldn't breathe.

Buddy seemed to understand her sadness. He sat before her and nudged her cheek with his cool nose. He licked tears from her face.

She wrapped her arms around this dog's neck, felt his warm body and his good heart, and sobbed.

"Diana?" Gus's voice. "Diana? Are you okay?" He scoffed. "No, obviously, you're not. Diana?"

Diana. It was her name. She was Diana.

Diana looked up from Buddy's sodden fur. Gus stood before her, wobbling slightly, using the ski poles to keep his balance on one leg. She saw his expression and understood it as worry and compassion.

For her. He felt those things for her. For Diana.

"Okay," she said and sniffed her tears away. "I'm okay." The words were right there, waiting to be said.

"Now that you're talking, can I ask you something?"

They'd already skinned and butchered the fox, and they had it on a large grate across the patio fire pit, frying on the grate itself and in the last skillets the houses on this lane offered. She'd found lots of uses for pots and pans at the homestead and had liberated most of them from these kitchens.

Buddy lay near the roasting meat, occasionally taking deep, sensual sniffs.

Diana looked up from Gus's foot, where she'd just finished rewrapping the strips of towel around the splint. The towel made a much better, and more comfortable, binding than the strips of sheet had.

Her ability to speak, or even to think in a way that would make words, had atrophied, and every sentence she tried took ages to assemble. She'd been alone, and lost in her head, for so long that the words she knew were all tangled together.

But as she picked at the edge of the duct tape, she answered his question with a nod. She'd try.

A pleased smile shaped his words whenever he spoke to her. "Where do you come from?"

At first, Diana didn't understand what he was asking. Then, she didn't know how to answer. Finally, she decided on, "Up."

"Up the mountain?"

She nodded and kept wrapping tape around his ankle.

"And you're alone up there."

There was no upward lilt to the end of his words, it wasn't a question, but she nodded again. "Alone." She peeked up to see his expression.

His smile was gone, but his compassion wasn't. "For how long?"

Diana didn't know. She'd kept track once, but not anymore. All she knew was that tomorrow was Fish Day. She didn't know how long it had been since Fiona's death. It had been spring, she remembered that, and not the most recent one. More than a year, then. As for how long she'd been up in the mountains, it seemed like forever.

When she didn't answer, he asked, "Since the Sunstorm? Have you been up here alone all this time?"

The Sunstorm. Was that what it was called? She remembered the lights in the sky, how they'd lasted so long and been so beautiful, how people hadn't realized that they'd meant the end of the world.

As a child, she'd once seen the aurora borealis, the northern lights. Those lights had been beautiful and breathtaking—and not as bright or as long-lasting as the lights in the California sky at the end of the world.

"Yes," she answered Gus. "Since then."

"Alone."

Except for Fiona, but she didn't want to talk about her. She nodded.

"Jesus, honey."

Finishing the cast, she set the tape aside and went to check on the meat. It sizzled in its fat as she turned the pieces over, and Buddy sat up to watch.

She smiled and used the fork to scoop a small, stray piece from a puddle of fat. When it was cool enough, she tossed it to the dog, who caught it with a loud, hollow snap.

"Good boy. Good Buddy."

When she went back to sit near Gus, she tried a longer sentence. "You were down there."

"Yeah. I was in Manhattan when it happened. Wandered around for a few years, just focused on keeping alive. Hooked up with some good folks, and we tried to find a way to live, but that didn't work out. People kept talking about the west coast, saying it was better out west, so I started walking that way."

"People. There are people?"

He cocked his head. "Yeah, sure. Haven't you seen *anybody*?"

She shook her head. "Only monsters."

His eyes steadied on hers, and he simply studied her. She studied him back, trying to make sense of this tremendous change in her world.

"Yeah," he finally said, his eyes locked with hers. "There are those, too."

The way he looked at her made her head hurt. She hadn't been seen in so long that she didn't remembered what expressions meant. She had to reach back into disintegrating boxes of decomposed memories to understand.

Breaking the confounding moment, Gus leaned back and stretched his arms out across the back of the stone wall behind them. His hand came within inches of Diana's shoulder, and she moved away. She could touch him to help him, but the thought of his hands on her made her ill.

If he noticed her move, she couldn't tell. He said, "There aren't anywhere near as many people as there used to be. A lot of folks died in the beginning, and it's harder to stay alive the way things are, so people keep dying. Not many are having babies ..." his words faded out, and he turned away, looking out toward the woods.

Diana sat and watched him, waiting, not knowing if he'd finished speaking or had simply paused. She remembered a phrase: 'lost in thought.' Gus seemed lost in thought.

With a brisk shake of his head, he turned back to her. "There's not a lot of kids in the world. All the nuclear reactors melted down when the storm fried the power, and I think everybody down there's breathing some kind of radiation—was, and maybe still is. I don't know how long it lasts in the air. I heard the east coast is just a wasteland now." He sighed. "Anyway, there are people, but it's hardly crowded."

He leaned forward; Diana thought he meant to touch her. She shrank back, and he sat back again. "What's it been like for you?"

What words would form the answer to a question like that? None. Or too many. More than she remembered. She lifted her shoulders instead.

There was another bewildering moment when he only stared at her. Hazel eyes, like her father. Long, wildly tangled hair, dark except where the sun slanted across it, showing gold. Heavy, dark beard.

Wanting the moment, and her confusion in it, to end, Diana made a sentence to say. "Winter is coming."

He laughed—a bright, surprised, full-throated sound. Not understanding why her words had been funny, she cocked her head.

Buddy came over, alerted to fun by his man's laugh. He brought his ball to Gus, who tossed it toward the trees. Buddy bounded after it. Diana felt the ache in her heart, but she was happy to see Buddy play.

"Do you remember *Game of Thrones*?"

After a moment of riffling through her old memory boxes, she did, and she smiled. She'd said the Stark words. As Gus's laugh picked up again, her own humor caught hold of it, and she laughed, too.

Something seemed to shake loose inside her as her chest vibrated with that strange chuckle.

"God, I miss TV," Gus said as his laughter subsided. "And movies. And video games—that room inside has just about every game I ever loved in my whole life. What I'd give to spend an afternoon like that again."

She'd written some of those games, she remembered. But she couldn't think how to say it or if it was worth saying. So she only smiled, then tried to say the thing she'd meant before. "Winter soon. A lot of snow here."

Gus tossed the ball for Buddy again and focused on Diana. "Yeah, I know. I guess Buddy and I are staying the winter, since I'm not going anywhere soon." He nodded at his cast.

"I'll help you," she said. She didn't know exactly what she meant, but she did know that the words were right. She'd forgotten what it was to be in company with someone. To have a conversation. To share a joke.

He smiled, and she liked to see it. He was a good-looking man. She'd forgotten that feeling, too.

"Thank you," he said.

Buddy brought the ball to her, and she threw it toward the woods.

After they'd eaten, Gus went a ways into the woods to handle his business. Buddy went with him, right at his side.

Diana cleaned up, wrapping the last of the meat, cooked dark and dry, in a clean cloth. It was the best she could do to keep the meat down here. It would be edible for at least another day. Then they'd have the jerky, eggs, and vegetables she'd brought.

Without smoked meat, he'd have to hunt in the winter, but even the animals that didn't hibernate in the winter hunkered down and made themselves scarce. She'd help as much as she could, but eventually she'd be snowed in, and Buddy and Gus would be on their own.

There was only one solution to that problem that Diana could see, but it was far too big and frightening to be contemplated. She shunted it aside and cleared the rest of their leavings.

Buddy trotted ahead of Gus as they came back from the woods. Diana could see that so much walking on one leg had worn Gus out. Even with the crutches she'd brought him, he struggled on the uneven terrain—and he was four or five inches taller than she, so crutches she'd made for herself didn't fit him very well.

She gathered up the big barbecue grate and the skillets to take to the stream for a wash. It was important not to leave meat smell around the house, or Buddy and Gus might get a large, hungry visitor in the night. Gus headed inside, heaving his body forward on the crutches. Buddy followed him to the door but didn't go in. Instead, he swung his head back and forth, to Gus and to Diana, not knowing which way to go.

Diana didn't call him, but she didn't leave, either. She waited. With a sweet grin, Gus waved Buddy toward her, and the dog trotted her way.

She figured it was the meat more than her company he sought, but she was pleased nonetheless.

She stacked the skillets beside her as she knelt at the edge of the stream to wash the big grate first. Buddy did his part by licking the top skillet clean with extreme attention to detail.

Then he did his bravely fearful whine-growl noise and dropped his belly to the ground at her side. Hunched over the rushing water, up to her elbows in its icy current, Diana heard a grunt across the stream and knew it as a bear.

Without moving enough to look for the danger, she slid the fingers of one hand through the grate, and slowly, slowly reached her other hand to the hilt of her knife. She drew it out inch by inch. When she had the grate gripped like a shield and the knife gripped like a weapon, she lifted her head.

Her heart leapt into her throat. She hadn't seen him in more than a year, but there was no question at all that she faced Shrek.

"Hey, boy," she said, her voice low and conversational. "Missed you."

He extended his nose and took a whiff of her. Without Fiona, she didn't know if she smelled the same.

Buddy whined again, and got Shrek's complete attention. He took another big, noisy sniff, and then grunted and shook his head.

He was confused. Buddy smelled like dog, but not his dog. Not Fiona. Diana understood his confusion completely.

She holstered her knife, still moving slowly, unsure how much Shrek remembered of her. She made the gesture she'd taught him and Fiona, for 'down.'

He grunted again and did a little dance with his front paws, like he couldn't decide. Then he lay down, putting his big front feet in the stream.

"Good boy, good boy," Diana murmured. "That's my boy. Missed you, buddy."

Buddy looked up at her and whined.

"It's okay, Bud."

Not liking the diversion of her attention — typical —
Shrek stood and crossed the stream, splashing through the
current. Buddy yelped and hid behind her.

Shrek stopped when Buddy hid. He made a soft
roar, and Buddy whined back.

"Buddy, it's okay," she said again. "Shrek, easy. Be
easy." She made the sign she'd used when he got too
rough with Fee, for 'gentle.' He remembered that one, too.

After a minute of Buddy's curious fear and Shrek's
wary interest, Diana managed to broker a meeting. Buddy
inched forward, and Shrek stretched his big head, and two
noses got within inches of each other.

Satisfied that no one was going to get hurt, she
picked up two greasy skillets and laid them on the bank
between dog and bear. Shrek sloshed over immediately.
Buddy, who'd been eating all day, stared longingly at the
one Shrek wasn't snuffling in. Finally, he couldn't stand it
and he made his way to the skillet and ate beside a bear.

Happier than she'd been in longer than she could
remember, Diana sat with them and scratched an ear with
each hand.

Shrek stayed for a while and let Buddy sniff him
while he licked the last skillet. Then, as he always had, he

ambled off without warning when he was no longer interested. Buddy sat and watched the bear go, just as Fiona always had.

Diana finished the washing, and they went back to the house. By then, the sun was low — too low for the hike she had back to the homestead. The days were shortening. If she left right away, it would be close to full dark by the time she made it.

As she opened the door and let Buddy in, she heard a strange noise. She tried to place it but couldn't. Not a threatening sound. Sweet and sad. She stepped deeper into the house and closed the door. Buddy had trotted off right away, so she stood alone, holding a stack of stream-washed skillets, and listened.

Music. Gus was playing that violin he kept beside the bed. The one from the game room closet. She set the skillets on a nearby table and followed the sound.

She didn't know classical music and didn't recognize the piece he played, but she knew it was beautiful — slow and graceful and … mournful. Like a song for things lost. It made her ache.

He sat on a chair in the little game room, playing softly, his eyes closed, his arms moving with fluid grace, his fingers strong on the neck. Stopping in the doorway, Diana watched.

After a while, he must have sensed her presence. His eyes opened, and he smiled. He played for a bit longer, reaching what sounded like an ending, or at least a pause, and lifted his chin from the rest, still smiling.

She wanted to tell him it was beautiful, that it had made her feel something she couldn't remember feeling before. She wanted to tell him about Shrek and Buddy. She wanted to tell him that she'd been happy on this day. But she didn't know what words to use.

"I have to go," she said.

His smile faded. "Diana ..."

With no idea what he might say next, but afraid of it anyway, she shook her head. "I have to go."

She turned and went to collect her things. If she hurried, she could get back to her world before full dark.

Fifteen

The sky rained pastel fire, and it was the most beautiful thing Diana had ever seen.

The world around her had gone completely dark and, for a single, frozen moment, completely silent. The only lights in the world were in the blazing, dancing sky.

She'd been driving home from the office, in the same foul mood she was always in after a day spent there. As a game designer, she was able to do a lot of her work from home, especially during the early stages of a new game. When concept became execution, the job required a lot more time on site. Most of the people she worked with were a lot like her—socially awkward and thin-skinned. Also extremely smart and arrogant about it. And mostly male and not entirely convinced that women made good gamers, much less game designers.

After a few weeks in that kind of social experiment, Diana was usually fantasizing about the zombie apocalypse.

And then the sky caught cold fire.

Her Nissan Leaf went suddenly dead, and she briefly thought she was trapped in her car when the electric door locks wouldn't disengage. But then she remembered that her window was open, and she clumsily pulled herself through.

All she could think of in those first few moments was to get into open space so that her view was unimpeded. Her parents had taken her and her sister to Scandinavia one summer when she was a teenager, and she'd seen the Northern Lights. Aurora borealis. The sky had been lovely – soft, swaying and rolling pastels, the night turning into the light, liquid texture of watercolor.

What was happening in the sky on this late-March evening was like the Northern Lights as painted by Vincent van Gogh on LSD and Ecstasy and heroin and meth all at once.

And she was a block and a half from her home near Los Gatos, California, fifty miles south of San Francisco.

Her neighborhood was quiet, and she had been the only moving car on the road. But she could hear neighbors coming out of their homes, their voices excited, almost reverent. Diana didn't look around. She simply stared up at the electric, frantic sky, her mouth open, transfixed. But then her brain began to work again.

She really did think a lot about apocalypses – plural. As a resident of California, in a town right on a major fault line, *she'd kept an earthquake preparedness kit packed for years. As a game designer, diehard gamer chick, and all-around nerd, she had imagined, created, LARP'd, RPG'd, and prepared for all manner of fantastic and apocalyptic scenarios. Thus she had studied widely and deeply the real possibilities for real apocalypse: disease, war, act of humanity, act of nature, act of God.*

What she was witnessing in the brilliant sky above her, and in the utter darkness of the street around her, was a solar storm. One of cataclysmic proportions. Diana didn't resist the idea; she didn't refuse to believe her eyes. She knew what she was seeing.

The apocalypse.

And it was beautiful.

And then a jet — maybe a 737 — fell out of the sky like a screaming stone. It exploded on impact, dimming the lights above.

Diana reached into her Leaf, grabbed her backpack off the seat, and ran.

All of her neighbors ran toward the explosion. Diana ran to her house. She understood what a solar storm of this magnitude, suggesting multiple flares in succession, meant. Every single thing that ran on electricity would be dead. The whole world over. And not dead until the power came back on. Dead as in fried. Kaput. Would never work again. Anything that used an electric charge — battery operated, AC/DC, solar, wind, water, it made no difference. The circuits would be fried.

Everything would have to be built from scratch. Any information stored digitally was lost forever. On this night, the world had been thrown forcibly back to an era before the light bulb. Before the telegraph. Early nineteenth-century technology.

Generators wouldn't work. Anyone being kept alive by a device that used electricity, from a pacemaker to a ventilator, would die. Anyone being kept alive by medicines that required refrigeration would die.

Diana knew all these things to be true. She also knew that the world had had eight minutes — the amount of time it took for light to travel from the sun to the earth — to prepare for the end of itself, from the time of the first flare until its arrival in the atmosphere. She wondered, if she had been listening to satellite radio instead of Pandora on her iPhone, would she have known it was coming? Had there been warnings transmitted? From the vantage point of her bungalow's front porch, no one yet seemed particularly worried about anything other than the crashing plane. No one seemed to understand what that meant.

But Diana knew that every plane in the sky at that moment would have fallen to earth. The 737 a few blocks away just happened to be the closest.

Her parents and sister were in Europe. Would they survive? Would she ever see them again?

Forcing her brain into survival mode, she set aside such unanswerable questions and ran onto her porch. She unlocked her door and went in.

When Diana had left work this evening, feeling frustrated and overwhelmed, she'd thought she'd order a sausage and mushroom pizza and curl up with her Xbox to stream some Buffy the Vampire Slayer *until she felt normal again.*

Instead, she was feeling her way through a dark house, the only light coming from the still-swirling sky. Buffy and Angel were obsessions of the past. Now she had to plan and pack.

Diana's opinion about people, as a species, was that they sucked. Her research into apocalyptic events had done nothing to disabuse her of her opinion. So she knew exactly what she was going to do.

In a situation like this, people, as a whole, fell into two categories of early response: seeking help or exploiting helplessness. People either waited or went for 'help,' or they looted and robbed, becoming part of the problem the others needed help from. In the apocalypse, neither case was productive. The seekers and waiters lost valuable time. The authorities would be overwhelmed — and impotent. Rescue and protection services would be nullified. There was no help to be had.

The exploiters stole a whole bunch of now-worthless shit and did lots of additional hurt while they were at it. There was plenty of hurt to be done.

To survive the apocalypse, in Diana's studied opinion, one needed to get clear of the chaos. Find a place to be alone and safe and wait it out.

And Diana had that place already.

She had a pack ready, too – a sturdy backpacking pack that had supplies for a minimum of ten days, assuming she could get clean water on the way.

Though she was hardly a fitness freak, her family was outdoorsy, and she was an experienced hiker and camper. In the dark, she changed into good hiking clothes, lots of thin layers, and her sturdy boots.

And then she armed herself. Her registered Sig Sauer P226 handgun. Four boxes of ammunition. Her father's prized Bowie knife. Standing in her little home office, surrounded by the collected treasures of a lifetime of geeky obsessions – her Star Wars collectible plushes, twenty-five long boxes of meticulously sleeved and filed Marvel and Dark Horse comic books, her Whedonverse action figures, her Lord of the Rings chess set, her Game of Thrones Pops, her complete set of Harry Potter wands, all of it – she swallowed hard and turned to the wall behind her computer. She had an extensive collection of replica swords from her years of LARPing and hanging out at Ren Faires. Most of the blades were blunted, for show only. But her Viking axe was battle ready.

Before she walked out of her bungalow, she turned and stared back into the dim space. She hated to leave it. She loved her little house and all her toys. She'd had a quiet, comfortable, contented little life.

But hey – maybe, like everybody thought, she was crazy, everything would be okay, and she'd just end up taking a long walk for no good reason and then come right back home.

Before that thought had left her head, she heard gunfire.

She holstered her Sig, strapped her knife to her leg, put her axe on her back, and shouldered her pack. She locked up her house and set out northeastward. To her family's little cabin on a little lake in the Sierra Nevada Mountains, above Lake Tahoe.

Sunspot Lake, it was called. Nearly three hundred miles away.

Diana sat on a creaky rocking chair on the front porch of her cabin and sipped at her hot olive tea. The morning had broken cold, with a faint dusting of frost smudging the world. She watched as the sun came through the trees and glinted on that cool rime for just a breath of a moment before it melted away. The day would be almost summer-warm, but the nights were cold. Summer was over, and autumn didn't last long on the mountain.

There were things to be done. But for now, she sat and sipped her tea while her mind busied itself cleaning up its mess.

She had the same dream almost every night now, memory more than fantasy, except for its soft edges and slow motion. Its vivid images lingered in her mind each morning, ransacking her room of boxed memories, tossing them up and leaving them to flutter to the floor, where she'd step on one and be filled with recollection.

In her mind, every day, she relived parts of a whole life lived, a whole past, and remembered everything that had been lost. Her parents and her sister highest among them. She mourned as if the loss of them was new.

But in the turmoil of that painful pillaging, Diana felt herself filling in again, and she understood how much of her had been missing. Since she'd lost Fiona, she'd been barely human. But she hadn't been Diana since long before that.

The memories were worth the pain of their rebirth. Becoming herself again was worth the price of recollected loss. But only because she once again felt, once again could name, could recognize, things like happiness and hope.

It was Rest Day, the fourth one since she'd met Buddy and Gus. She'd been working hard to keep closer track of the passage of time. She went to see them two or three times a week, on days that she had time to spare, and on Rest Days. Gus's ankle was healing, but he could only put moderate weight on it yet. He still needed her help, and it made her feel good to help him. It made her feel good that Buddy and he were glad to see her. It made her feel present. It made her feel alive.

It made her feel human.

She finished her tea and stood up. There were things to be done.

When the storage house was only a rooftop down ahead, Diana could hear the trouble. Buddy barked furiously, occasionally yelping in either pain or fear. Packed lightly, with only supplies for her trek, provisions for Buddy and Gus, and defensive weapons, she pulled her axe from her back and ran down the hill.

Gus was on the road; she saw him between the storage house and its nearest neighbor. His leg was still in a makeshift cast—he made his own now—but he stood on it; he had no choice. He had his katana in his hands, and he wielded it against a monster. Buddy ran around them, snarling and barking and yelping.

Charging forward, Diana called up a roar from her chest and let it loose. As she neared the fight, she brought her axe back and to the side. Gus saw her and dropped his katana, then ducked, and she sank the axe into the neck of the monster as it turned toward her. A crossbow bolt stood up from its chest, just below the grimy notch of its throat. Her axe sliced downward, into its chest, carving a long path below the bolt. She felt the blade cut through bone.

The monster gaped at her as blood gushed from a mouth full of black teeth. Long grey hair matted into ropes and thick with grease and dried blood surrounded a skeletal face, its cheekbones like razor blades beneath red-rimmed, rheumy eyes. It stank of death and foul meat.

Still standing, even as Diana struggled to pull her axe free from the center of its chest, it lifted an arm and brandished a strange hammer at her. Made from stick and stone and rope. She frowned at that caveman's weapon, and it swung.

"NO!" Gus shouted, and Diana saw the thin blade of his katana as it sliced through the monster's shoulder.

The monster's arm dropped, and the hammer thudded to the road. Diana pulled her axe free, at last, and the monster dropped.

Buddy barked ferociously at it, his fear gone now that the monster was dead. Diana looked over the body at Gus, who stood with the katana clenched in both hands, stuck in his downswing. Blood washed over his face from a cut above his eyebrow, but he asked, "You okay?"

She nodded. "You're hurt."

He waved her off and turned around to study the road. The movement hurt his leg, and he hopped a little on his good foot. "I think he's alone. Never seen a Feral alone before, but if they were around, they'd've ganged up on us." He looked over his shoulder. "Especially when they saw you."

Feral. Gus had told her about Ferals. Monsters who prowled the world below.

But this one was on her mountain. Her brain skidded sideways as she stared at the befouled corpse.

"No," she said. "No more monsters. Not here. No."

"Hey." Gus limped to her and brushed his hand over her arm. "Easy. Don't go away. I think he's alone. Just a stray."

She focused on his words. "You said they don't go alone."

"They don't. Maybe this one's the last of his group." He grinned suddenly. "I could see the Rennies taking a whole band of them down. Those guys have their shit together."

"Rennies?"

"Yeah. It's a substake down toward the base of the mountain. I told you about substakes."

She nodded; he had. People who lived together in a guarded community, making little self-sufficient towns. He'd also told her about what had happened to cities. She'd been right to go up the mountain and away from what the world had become after it died.

"They're a bunch of people who traveled together to work Renaissance Faires before the storm. You know about Renaissance Faires?"

This time, when she nodded, she smiled. "I used to go to them." She lifted her axe, dripping with the blood of the monster — the *Feral*. Not a monster but a monstrous man. "I bought this at a Renaissance Faire down there."

"Yeah? Huh. I bet those guys worked that faire. That's wild." He wobbled and used his weak leg to balance himself. He didn't have his crutches, just his katana. "Ow, damn."

"You need to get off your leg." She scooped her arm around his waist, and he dropped his arm across her shoulders, giving her some of his weight. "And you bleed."

"Saving me again, Diana. How many times would I have died if I hadn't been Goldilocksing your storage house?"

"Only once," she said and helped him to the house. They left the body in the middle of the road, at least for now.

"You're good at this. Barely hurts." He winced as she pushed the needle through the skin at his forehead again, making a liar out of himself.

"My dad was a doctor. He taught me some things." She'd learned more getting a biology degree and spending a year in medical school herself, but those were new memories she was still getting used to, so she kept them to herself. She tied off the last stitch. "There."

Gus turned to the bathroom mirror. "He taught you well. It looks good." His hand came up, and his fingers reached for her face. Surprised, she ducked away. He'd never touched her face before. That was too much, somehow. The thought made her knees unsteady.

"I'm not going to hurt you, Diana."

"I know. Just ..." she sighed and didn't finish. Words came more easily now, but they didn't flow. Holding a conversation took exhausting effort.

"I was just going to ask if the scar on your forehead — did you sew that up yourself?"

The attack on her homestead. The day that Fiona had been killed. When the monsters — the men and women — tried to take everything from her. The last time she'd seen humans until she'd met Gus.

Those memories were too powerful for words, so she only nodded.

"You're one tough chick. It doesn't surprise me at all that you've survived alone."

Alone. Since she'd met Gus and Buddy, since she'd had this chance to know another person, to grow to like him and enjoy his company, to have the trust and affection of Buddy, Diana had felt a hollow ring of loneliness throughout her homestead. The home that she'd worked so hard to make, that she'd protected fiercely, that she loved, felt empty now, as she remembered more and more what companionship was. The times that she could come down to see this man and his dog were her favorite times. When she went away from her home.

It hurt and confused her, but she understood enough to know the solution. It carried a heavy risk, but everywhere around her was risk, and this was both the greatest and the least of them all.

"Gus," she started, and then words dried up and left her tongue stuck.

He cocked an eyebrow in query, winced when it wrinkled his fresh stitches, and waited.

She closed her eyes and sought the words. "I … will …"

After a few seconds, he asked, "You will what?"

She shook her head; that was wrong. "There was frost today."

He frowned. "Was there?"

Maybe this far down there hadn't been, but she nodded anyway. "Winter's close."

"I know." Still frowning.

In a deep breath, she found the words. "Come with me. Up."

His frown deepened, and he cocked his head. "Up? To your place?"

Relieved, she nodded. "Safer there." Her heart raced with uncertainty and fear, and the throb of her pulse stymied her words. She could barely make a coherent thought.

He leaned against the back of the toilet, where he'd perched while she'd closed his wound.

"You want me to go up the mountain with you? For the winter?"

She nodded.

"Diana, you won't even spend one night in this house with us." He'd asked a few times, when she'd stayed dangerously late, and there were lots of bedrooms, but she'd always refused. This wasn't where she slept.

She didn't know what to say. So she looked away and busied herself cleaning up the first aid supplies.

His hand wrapped around her wrist, and she froze. "Diana. Look at me." She looked. "Now talk to me."

Again, she closed her eyes and sought the words. She made them make full sentences before she began to speak. "The snow gets very high. To the rooftops. It's hard to hunt, and the stream freezes. Winter is dangerous. But I have provisions, and a deep well that doesn't freeze. I work all year to make sure the winter is safe."

"That's not what I'm asking. It's pretty obvious you're set up well up there. I'm asking if you really want us there with you. In your place."

She nodded at once. That was what she wanted most of all. Someone to talk to. A friend.

His grin eased her mind and her heart. "Okay. Buddy and I'd be happy to spend the winter with you. I'm not sure I can hike uphill on this leg yet, though. It's still pretty weak. I could use another week before I go mountain climbing."

She felt suddenly and inexpressibly light. "That's okay. There are things to be done first."

Book Four: Protector

Of all things visible, the highest is the heaven of the fixed stars.

~Nicolaus Copernicus

Sixteen

Gus leaned back and took a deep breath as Diana set the splints aside and rested his ankle on her thigh.

"I'm sorry I'm so slow."

Without looking up at him—she only met his eyes when she had something to say or something to understand—she shook her head and began to rub his ankle with smooth, firm sweeps of her thumbs.

The woman was a puzzle. From the start, once she'd decided not to kill him, she'd taken care of him: healing his ankle, bringing him and Buddy food and supplies, taking care of the chores he couldn't do on his own. She'd kept him alive, and probably Buddy, too. Now, she was taking them to her home, this mysterious, bountiful place, so they'd be safe through the winter.

But she could barely stand even the most casual touch, and she only spoke when she couldn't avoid it. Which was a substantial improvement over her silence of the first few days. She was skittish and hesitant, digging those blue eyes into his whenever he asked her a question about herself, then jerking them away, and only giving him answers in broken fragments. Even when they sat side by side, she seemed to hover on the edges.

Except where Buddy was concerned. Buddy was the reason she hadn't killed him on sight, and he was the reason she'd kept coming down to help them. In her interactions with Buddy, Gus saw hints of the woman she truly was. She loved his dog and gave that love freely. She'd even helped him make friends with a fucking bear.

That had been something, seeing that bear saunter up to the patio like he lived there. Gus and Diana had been sitting on the bench against the wall, taking turns tossing Buddy's ball for him, and then there'd been a bear walking out of the woods, right behind Buddy.

He'd reached for his crossbow, but Diana had set her hand on his arm and said, "That's Shrek."

The woman had a fucking pet bear, and somehow Buddy knew him, too. When he'd asked how the hell his cowardly lion of a dog hadn't simply shat himself and then been eaten by a bear, Diana had stared at him for a long time. He'd seen her brain trying to make the explanation. But she'd only shrugged and said, "I know him."

Well, obviously.

Yeah, she was a puzzle. He thought they'd become friends over the month or so of their acquaintance, this bizarre month he'd spent living in an elegant ski chalet, above the end of the world. She'd come down to them often, and she'd listened avidly as he'd spoken about the world below. But what she'd told him of her own life wouldn't cover a single page, even if he tried to fill in the spaces between the pieces she'd shared.

Her massaging fingers eased the ache in his weak leg and foot, and he sighed with relief. "Thank you."

She lifted her eyes then and smiled. Gus wondered if she knew what she looked like. Did she know she was beautiful?

"I'm sorry this hurts."

"You're not hurting. You're helping."

"But the walk hurt." She pulled the old tape from the strips of soft towel they used as binding and began to rewrap his ankle. He could do it himself now, but she did a much better job. The thought of binding up a freshly-swelling foot made him sigh again, this time not in relief. He'd been thrilled to get the damn thing off for a little while.

He shrugged. "I'll be glad when it's over, yeah."

They'd been walking for almost four hours, and she said they had two or three more to go, at the pace they'd been moving—which was, to put it mildly, leisurely. He wasn't on crutches, but he still limped, might always limp now.

They stayed on the paved road as much as possible, but they climbed a steep incline into thin air, and a month of sitting on his ass with a broken ankle had knocked his fitness all to hell. Not to mention that his ankle wasn't fully healed. The bones had set, but the soft tissues were weak and sensitive and not at all loving this walk.

A rustle of leaves not far off got everyone's attention. Buddy perked up his ears, Gus clutched the crossbow at his side, and Diana threw her hand behind her to grab her axe. But it was just a little rodent, like a large hamster, nosing through the leaves for nuts or something. It paid them no mind.

Now on alert, Diana kept her hand on her axe. She turned and scanned the area around them. They were just off the road. Setting his leg gently aside, she went to stand on the fading, pitted asphalt and study the path they'd already taken. The leaves of the deciduous trees had turned on their autumn charm, from fiery red to gleaming gold. They shimmied from their loosening stems in a breeze coated with chill.

The breeze blew up the road and made the strands that had escaped Diana's long blonde braid whip around her face. She tucked them behind her ears and peered down the hill.

Gus turned and looked in that direction as well. "We're okay, Diana. There's nobody this far up. I haven't seen anyone in weeks. You haven't seen anybody but me in longer than that."

"The monst—the Feral," she countered, coming back to kneel before him and pick up his foot again.

Monster, Feral, Fiend—three names to mean the same thing. "Just the one, and he was just about starved to death. He doesn't count."

"He almost killed you."

"But you killed him, and there were no others. He was just a stray, and now we're going even higher. Things are okay here. Monsters won't come this high."

"They do. They come."

And that was the closest she'd ever come to telling him what had happened to her.

"Diana." He leaned forward, reaching to catch a loose lock of her hair, but she reared back before he could. Sometimes, she'd let him touch her, but she had to know he was coming and gird herself for it. He hoped her mysterious cabin was a mansion, because the woman needed her space.

Keeping her attention focused downward, she tore off a strip of white duct tape and began setting the binding around his leg.

Buddy chewed a bur from between the pads of a front paw, then yawned loudly and flopped his head to the ground. If this dog was that chill, there was no danger around for miles.

Gus laughed and rubbed his belly. "Okay. We'll be careful and keep an eye out. The one guarding skill Buddy has is that he's afraid of absolutely everything, so he alerts to the smallest odd sound or smell. He'll tell us when trouble's coming. He told me about the Feral. That's how I was able to get up and armed and fight him off."

"Good boy, Buddy." She smiled at the dog, who thumped his tail on the ground.

As they came around a gentle bend in a smooth dirt lane, Gus saw the cabin. He saw most of the property, what she called her 'homestead,' and it wasn't at all what his mind had conjured. He stopped dead in the middle of the lane as his brain reprogrammed itself. Pieces began to settle into the puzzle of a woman beside him.

Off to one side, he saw a large garden, enclosed in a tidy, but obviously handmade, picket fence. Behind that, he saw the edge of a building he thought was a chicken coop. To the other side, there were tall reeds, with sun-glimmering water shining behind them. An elaborate grove of poles and ropes between the water and the cabin made a laundry-drying area. A washing board hung on one pole, with a steel washtub upended on the ground beneath it.

And the cabin. Not a mansion at all. Just a small log cabin, with plaster between rough wood beams. A quaint little porch on the front held two high-backed rocking chairs and a tall, rusting metal milk jug. On the high peaked roof—it was shingled in wood shake, or a composite made to look like wood shake—was a tin smoke stack at one end and a stone chimney at the other. Cookstove and fireplace, he assumed.

Jesus. The place could have been on the cover of a magazine. One of those 'simple living' things his mother had liked.

"Gus?" Diana looked up at him; he saw doubt in her eyes and realized that it might look like he was having second thoughts.

"It's wonderful. I had something else pictured."

She frowned a question at him. A lot of her conversation happened with body language, something he was used to, even without ASL. He was fluent in body language. "I thought it would be more like the house we were at."

At least. Her father had been a heart surgeon in Silicon Valley. Gus had expected a rich-and-famous kind of second home, not something out of *Little House on the Prairie*.

But it was beautiful, and it was, in fact, a home. Everywhere he looked, he saw that. This little homestead was a world unto itself.

Eventually, she gave up on him and went to the door without him. Buddy followed her; he had two people now. Gus trailed after them, still marveling at how she'd singlehandedly made a way to live here—to live *well*.

And then he went through the front door, and he stopped dead again. Jesus.

Clearly, though he hadn't noticed wires outside, the place had had electricity. There was an electric range and a refrigerator in the kitchen. But there was a pump at the sink, a Franklin stove between the kitchen and the main room, and a fireplace across the main room. That was all the cabin was: kitchen, large main room, and a loft with a sturdy ladder. His sense of the exterior compared with interior suggested the few doors in the walls were closets, not rooms.

Gus could see that it had once been a cozy vacation cottage. The furniture looked like castoffs from a 'main' house, and family photos hung on the walls and a few knickknacks stood on flat surfaces. A wall of shelves seemed primarily filled with paperback novels—and a couple of shelves of kids' board games, like Sorry and Clue. There was no television. An ancient red and white plastic radio sat on a long table under a back window.

There was no dust anywhere, no untidiness. The place was cluttered, but neat as a pin, as his mother might have said.

Though it still showed its past life as a vacation cottage, Diana had fitted it out as a pre-industrial home. Instead of lamps on the tables and the mantel, there were kerosene lanterns and candles. A large cast-iron skillet sat on the Franklin stove, and there was a large pot, so big it was nearly a cauldron, on the hearth.

But it was the kitchen that truly astonished Gus as he shrugged off his pack and limped to that side. Instead of cabinets, the walls were lined with shelves and hooks, and every one was packed. In addition to the usual kitchen gear, the shelves were full of non-perishable food, all in tins and jars marked with careful handwriting in black marker. She had different kinds of flour, and salt, and pepper, and even some sugar. A floor-to-ceiling unit that had to be handmade was filled with preserved vegetables and fruits. Everything was arranged in neat rows and stacks, and as he studied it all, he saw that it was all sorted by alphabet and date.

Diana wasted absolutely nothing, so, curious, he opened the refrigerator, to see what she'd done with that space. When he saw, he stepped back, shocked.

Guns. The fridge was full of guns. She'd taken out the shelves. In that large area, she'd stored ten rifles, including a fucking M16 or something like that. The door shelves were stacked with ammunition. In the freezer: pistols and ammo. The ice bin held a half dozen goddamn grenades.

He wasn't sure he seen so many weapons in one place ever, before the end or since. She could have a war all to herself up here.

"Diana, what the hell?"

When she didn't answer, he turned in the direction he'd last seen her. She stood in exactly the same place, with her pack leaning against her legs. She hadn't moved at all, and she stared off toward the back of the main room. Her expression was slack, like she'd gone off and left her body behind.

"Diana?"

Again, she didn't respond, so he limped over to her and touched her arm. She jumped and came back. In her blinking eyes, he saw sorrow and confusion at war. He turned to see what had her so fraught.

Buddy. Standing on a stack of blankets folded in quarters, sniffing thoroughly, like a cokehead at a long line of pure blow. It was a makeshift dog bed. An empty one.

He'd suspected she'd had a dog.

"What happened?" he asked.

"Monsters killed her. She was my friend." Still snorting, Buddy lay down on her dog's bed, and she let loose a long, shaking breath.

"I'm sorry, honey." He wanted to touch her, offer her comfort, but he knew better than to try now. When she needed it most, she reacted hardest against it. Instead, he redirected her to the question he'd meant to ask. "Why do you have all those guns?"

She blinked and refocused. "Protection."

"But you haven't used it." Something terrible had happened to her, and her dog, and he'd lived in the end of the world long enough to know what terrible things happened to women on their own, but this dead fridge was full of all kinds of protection. Unused, as far as he could tell.

She closed her eyes, preparing to speak at some length. She always had to psych herself up for that effort. "Guns are loud. They tell people to look. Quiet weapons are better. It's better to be quiet."

He agreed. "But why have them?"

"If I do, others don't. That's protection, too."

And that was fucking brilliant. The wisdom of staying in one place finally revealed itself: she only had to carry things for as long as it took her to get home. With the rest of the world so far away, she had time to scavenge far and wide, and over time, she'd made a radius of emptiness around her. Like a firebreak.

"That's fucking brilliant."

She grinned, and the sorrow faded from her eyes. "You should sit and rest your leg. I'll start a meal. You can see the rest later."

He limped over and sat on a old floral sofa next to the dog bed, and she went to the kitchen, going over to give Buddy a pat first. "Good boy."

Diana with something to do was a much more centered, a much more *present*, Diana.

While she'd cooked, he occupied himself at her bookshelves, and filled in more pieces of the Diana puzzle. Most of the books were paperbacks, and at first he'd thought they were all novels—science fiction, fantasy, mystery, romance, lots of genre fiction and very few classics. Vacation reads. But toward the bottom were shelves of how-to books. Cookbooks, home-repair guides, books on gardening, hunting and fishing, game meat preparation, even building. Several books about 'simple living' and 'living off the grid,' all with cheerful, colorful covers, made to appeal to people who dreamed about rejecting the modern lifestyle and all its pressures to live the fantasy of a simple life.

News flash: a life off the grid had pressures of its own. Not that simple at all.

All those books helped Gus understand Diana and this place a little better. Some of the books had name plates in their covers or inked names that were not Diana. His best guess: she'd scavenged a lot of these. It had never once occurred to him to check the shelves of the places he'd scavenged in, to look for books that would help live better this way. No one he'd wandered with had, either. They'd all discarded books as overweight space hogs.

A couple of the carefully organized shelves each held a family photo at the end of a row of similarly-themed books. Gus picked one of them up and studied it: An older man and woman, nicely dressed, with carefully styled hair. Two pretty teenaged girls, both blonde, standing before them. None of the four wore a smile, not even the plastic 'Say cheese' kind of smile. A golf course or something like that provided the background. The older girl was obviously Diana at about sixteen: he recognized the arch of her brows over striking blue eyes and her soft, sensual mouth. Her hair was shorter, and he'd never seen Diana's hair loose, but it was her. She'd been heavy. Not obese, but definitely overweight—what his mother would have called 'pleasingly plump.' Now, as far as he could guess, under her layers of sturdy clothes, she was thin— and she was strong as hell, thus muscular, he imagined. She'd picked him up and carried him once, fireman-style, shortly after they'd met, when he'd fallen off his ski poles and nearly fucked his ankle up again. He was not a small guy — six-one and a best guess for his weight was probably one-seventy-ish. So she wasn't frail. But she wasn't plump, either.

This wasn't a world where people had a lot of chance to be plump.

The other, younger girl in the photo was rail thin, with an ethereal kind of beauty. Diana's sister. What kind of family had these beautiful people been? He set the photo down. Another one on another shelf showed Diana arm in arm with her father, this cabin in the background. She hadn't been smiling in the first photo, but in this one, she was. She looked happy. So did her father.

Gus had bent low to check out the books on the bottom shelves when Diana came up to him.

"There's food now." She took the book he'd pulled from the shelf — the cover was blank, and he'd just realized it was a journal — and restored it to its place. "Come eat."

"You keep a journal?" If all those books were journals … Oh, to know what went on in her guarded mind.

"No," she answered and walked away.

She didn't have a table and chairs indoors, so they sat side by side on the sofa and ate the meal she'd prepared: smoked venison, roasted potatoes and zucchini, and what she called skillet bread and he recognized by smell and taste as fry bread. Back in the long ago, he'd dated a pianist who was a member of the Chippewa tribe; she'd introduced him to the delights of fry bread. What Diana had made was close enough to the real deal. She hadn't kept herself plump with her cooking, but she was going to fatten him up like a Christmas goose if this was the kind of meals on offer.

Buddy, too—he devoured a bowl full of meat and vegetables and then belched like a professional.

It was near dark by the time they sat down, so Diana lit a couple of candles. The burnished gold hue of the dim light made the room seem even warmer than the cookstove did.

After dinner, Gus helped wash up and saw right away that she had rigid routines for how things should be done. He let her show him her way; he followed her lead. Her house, her hard work, her generosity, her rules. She'd heated water on the Franklin while they'd eaten, and they washed the dishes and set them on a wooden rack to dry.

It was all so domestic and homey, Gus felt dizzy. There was no apocalypse here. There was only simple living.

That day they'd walked hours and miles up a mountain, Diana had walked the same distance twice, and the night was dark. In this world of scant resources, sleep came when dark did. But Gus had only seen a narrow daybed. "What are the sleeping arrangements?"

Diana went to a door near the fireplace and opened it—a closet. She pulled blankets, sheets, and a pillow down and set them on the low table in the middle of the room. "The sofa opens out. I sleep on the daybed." She looked up to the loft. "Luna and I used to sleep in the loft, but I use that for storage now."

Luna, he assumed, was the ethereal young beauty in the family photos. Her sister. Girls named for goddesses.

They opened the sofa and made up the bed together. Then Gus limped toward the front door. It was dark, but she'd shown him around a bit out there, so he figured he'd manage to find a place to take care of business.

"Where are you going?"

"Nature calls."

"There's—wait." She came around the opened sofa bed and went to another door that he'd assumed was another closet.

It wasn't. It was a bathroom, with a little pump sink, a deep metal tub … and an outhouse commode? He turned and lifted an eyebrow to ask the question.

"Composting toilet. My dad wanted this place to be self-sustaining. He didn't want to owe anybody for anything up here. The only reason we had wired electricity was my mom. He wanted solar, but she thought it was ugly."

"Solar doesn't work, either. Not what was installed before the storm. I don't know, maybe somebody's got solar going somewhere now, but that was all fried, too."

She nodded. "It's the circuits. Made a whole chain reaction. As long as the storm lasted, it must have been an incredible succession of solar flares. Long enough to fry the whole world, like a huge EMP."

Here in her cabin, her place of comfort, they were having their first actual conversation. "Yeah, that's what I heard. How'd you know?"

She shrugged. "I read about solar flares in the world before."

She walked away and left him to use her old-fashioned, new-world bathroom.

The sofa bed wasn't as comfortable as the expensive California King he'd spent the past month or so on, but the room was cozy, and the blankets were soft, Buddy lay curled at his side, and Diana lay in the iron-framed daybed across the room. He wore only a pair of new-to-him sweatpants. Even his leg was free, for the night. It felt like the best night he'd had in six and a half years, and he hadn't even fallen asleep yet.

Gus relaxed into a deep breath and rolled to his side, laying an arm over Buddy's warm body.

Diana had made a home for herself, and now she'd shared it with them. Already, he felt at home here, and that sense that the end of the world had happened below, elsewhere, filled him up. He could think of Erin and Michael, and Michaela, and his parents, and not feel rage for how he'd lost them. Without the rage, the melancholy of the loss flowered into fullness, and he could finally mourn them properly. Easing into that sadness, he felt comfort.

He could be still here. He could stay. Him and Buddy. Maybe this was what he'd been looking for all this time. They could stay, if she'd let them.

"Diana," he said, quietly, unsure if she was sleeping.

"Hmm?"

"Thank you."

She answered with one soft word, which was the wrong word for the conventional response, but the right word for the meaning that moved between them.

She said, "Yes."

Seventeen

Sweat slid down Gus's back, rivulets converging from his shoulders to make a stream down his spine. He set the axe against the stump they used as a chopping block and pulled his t-shirt up over his head. Already he'd shed a hoodie and a flannel as he'd worked at this chore. He'd run out of layers to remove.

He thought it was late October, maybe early November, somewhere in that ballpark. Not too much later than that, anyway. They'd had a spate of days when winter had loomed right outside the door, but then, for the past week or so, they'd had this resurgence of warm weather.

They were making the most of the chance. Diana was worried about how supplies would hold out now that he and Buddy were with her, so she'd spent these couple of weeks since they'd come up the mountain in a frenzy of work: canning, fishing, hunting, chopping, enclosing, foraging.

He'd followed her around at first to understand her ways—he'd been right; her routines were rigid as steel. Every day had a purpose, and every job had a way to be done. Thinking about her alone up here all these years, it wasn't hard to understand why routine would have become so important. It was obvious that she'd forgotten most things about her life before. Sometimes, he'd say something about the old world, and she would simply stare at him, blankly at first, and then with dawning comprehension; in her eyes, he saw recollection stir to life and take a new breath.

She'd been losing herself steadily, losing all her moorings. Routine had kept her tethered to life itself.

So, no, he wasn't going to quibble with how she did things. He asked her what needed doing, and he helped her do it.

He tossed his t-shirt back without looking and heard an irritated cluck. One of the chickens had gotten out of the yard outside the coop, and his shirt had landed on her head.

"Sorry, ma'am." He lifted the shirt and picked up the hen. "Let's go see how you got out."

Buddy had pulled the chicken wire loose at a corner, trying to get into the yard—not to eat them. Just to play. When Gus came up, he sat like a gentleman and ducked his head. He knew what he'd done.

"Buddy!" He put all the disappointment he could into the name, and the dog drooped his head more and looked up under his brows, a portrait of shame. "You know better." He waved his hand. "Go find Diana. Go on."

She was hanging the winter shutters over the windows, up front, far from the chickens. This was 'Protect Day.' That morning, they'd walked the perimeter of the property and checked the conditions of the weapons she kept stashed in various tree trunks and nooks among rock formations. Then they'd seen to the weapons they used and kept handy: honing blades, treating leather, repairing reclaimed arrows and bolts. This afternoon, they were winterizing: filling the woodshed to capacity, putting the walls on the chicken coop, hanging the storm shutters that would close over the cabin windows in foul weather.

Buddy trudged off like he'd been grounded, and Gus set the hen over the fence. He crouched to take a look at the dog's damage. Not much to fix, just needed a hammer and nails. Diana had built this coop and fenced yard on her own. It looked handmade, but it wasn't weak. She'd started from as scratch as possible, chopping down the trees herself. The wire, she'd found at an abandoned hardware store in a town the other direction down the mountain from whence he'd come, but she hadn't been able to lug the wood up. So she'd made her own lumber.

Signs of her strength, her fortitude, her ingenuity abounded everywhere he looked. She'd built her own smokehouse, using the ancient woodstove her father had replaced when he'd bought the cabin. She cured her own meat and tanned her own hides. She'd built the coop—and wrangled stray chickens. She kept a nightcrawler farm for fishing. She grew vegetables and canned them. She foraged wild fruits and made them into sweet jams.

She'd taught herself all of that from *books*.

The one skill she hadn't learned was knitting. She had a book on that, too, but she hadn't found any needles or yarn.

Gus had admired her from the moment she'd set his ankle. Now that he was here and knew her so much better, he was in awe.

He knew her better, living in her world, but he didn't know her well. She wasn't reluctant to speak about herself or her life so much as she was unable. He could see it, her struggle to remember herself, or even to choose words that said what she wanted to say. He had to fill in the wide, deep gaps between her words and create his understanding from his observations and experience of her.

But some things, he could only imagine. He finished the repair of the chicken yard and went back to the chopping block. As he picked up the axe, he fixed his eyes out ahead, to the ravine that ran along the edge of the homestead, marking the line of the forest.

There were bodies buried in that ravine, and not deeply. Only a few days after they'd arrived, when Gus was limping around, getting to know the place, Buddy had run down and dug at the bottom. He'd uncovered the bones of a hand.

Gus had struggled down to the bottom to cover it back up, and found other bones uncovered. He'd reburied them all and not said a word about it. Diana spoke of monsters who'd come here, and yet she lived. He knew quite well that the bodies in that ditch were all that remained of her monsters. Whoever they'd been, whatever they'd done to her, she'd won.

And he was in awe.

"I still can't believe you have a pet bear."

Diana smiled and looked to the far shore of the tiny inlet of this small lake, where Buddy and Shrek were chasing fish. "Not a pet. A friend."

"He knows commands. That's a pet." Gus lay back on the grassy bank and stared up at the sky. Clouds moved briskly over the bright blue span — white clouds with grey bottoms. Bringing a change in the weather. This might be the last warm day.

It wasn't exactly balmy. He and Diana were both wearing a few layers of clothes, and they buried their cold hands in mittens between jobs. But the sun was out, and the wash billowed on the lines. The dry grasses at the shore ruffled in the breeze, a sound almost like an audience before the house lights went down. Gus closed his eyes and opened his senses to this calm, fragrant world.

"He was Fiona's friend more than mine." Her words were almost too quiet to be intentional.

Gus opened his eyes and tilted his head to see her. She sat beside him, braiding reeds she'd plucked from the ground. The sunlight caught the stray strands that danced around her head in the breeze and made a glowing halo.

He sat up but said nothing; when she was caught in a recollection, she'd speak more if he didn't interrupt.

"I found Fiona not long after the world ended. She was just a little puppy, locked in a dog crate in an abandoned house. I don't know what happened to the people who put her there, but she was almost dead from hunger and thirst. I brought up here with me and made her well. Once she was big enough to be safe, she went with me everywhere. She was my best friend."

After a moment's quiet, she went on. "She was like your dog, I think. The one on your chest."

He brushed the left side of his chest, where his first tattoo was. "Mudge? A Newfie?" An ancient wound pulsed. Oh, man. He knew exactly what kind of friend Fiona had been.

"I think so. I found a book about dogs once. It was too big to take, but I looked through it. I think she was that. A Newfoundland. Like a bear. But she was black and white."

"That's a Landseer. It's a variation of the breed." He had such a vivid picture in his mind of her dog that tears bubbled at the corners of his eyes.

Across the lake, Shrek caught a fish, and Buddy jumped up, trying to grab it from the bear's mouth. Shrek lifted one enormous paw, and Gus had a bad second of fear. But the bear only set his paw on Buddy's head and pushed him into the lake.

Friend or pet, he was gentle with his pack or herd or whatever a group of bears was called. Was there a collective noun for bears? Did they collect?

"I came back from foraging one day a few weeks later, before Fee was old enough to come along, and there was a little black cub on the porch, trying to dig through the front door. Fee was on the other side, whining and scratching. He was tiny and skinny, and there wasn't a mama around, so I let him come in."

"And you called him Shrek because of the movie," he murmured.

She looked over her shoulder at him, frowning. "Movie?"

That surprised him. "Yeah. *Shrek*. The animated movie about the ogre. His true love was Fiona."

"Oh." She frowned and stared down at the braid of reeds in her hand. "Oh. *Oh*. Yes. I remember. Yes, I did. Name him for the movie." She turned back to him. "It's not really his name. He doesn't come when it's called. He's not a pet."

"He's a friend."

She nodded. "He stayed and let me take care of him until he could do it on his own, and then he went off to the woods. He comes and goes when he pleases. I didn't see him at all after Fiona … after she died. Not until he came to meet Buddy. It's dogs he really likes, not people."

Focused on the reeds again, she let her words die off. Gus leaned back on his elbows and watched her. In the midst of all this calm, a coil of anger heated in his gut. She'd made a heaven above the end of the world, and the thought that the filth from below had made its way up here and violated her safe haven infuriated him.

It was one thing to live in the end and fight for survival. But up here, this wasn't survival. This was *life*. Or it should have been. This was a place for a beginning to sprout, in this fresh air and clear sun, in this quiet and peace. This was where the world could begin again, because here, it had never ended.

But the end had found this place, and turned a woman into a ghost.

"Diana." He reached out and brushed his fingertips lightly over her sweater-clad arm.

Her blue eyes met his and waited.

"Will you tell me what happened?" When she only stared, he took a dangerous risk and added, "In the ravine. How did that happen?"

Her reaction was gradual; he saw the memories fill in and clamor in her eyes. Then she flinched hard and dropped the reeds.

As she scrambled to stand, Gus stood, too, and reached to take her arm. "Hey, I'm sorry."

She yanked free and reeled back, but then she stopped. Her arms locked against her sides, and her fists curled into knots.

All around them, the peaceful afternoon continued, but between them, a storm had erupted. "Diana, easy. You don't have to say. I don't need to know. I'm not ever going to hurt you—you have to know that by now. You have to trust me by now."

In the lake, Buddy and Shrek had gone quiet. Gus darted a look in their direction and saw them both watching. The sudden shock of tension between him and Diana was powerful enough to reach across the water.

He took two steps closer to her. She watched him with eyes pinched in suspicion.

"You can trust me. You know that, right?" Her nod brought the crisis level down a degree. "I'm sorry I asked. I don't need to know." He didn't; he knew enough. He'd lived in the dead world that her monsters had brought up the mountain. She didn't need to utter words for him to know what they'd done.

Why had he asked, then?

Because she'd been remarkably expansive for that brief time, and she'd spoken of her dog, and her dog's death, and he'd hoped that she'd say more. He wanted more. He wanted to know more of her—he wanted her to *offer* more of herself.

Why? They shared close quarters, yes, but there was no real reason they needed to be close friends. Except that they already were, weren't they? They'd shared life and death together already. He owed her his own life, several times over.

And he thought maybe she owed him hers. Not her survival, but her life.

There was responsibility in saving a life. There was a bond. He'd felt it for Erin, though he'd failed her in the end. He felt it for Diana now. Like a second chance. He wouldn't fail again.

"Diana. I would like to hold you. Will you let me?"

She held herself instead, crossing her arms over her belly. Then she shook her head.

Gus nearly grunted at the sharp pang of that disappointment, but he let it go. "Okay. I'm sorry. I promise I'll never hurt you."

"I know," she finally said, and the steely angle of her shoulders softened. "I know."

It was enough.

That night, after a brilliant, warm bath—something he'd never take for granted again in his life—feeling fresh and at ease, Gus came out of the bathroom into a cozy-warm room glowing with flickering firelight. Sleet ticked against the windows. They hadn't closed the shutters because the wind hadn't boded a hard storm, but the brief second summer was over. Those heavy-bottomed clouds hurrying across the sky that afternoon had been the last of it.

Both beds were made up, and Buddy was curled up on his pad before the hearth, snoring. Diana was dressed for sleeping, in her favorite set of faded pink thermal underwear. Her loose hair draped over one shoulder. She sat in an upholstered rocking chair, her legs curled up on the seat, reading a novel by firelight, twisting one lock of hair around her finger.

Golden hair and sky-blue eyes, high cheekbones and soft lips. Living like this, he knew more about her body now, though he'd never seen it bare, and knew her strength came packed in sleek muscle.

She was beautiful. He'd seen that even the first time he'd seen her, when he'd momentarily thought her a Feral. It was her beauty and freshness that had shown him the truth. He'd always enjoyed looking at her. He'd wanted to know her, to be her friend, not long after that first day. Since she'd started to open up and reveal herself as she remembered herself, since she'd brought him here, to her home, he'd come to think of her in another way. But she was a far, far distance from feeling the same. Her reaction at the lake had drawn a bold line under that truth.

Wearing a pair of sweatpants and nothing else, Gus looked away before things got awkward. Thankful of the low light, he went to the front window and looked out into the dark. The dim room was good for more than simply obscuring inappropriate body parts. He could see fairly well beyond the window, though the night was dark and stormy. Heavy sleet slicked the windows and the porch, and the wind made the forest shudder. He'd spent many a night huddled in scant shelter while weather like that growled and snapped at him. And here he was, with a cheerful fire warming his back. A full belly, a clean body. A faithful dog, a soft bed, and a good friend.

This was a beginning.

"Gus?"

"Yeah, hon?" He turned toward the snug scene at the fire. Diana faced him directly, the book resting on her lap.

"I'll tell you. About the ravine."

"You don't have to. I'm sorry I asked at all." He crossed and crouched before her and Buddy. "I mean it. It's not my business."

She closed the book and offered him a tiny smile. "I think I do have to. For me, not you. Sometimes, my mind feels like things aren't in the right places. I think I have to remember bad things so I can have the good things back and know what they mean. So everything goes back where it belongs." She dropped her eyes and fiddled with the pages of her book. "I don't know if I'm saying what I mean."

"I think I understand." He stood and went to sit in the matching rocker that faced hers. "I'll listen. Tell me anything you want."

With the warm fire and the cozy dog between them, speaking slowly as if she plucked each word carefully from unfamiliar boxes, Diana told him about her monsters.

Gus lay in bed and stared into the dark. The sleet had become snow as the temperature dipped, and the world around the cabin had gone quiet. They'd banked the fire to embers and closed the screen. Now they lay under wool blankets and tanned furs. Gus had Buddy under cover with him, so he was snug and warm.

But he doubted he'd sleep, at least not for a good long while.

Once she'd begun her story, she'd told it vividly, albeit slowly. He now knew, he thought, every detail she remembered about that span of two days and a night — and another day years before that. Twice, she'd been attacked. Her monsters hadn't been Ferals, or they hadn't yet been. He'd have liked to think they weren't human, either, but that was the great lesson of the apocalypse, wasn't it? Humans were shit.

All the Sunstorm had done was kill electricity. That was bad, it was cataclysmic, in itself, but it hadn't ended the world. Millions had likely died in those first few days, from the lack of power alone. Then the core meltdowns had fucked a whole quarter of the US at least, and who knew what had happened around the globe. But if people had kept their shit together, the world itself would have recovered. A year or two, maybe, while the builders and thinkers rebuilt the tech. Then a big, ceremonial flip of a power switch, and a new version of the modern world could have gone back to humming. That was what Gus had imagined in the first days and weeks after the storm.

But people were shit, as a whole. At best, they were entitled and useless, literally unable to function without their fucking smartphones, and prone to panic at the slightest discomfort. They were the ones killing themselves and each other first—the suicides as well as the idiots with guns, shooting to kill every time something startled them. At worst, they were depraved, leaping on the first chance to take from someone else. The assholes who'd started looting while planes were falling out of the sky—Gus would place good money, if money still had any value, on the bet that those sons of bitches had gone Feral right quick.

So the people who'd terrorized and savaged Diana were very much human. And so were the Ferals down below. That was what humans became when you took their electronic pacifiers away from them. So what was the fucking point? Humanity deserved to get fried off the face of the earth.

He sighed at himself for his nihilism, which made no room for people like Carver and Talia, or Mara and her kids, or Sarah and the Rennies. Decent people who stayed decent, who helped each other, who loved and laughed and forged communities and found something worth living for.

And Erin. Who'd moved through the world as if it hadn't changed. Who'd loved a baby made from pain and horror. Who'd loved him. Whom he'd loved.

And Diana, who'd persevered through horror and pain, and the endless torment of thinking she was entirely alone in the world. Who'd built a new world of her own.

They were humanity, too. The true best of them.

Erin had never told him the precise circumstances of her rape. He'd had no need to know—less even with her, who'd been so open with him from the start—but with Diana's story clamoring in his head, he imagined Erin's more vividly as well. He could only imagine. He'd no experience of his own that could compare.

There were seven bodies buried in the bottom of that ravine, and another buried somewhere she didn't know. Twice, Diana had been attacked, and twice, she'd killed them all. The last time, she'd been set on by five people, and yet she'd prevailed. He had no cause to doubt her story. In fact, watching her face in the flickering firelight, he'd known for a certainty that every word was true and that she'd relived the story as she'd told it. It was that—the play of pain on her face—more than the story itself that had him sleepless now.

She'd fought off all those people, five of them men who'd hurt her terribly. She'd killed them. And then she'd buried their bodies and cleaned up their mess. She'd erased them from her world and carried on living in it.

If the last monsters hadn't killed Fiona, he might have met a different woman the day he'd broken his ankle. But they had, and she'd been utterly alone above the end of the world. Her tether to her own self had frayed badly.

Across the room Diana gasped and sat up. It wasn't unusual for her to dream actively, and badly. She didn't like him to notice when she woke from a nightmare, so he lay still and listened. The sound of her breath, heavy and fast, carried so much vulnerability that Gus clenched his jaw to resist calling out to her.

Then the rustle and creak as she rose and crossed the wood floor. Buddy jumped down from the bed to check on that new development. Expecting her to be headed to the bathroom, Gus closed his eyes. But the creak of the floor stopped near his bed.

"Gus?" she breathed. If he'd been asleep, he wouldn't have heard.

"Yeah?"

"I think I'd like you to hold me now."

Not daring to question her, not even to ask if she was sure, he turned the covers back. She stood at the side of the sofa bed long enough that he felt the chill in the room cooling his sheets. Then she slid in beside him. She'd brought her pillow with her.

At first, it was like holding a cattle prod; she was stiff as iron and jerked wildly at every slightest move or touch. Coaxing her gently but firmly around those violent shudders, he cradled her head in his hand and settled her on his chest, wrapping his arm around her shoulders. But she remained stiff and nervous.

Then Buddy jumped up on the bed, nosing himself under the covers, and settled in the narrow space between their legs. Diana reached down and scratched his head, and she relaxed entirely on Gus's chest.

He lay still and felt the warm weight of her against him. It had been a long time for him, too, since he'd felt the comfort of intimate closeness. When he sensed that she'd fallen back to sleep, he kissed the top of her head.

She wasn't alone now. He intended that she never would be again.

Eighteen

The next morning, Gus woke before Diana. They lay in the same position they'd fallen asleep in the night before, though Buddy had abandoned ship at some point and slept on his pad by the banked fire.

He'd slept deeply and well. His back ached stiffly and he had to pee, but had no desire to move, not as long as she was quiet and calm, at ease and in his arms.

Did he love her? He didn't know. He was in awe of her. He was attracted to her. He felt responsible for her, protective of her. He was grateful to her—for her care, for her home, for her company. For her trust. The feel of her body on his was a comfort. And an enticement. But there was so much he didn't know of her, so much he could only imagine.

The sun was up and shining brightly from a blue sky; the storm had ended. Mac, the rooster, had been quiet, however. Normally, he shouted them awake while the sun was still wiping sleep from its eyes. Maybe the newly hung walls around the coop had him fooled into thinking it was still night.

That would be okay by Gus. Mac was a pain in the ass. It was like he knew how important he was to their little ecosystem.

Diana sighed and woke. When she understood where she was, she startled like that cattle prod had gone through them both, and she rose up on her elbow. Inside the shelter of her hair, her eyes were wide open with surprise and maybe some worry.

He offered her a smile to ease that disquiet from her sleepy face. "Hey. It's okay."

She let out a tense breath and tried to return his smile. Hers shook a little at the corners. When she pushed away, ready to get out of bed, he tightened his hold across her shoulders. Just enough to let her know he didn't want her to go.

"How do you feel this morning?"

"Better. Thank you."

"I'm glad you came to me. It was a good night."

Her smile steadied, and then she pushed back more firmly. "I need to get the fire going."

He eased his hold and let her go.

About six inches of powdery snow lay over the ground in a white puff, quieting the world to a whisper. The ice that had fallen first made cut-crystal figures of the trees, glinting faceted sunlight that dazzled the eye.

It wasn't bitterly cold; the mercury thermometer nailed to a porch post read twenty-nine degrees, and the storm had blown itself breathless, so the air was still. The perfect weather to enjoy the first kiss of winter. The sun would warm throughout the day, and by nightfall, most of the snow would be gone.

Gus stood on the porch, bundled in the sweater, scarf and beanie that Erin had knitted for him, sipping eucalyptus tea while Buddy plowed his nose through the snow.

"We should shovel." Diana had come up behind him and stood in the open doorway. "It's important to stay on top of the snow, or we'll be buried in it."

He reached back and picked up her hand. She didn't pull away. Tugging gently, he coaxed her onto the porch to stand at his side.

She looked out to the yard and smiled. Gus turned as well and saw Buddy on his back in the snow, wiggling back and forth as though he were trying to make the world's most deformed snow angel.

"He's got the right idea. We should take a walk or something. Enjoy this before it buries us."

"We should shovel."

"This snow won't last the day. Besides, it's Rest Day, right?"

"It's better to shovel. What if another front comes through this afternoon and it gets colder instead of warmer? That happens sometimes. We can't let it pile up. I can shovel, though. You can take a walk, if you'd like."

Though he knew she meant that honestly, it wasn't a passive-aggressive move to guilt him into doing what she wanted, he sighed—quietly, subtly, letting the frustration out without making a passive-aggressive statement of his own. Passive aggression was a luxury of the long ago. This world made no quarter for such interpersonal manipulations.

Still, he was frustrated, with himself as much as with her. The night before—what she'd told him and what she'd asked of him—had unlocked something between them, and he wanted to explore the new territory, but he was afraid to spook her. He felt like a teenager, worried about rejection and reading it into every iota of resistance from her.

She'd let him hold her hand—he still held it—and pull her out to the porch, but she clung to her routine like a ship's mast in a storm. Willfully or innocently, she'd missed the import of his suggestion for a walk and had made it about the priorities of work and play.

"Okay. We'll shovel. And then you'll take a walk with me. Just a walk to enjoy the beautiful day—no hunting, no checking the weapons, just a walk. Because it's Rest Day."

Her eyes came to his. "Why? We walk all the time."

"Because it's been six and a half years since I took a walk in the woods without trying to get somewhere or find something or kill something."

"We have to take weapons. We can't ever assume we're safe."

"I know." After all this time, he was fully aware of the dangers in the world, and kept watch around him always, almost unconsciously. But this morning, he resented it. He wanted this place to be truly above all that. He wanted the horrors Diana had told him last night to be locked in the past. He wanted to have found the end of the end. "Diana, come on. Let's play in the snow today. Before it's everywhere and we hate it. Let's have one afternoon that's more than survival."

Her teeth worried at her bottom lip as she scanned the vista before them. "Okay. After we shovel and do the daily work."

Gus squeezed her hand. "Thank you."

A walk for its own sake did indeed feel like an extravagance. Even Buddy seemed to sense the difference; he ran out ahead, kicking up snow, circling trees and dropping gleefully into small drifts. Gus kept an eye on him, wary despite himself, and he carried his crossbow and quiver, as well as a knife at his hip. Always on the alert, even when he tried not to be.

Gus tossed the rattiest tennis ball out, and Buddy charged for it. That ball had a sad story, it turned out. Fiona had been the first one to play with it, and the tube with its mates had been sitting on a shelf in the cabin, unused until Buddy.

They walked through the woods, their boots mostly silent on the melting snow. Dripping trees made a pitter-patter like raindrops around them and occasionally dropped a cold surprise on their heads.

Buddy ran back with the ball, and Diana took it and tossed it again. She watched him run after it and then scamper off to take his long, circuitous, happy way back. "I never had a dog when I was a kid. My mom thought they were dirty."

From the smattering of words she'd uttered about her mother, Gus assumed that the relationship had been troubled. As usual, when she talked about herself, Gus went as quiet as he could, but she didn't go on. She just let that tiny statement sit there, took the ball from Buddy and tossed it again.

Gus reached for her hand, and she let him hold it. He hoped that would draw her back to him, maybe get her to say more, and it did. She glanced down at their linked hands. "They were in Europe when it happened. Visiting my sister. She's a doctor in the Army. I don't know what happened to them." Her eyes came up to his. "Do you know about your family?"

Though he'd shared a lot, comparatively, about himself, and he'd spoken at length about Michaela, they'd never talked about the loss of their families in the Sunstorm. He nodded and took a breath, aware that the bleakness of his story could shut her down and end this moment of sharing. "They're dead. When I got home to Philadelphia, everybody was dead. My sister was buried in the back yard, with a handmade cross for a marker, even though we aren't religious at all. My mom and dad were in their bed, shot in the head. There was a pistol on the floor. My parents never owned a gun, but I don't think anyone who might have killed them would have left their weapon behind. So I figure Michaela died right after the storm—she wouldn't have been able to live long without power—and my folks couldn't deal with that, so my dad bought or traded or just stole the gun, and they did a suicide pact thing." He shook off the weight of the memory and cleansed his mind with a view of the fresh winter woods. "That's what I made of what I saw, anyway. They didn't leave a note for me. Maybe they thought I was dead, too."

He felt Diana move closer and brought his attention back to her. She stood right in front of him, holding his hand. The emotion in her eyes — empathy and sympathy, compassion and concern — was like a salve over the wound he'd reopened. A drop of water came down from a tree branch and plopped on her cheek. She flinched and then laughed.

Laughing, he brushed the wet from her cheek with his thumb — and then he left his hand there, cupping her cheek, staring into her eyes. Their laughter faded away.

At the precise moment that he would have bent down and kissed her, she stepped back and tugged on his hand. His disappointment at the broken spell, however, didn't dampen his awareness that she hadn't skittered or flinched. She'd only stepped away.

She wasn't afraid any longer. She simply wasn't ready.

"What was it like, playing in a symphony?"

Gus looked up from the bow he'd been tightening. He played only occasionally, keenly aware that, with two sets of strings and two bows, and one rosin cake, his time with this instrument had an expiration date, and then he'd be lost in the world without music again.

He smiled as she sat on the rug before the hearth, next to Buddy, both of them at his feet. "You play a symphony. You play *in* an orchestra."

Her answering grin was surprisingly wry. Humor wasn't something Diana had quite remembered yet. "Actually, *I* don't play in either."

A joke! He laughed, because it was funny, and because he was delighted to see that spark of wit. "I sounded like a condescending asshole didn't I?"

She didn't deny it, and her grin didn't fade. "What was it like?"

He set the violin on his shoulder and put his chin on the rest. "It was …" Without thinking much about it, he began playing, slow and soft. "While we played, we couldn't see much of the audience. The stage lights were on us, and the house lights were down, so beyond the conductor was mostly black space. Sometimes, an asshole would take a flash photo, and at least a few times a week, somebody's phone would ring during a quiet moment in the number, but for the most part the audience was only the applause at the end. While we played, it was just us. For me, it wasn't even that. When I played, the whole world closed down to just me and my violin. Even the conductor just flitted at the edges, something to hold me in the world but not much more than that. I could play in an empty room or at the Kimmel Center and wouldn't know the difference until I lifted my chin off the rest."

Without realizing it, he'd begun playing the notes to Dvorak's 'Four Romantic Pieces' — not really playing the piece, not while he also talked, but bowing the notes. He stopped and rested the violin on his thigh. "That's not entirely the truth, though. I loved playing for the big audiences at the Kimmel. A lot of the musicians would stay as far from the stage as they could before a performance, but I liked to stand offstage and watch people come in. You see all kinds of folks at a symphony performance — dressed up in evening gowns and tuxes, or looking like they just came from the office, or in jeans. I always liked the people in jeans the best. People think classical music is only for snobs and rich people. But I knew a welder who had season tickets for most of the time I was in the orchestra. Him and his buddies. They came without their wives and went for beers after."

He set the violin and bow back in the case but left it open. "What did you do, before? Your dad and sister were both doctors, right?"

She nodded and turned to stare at the fire. "He wanted us both to be doctors. I went to med school, but I dropped out early in my second year." Her attention returned to Gus. "I wrote video games."

"What? You're kidding."

"I know. It's hard to remember all the reasons why, but I didn't like med school. It wasn't about patients like I thought it should be. My dad, he always knew so much about the people he helped. He was a heart surgeon. Lots of surgeons barely know their patients' names, but he talked to them, got to know them, worried about their families. I thought that was what medicine was. Med school wasn't like that, though."

"Then how'd your dad get to be the doctor he was?"

She shrugged and looked away again. "I wanted him to be happy, though, so I went to med school and tried to stick with it. Then I started to write this study aid for my cohort. Just a simple little game to simulate contexts and aid with memory. I'd been coding since I went to computer camp in summer before sixth grade, and I loved that. I made the game, and it was fun, and it really helped, so I made another one for another class, and then other students asked me for games, and then I was coding instead of studying, and I … dropped out before I washed out."

Diana went quiet again, as she often did after a long burst of spoken recollections. Gus intuited that the memories came at her while she spoke of them, the first threads spooling out until the tapestry was complete, and he supposed she needed some time to comprehend what she'd remembered.

He picked up the violin and began to play. When he'd played the piece truly and all the way through, she hadn't moved; she stared at the fire, absently stroking Buddy's head in her lap.

Setting the violin across his lap, Gus asked, "What games did you write? Do you remember?"

Still staring at the fire, she nodded. "I started with educational games, like the stuff I'd made for studying. One of my cohort had a friend in the business—we were at Stanford, and everybody had a contact in some kind of tech—and they bought my study games and hired me. I wrote those kinds of things for a while, then pitched an idea for a big-budget game. They went for it. It was *Dead Spring*."

Gus almost dropped the violin. *Dead Spring* was a massive bestseller with one equally popular sequel. Another had been in the works to complete a trilogy. Gus knew because he'd played the shit out of that game and had been following developments on the third installment. "Are you shitting me? You did *Dead Spring*?"

As she nodded, it dawned on him. *Dead Spring* was a post-apocalyptic horror/survival game. The apocalypse event had been a contagion that wiped out eighty-five percent of the earth's population. Another five percent or so had been turned into a gooey kind of zombie called the Defiled.

But the story wasn't about the Defiled. They were just boogeymen, the thing that kept the characters in constant danger and provided plenty of sudden scares and intense fight scenes with vivid gore. The real story was about the people—the players as much as the characters. Every engagement had some kind of survival choice with murky ethical implications, always asking the player to decide how far they'd go to stay alive, and shaping the game with their choices. At the end of each installment, the final choice was really about the very value of humanity itself, and the final cinematic was wildly different depending on the choices the player had made—which, in turn, shaped the next game as well, if they loaded their progress into it. The internet had been on fire with fanboy fights about what choices were right and why. Gus had participated in a few of those fights.

Dead Spring, both I and II, had won just about every award there was to win. And Diana had conceived it. Jesus.

"That's why you came up here, away from people. That's how you knew we'd devour each other down there. Because you'd been making that game."

She turned and looked up at him. "Lots and lots of people make a game. But yes. It was my idea, and I wrote the bulk of the narrative and characterization. I did a lot of research about different kinds of cataclysmic events and about crisis psychology. The theory of reciprocal altruism suggests that people will cooperate for their own good, but on a large scale, that idea breaks apart when it hits the phenomenon of mass panic. What you get instead is small, insular cooperative groups antagonizing among each other."

Her eyes slid back to the fire, and she stared at the flames. Gus watched her, sorting through the mountain of words she'd offered him. He'd unlocked a trove of insight. She was right, of course—up here above it all, she'd known exactly what would happen down below. People had panicked, and they'd done at least as much damage to each other as the loss of power had done. The ones left standing clung together in small, trusted clusters and suspected everyone else. Even the Ferals had formed cooperative groups.

Those who'd stayed in the big cities had become enslaved in exchange for an illusion of security. Those who'd rejected community and wandered alone fought every day to survive. Small groups were the only true communities left. At one point or another in the last six and a half years, Gus had seen every iteration of community or isolation. She'd been exactly right.

"I knew people would tear the world down, yes," she murmured, still staring at the fire. "So I came here. But this wasn't a better life. It was just a better survival."

All at once, Gus could see Diana clearly. He had all the pieces he needed of her puzzle. The girl with the disapproving mother and doting father, the young woman who'd risked that father's disappointment to follow her own path, the brilliant creator who'd made a piece of entertainment that challenged people to think about who they truly were, the powerful survivor who'd outwitted an apocalypse and overcome its worst, the enigmatic cipher who'd stored all of herself away so she wouldn't go mad in an empty world. The beautiful, complicated, heartbreaking woman who'd come back from all that and offered him her trust.

He set the violin back in its case, slid out of the chair to his knees, and wrapped his arms around her.

She didn't resist his embrace at all. In fact, she leaned into it, and he felt her arms circle his waist.

Nineteen

Gus took down the first wall on the chicken coop. Every bird—six hens and a rooster—had gathered against the wire, and they all clucked at him indignantly. They didn't like being cooped up in the dark.

"Don't bitch at me, ladies. You should be nicer to the man bringing you sunshine again."

A storm through the day and night before had dumped about two feet of fresh snow on the ground. Diana had been right, of course, about the need to stay on top of the shoveling. Though he'd spent the winter before in the mountains, too, he hadn't had the supplies for shoveling, or much else, and he'd been in such a broken mental state that he could barely remember how he'd weathered the season. He remembered snow, a constant state of blinding whiteness, but he couldn't really remember how he'd kept himself alive.

Here, though, there were, as Diana said at least once a day, things to be done. The work never seemed to be done, and that was a good thing. For years, whether he'd been wandering alone or with a group, he'd spent almost every day walking, scrabbling for survival. With the exception of his brief time with Erin, his existence had been vague, unmemorable, unlived.

Here, though, with Diana and all the things there were to be done, it felt substantial. Each thing they did made them stronger, safer, more comfortable, and every night, they sat together in a cozy room before a warm fire, and enjoyed the fruits of that labor. Every day was full of work that had a purpose beyond the next meal or the next shelter. The work they did made a home.

She'd said she'd only been surviving up here, as he'd only been surviving down there. Maybe she was right. Maybe it was that they were together, sharing the experience, that made it living.

He leaned the wooden wall from the coop against the wall of snow at his side. Here at about the midpoint of winter, the snow was nearly five feet high, and there'd been enough melt and rebuild over the course of the season so far that the pack was just about perfect.

They had lanes shoveled all around the cabin: to and around the chicken coop, to the woodshed, to the smokehouse, to the compost. They kept those as clear as they could. Yesterday, they'd spent a total of six hours shoveling, and another two this morning. And Gus had been on the roof, clearing the new fall off. He was exhausted.

Now, with the sun shining down on the glittering, nearly soundless world, Gus was opening up the coop and giving the ladies and their gent a couple of hours of fresh air and sunshine. The temperature was only a couple of degrees below freezing, and the breeze was light. The storm had spent all of Mother Nature's energy, and today, she rested.

As fascinated by the chickens as ever, Buddy tried to shove his big, dumb nose through an octagonal space in the chicken wire, and one of the hens welcomed his intrusion with a sharp peck. He yelped and jumped back, hitting the wall of snow behind him. Gus laughed.

"Dude, they're never going to like you. You jump around like an idiot and piss them off."

Buddy whined like he'd understood. Then stuck his nose in the wire again. With a similar result. Now his nose was bleeding. He lifted his paw and tried to rub the sore spot.

Gus crouched down and wiped the blood off with this gloved hand, then took a little snow and rubbed it on the tiny wound. "I love you, Bud. But sometimes you're a bulb or two short of a chandelier."

Buddy licked his face.

He came in the back door and sat on the little wooden stool to get his wet boots off and hang his coat on a wall hook. Diana had been methodical and thorough in figuring out what supplies he would need for the winter at her cabin, and she'd used his last week down at the 'storage house' to make sure he had everything: clothes, boots, coats, weapons, bedding, extra tools, the works. By the early afternoon of every day of that last week, she'd arrived from her mountain aerie, and she'd gone back up with a load of supplies. By the time he could walk well enough to struggle up her mountain, she had her cabin tricked out for him. The houses on that circle lane were damn close to empty now.

Buddy sniffed around the kitchen and then wandered off to the other room, probably for a nap. Aggravating the chickens was hard work.

"Smells awesome. What're you making?" Gus set the single egg he'd collected in the little reed basket on the butcher-block worktop. The chickens never laid well when they were closed up longer than overnight. But they could go a couple of days without eggs. There were still five in that basket from earlier in the week.

"Butternut squash soup. Biscuits," she nodded at the glass jar on the worktop. "And pickled tomatoes."

He grinned. "I'm still amazed by the stuff you managed to get up here. Spices, sugar, flour." They were getting low on all-purpose flour, and what was left was pretty stale, but Diana had started grinding her own barley and acorn flour, and cutting it into the packaged stuff. They didn't have yeast, or an oven, so bread didn't rise, but still, it was far lighter and fluffier than what he'd been eating on the road. "Stuff everybody else left behind, you knew to take. Real food feels like a miracle to me."

He stood behind her and looked over her shoulder as she flipped the biscuits in the skillet. Next to the skillet was a cast iron pot, with aromatic, pale orange soup bubbling enticingly.

Reaching around her, he held his hands above the stove, letting the heat warm the numbness from them.

She shrugged. "I didn't take that stuff first. I had time to think about what I needed and go back for it. Do you want eucalyptus, barley, or olive tea?"

"I miss real tea. Like English Breakfast. Or Darjeeling."

"I miss Cherry Coke."

He'd never been a soda drinker himself, but he smiled and went with the trend of their conversation. She'd become much more comfortable speaking fluidly as the winter had deepened, but she was hardly gabby. "I miss popcorn."

"Tacos."

"Oh man," he groaned. "Tacos!"

With a flex of her hips, she nudged him backward, pushing her ass against him. "We should stop talking about food we can't have, or the food we have won't seem good enough."

Gus dropped his hands and stepped back, but he didn't answer right away. Her touch had gone through him like an electric shock.

Diana's comfort with him and recollection of herself had increased steadily over the months he'd been sharing her cabin, and Gus had found himself in a predicament. The more ease she had with him, the more she opened up to him and enjoyed his company, the more he learned about her, the more he liked her. No use evading the truth: the more he wanted her.

He was fairly sure he loved her, or was on his way, and there were signs that she felt something, too. Every day, there were signs.

But comforting hugs were all she wanted—or, maybe more true, all she could handle. They slept in separate beds each night, Buddy moving back and forth to hog each bed in turn, and she pulled away from any intimacy that began to tip over into the territory of attraction.

Gus wasn't remotely tempted to push the issue—hell, he hadn't even brought it up. He knew what she'd been through, and how long she'd been alone, and if she never wanted, or could handle, anything more, he'd be her good friend. They made a strong team up here, the three of them.

But when she touched him, especially a touch like that, he felt it. Everywhere.

He'd been quiet and still long enough that she glanced over her shoulder at him. Getting himself back in the game, he smiled and remembered to respond to her. "The food you make is more than good enough."

On the roof a few weeks later, Gus stood straight and stretched his back. This was his least favorite job, shoveling the snow off the roof. The peak was fairly high and sloped sharply forward at the front of the cabin, so the snow didn't accumulate ridiculously there. But it was almost perfectly flat at the back, over the loft, and they were at nearly six feet of snow now. The roof might have caved in if they'd let all that pile up.

Which was why he didn't like this job. The cabin was old and, though it was well kept, there was only so well one could keep anything after the end of the world.

As he pushed heavy snow off the side, he half-expected that each step would put him through and leave him dangling through the ceiling.

Down below, Diana carried wood from the shed, walking along the narrow corridor walled with snow. Buddy cavorted atop the snow, sinking in just enough to be able to plow his nose through the freshest, loose stuff. As Gus watched, she came back out of the cabin after depositing a load of wood, and Buddy, covered in snow, barked at her and hunkered down into his play-with-me pose. Diana laughed and made a snowball. She lobbed it, and Buddy caught it and then, when it disintegrated as he bit down, he spun in a circle, looking for the ball.

Still laughing, Diana climbed up one of the sets of rough steps they'd carved into the snow and got on top with the dog. She bent forward and, with her hands, shoveled a big mound of it at Buddy, who danced around as it fell on his head and shoulders.

Feeling left out, Gus dipped down and made himself a snowball from the fresh fall he hadn't cleared yet. He tossed it toward Diana and Buddy, aiming for the dog.

And hit Diana square on the back of the head. She spun hard, instantly on the defensive, her hands up and ready to fight, her face drawn into a fierce scowl—then, as she realized what had happened, she blinked, and looked up at the roof. Her expression eased in increments, until she finally smiled. Just a little one, but something.

"Sorry!" Gus called down. "I was aiming for Buddy!" Idiot. He'd broken a moment of peaceful joy because he hadn't been part of it.

But then Diana's smile went wide and bright, and she picked up a big mound of snow. While she stared up at him, she packed it into a hard ball, then bounced it in her hand a few times.

Gus laughed. "That's too big. You won't get it all the way up here."

She juggled the ball back and forth in her hands, then, like a big-league pitcher, she cocked her arm back and her leg up, and she hurled the snowball to the roof.

It hit him on the thigh, and had a little power behind it still. "Okay, okay. It's on now!"

"You still have work to do!" she called up, hands on her hips.

"You're right, I do." He picked up the shovel, already filled with a load of snow, and flung the load off the roof, so that it dumped right on Diana and Buddy both. "Look at me, three birds, one shovel!"

Diana brushed the snow from her eyes and grabbed up another handful.

She was giggling, and Gus thought his heart would explode. What a beautiful sound.

A few days later, after a spate of clear, cold weather that had hardened the snowpack, Diana put her snowshoes on and went out to check the perimeter weapon stashes. It was Protect Day. She took Buddy with her; he enjoyed that long walk in the woods. Gus stayed back, to tend to the handy weapons.

Diana and Buddy had been gone a couple of hours, and Gus was expecting them back any time, while he stood at the kitchen worktop and re-fletched a couple of worn crossbow bolts. He'd taught himself how to make his own bolts, but he recycled and repaired as many as he could. Waste was risk in a world like this.

Last week, he'd shot two bolts while he'd been doing the Protect Day walk, at a fox he'd encountered behind the cabin. It had been stupid to shoot at a fox at that distance, unprepared, but the prospect of fresh meat, not smoked or cured to within an inch of its edibility, had been too much. He'd missed with the first bolt and had nocked and fired again, trying to redeem his attempt.

That wasn't something he *ever* would have done in the world below. Because waste was risk. Up here, though, he was losing his edge. Every day had a little more enjoyment, more *joy* in it. Every day felt a little more like a real life.

He'd just put the repaired bolts in his quiver when he heard a sound that shocked him. A roar — but in Diana's voice. Diana had *roared*.

That could only mean trouble. Gus grabbed his quiver and crossbow and yanked open the front door. He had only his workboots on, and no coat, but he barely noticed the cold. As he ran up a cut-in set of snow steps onto the top of the hardpack, he saw the trouble, about twenty yards away, just past the tree line.

A mountain lion — huge and gold and gorgeous, making a point of a triangle with Diana and Buddy. The lion faced Diana, who stood with her big axe in her hands. Buddy crouched, caught in his usual conflict between bravery and cowardice.

Gus nocked a bolt. As he did, the frozen scene before him broke. The lion advanced on Diana. In defense of his friend, Buddy found bravery and barked, running forward. Just as Gus aimed, Buddy's courage faltered, and he tried to turn and run, but he'd drawn the lion's attention. The beast charged after Buddy and swung a great paw. Buddy yelped and went flying, landing in a motionless heap several yards away.

In the midst of those three seconds, Diana screamed "BUDDY! NO!" and leapt forward as well, running in her snowshoes. Before she could get in his way, Gus fired. The bolt struck the lion in the neck, and the beast shifted directions again, away from Buddy and Diana. He charged for Gus instead.

As the distance between them shrank, Gus managed to nock another bolt and fire. The range was far too close, but he struck the lion in the chest just as it leapt at him. The animal landed on him, taking him down into the snow as he fell.

Gus began to fight immediately, but the lion was still — breathing, but barely, straining for each bloody gasp of air. As Gus lay under him, the lion died.

In the woods, Diana screamed Buddy's name, over and over.

Oh no. Oh God. Buddy! Gus pushed the heavy body off of him and got to his feet. Over the hard, slick snow, he ran.

Diana was on her knees, next to a soft golden body, furry and sweet and too fucking still. Jesus *Christ*, not Buddy. He landed on his knees beside her. She had Buddy's head on her legs, stroking him.

"Buddy! Buddy! Buddy!" she wailed.

His fur was wet and red, glistening with running blood. A gaping wound across his shoulder showed muscle and bone. But he was alive. His side rose and fell with deep, erratic breaths.

"Diana, stop! Hush! He's not dead! He's not dead!"

She kept screaming, and he grabbed her and gave her a hard shake until her eyes focused on his. "He's hurt, not dead. We have to help him."

Her eyes went to the dog. "Buddy?"

"Don't go away, honey. *Please.* Keep it together. Let's get him inside." He pushed her out of the way and picked up their dog. Buddy whined in pain, but Gus was glad for the sound; it meant he was still with them. "It's okay, Buddy. We're here. We're gonna make it okay." He kissed a soft ear. "You stupid, stupid dog."

Her eyes blank with shock, Diana stood and followed him back to the cabin.

Back in the cabin, with something to do, Diana focused. While Gus sat on the floor, holding a folded towel to the wound as Buddy rested his head in his lap and whined, Diana put together the supplies she needed to stitch him up.

Aside from the blow Buddy had taken when he'd landed on the ground, the only injury they could find was across his shoulder — two slashes, one long and deep, the other shorter and shallower.

Diana sat on the floor with them and set up her first aid supplies. First, she shaved away enough of his fur that she could stitch his skin. Without the fur, the gashes both looked much worse. Next, she washed the wounds with rubbing alcohol—Buddy's head came up fast at the first sting, and he whimpered and licked Diana's hands as she gently laved the wounds, but he didn't fight her. He simply licked her hands, as if he wanted to remind her how much he loved her and ask her to stop hurting him.

Her tears dropped on her hands and on Buddy's fur. Gus's soaked into his beard.

"You're doing great," he said, offering the encouragement he could. "Both of you."

When she made the stitches, Buddy fought, just a little. He tried to pull away, but Gus held him firmly, making the hold as close to a hug as he could. "It's okay, Bud. It's okay. We're here. It's okay, it's okay, it's okay." He whispered that soothing croon while Diana worked, keeping Buddy calm through the pain. Each small, long whine, high as a puppy's pitch, made a gash in Gus's heart.

Finally, she was done; she sat back on her heels and stared at Buddy, her bloody hands slack in her lap. Gus let him go, and the dog scooted slowly, his head low, to Diana, looking up at her with those soft, sweet eyes. She fell forward and laid her head on his. "I'm sorry," she whispered. "So sorry. Please don't leave me."

Gus crawled over and wrapped them both in his arms.

Twenty

As Diana stood and stepped back, Gus choked down a chuckle. "I think that'll work."

She'd found a round velvet pillow, one of those things people had used to sleep on airplanes, in the loft. It had a pattern of brightly pastel daisies. Now, Buddy wore it. Lying on his pad before the fire, he looked up at them both with true betrayal in his brown eyes, as if this humiliation was the worst pain he'd experienced in all of this hard day.

"I'm sorry, Bud," Diana said, crouching to the dog's level. "You can't chew your stitches." She scratched behind his ears and kissed his nose.

He accepted her apology and affection with an unenthusiastic wag of his tail, then let his head drop to the pad. When the pillow got in his way, he fussed around.

Gus almost believed the dog's evident lack of comfort was meant for show. Finally he found a position where he could lie comfortably and still send guilt daggers with his puppy eyes.

It was long past dark, and they'd had candles and lanterns burning for hours. A strong wind drummed at the shuttered windows, boding another storm. Gus took Diana's hand and gave it a pull, drawing her attention from Buddy. "We need to shut down for the night."

She looked around, as if remembering where she was. For hours, she'd seen only Buddy. Even as they'd worked throughout the afternoon and evening, her attention hadn't strayed far from the dog.

"There's so much we didn't get done today."

There was so much extra work they *had* done: healed Buddy, butchered a mountain lion, tanned a hide.

"It's okay. We got the important stuff done. We're a little low on wood for the night, but we'll manage." In fact, there was no way the fire would hold out until morning; they were in for a cold sleep. But they didn't go out after dark unless the moon was bright enough to see by. Tonight, the sky was an impenetrable mass of deep blue clouds. "And we got the Protect Day work done."

She sighed, and Gus saw that she was very near another breakdown, though Buddy was okay. If they were careful about treating his wound—and they would be— he'd be fine. He'd forgiven them for the pain they'd caused him. It might take him a minute to get over the collar, though.

He tugged on her hand again. "Hey. It's okay. Everything's okay."

"He almost died. He was with me, I was supposed to take care of him, and I let him get hurt."

She'd described the scene he'd jumped into the middle of that afternoon—she and Buddy, finished with their perimeter check, heading back to the cabin; the lion leaping down from a tree. He'd been lying in wait up above, and she'd been watching for trouble at ground level. Because that was where human trouble came from. Below.

Gus pulled until her body met his. "Stop. Buddy's going to be okay. You're okay. We won that fight. You can't see everything in every direction at every moment."

"We have to. We're forgetting that."

He *wanted* to forget that. He *wanted* to stop living like he had to fight for every day. He was willing to trade some safety for the chance to have days like they'd had this winter: snowball fights and aimless forest walks, playing fetch with Buddy, spending quiet evenings with books and music. Spending whole days tucked up in this comfortable cabin while storms howled just beyond its warm glow. Not giving up all caution, but not letting it rule them.

This wasn't the end of the world anymore, not here. This was the beginning of the next one.

With that thought in mind, Gus slid his hand along Diana's jawline until he cupped her face. "It's time to stop surviving, Diana. It's time to live again." He bent his head and touched his lips to hers.

It was the first time he'd kissed her like this, on the mouth, with his desire and his intention at the fore, the first time he'd leaned in and made it all the way to contact, and he expected her to bolt. In the brief second he had, he savored the touch.

She did pull away, but she only tipped her head back to do it. Her head remained in his hand, her body in his arms. Her eyes lased into his, and he let her look. If she turned out of this embrace, he'd leave her alone.

But she didn't. Instead, hesitantly, her hand came up and brushed over his cheek. She studied his face, watching her trembling fingers as they moved over the edge of his beard, across his mouth, to his chin, and then along his jaw, in the same way that his hand held her.

"Gus," she whispered.

He turned his head and kissed her palm. "I want to live with you, Diana."

"I don't know how."

"You do. You already are."

"I'm scared."

He made some distance and took a breath. "I don't want to scare you. I'm sorry." He dropped his hand from her face.

She caught it and held on. "I don't want to be scared. I want to be strong."

She was one of the strongest people he'd ever known. In fact, that list was all women: Michaela. Erin. Sarah. Diana.

Stepping close again, bringing her body against his, she rose up on her toes and pressed her lips to his. "I ... I want to live with you, too."

This time, when he kissed her, there was no hesitation. He made his intentions completely clear, pushing his tongue against her lips. She opened her mouth and let him in.

They made up the sofa bed and then undressed slowly, standing near the fire, each removing their own clothes. Gus watched her while he pulled his sweater off, his t-shirt, opened his jeans and let them drop. He kept his boxers on and shed his socks. Already the room had taken on a chill; they'd banked the fire to try to preserve it through the night.

Diana kept her eyes on herself, removing each piece of clothing with particular care. Even in these tight quarters, the most Gus had seen of her body was her arms and shoulders, and then only rarely; she dressed in the bathroom. He'd held her, though, and knew her body's contours. She was lithe and strong and beautiful. Her fair skin bore the scars of a life of hard survival—and some marks of her previous shape, in a previous life.

Standing in a pair of blue cotton panties and a white tank that was considerably too small for her, she finally put her eyes on him. She started at his feet and worked her way up.

He'd been less careful about how much skin he'd shown around the cabin, not for any reason but that he hadn't thought much of it—and that, to be carelessly undressed again, was a gift he cherished. Generally, in deference to her reticence, he dressed in the bathroom, too, at least to cover his bottom half. His chest, he'd covered to keep warm above all other concerns, and if it was warm enough in the cabin, he'd sleep without a shirt. In the long ago, when he'd been trussed up in a tuxedo half of his life, he'd preferred to be as undressed as he could be, when he could be. He'd slept in the nude, and, alone in his apartment, he'd spent whole days off in only his underwear, even answering the door to collect his food delivery in that state.

He'd been a boxer-brief man in those days. These days, he was a 'whatever he could find' man.

Diana's eyes worked their way up his legs and stopped at the level of his hips. Though he still wore his boxers, she had to see the effect she'd had on him. She hadn't needed to be nearly naked to have that effect on him. Lately, he got hard for her at every moment of intimacy. Any time she opened up, he rose to the occasion.

After lingering on his boxers, Diana lifted her eyes to his chest. That, she'd seen often in the months they'd lived together, but she'd never touched him. On those nights that she came to him after a dream and slept in his arms, he wore a t-shirt. If he hadn't been wearing one, he'd put one on. For his sake as much as hers. She hadn't touched his chest since they'd first met, when he'd been lying helpless and hurt in bed, and his tattoo of Mudge, inked over his heart, had drawn her attention.

She took the few steps of distance between them and set her hands on his chest, pushing her fingers through the hair across his pectorals. Then her fingertips traced a pattern over his skin. Her touch left tracers of energy in his sinews strong enough to make their own light. He could illuminate the cabin on the power of this moment.

Still watching her eyes, his attention consumed by his rioting senses, he didn't understand at first that she was tracing his tattoo. It was an old piece, acquired in college, and had faded with time.

Laying one hand over hers, he reached out with the other and pulled the band from the bottom of her braid, drawing his fingers through the weave to set her hair loose. "Come to bed with me."

When she nodded, he took her hand and led her to the open sofa bed.

Turning back the heavy layers of covers, Gus waited for Diana to climb in first. Before she did, she checked on Buddy, and Gus looked over at the fire as well. The dog slept, curled in his usual sleeping position, not too badly disturbed by the pain of his shoulder or the indignity around his neck. His side rose and fell in a comforting, familiar depth and rhythm.

Still in her underwear, Diana slid between the sheets. Gus left his boxers on and followed her in.

The sheets were chilled, and he went tense at the contact on so much of his skin. But Diana was right there, her body warm and soft and welcoming. He turned and blew out the last lit candle, and the room became nearly full dark, with only the reddish glow of the banked fire providing any light, closed in as they were inside a storm-shuttered cabin.

This first time, they would experience each other by other senses than sight. An image illuminated in his mind of Erin, blind and deaf but also sweet and strong and stalwartly hopeful, moving through the end of the world on the power of faith and trust.

No amount of faith and trust had saved her.

He closed his eyes until her image dimmed.

Diana's hesitant hand found his face in the dark, and she stroked his cheek. He returned to this moment, to this strong, sweet woman, without hope but with a fierce will. Catching her hand in his, he pressed her palm to his lips and felt the tremble under her skin.

"We can just sleep, Diana. That's enough."

"I don't want to sleep yet. But I don't think ... I don't ..." She took a deep breath; in the quiet cold it seemed loud and heavy. "The words don't sound right, but...I don't think I remember this. What it's like."

"Have you had sex before?"

"Yes. I had boyfriends. I just ... since the world before, I only ... it was only ..." She breathed deeply again. "It wasn't this."

She'd been raped. She was trying to tell him that the only times men had been in her body in the past nearly seven years, they'd been there against her will, brutally. She didn't remember what it was like to feel cared for in this act. To feel loved.

He laid her back on the mattress — warm now with the heat of their bodies — and hovered over her. Though he was unable to see her, he stared hard into her eyes. "I won't ever hurt you, Diana. I'll do everything I can to protect you from ever being hurt again." He kissed her, finding her mouth easily, tasting her lightly with his tongue, brushing his beard gently over her soft lips.

Then he said the thing he felt. "I love you."

A tiny whimper rose up from the bed, and her arms snaked around his neck. Her mouth found his again, and she kissed him, no longer simply open to his exploration but seeking on her own.

Gus woke, shivering, into a dark room, alone. The space beside him was still warm, but cooling. The scent of their sex was strong in the air.

Had she moved to her bed? The thought worried him—and hurt, too. He'd thought they'd made something special between them.

He sat up. "Diana?"

"Here." Her voice came from near the fireplace, and he squinted at that faint red light and made out the barest silhouette.

Buddy. She was with Buddy. "He okay?" Gus turned the covers back and got out of bed—shit, the floor was cold.

"He was crying in his sleep, but his wound seems okay. I think he's cold, and it's making him hurt more."

He was also used to sleeping in bed with one or both of them. He probably felt sorry for himself — sore and cold and alone while his people did weird things in the dark.

"You want to bring him up with us?"

Though she was little more than an impression of a shadow, Gus felt her smile. "Is that okay?"

"Of course. Keeping each other warm through the long nights is what we do." He made his way in the dark and picked Buddy up, getting a wet lick on his neck for the effort. The dog could walk, but with evident pain. Gus imagined him lying there, wanting to climb into bed with them, maybe limping over to try, and being unable. Then going back to his pad by the dark fire and feeling abandoned.

"Sorry, Bud. My bad." He set him on the bed and removed his collar of shame, then went back for Diana and took her hand. "How are you?" He'd given her pleasure, he knew that, and she'd given him the same and more, but now, in the cold dark, how did she feel about how things had changed?

She stepped up until her body touched his at nearly every point, leaning her forehead on his shoulder. "I feel good. I feel … happy, I think."

Gus couldn't think of a response that would have pleased him more, unless she were to give him back the words he'd given her. He kissed her head. "Me too." Wind kicked up and gave the shutters an angry shake. The sound made the room seem suddenly even colder. "Let's go to bed and keep each other warm."

They fell asleep with Buddy between them, sheltered in their arms.

When Gus woke in the morning, he was cold, but he wasn't alone. Buddy and Diana slept quietly at his side. He smoothed a hand over Buddy, finding ease in the warmth of his fur and the rise and fall of his chest. The swelling around his wound had receded; Diana had done well with her care of it.

The cabin was swathed in deep grey darkness, but sunlight pushed through the seams between the shutter boards like lines of fire, offering evidence that the storm, and the night, had run their course. He wondered how much snow he'd have to heave from their paths during the day. It was Rest Day, but they had work to catch up on, and probably a few hours of shoveling to do. It was time to get moving, but the moment was too peaceful, and too warm, to break.

On Buddy's other side, Diana slept. Her long, blonde hair swept over her shoulder and obscured her face. Strands quivered with each calm inhale and exhale.

Yes, he was happy. Despite the stress and fear of the day before, he was happier than he'd been since the Sunstorm. He'd loved his life before, excelling at a job, an *art*, he adored, traveling the world, meeting famous and important people, performing in exquisite halls. More than all that, each day, when he'd picked up the tools of his trade, his bow and his violin, he'd made the world a more beautiful place. If only for that moment, he and his fellow players had brought beauty into the world.

It had been a world that needed all the beauty it could get. A world of war and suffering and pain, of poverty and torment, of terror and greed, of cynicism and corruption, of haves and have-nots.

That world had had its Ferals, too. They'd occupied thrones and capitols and corner offices. They'd been the people in the audience in the most elegant eveningwear and expensive tuxedos.

Suffering dominated the world below, the world after, as well. New kinds of suffering as well as the mundane kinds many had known before. Hunger and need, a silent plague on the modern world, was the way of the end of it; no longer could people pretend that the world was good because their own bellies were full. Illness and death stood akimbo in the path of every soul and demanded to be acknowledged.

It was a hard life, living in an ancient past reborn. No denying that.

But the Sunstorm had stripped people of their trappings, exposed them for who and what they truly were. There had been a kind of comfort in that simplicity: you could walk through the end of the world and know where the danger lay. When you encountered Ferals, you knew them for what they were. You knew what would happen to you in a city. You could tell a good wanderer from a troubled one over a single campfire. Substakes each had their own ways, and those ways were clear at the gate. The end of the world had no time for artifice or prevarication. You could take it at its face.

From his perch here, high on this mountain, in a place of peace, in a home, with a family, Gus could see the world below more clearly. These years had been a reset, like rebooting a crashed laptop. The power had gone out, and in the restart, the world was going through its files, finding the corruption, sending it to the trash bin.

Eventually, someone would get the power on again, and when that happened, the return to the modern world would likely be swift: the technology was there; it had only to be rebuilt, not reinvented. But there were dramatically fewer people now, and they had been fundamentally changed. Maybe the new world would remember the mistakes of the old one.

Probably, at first, it would. But future generations would eventually forget a past that had become history, and the world's files would become corrupted again.

If there were future generations.

Gus thought of Michael, born without most of his head. He thought of how few pregnant women he'd seen since the Sunstorm, how few children younger than the end there were in the world. In all his years of wandering, he could count the healthy young children on his hands.

He thought of Diana. In all the months he'd been here with her — four or five, at least — he didn't think she'd had a period. He'd know — there'd be no way, in their close quarters, he'd have missed that. He'd come inside her twice last night, without any qualm at all. She was probably infertile. He was probably sterile. Several dozen nuclear reactors in the US had melted down, probably very close to all at once.

He'd been west of the thickest concentration of nuclear plants by the time the cores went past their safe zone, but it had been years before he'd wandered west of the Mississippi. He had no clue how long radiation poisoned the air. When he'd been with Carver's group, they'd met a wanderer who'd called herself a nuclear scientist. She'd tried to explain, but she hadn't been so good speaking in plain terms, so she hadn't really clarified much. What Gus had taken from her mumbo-jumbo was that it didn't matter how long radiation was in the air. Even if you survived that, it was still inside you. More importantly, it was in the soil, changing the cellular structures of the plants, changing the animals who ate the plants, and the people who ate the animals and the plants — changing everything.

If you hadn't died right away or gotten morbidly ill from the direct radiation, you were likely mutated on some cellular level. If you weren't infertile, your mutated cells would carry on to your next generation.

And make babies without all their parts.

Almost seven years after the end of the world, Gus felt strong and well — more now, in fact, that ever since the storm. He'd seen people succumb to radiation sickness and, later, to various horrific cancers, and he knew what to expect, but he'd avoided that torment.

Diana seemed well, too. She'd been tucked snugly into her mountain retreat by the time the nukes went down, and she'd been here, straddling California and Nevada, with no US reactors at her back. And still, she was apparently infertile.

There would be no future generations. Humanity was dying out.

They deserved to. They'd shat all over the gift of this beautiful planet.

Nowhere was Earth's magnificent beauty more striking than here, on this mountain on which he lived. It was as it had been, almost untouched by human hands, and it thrived.

So yes. Gus was done living in fear. He didn't want to watch everything in every direction at every moment.

There was no point in surviving, no legacy to build, nothing to come next.

There was only living, making the most of the world they had left.

Reaching across Buddy's still sleeping body, Gus brushed a long tress of Diana's blonde hair from her face. Her eyes opened and shone at him, a blue light in the dim room. She smiled.

There was only this.

Home.

Book Five: Settler

To know that we know what we know,
and to know that we do not know what we do not know,
that is true knowledge.

~Nicolaus Copernicus

Twenty-One

"Buddy! Stop it, you dork!" Diana laughed and looked around the yard for a stick or a bone or one of his filthy tennis balls, something to distract the dog from dismantling the clean laundry on the line. She picked up a big stick he'd dragged back from a walk. "Here, boy! Come!"

Pushing through the tangle of sheets he'd made, Buddy came, tail wagging and tongue lolling. He saw the stick and did his fetch dance. Diana threw the stick as hard as she could toward the lake and then hurried to get the dry sheets off the line before he came back.

She just made it, stuffing the last sheet into the basket as he came up, trying to balance a stick that was practically a tree branch in his mouth. Not the stick she'd tossed. He lay down in his favorite spot, and began gnawing.

His favorite spot was the soft patch of sandwort under the swaying shade of the willow tree. Fiona's grave.

But it didn't cause her heartache to see him there. She liked it, in fact, to think of both her beloved dogs sharing space at her home the way they shared space in her heart. "Went for an upgrade, huh?"

His tail thumped once, as if in answer.

The mountain lion's swipe hadn't done much lasting damage, thankfully. Some evenings, after a long day of walking, he'd pick up a slight limp, and he'd lie on his pad and worry at his shoulder a little, but otherwise, he was the same Buddy. His fur had grown back fully and covered the scar so well that, if they went looking for it, they had to really look.

Since that frightening day, they'd had no other dangerous visitors. Only Shrek, who'd made his first spring appearance while there was still snow on the ground and had been by every few days since. He liked Buddy almost as much as he'd liked Fiona, though Buddy was smaller and not as tolerant of his rough play as Fee had been.

Sometimes in their play, Buddy would yelp and back off. When that happened, Diana always got the feeling that Shrek would have rolled his eyes at the dog if he could have. But he'd be more gentle after.

It had been a while since they'd seen him, actually. Diana picked up the laundry basket and set it on the picnic table, then went for the big steel buckets and the yoke Gus had made. The spring had been dry so far, with almost no rain — the winter had been dry, too, comparatively, with less than eight feet of snow at its highest point. In previous winters, the snow had been well higher than the eaves at the front of the cabin, and a couple of times had topped the eaves at the rear.

Summers were always dry here; it was in winter that the water table was replenished and the lakes filled. So a winter with half the usual snowfall had Diana concerned. Still, it was only the three of them up here, with a good well and the little lake. They wouldn't dry up.

With such dry conditions, however, Diana couldn't rely on the earth to nurture her garden as it should, and they needed the vegetables to stay healthy. So Gus had made the yoke, and they toted pails of water up from the lake.

It was a long walk, made several times every other day, but they didn't want to use the well and fill at the much closer pump, just in case. They'd loosened up a few of Diana's old routines and had considerably more time for leisure, but it was still important to be smart about their resources.

Her routines had been almost as much about having things to do as they'd been about keeping herself safe and well, but they'd been no less important for that. Even keeping as busy as she had, Diana knew now that she'd been going honestly crazy, up here all alone, especially after Fiona's death and the last attack of the monsters.

With Gus and Buddy, she didn't need things to do to keep herself sane. She had them, and she was happier than she'd ever been in her whole life — including her life in the world before. They still kept her calendar of days, but no longer did Clean Day mean scrubbing every shelf, every glass, every jar of preserves. It didn't mean organizing and reorganizing her books or scrubbing the windows and floors every single week. Now they did the work required to keep their resources up, their protection strong, and their home clean.

And the rest of the time, they enjoyed the life they'd made. A home and a family.

After she finished watering the garden and harvesting the ripe vegetables, she picked up the laundry basket, called Buddy, and they went inside to get ready for lunch. With the laundry basket on one hip and a basket of greens and tomatoes on the other, she jostled her way through the back door.

Gus heard her and came around the corner, taking the laundry from her hands. His somber expression made her belly clench, and she sat the vegetables on the worktop. She didn't face him when she spoke.

"Is it that bad?"

His hands hooked over her hips; he must have sat the laundry down. "I love you. God, Di. I love you so much. You're so fucking strong."

He was reading her journals. On the day he'd arrived, he'd asked about them. She'd been violently unable even to think about them, and in no way, then, had she had the words to speak of them. Since then, all this time, through a whole winter, he'd never asked again. He'd understood, with that one question and her stunted answer, that they were not a topic for discussion.

Until a few days ago, when she'd gone to them to try to find an entry and jog her still-faulty memory.

She'd gone to them without a thought, not realizing until she had one in her hand how momentous the event was. Since Fiona's death, since that time that she meant to forget but could not, she had never written in them again. In fact, she'd grown to *fear* them, the strange annals of a dead life, as if demons might have been conjured had she read the words.

And then, speaking of the garden growth, she'd mentioned a particularly bountiful year and simply walked over and scanned the shelves, looking for the right journal for that time.

There were no longer demons to be summoned. Not since Gus and Buddy.

So when Gus asked — tentatively, carefully — about her journals, she'd felt no qualms about offering to let him read them.

It had taken him three days to finally do so, and he'd spent the whole morning with them. Diana had been glad that there were things to be done that had kept her out of the cabin for hours.

"You read about it, I guess," she said, thinking about the first time monsters had tried to hurt her and Fiona and take what was theirs. That attack, when she and Fee had been both standing after, she'd written about, in detail. She'd wanted to remember, to never forget what had happened, so that she would be vigilant about what could happen.

And yet she had failed.

She felt Gus's lips on her bare shoulder, his soft beard caressing her skin. "I love you," was his answer.

"I love you, too." She rested her head against his. "I'm okay now. With you and Buddy, what happened before can't hurt me."

He turned her and stared into her eyes. Diana remembered finding him handsome almost from the time she'd first seen him, but now, since she'd come to love him, he was beautiful. The soft curve of his mouth, the dimples under his beard, the soft waves of his long hair. His clear hazel eyes that crinkled at the corners when he smiled—the love in them, love for her, shone always. Sometimes, when she thought of what had been, before him, and what was, with him, she could almost remember believing in God. Because he was like an angel.

"I hate what happened to you. I hate that people can do such things. That they're even *capable* of it."

She didn't want to relive that time, or any time before him, and she knew of the perfect way to distract him from those thoughts and to remind him that she truly was okay now. She had survived, and now she lived. Offering him a particular smile, she pushed her hands under his t-shirt, up the solid muscle and soft hair of his belly, over his firm pectorals, his strong shoulders, bringing his shirt up on her arms. He moaned quietly and helped her take his shirt off.

"I don't think about those journals anymore because the past doesn't matter. I'm happy now, Gus. I have everything now." She looped her arms about his neck and pulled his head to hers for a kiss. "We can fold the laundry later."

Gus leaned forward and unlaced his boot. "We'll go farther down next time." He pulled off the boot and his sock — there was a hole in the toe — and sighed out a groan as he flexed his ankle.

The fracture had healed well, considering their limited options for treating it, but it ached in cold weather, and, like Buddy, he picked up a noticeable limp after a long walk. They'd walked very far today — the whole morning down the mountain, the high hours of the afternoon around Pinon Valley, and now halfway back up.

Diana sat on the ground before him and lifted his leg onto her lap so she could rub the ache away for him. When his next sigh was one of relief and comfort, and he leaned back and closed his eyes, she smiled. It felt good to make him feel good. In this way and countless others.

A breeze rose up from the mountain pass, and Diana closed her eyes and turned into it as it cooled the hot sweat from her brow. The summer wasn't yet at its peak, but the air, even at their altitude, felt oven-hot when it was still. Breezes ran cool as ever, though, lifting up the chill of Lake Tahoe and sending it high.

Gus offered Buddy some water. He hadn't perfected the art of drinking from a bottle as Fiona had, so Gus poured it into tin camp cup that they carried for the purpose, and the dog lapped daintily at the water, letting only a few drops fall to the dusty ground and leave dark circles to soak quickly into thirsty earth.

"We went as far as we can go and still get back home before dark," Diana finally said. "We left at dawn as it is." She looked at the sun, already sliding behind the peaks of taller mountains in the range. "It's too dangerous any closer to the bottom."

There had been a new body in Pinon Valley — not simply a skeleton, but one that still had quite a bit of rotting flesh on its bones. A month old, maybe less. They were already too far down.

She'd avoided Pinon Valley since early in her time on the mountain. Before the Sunstorm, it had been a lively little town, with a general store, a couple of souvenir shops, a diner, and a little Gold Rush museum, with the typical cluster of vacation homes around it. It had been full of precious post-storm resources.

It had also been full of bodies. Mounds of them lined up along the sides of Pinon Street, as if somebody had pulled all the townspeople out into the street and mowed them down.

Diana hadn't lingered there, and she'd never gone back. Not until today. The ghosts of that town were too strong, and the dangers seemed to great. Menace lurked in every shadow, and she'd had other places to forage.

But over the course of seven years, and especially since Gus and Buddy had been with her, she'd stripped bare all the areas she could easily reach. Nothing was left of obvious use.

So they'd come to Pinon Valley, which had also been stripped. Not by Diana—which was at least as worrisome as the rotting body. Other people had been there, and if they'd killed that woman who was rotting on the decayed boardwalk, they were monsters.

"We can't go farther down," she repeated, rubbing Gus's calf. "We're not safe."

He shifted and sat up again. His fingers brushed the side of her face. "Okay. I won't let you get hurt."

She smiled at him, though she knew, as he did, that there was only so much they could do to protect each other. The primary thing was to stay away from people.

"What things do we need that we don't already make for ourselves, and how can we make them?" He took his foot from her and pulled his sock back on. "I need to mend my socks. I think I'm out of whole socks."

"Clothes," Diana said at once. "We have tools and weapons enough to keep us for many years, and we know how to keep them in good shape. The garden is self-sustaining." She got seeds for the next year from the current year's crop. "As long as we can hunt and fish, and grow vegetables and fruit, we're okay. The chickens, too. Mac keeps the flock growing, though we should let a cockerel mature soon, I think."

"If Mac'll let him grow up. That rooster is a bastard."

She laughed and lifted her arms so Buddy could flop his head onto her thigh. "I know. Maybe we can build a cockhouse and keep them separate."

"We don't have enough chicken wire for another house, and we need what we have for repairs."

"There's a hardware store in Hatterville. They might still have plenty. But it's farther down."

Gus shook his head. "We're thinking about ways not to have to scavenge anymore, right? To keep going at home for as long as we can. So if we build a cockhouse, it has to be from what we already have or can make. Let's set that one aside. You said clothes is the biggest problem. Can't we make our own?"

"From what? We have plenty now, but eventually, things will wear out. Look at your socks. There aren't any more socks, and you'll only be able to sew up the holes for so long. We only have so much thread, and I don't know how to make more. We don't have sheep for wool. I wanted to teach myself to knit, but I've never come across any yarn or knitting needles. And what happens when the spools of thread we've found run out?"

Diana felt herself working up to real worry, but Gus grinned at her. "Honey, you can tan hides. I bet we could make something like thread out of strips of leather, and a kind of needle with bone. We might end up dressed like extras from *10,000 Years B.C.*, but we won't be cold or naked—unless we want to be." He took her hand. "We don't need other people's old shit anymore. We have everything we need at home."

Her mind conjured an image of Gus's lean, muscular body in a deerskin loincloth. It was a remarkably compelling picture—and not entirely outside the realm of the possible, if they did stop foraging for old world supplies.

He laced up his boot. Their shoes would wear out eventually, too. Could they make their own boots? Unlikely.

But for Gus, the matter seemed to be resolved. He stood and held out his hand. "In fact, let's get moving. We're wasting the sun."

Diana trailed her hand over Gus's belly, tracing the contours of each muscle, drawing a spiral through the line of soft hairs to his navel. Each time she hit a particularly sensitive spot, his muscles spasmed lightly, and his fingers paused in the circles they drew on her shoulder.

Thunder rumbled outside, and Buddy whined at her back.

"It's okay, Bud. We're snug and safe, and that's far away. No monsters here." She reached back and patted the dog's rump, then resumed her fingers' travels over Gus's terrain. Another flutter of distant lightning gave the sky a flash of pale glow. Several seconds later came its answering rumble. "Miles away. We're okay."

Summer thunderstorms on the mountain happened occasionally each year; sometimes, the rains they brought slammed punishingly down so that she had to hang the storm shutters again. This summer had brought no storms until now. Diana hoped that this would be a good soaking rain, to ease the crispness of the dry spring and summer and replenish the well and the lake. She worried vaguely about the lightning, but it was so soft and so far; this promised to be a gentle storm. A complaint, not a tantrum.

Her fingers wandered over the carved muscle at Gus's hip and trailed down, following it inward. He chuckled and laid his hand over hers. "Bud's not going to want to get down while it's storming, but you keep that up, and I'm not going to care if there's a dog in bed with us."

She could feel how much he wouldn't care. She didn't care, either. Sliding her hand from under his, she finished her journey and took hold of him. He groaned, a particular kind of sound that he only made in bed, rough and guttural, full of need and want. With a smile he couldn't see in the dark, she scooted down his body, under the cover.

"Diana," he moaned in that rough, sensual tone. He grabbed a fistful of her hair and said no more.

If Buddy minded, Diana didn't notice.

Diana woke with a start. Buddy sat up on the bed; he'd gone on alert, and, although he was quiet, the tension in his body must have pulled her quickly from sleep. Something was wrong, she could sense it as Buddy had, but she couldn't puzzle out what it was.

It must have been near dawn — a gold light pushed through fog outside the window. Fog boded well; there was moisture in the air.

But something was wrong.

Buddy whined and jumped down. He went to the door and scratched at it. The only time he'd ever woken them in the middle of the night to do his business had been the night after he'd found a half-eaten pika in the woods and had taken several bites before they could stop him.

That had been a long night. Dopey dog.

He whined again, then turned and came back to the bed and stared at her, panting.

"Gus," Diana said and patted him. "Wake up."

He sat up right away. "What's up? Trouble?"

"I think so. I don't ... something feels weird."

Without another word, he got up and yanked his jeans on. Diana got up as well, and pulled her jeans back on. They stepped into their boots. Gus picked up his crossbow and nocked a bolt; Diana grabbed her axe.

As they went to the door, Diana glanced out the front window again. "Oh my God. That's not fog. That's not sun."

She leapt in front of Gus and yanked open the door.

It was smoke. Not fog, smoke. The strange glow came from the lake side, and Diana ran off the porch and across the yard until she could—"Oh my God! Oh my God!"

"Jesus," Gus muttered. "Jesus Christ."

At the far side of the lake, the forest was engulfed in flames. The strangeness she'd sensed was the noise. None of the right sounds of their world—no animals, no birds. Only the sound of fire eating forest. And wind, a strong wind, blowing right in their faces, driving the fire to them, filling their breath with acrid smoke.

Buddy whined and brushed his snout with a paw. The smell must have been exponentially stronger for him.

"We have to go. Right now." Gus grabbed her hand hard.

"NO! There's no place to go!" Her frantic mind tried to plan a way to protect her home. All these years, she'd planned so hard, for everything. But she'd never planned enough. Always, there was something to come and hurt her anyway. "NO!"

"We'll go down the mountain. Come on, honey. We don't have much time." He tried to draw her back into the cabin. "Buddy! Come!"

"We can't go down the mountain! It's not safe!" She knew she didn't have a choice. She knew they had to go, but she couldn't leave. This was the world she'd built with her bare hands! This was where she had Gus and Buddy. This was where she *lived*!

Grabbing her by the arms, Gus got in her face and shook her. "Stay with me, Di. We have got to go. Look how fast it's moving." He turned her forcibly in the direction of the fire, which had reached the far shore of the lake and begun to find its way around the sides. "Our only shot is to get down to the river and cross. The lake will slow it down and give us time to get ahead of it, but we've got to run NOW."

"Shrek!" He'd get burned up — he might already be. Oh God!

"We can't look for Shrek. He'll have to take care of himself, like he always does. It's you and me and Bud. Right now." Keeping firm hold of her hand, he dragged her back to the door of the cabin, reached in, and grabbed a ready pack from the floor just beside it. "Take this."

He let her hand go, and she took the pack, numbly hooking it over her shoulders. He put on the other pack and grabbed his quiver. When they were loaded up, he grabbed her hand again. "Now. We run. "

They ran.

Diana didn't look back. To look back would have been to see the end of her life.

Twenty-Two

The fire burned faster than they could run.

They had the head start of the length of the lake and the hundred feet between its nearest shore and the cabin, but it wasn't going to be enough. The fire's roar and heat chased them down, licking at their backs by the time their stinging, watering eyes could see the river ahead of them. The blaze was so close that its reflection had turned the water a wavering orange.

They'd still been close enough to the cabin when the fire reached it to hear the ammunition explode.

They wore only jeans and boots and the packs and weapons on their backs. Gus was bare-chested; Diana wore a scanty tank. Her arms and shoulders stung, seared by the heat that the flames pushed forward. A particular rank odor wafted around her nose as wisps of her loose hair crisped in the heat.

They'd kept to the road, following its crumbling path downward, trusting its limited value as a firebreak. Forest creatures ran with them, some of them—jackrabbits and foxes—tearing past them, able to move more quickly. Others, pikas and voles, scurried underfoot. No sign of Shrek. Diana once thought she'd heard him crashing along just behind them, but it had been trees falling into the flames as the fire had found a particularly hearty meal and leapt forward, gaining ground.

She hoped Shrek had run out already and was safe. She couldn't think of the alternative.

They didn't try to speak as they ran; the smoke and their efforts made breathing difficult as it was, so they relied on their trust in each other to know what to do. They ran for the river, together.

Buddy ran with them, keeping up, as frightened as they. But his weakened shoulder gave out, and he faltered just as they came in sight of the river, just as the flames behind them surged closer. As Buddy went down, Gus didn't hesitate; he seemed not even to break stride. He scooped the dog into his arms and kept running.

An animal darted past, shrieking and on fire. A fox, she thought it was. Then another, a rabbit, also burning.

The river was just ahead. A hundred feet, maybe less. Gripping Buddy, Gus surged forward, faster, and

Diana dug down for the last of her strength and found more speed, too. She didn't dare look behind her; the sting in her arms, the smell of her hair, the weight in her lungs — she knew how close the flames were, and to see it would only bring despair.

She kept her eyes on Gus and ran.

The road bent at the river, and Gus jumped off the pavement and slid down the steep, rocky slope to the bank. Diana followed, but she hit a large rock protruding from the slope, and it sent her end over end, rolling down the last ten feet and into the water — it was warm, the water, and only about six inches deep at this rocky bend full of small pools, but so much cooler yet than the air, and the current ran over her sore skin and gave her a moment of hope that they might survive.

She lay still, on her back, and tried to breathe through her thick lungs. A cough that hadn't found a way up while she ran now clenched her chest and wouldn't let go.

Coughing too, Gus splashed over to her. "Are you hurt?"

She shook her head. Above them, at the top of the slope they'd come down, flames shot into the air and sought passage down the hill. "I'm okay, I'm okay." She held out her hand, and he took it and helped her to her feet. Buddy stood at Gus's side, his tail tucked tightly against his belly, favoring his sore leg.

"Are you guys okay?" she asked, trying to cough out the smoke.

"Yeah." Gus looked up, and Diana did again as well. The fire had found small outcroppings of dried plants at the top of the slope and begun to creep down the rocks. "We're not safe yet. If it finds its way across the water, we're dead. We have to keep running."

"Can you? What about your ankle?" It would never be as strong as it had been before the break, and it hurt him badly when he worked it too hard. They'd just run miles at full speed without stopping.

Grim determination filled his eyes, and he picked Buddy up again. "I'll deal. Let's go."

"Let me take Buddy, at least." If she could carry a deer on her shoulders for miles, she could carry Buddy.

"I got him. Let's go." This time, he swung the dog over his shoulders. Buddy let him, too afraid and confused to protest being carried like a kill.

Together, they climbed out of the water and up the other slope, and they ran.

The rain that the lightning and thunder had promised earlier, while they'd shared a last blissful moment in bed, finally began to fall.

The rain sliced down over them, carving into earth that had been dust, churning it into a muddy froth. Like curtains of glass shards, the downpour obstructed their sight and their progress, but it was the most wonderful, miraculous rain Diana had ever experienced. The chill wet cooled her skin and cleared her lungs and her eyes. It killed the flames behind them and saved their lives.

Their existence, at least. Diana wasn't sure she had a life without the cabin.

They sat huddled in a tiny cave formed by a cluster of prehistoric boulders and waited the rain out.

Before Diana's mind could fix on the loss of her life and dive into despair, she found something to do. She opened her pack — the webbed nylon fittings had melted — and pulled out the flannel shirt she kept inside it. Gus followed her lead and took the shirt from his pack.

After she was more fully dressed, she took out a bag of water, a plastic cup, and a pouch of venison jerky.

Buddy's breath worried her; it came in rasping husks, each exhale ending with a coughing chuff. But he perked up at once when he caught the scent of the jerky. She gave him a piece, holding it between her fingers, and then poured some water into the cup. Then she handed the bag and pouch to Gus. He drank down a third of what was left and handed it and the pouch back.

"You should eat, too," she admonished, but he shook his head.

Diana took her drink and offered Buddy the rest. She tried to nibble on some jerky, but her taste buds were full of smoke and fire, and she couldn't get more than a bite down. She put the pouch away.

Then there was nothing more to do.

Their home was gone. She didn't have to see the devastation with her eyes to know it in her mind. She could imagine exactly what was left: nothing at all. Maybe a few charred-black shards, reaching up into the smoky air. No cabin, no garden, no smokehouse. No chicken coop.

Oh, the poor chickens.

She'd seen the images of wildfires. Northern California had a wildfire season, like other parts of the country had hurricane or tornado seasons. Even when armies of specially-trained firefighters battled forest fires, the destruction was nearly complete. A fire like this, left to take its fill, ate everything, absolutely everything.

Everything was gone. The whole world she'd made. The home Gus and Buddy had brought her. Gone.

Shrek. Oh Shrek, please be okay.

Gus's hand brushed her face. "Diana. Don't go away, honey. Hey."

She blinked and found his eyes, watching her under a furrowed brow.

"Everything's gone." Her voice felt stunted and surreal.

Gus shook his head. "We're not. We're here." He stroked the top of Buddy's head. "We're together."

"We have nowhere to go."

He took both her hands. "Buddy and I wandered the world below for a long time. If we have to wander again, we know how to do it, and we'll keep you safe. But I don't think we have to do that. I know where we can go, and I think they'll let us stay. Remember the Rennies? They offered me a place, when I met them. Maybe they'll offer again. Either way, we're together, and we'll be okay."

"People?" The thought soured Diana's stomach.

"Good people. No monsters." He tugged on her hands, drawing her into his arms. "Trust me."

"I do.

She trusted him completely. But how could she ever trust anyone else?

"We should find a place to bed down."

Diana looked up at the sky—still a strange shade of murky grey from the smoke that lingered in the air, even after the hard storm, but that grey shone pink and purple with the sunlight behind it. The mountain above them was a bare, still smoldering desolation, nothing but scattered black spikes that had once been mighty, ancient trees.

They'd slept in their little cave and awoken to a muddy, charred landscape. Now, well past noon, Diana was much farther down the mountain than she'd been since the end of the world. They hadn't seen any people, but they'd seen signs that other people had passed through.

She didn't like the thought of sleeping out in the open here, where they might be set upon by monsters. The Rennies scared her, but she trusted Gus, and he'd promised her they'd be safe there. It was the only place she could conceive of going, and she didn't want to stop until they'd gotten there.

"Already? We've got a few hours before dark yet."

Gus nodded. "If we pushed it, we could probably make it to the Shire today, but it would be past sunset, and I don't want to come up on them in the dark."

They were nowhere near a town or any homes that she could see, and when she tried to search her memory, reach back to the world before and see the trip to the cabin as it had been when her father had driven the Land Rover up, she hit a vast, empty black space. The world below had disappeared.

"We'd have to stay outside again." Since she'd reached the cabin after the Sunstorm, she'd only spent a handful of nights away from it—and none in years. She'd known what to do, where to go after the storm, how to survive—but not down here. Not with people. Away from them. She'd survived because she'd been away.

Stepping right in front of her, blocking her fretful view of the way down, Gus cupped his hands around her face. "Diana, it'll be okay. We'll find a sheltered spot we can defend, and we won't build a fire. If anybody comes up on us, we'll be ready. I did this for a long time. I can keep us safe."

Buddy jumped up then, on full alert, and a second later, Diana heard the rustle of heavy feet moving through drifts of trees. Gus heard it, too, and they both turned, drawing their weapons.

Diana saw who was coming and dropped her axe. "Shrek!"

Buddy jumped forward and ran toward the staggering bear.

"Bud, no!" Gus grabbed Diana's arm. "Are you sure?"

"I raised him from a cub. I know him! Buddy knows him!"

He dropped his hand, and Diana ran. She stopped several yards away, so she didn't make him wary, but she was close enough to see that he was hurt. The fur on his back end had burned away and left raw skin.

He and Buddy snuffled a greeting, and then the bear turned to Diana and made a grunting groan. A plea.

"Okay, baby. Come here. Let me see. Gus, I need some meat and water." They didn't have much to spare, but she'd go thirsty and hungry for a day and give Shrek her portion.

Shrek hadn't fully committed to Gus yet; he'd hibernated through most of the months she'd had a family at the cabin, so Gus was still almost a stranger. The bear kept a suspicious eye on the man as Gus brought food and water.

Diana poured water on the bear's tongue, and he lapped it greedily, then snapped up a piece of jerky. "Here, you feed him," she said to Gus, handing the food and water back. "I want to check him out."

The burn on his back end was large, covering most of the right side of his rump, but the skin was mostly intact—first- and second-degree burns, with a few open sores, the largest of which was about the size of her fist. She had enough first aid supplies in her ready pack, including her homemade salve.

He was shifting back and forth on all his paws, though, so when he took his weight off the leg she was near, she caught it and lifted it—the pads were burned away, leaving raw, bloody, muddy meat. "Oh, baby boy."

As she walked around his rear to check his other back paw, he made that plaintive grunt again and turned his head to huff at her.

"I know it hurts. I'll be careful." That paw was burned, too.

All four of his paws were raw meat. Diana stood at his head and scratched his ear, the one with the thick notch in it, and turned her mind to the problem. There had to be something she could do for him.

"Maybe I can use the emergency blanket to wrap his feet." She had a shiny silver blanket in her ready pack, a holdout from the family earthquake preparedness kit, when that had been the worst crisis they could imagine. "But I don't know if he'll be able to get where he needs to go if his feet are covered with that."

"I have an idea," Gus said and went back to their packs. Diana followed, leading Shrek with a hand on his neck. The bear came docilely with her, and Buddy trotted at his side.

With Gus's ingenuity and Diana's first aid supplies, they fashioned pad-size bandages of duct tape, emergency blanket, and homemade antiseptic salve. Shrek lay quietly and let them tend to him, only swiping halfheartedly a few times, when they found an especially sore spot.

The bear lay with them as the sun set and shared a meal with them in the dark. When they curled up against the shelter of redwood deadfall, Shrek was still with him.

He left in the first strands of dawn light. Diana woke and watched him amble off, heartbroken but relieved. The duct-tape bandages would wear off eventually, but by then maybe new skin would have grown. He'd felt well enough to walk away, and he was better off on his own, away from the people they were about to join.

She knew she wouldn't see him again, not in the world below.

Diana knew when they'd gotten close to people. Gus's posture and attention changed, his body pulling inward subtly as his eyes sharpened and scanned their surroundings constantly. And he was quiet, speaking rarely. The calm demeanor he'd taken on at the cabin was gone; he must have been like this as a wanderer—watchful and terse.

Buddy, too, seemed to remember the dangers of this world and kept himself close. Diana followed the lead of their experience, and they moved down the road in a tense knot.

They didn't see anyone, though—and few signs that people had passed recently. Not until a rough fence rose up in the distance ahead, along the side of a road that had gone straight, rolling downward in a ribbon.

"That's it," Gus said, visibly relaxing. "That's the Shire. It's still here!" They picked up their pace, but kept a wary watch until they neared the fence and could see it clearly.

The fence was made of bark-covered poles carved to points at the top, like an old Army fort from pioneer days. Men stood behind it, their heads and shoulders above the pointed poles, obviously standing on a sentry walk. They bore old-fashioned crossbows like Gus's, and they wore simple cotton lawn tunics, the kind Diana remembered seeing everywhere at Ren Faires—the kind she'd owned, in fact, to wear under her peasant dress or her pirate costume.

Gus had told her about meeting 'the Rennies,' and the way they lived as if in the Middle Ages.

As they approached, all three crossbows were aimed at them.

"Hang tight. I don't know these guys," he muttered. He put up his hands up and faced the guards. "I come in peace, friends. I was here about a year ago. You offered me and Buddy here your hospitality. We're in need of it again."

"You say we let you in?" The nearest guard, broad-shouldered and black-bearded, asked.

"Yes. Buddy and I had a fine meal at your fire."

"Who d'you know here?"

"Sarah. Howard. Danny. And more." He rattled off the names at once, then turned his back to the fence and looked back over his shoulder. "Howard gave me the crossbow."

The guards conferred, then one of the other guards disappeared behind the fence, and the black-bearded guard turned back. "Hold. We're going for Sarah."

While they stood on the road with their hands up, with crossbows aimed at them, Diana stared at the guards. She'd seen no other human but Gus in more than two years, and she found them fascinating and terrifying. What was to say that they wouldn't simply shoot them? Why was putting their hands in the air enough to keep the bolts in their crossbows? Was that social compact still in place here?

No, it couldn't be. In seven years, only Gus had been trustworthy. Every other human being she'd encountered had been a monster. They'd hurt her. They'd killed her only friend. They'd tried to take everything from her.

But now she had nothing left to take.

No, she had Gus and Buddy. They could still take them.

As her mind began to skid on the ice of those thoughts, Diana let her arm rise, and she reached back for her axe. She'd lost her home, but she wouldn't lose her family.

"Diana, no," Gus barked under his breath. "Easy, easy. Please, honey. It's okay. Trust me."

At his last words, Diana took a deep breath, and her mind found its traction. She let her hand slide back into place, still raised, waiting. "I'm scared."

"I know, honey. But we're okay."

A grey head rose up behind the fence, and an old woman squinted down at them. "Gus! Glad to see you well and strong. Your wandering has brought you in a circle, I see. And you've picked up a friend on the journey."

"Hi, Sarah." Gus dropped his hands, and so did Diana. "This is Diana. We'd be grateful for your help, if you can spare the offer."

"Never turn down a friend in need, lest you have need of your own some day." She nodded at the black-bearded guard, and she and he dropped behind the fence. The gate opened.

Sarah met them at the gateway and offered open arms to Gus. "Those of us whose lives you saved are still in your debt, my friend," she said as Gus hugged her.

She bent low and greeted Buddy — who welcomed her attention as if he remembered her — before she stood straight again and smiled at Diana. "And welcome. We are glad to have you as well."

Sarah didn't offer Diana a hug, or a hand, and she was relieved. Her mind shouted at her, too many thoughts to comprehend any of them. Inside the fence was a town — a community, a whole world — full of people and animals, work and play. Even standing here at the entrance, the bustle terrified and overwhelmed her, and she took an unwitting step back toward the road.

Gus caught her with an arm around her shoulders. The sting of his skin on hers, crisped from the heat of the forest fire, brought her back and honed her focus. "This is Diana. She's been up at the top of the mountain since the Sunstorm. She's not so used to people."

The old woman named Sarah nodded sagely. "I understand. This is a safe haven, Diana." She gave her that steely squint again, then turned it on Gus. "You came from up the mountain? You were in the fire, then."

"Yeah," Gus answered. "Barely made it out. We lost everything."

"No, you didn't. You saved each other."

"Yeah, you're right. Everything that matters."

Diana felt Gus's lips on her cheek. She turned and found a question in his eyes. Afraid or unsure of any options, and without the strength to speak, Diana gave him her answer with the tiny smile she could muster, and

Gus turned back to Sarah. "Sarah, we'd like to stay now, if you'd have us."

"Come on," Sarah said, stepping back. "We'll get you fed and rested, and we'll talk."

Gus took a strong hold of Diana's hand, both reassuring and directive, and drew her forward, into the Shire.

The gate creaked closed behind them.

Twenty-Three

Inside the fence, what had clearly been a cabin motel — several cheap log cabins of different sizes scattered around, following a gravel lane, with a log cabin office and manager suite in the center, OFFICE sign still showing — had become more like a medieval English village. For every person wearing jeans and a t-shirt, there were two in tunic and breeches, or in long peasant dresses.

Folded in among the log cabins were other buildings, more roughly built, that seemed to be like shops, or maybe other little cottages, or maybe both. There were so many *people*, doing so many *things*. This world was loud and chaotic, and Diana's brain tore around inside her skull, seeking somewhere safe and quiet and familiar.

There was only Gus and Buddy. Only they felt right.

With both hands clamped around Gus's hand, Diana let him lead her forward, deep into this terrifying new world, following Sarah. Buddy trotted along with them, veering off suddenly when another dog barked.

The sound startled Diana, and she jumped. Gus squeezed his hand more tightly around her fingers and sent her a smile to reassure her. It didn't work.

She watched Buddy run to meet a black and white dog who stood in the middle of the compound. They sniffed at each other carefully, then began to play. Buddy knew that dog. Gus knew the people. Buddy knew the people, too.

Diana was the only stranger here, among all these strangers.

She didn't know what to do or what to think. For more than seven years, she'd known what to expect from other people, and what to do when she encountered them: protect herself. Only Gus had been safe, and Buddy was the only reason she hadn't killed him on sight.

So she clung to Gus and tried to find comfort in his comfort here, and in Buddy's.

Sarah led them behind the building with the OFFICE sign, where a large, rough shed stood. Two women and a man worked inside, and Diana realized quickly that it was like a dry, outdoor kitchen, with bins of food and cooking supplies. The people working weren't cooking, but they were preparing the supplies. The man was grinding some kind of grain into flour, using a wooden grinder with a metal crank. Diana felt a spike of envy make a path through the unfocused noise of her mind: she'd been grinding grain with a homemade mortar and pestle.

The women sorted greens into bins, chatting as they worked. The man and the older woman wore old-fashioned clothes, both in breeches and tunics, though the woman wore hiking boots.

"Cammie, honey?" Sarah asked, setting her leathery, age-spotted hand on the younger woman's shoulder. She was dressed very like Sarah, and like Diana, too: jeans, t-shirt, flannel. She turned, and Sarah said, "This is Gus and Diana. Gus visited us last year. Put together something for them to eat, please. I'm going to talk to Dennis and find them a place to bed down for the night."

"Yes, ma'am," Cammie answered with a smile and a nod.

Sarah focused on Gus. "I'll be back, and we'll sit for a while and talk. You two keep together, okay?"

"Thanks, Sarah." Gus tugged lightly on Diana's hands, and she took a step closer, so that they were in full contact.

With a nod, the old woman was gone, and they were left in the smiling company of Cammie. The other woman eyed them suspiciously over her shoulder, and the man offered only a curt nod, but Cammie seemed genuinely friendly. Holding Gus's hand, Diana wanted to trust that friendliness, but she could only trust Gus.

"Hi. I can make you a tomato sandwich, if you'd like—we've got plenty of greens, and a brown mustard that Jerry makes. And there's still some fresh milk from breakfast, if you'd like that to drink. Or water, of course."

Milk? They had milk? What kind? It didn't matter. *They had milk.* Diana tried to speak, but her mouth wouldn't work.

Another reassuring squeeze from Gus. "Sandwiches and milk sounds like manna from heaven, Cammie. Thank you."

"Of course. Why don't you go ahead and have a seat over there"—she indicated a common meeting area, like a town square, with tidy rows of simple wood tables and a cluster of stumps around a large fire ring surrounded by neatly place stones—"and we'll bring it right over."

"Many thanks, Cammie."

Gus led Diana away from the kitchen and sat her down on a stump. They were alone there, to a reasonable extent. People moved around them, going about their business, eyeing the strangers on the way, but no one stopped to interact.

Gus crouched before her, still holding her hand. She still had both of hers wrapped around his. "Hey. You doing okay?"

She tried to speak, and finally could only shrug. Buddy trotted over, finished with his dog play, and sat on the ground at her side. She unwound one hand from Gus so she could pet the dog.

"I won't let you get hurt, Diana. These are friends."

It wasn't that she was afraid they were monsters, exactly. She did trust Gus, and she did recognize the welcome they'd received. She couldn't stop being wary, but she wanted to relax.

There were just so *many* of them. There was so *much* going on. "Too many," she pushed out through her knotted throat.

She could see that he understood, and Diana felt a fraction of ease. "Just stick with me. I'll be your people shield. Okay?"

"Yes. Love you."

He grinned. "Love you right back."

"GUS!" An enormous mountain of a man charged up, and Diana flinched so hard she almost fell backward off her stump seat, and would have if Gus hadn't been holding her.

Gus stood up and let go of her hand. "Howard! Good to see you." The two men hugged, and then the mountain named Howard crouched down to give Buddy a greeting as well.

He smiled at Diana. "Milady."

"This is Diana. Di, this is Howard. He's a very good guy. And a blacksmith. He made my crossbow."

Howard held out his hand. After a second's inner turmoil, Diana forced her hand forward and let him grip it in a palm made of granite. He bowed over it and said, again, "Milady."

Somehow, that helped. She could almost feel that he was decent simply in the touch of his skin on hers. She managed a smile, and he returned it. The expression was remarkably kind on his wide, thickly bearded face.

"Sarah says you've been up on the mountain alone ever since the lights went out."

She nodded.

He said nothing more about it, but he gave her hand a lingering squeeze before he let it go.

"Didn't think we'd see you again, friend," he said to Gus. "I thought you were for the coast."

"Had a little mishap on the way, met Diana when she helped me," he turned and smiled at her, "and then the coast just wasn't that interesting anymore."

Howard nodded. "Family. That's all you got to get to, and then you're there. Well, I'm glad you found your way back here. And you want to stay, I hear?"

"If you'll have us, yeah."

"You got my vote." He slapped Gus's back hard enough to make him take a step, then noticed the axe

Diana had leaned against her backpack when she'd sat down.

"That axe—"

Diana gripped the handle, suddenly suspicious again.

"That's yours?"

She nodded.

"That's my brother's work—that's Doug's mark."

"I knew it!" Gus crowed. "She bought it at a Ren Faire. I thought maybe it was one of yours."

"Don't you talk, sweetheart? It's okay if you don't."

Again, Diana opened her mouth and tried. Gus didn't jump in, so she tried again. "S'hard," she managed.

Howard's head moved as if he understood completely, more than a simple nod. A whole essay of empathy. "Lot of new stuff going on, I guess. No worries. We're all a band of oddballs, anyway. Well, I gotta get back to work. Sarah's working on getting you squared away for the night, at least." He offered his hand to Gus. "I'm glad you made your way back."

"Thanks, man," Gus shook. "Me, too."

After a good meal—the milk was goat, from the Shire's small herd, and to Diana's palate, it was almost too rich and fresh to be enjoyed—Sarah came for them and led them to a wood-framed tent. "If you stay with us, we'll all help you build up a hut. In the meanwhile, this'll keep you. It's summer storage, but I had some of the young ones make it up for resting. There's a few buckets of good clean water in there—it's not hot, but it'll get you clean, and maybe the cool'll feel good after what you've been through. There's clothes, too—I'm sorry, but it's Rennie garb. If that's not your bent, and you stay, we can try to get you fitted out more comfortably. But breeches are easier to make than jeans, is what it comes to."

"You ..." the word was out before Diana's addled brain knew it was coming, and its passage left the way open for the rest. "... make your own cloth?"

Sarah's broad smile warmed the air around them. "We do, yes. We traded some weapons for a few sheep, and we've got a spinner and a couple of knitters. I'm a weaver. You'll see a lot of people in patchwork, but nobody's cold or uncovered. We keep everything, no matter how broken or worn out, so we manage to make new out of old every day."

"How'd Aidan do with his light bulb?" Gus asked, and Diana turned to him, shocked. Power? They had power?

But Sarah let out a sigh with a shake of her head. "He's made three bulbs and bases, and they give light for about five minutes a crank. They help a little, but the materials he needs aren't easy to find, and without a real power source, it's not much. He and Howard have been working on a bigger crank for more power, and Aid's still working on the bulbs, too." She pulled back the flap on the tent. "When you're ready, I'll be up in the central cabin, and we can talk."

Gus took the flap from her, and she strolled off.

Diana stood at the front of the tent and scanned the Shire again. From here at the back, it seemed even busier. Here was where people worked: she saw Howard at an anvil, and realized she'd been hearing the *clang-clang-clang* of hammer on metal; she saw Cammie and the others in the kitchen. Off to the side, tucked in among the trees, was the mixed flock of goats and sheep. Across the way, three women, all in cotton dresses and long braids, sat before a bare-wood hut, knitting — and watching Diana and Gus.

When Diana faced them and stared back, one of the women tipped her head in a cautious greeting. Diana returned it.

"Come on, honey. Let's have some time to ourselves here." Gus tugged lightly on her braid, and she turned and went in with him to the tent. Buddy followed on her heel.

Most of the tent was stacked with baskets and wooden bins, but there was a roomy sleeping pallet of linens, cushions and furs, a few bins and baskets of clothes and towels — and two big buckets full of clear water.

Buddy ran to the closest bucket and took a long, sloppy drink, his tail wagging in time with his slurps.

Gus stood before her and framed her face with his hands. "Can you talk to me?"

Closed in alone in the snug tent, her throat loosened and her chest lost its burden. Diana nodded, then smiled as she realized the irony in the gesture. "Yes. Here, I can. I'm sorry."

"Don't be sorry. I want to help. I guess it's hard to be around all the people."

Again, she nodded. "Only monsters before."

"I don't know everybody here, but they're not monsters, hon. I feel like I can promise that. They wouldn't let monsters stay."

"I know. I just … don't know how to be. I don't know this place." She'd had a home, a place to make a life. She'd worked hard to make it. But the universe had eaten that life just as it had the first. The trauma and fear of the past couple of days landed on Diana's shoulders all at once, and her knees gave with the force. "It's all gone. God, it's all gone."

Gus clutched her close and tucked her face against his neck. "Not all of it. You still have me and Bud. We're together, and we made it here. We can make a different kind of home here."

"If they'll let us stay." They were dependent on others, on people she didn't know. Diana didn't know how to rely on strangers. Even in the world before, she'd hated it, not having that control over her own life. Could she stay here, among all the people, and become one of them?

"I think they will. But if they don't, we're still together, and we'll work it out. We'll go west, to the coast, like I'd planned before I met you. It's supposed to be better there." He shrugged her head off his chest and smiled. "Okay? Trust me?"

On the mountain she'd trusted him, but she hadn't had to depend on him. She'd known how to live alone. Down here, she didn't have the first clue how to live. She would need to trust him to take care of her. All the promises he'd made to take care of her and keep her safe, now they were more than love words. Now she had to believe them.

Did she?

Had she any other choice?

"I trust you."

Gus bent his head and rested his forehead on hers, and for that moment, at least, Diana felt safe.

"Here in the Shire, we work like a family. That was how it was in the old world and in this. Just like a family, we don't all get along all the time, but we all take care of each other, and we're all working to keep our home and each other strong. Toward that, everybody does what they can, and everybody takes what they need." Sarah sat back in one of the fake-leather armchairs that must have once made up the little lobby area in the motel office. "So to bring you before the community for a vote, I need to know what you can do, how you'll pull your weight."

She fixed her eyes on Diana as she finished her sentence. Gus had jumped in to speak for her several times during the day, but he stayed quiet now. He understood, as Diana did, that Sarah would only be satisfied to hear her speak for herself.

He looked good, dressed in a loose pair of brown pants and a plain, not-quite-white tunic. The contours of his strong body showed against the thin weave of the fabric, and the deep notch at the base of his throat, a feature Diana had always found especially compelling, lay inside a split at the neckline. He looked like he belonged here.

For her part, she hadn't worn a dress in so many years that she felt half naked in this simple blue shift. In the world before, she might have owned a dress just like this, and worn it in a place not much different from this, when she road-tripped to the mountains to spend the weekend pretending to live in the distant past. In a world where there was the luxury of leisure and fantasy, where one could imagine that the past had been a simpler time.

Diana plucked at the nubs in the weave of the dress. She was still wary — no, she was afraid. Was this what she wanted? To live in this place, among all these strangers? So close to the world that had been?

No, it wasn't. She couldn't have what she wanted. The fire had taken it. Now, if she was going to live, she would have to do it here, in the world of strangers and monsters. She knew nothing of this world, but Gus said that here was the best place. He wanted to stay. So she would stay.

"I …" Her voice died before the single syllable of that word could finish. She cleared her throat and tried again. "I can …" What could she do? How could she be of use? "I can hunt. Cook. Fish." She couldn't think of anything else. Except: "Work hard."

When she finished, neither Sarah nor Gus spoke. The air in the little office, which was still set up like an office and seemed to be still in use as such, went still and thick with waiting. But Diana didn't know what more to say. She felt like she had to validate her existence, and she didn't understand what of her was of value in this world.

Eventually, Gus said, "She's selling herself short." His eyes met Diana's, and she saw a hint of impatience sparking in their depths. "May I?"

With a shrug and a nod, she gave him her voice.

"Diana can do almost everything. She's a dead aim with a bow, and she can field dress a deer faster than anyone else I've seen. She's good with all manner of blades. She can brain-tan hides. She kept a lush garden from seeds she harvested, she kept a worm farm for fishing. She built her own smokehouse, a chicken coop, a fence around her garden. She's the best damn scavenger I've ever known, with a keen eye for what's of use. She kept her cabin going almost as if the Sunstorm didn't happen, all by herself, for six years. And she's as tough a fighter as any you have here. The only thing I haven't seen her do is knit."

"Couldn't find needles," she muttered, and Sarah laughed — she tossed her head back and opened her mouth and laughed hard, clapping her hands together in delight.

Diana didn't understand whether she'd been deemed hilarious or ridiculous.

When she'd reclaimed herself, but still smiling, Sarah asked, "Is that true, dear?"

"Yes. I can't knit."

Sarah's smile went wide and bright again. "But the rest — you can do all that?"

"Yes."

"And how did you get such a vast collection of skills?"

"Books. People left them behind. I took them and read them. I practiced. I learned." A bleak, painful recollection rose up before her eyes. "They're gone now."

Gus reached for her hand, and she wove her fingers with his. The image of her loss receded.

Sarah's smile receded, too; she stared hard at Diana with small eyes framed in the creases of lifelong sunshine and good humor. Their diluted blue was of the sky in a watercolor painting, lovely and abstract.

"You're resourceful and strong. It sounds like you can be of use wherever we have need."

Diana nodded. "I'll do whatever I can."

"And you, Gus? I know you're a strong fighter, and we always have need of that. The Fiends still pester us. Is there more that you can offer?"

Gus shook his head. "Nothing special, for this world. I'm a decent carpenter, and I'm good with a crossbow. I know a bit of the world— I was a wanderer for the first six years after the storm. I started in Manhattan and walked west. So I've got some knowledge about what's beyond the Sierras to the east. But Diana is the asset between us." His mouth twisted in a rueful shadow of a smile. "I was a violinist before. Not much call for that now."

"He sells himself short, too," Diana told Sarah. She squeezed his fingers, thinking of the violin he'd loved so much, how carefully he'd tended it, the beautiful music he'd made. Gus, too, had built a home and a life at the cabin, and had lost it in the fire.

"I know he does. I've seen him fight, and I've seen him make friends. A lorekeeper is important in a world like this. Somebody who can talk and listen and remember, somebody who knows the world beyond our fence. And somebody who remembers the old world enough to step in and help strangers. Somebody like that is good counsel for us all. You'd both be assets here in the Shire. It has to go to a vote, but I will speak strongly for you both."

Diana sat on the sleeping pallet and stroked Buddy's belly. Gus slept quietly at her side, on his belly. The covers slanted over his ass, and the pale moonglow through the open top of the tent carved shadows around the powerful contours of his strong back. With his arms crossed under his head and his dark hair trailing back over his pillow, he looked like a god in repose.

The sensation of his body on hers, inside hers, the suck of his mouth, the weight of him, the fullness of him and the mingled wet of them, yet lingered. It was a moment she especially enjoyed, lying wakeful after sex, her body clinging to the memory of their pleasure, the silken strands of that memory winding around older memories, awful ones, and throttling them into oblivion.

But here, in this place, those old memories fought back against the new, tried to drag themselves to the front of her mind.

Around this snug little tent, the air in the Shire rattled with noise, even so late at night. Hushed conversations and not-so-hushed, snoring sleepers, vocal lovers. The tramp and shuffle of guards on patrol. The occasional sleepy bleat from the herd, penned and watched by Eddie, the border collie Buddy loved.

So many sounds. So much life. It made Diana's skin creep and prickle. Every noise that was different from the world she'd made sent up a new shock of alarm; neither her mind nor her body could accept that she might be safe around so many people. There had to be monsters here. How could there not be?

But this was their home now. They'd been welcomed, accepted. Wholeheartedly.

If it was a trap, Gus would have seen it. Right?

"Diana?"

She looked over her shoulder and saw Gus watching her through sleepy eyes, his head now turned toward her. "Hi."

"Can't sleep?"

"Loud."

He listened for a few seconds to the quiet murmur of a town at rest, then nodded and held out his arm to her. "C'mere."

Glad to take comfort from him always, she tucked herself into his embrace. He shifted to his side, and she nestled her head against the tattoo on his chest, his dog so like Fiona. From the moment she'd met him, that image had been a touchstone, a sign to show her that she was safe with him.

"This is a good place, honey."

She trusted him. So she would believe him.

Twenty-Four

"No, sweetheart. Like this." Daddy wrapped his big hand around her little one and made the pole in their shared grip shake. The little red and white ball at the end of her fishing string danced in the water. "If you make it move around, the fish will notice your worm."

She'd felt bad about hurting the little worm. Worms were icky and slimy, but when Daddy had helped her push the hook into it, some goop had squished out, and she thought it probably hurt to have its insides squish out.

"You feel that?" Daddy asked, and Diana tried to think with her hands. It was like something was pulling. "Look!"

Diana looked to the water and saw her bobber go under. That meant that a fish wanted her worm.

"Remember what to do now?"

She nodded, because she remembered.

"Okay – quick, before he finishes his snack!"

She gave her fishing pole a sharp jerk and then lifted it until the end of the string came out of the water. There was a little fish hanging off the end, shimmering rainbows in the sunshine. The things on its side fluttered open and closed. That was how the fish breathed.

"Good job, Di!" Daddy helped her swing the line in. He caught the fish and laid it across his palm. He gave her a tight, one-armed hug. Even his half-hugs were perfect. "You caught a catfish!"

Diana giggled at that. What a silly name for a fish. It didn't look like a cat at all. Except it had whiskers.

"I want to show Grammie and Big Pa. And Mommy, too." Mommy probably wouldn't give her a hug, but Diana didn't want to leave her out.

"Okay. Let me get a picture first, though. Your first fish – that's a big deal!"

Daddy aimed the camera, and Diana grinned into the sun, holding her fishing pole in one hand and the string with the catfish in the other.

"Her name is Lisa! I'm going to keep her forever!" She ran off toward the cabin, to show her family her new fish.

Diana roused from the dreaming memory of her young self, running through tall grass toward the family cabin, dangling her little catfish before her. She tried to fall back into the dream, to see her father save the fish, but the morning light shone through her eyelids. The time for dreaming was over.

Before the melancholy of remembered loss took her over, as she brought in the deep breath of first waking, she felt Gus's beard on her bare shoulder, and his touch brushed the sadness away, leaving only the soft shape of the happy memory.

He'd trimmed his beard not long after they'd arrived at the Shire, so that it was still full but just skimmed his jawline, and he'd kept it neatly since. Without the heavy bush of beard, he was even more handsome than she'd known. So handsome that the woman she'd been in the world before would never have made eye contact with him.

"Good morning." His low voice rolled against her ear. "You were dreaming. You okay?"

"Mm-hm. It was a good dream. A good memory." She turned her head and found his mouth waiting. He pushed his tongue between her lips, and she caught a handful of his long hair and held him close.

Just as she began to roll toward him, and enjoy a more rousing morning greeting, Buddy shoved his cold, wet nose against her side.

She jumped at the chill and broke their kiss. "I think Buddy's ready to get moving."

"Buddy knows how to let himself out if he has business. Otherwise, he can wait." Gus pushed her to her back and moved over her, making a trail of kisses from her neck to her breast. He sucked her nipple into his mouth, and the surge of sensation pulled Diana's eyelids closed.

"Good morning," she whispered as her pulse found and matched the tempo of his mouth. She tangled her hands in Gus's hair and forgot about everything else.

There were always things to be done at the Shire. Every day was busy for all the hours of light. Just as it had been at the cabin. There was a comfortable familiarity to the shape of the routines here.

At first, Diana had worked wherever there was need of her, but by the time she'd begun to feel relaxed even when Gus wasn't near, she'd taken on a primary job at the garden. Darlene, the woman who'd started the garden, had taken ill and become too weak to manage the work. She had some helpers, but Diana had a knack for growing things and long experience. She'd made a couple of suggestions for improving the yield, and when they'd turned out well, Darlene had passed control of the growing to her.

She still sat in the sun by the fence every day and threw her two cents all over the place, however.

"Here. Bring those beans to me. Might as well string 'em while I'm sittin' on me bum." Darlene was one among the Rennies who'd made this world livable by turning it into the past. She wore peasant garb and spoke with a broad, probably not very authentic, accent which might have been Scottish or Northern English. Or Welsh, for all Diana knew.

Diana didn't need to wear a rough dress to know they lived in the past. She was comfortable in jeans, and she'd found a few pairs that fit her. But she understood why Darlene and the others like her were happier in their imaginations. From this vantage at the bottom, she could look up at the blackened spears of the decimated mountain forest and understand that she, too, had been living in a fantasy. Her world above the world.

Shooing a little group of nosy chickens away from the garden fence, Diana carried the basket of beans to Darlene and handed it over. "Save the strings and greens. Elsie wants them for a paste or tonic or something she's making."

Darlene nodded, but Diana saw, or thought she saw, a twitch at her mouth and a shadow at her eyes. A little bit of nostalgia, maybe, for a world where medicine and healing had been more than potions and tonics and poultices.

It was pretty obvious that what had made Darlene so ill, what was killing her, was cancer. Not long before Gus, Diana, and Buddy had arrived, she'd developed a lump under her arm. In the weeks that Diana had known her, it had grown so large that her arm stuck out oddly, resting on what was clearly a tumor. Darlene had once been heavy, even years after the Sunstorm, but now her skin hung on her in loose sheets.

A few others were ill, and in her weeks here, Diana had learned that the Shire had lost members to similar growths and wasting illnesses. Not many, not so much as a plague or even a crisis, but enough that they'd taken notice. Other illnesses took people, too, of course. A world without antibiotics was a deadly world. But there were more tumors and bloody coughs and stools than would have been normal in a group this size, in the world before.

Diana herself had developed a heavy cough and a low fever the second week at the Shire and scared Gus so much she'd worried about his sanity. But she'd gotten better and had felt well since. Elsie had deemed her healthy and decided that it was just her body getting used to being around so many people and their germs after all her years alone. That made sense, and she'd convinced Gus of its logic.

He'd worried that her illness had been a first sign of cancer. He believed that most people would eventually die of that disease, brought on by the meltdown of nuclear reactors. Diana didn't remember her limited medical study enough to know if he might be right. Could radiation still be a problem, seven years after its release? Unlikely. However, no matter the condition of the air now, there were types of cancers that moved slowly, that lay in wait for years before some obscure factor triggered their metastasis.

Maybe he was right. He'd obviously been right about fertility. There were only three young children in the Shire, and two of them had obvious birth defects — a girl whose fingers had never separated, leaving her with hands like paddles, and a boy with profound cognitive impairment. The third, a healthy, pretty blonde baby still young enough for her mother to wear in a sling, was treated in the community like a child savior.

For her own part, Diana's menses had all but stopped. Every now and then, she'd have a day or two, maybe three, of light spotting, so light she didn't need to bother with it. Other than that, it had been well more than a year since she'd had a real period, and several years since she'd had anything like a trackable cycle.

More to the point, she and Gus had never tried to prevent pregnancy.

Gus believed the human race was dying because it couldn't replicate itself. On the mountain, Diana hadn't thought much about whether he were right or wrong. On the mountain, in their own little world, it hadn't mattered. But here, amongst others, she could look around and see that he was right.

As Darlene plucked at green beans with bony hands that looked much older than they should, Diana turned and surveyed the garden of the Shire. Lush lettuces, ruffled kale, fluffs of spinach. Fuzzy carrot tops. Curlicues of vines for beans and squashes, cucumbers and zucchinis, winding elegantly around their wooden guides, showing pearly buds of new growth. The pungent fragrance of tomato plants, hung with bulbous fruits that looked nothing like the uniform balls in the grocery bins of the old world but tasted ten times better. Tall stalks of corn—the ears multicolored, red and blue and orange mixed in with white and yellow, like the maize of the oldest world. She was knee-deep in lush new growth, in the promise of life.

The world would live on without people.

That was the story of the Sunstorm. Not the end of the world. A cataclysm, but not the apocalypse. Simply the end of the human era. Humans were breathtakingly arrogant to think the world would end when they did. Try as they might—and they had tried hard—they weren't strong enough to defeat the planet. They'd behaved like frat boys on a spring break bender, and the earth was just shrugging them off.

Ice had taken the dinosaurs, and sun would take the people.

There would be another era. Maybe the next intelligent beings who evolved would do better. Maybe they would evolve a conscience with their consciousness.

Their cabin in the Shire would have fit comfortably in the main room of the mountain cabin they'd lost. It had no kitchen, no bathroom, no loft. The people of the Shire took their meals together, they shared the place for washing, and they took care of their bodies' other business in a tidily kept latrine at the back of the compound.

The cabins that had been part of the motel had bathrooms and kitchenettes, but those didn't work, and the larger cabins had more than one family in them. Diana preferred the tiny cabin that they'd built in the first days after their welcome to the Shire.

They had no bed yet, or chairs. Only a lot of furs and cushions and blankets, a low, wide square table that she had made, and three small tables made of tree trunks. A tiny metal stove, forged by Howard and Doug, would keep them warm in the winter nights. They had two candle lanterns and a kind of bureau Gus had made, which was simply a tall frame to fit wooden bins like drawers. Everything they possessed fit into those bins and two woven baskets.

But the cabin had two windows, one of which faced the woods, and a little covered porch. The sleeping pallet was comfortable and snug. It was their private place, and the best parts of each day were the first moments of morning — when she woke under the covers with her man and her dog, and she and Gus talked about their day to come, or didn't talk and found even better things to do — and the last moments of the night, when the Shire had gone into its noisy quiet of the sleeping hours, and she and Gus talked while they undressed, or didn't talk while they undressed each other, and eventually fell asleep wound together, with Buddy curled among their legs.

This snug cabin, redolent with the scent of fresh-cut pine, the place where only she and Gus and Buddy belonged — it was home, and curled together with them in the snug little nest in which they slept, Diana felt swaddled in love and belonging. She felt safe.

But when it was empty, it felt lonely and bare, and three times its size. Diana found reasons to stay away from the cabin when Gus wasn't near — or she'd sit on the porch with a book. There'd been a few books in the Shire when they'd arrived, but Diana had made it a mission to scavenge for more both times she'd gone out with the scavenge group. Even when she hadn't gone out to scavenge, she was collecting books — the others had started to bring them back to her.

She'd begun to think she might someday start a library, here in the Shire.

Gus was out on a scavenge mission, late one afternoon, and Diana had run out of things to be done. She hated when he was away from the Shire without her, and her mind still liked to dig itself into a hole when she got stressed, so to keep it occupied, she read. She sat on the step of their little porch and read a copy of *Magician*, by Raymond Feist, that she'd borrowed from Doug — a story she'd read several times in the world before. Buddy lay on her feet, exhausted, his paws still muddy from playing in the stream behind the compound.

Then he sat up, his tail dragging happily across the gravel, and Diana glanced up from the page. Sarah strode toward them, carrying a basket over her arm. Sarah dressed in modern clothes, but she most often wore her long, moon-grey hair in an old-fashioned wreath of braids. With the reed basket over her arm in that way, it was the jeans that seemed out of time.

"Hi," Diana said and closed the book. "What's up?"

"Scoot." Sarah waved her hand, and Diana scooted over on the porch so she could sit. She dug into the basket, pulled out a large ball of soft, newly spun wool, and handed it over.

"What's this?" She could see the different threads woven through the new skein. Nancy, their spinner, unraveled knitted goods that had worn beyond repair and recycled their threads into new ones. Some of the resulting amalgams were quite lovely. This skein was creamy with sparks of red and yellow and bright white.

Sarah produced another skein of a different blend of colors, and then two sets of knitting needles. She smiled. "I thought I'd teach you to knit. Then you'll know how to do everything."

Diana laughed and set her book aside. "Sounds like fun."

"I don't know what happened." Diana glared at the spot in her knitting that looked like the start of a runner in a pair of tights. They'd been knitting together, and chatting about the Shire — gossiping, really, but without malice — as the sun turned its sleepy shades of red. Diana had knitted nearly a foot of what might be a scarf — what would be a scarf, for Gus — and she'd been proud of herself for how quickly she'd developed this new skill. But now there was a hole.

Sarah glanced over. "You dropped a stitch. Here, just knit back and fill it in. Watch." She held up her own piece, twice as long as Diana's, and made a few stitches. "See? I dropped that stitch a couple back." The needles clacked as she speedily knitted the rest of the row, then another, and part of another, and Diana saw a similar fault in the pattern. Sarah stopped and pulled out another kind of needle. 'This is for crocheting, but it's great for this. Watch." She turned the piece over, hooked the smaller, hooked needle through the fault, clacked with her knitting needles again, and the fault was gone. "Now you try."

Diana had survived on her own on the mountain because she was a strong visual and kinesthetic learner. If she could see something done, envision her body doing the same work, then she could do it in reality. She'd watched Sarah closely, feeling the ghosts of the needles and wool on her own hands; now, she repeated her actions precisely and earned a warm, motherly grin from Sarah.

"Well done. If you catch it right away, you can just back up and redo the stitch. If you catch it after a few rows, and the ladder is small, you can do what I just showed you. Sometimes, you'll get going and not notice for several inches of work. Then you have to pull the whole thing out and start over from the dropped stitch. That'll break your heart, trust me."

Diana smiled but didn't respond. She picked up the rhythm of their knitting. Her heart, she knew, was much stronger than a dropped stitch could break.

As they set back to their work, Sarah asked, "Can I ask you something, sweetheart?"

When Sarah used an endearment, she either had bad news or hard truth. Diana looked sidelong through her lashes. "Sure ..."

"You went up the mountain after the lights went out, right?"

Diana nodded, her neck stiff, tensed as if Sarah's words might strike her like a fist.

"You had a place up there?"

"Yes. My family did. My parents. Just a little cabin, away from everything."

"Your parents didn't go up, too?" Sarah set her knitting down and ducked her head, finding Diana's downcast eyes, and Diana understood that the blow would hit her heart. She knew what Sarah wanted to know.

She dropped another stitch and set her knitting down, too. "I don't know where they are," she said, answering the question Sarah wended toward. "They were in Germany when it happened, visiting my sister."

"Oh, sweetheart. I'm sorry. That's your whole family?"

"Yes."

Sarah reached out her hand and grasped Diana's. "Maybe they're okay. Like you."

"I hope so. I don't know how I'll ever know."

"People will get across the oceans again. Maybe they already are. The Mayflower didn't need electricity to land at Plymouth Rock, after all."

"Gus says the East Coast is a wasteland. Radiation."

Sarah let out a long, somber breath. "Yes, I suppose that's true. Well, I'm sorry."

Not knowing what to say, and needing something to do before her mind started to dig a hole, Diana picked up her little strip of scarf. Sarah followed suit, and they resumed the rhythm of their needles.

"Can I ask *you* something?" Diana asked, after she'd worked her way around the question of whether she should.

"Of course. I owe you at least one."

"What about your family?"

Sarah set her knitting down again and stared out toward the center of the Shire. "I never had children of my own. I had a husband once, but that was over long before the lights. I had lovers, but never anyone I'd call family. These people are my family. That's been true most of my life."

"And you were with them when the world ended."

Sarah nodded. "Most of them, yes, I was."

"You're lucky."

"Yes. I am." She reached out again to squeeze Diana's hand. "And I'm lucky to have you now, too."

They'd stopped asking hard questions and gone back to gossiping when Buddy stood up, his posture tense. Seconds later, Aidan, one of the teenagers of the Shire, came around the bend in the lane, from the middle of the compound, running full tilt. "SARAH! SARAH!"

Both women set their knitting aside and went to meet him. "What's the trouble?" Sarah asked.

"The ... the ..." Aidan closed his mouth and held his breath for a moment, then tried again. "The team is back—they ... Fiends ... my dad's hurt!"

Not waiting for Aidan to make clearer sense, Sarah ran off in the way Aidan had come. Diana went with her. Fiends had attacked the scavenge team. Gus was on that team today.

By the middle of the Shire, they'd met a throng of people running toward the gate, but everyone made way for Sarah, and thus for Diana and Aidan.

Four of their people had gone out that morning with a list of resources to scavenge—mostly scrap metal and other materials for the craftspeople to recycle, some wild-growing greens and fruits that they couldn't cultivate well near the Shire, books, and other supplies. Scavenging was their most dangerous work, so the team was different each time, pulled from a pool of strong fighters with sharp eyes. In her weeks in the Shire, Diana had gone out twice, both times with Gus. He'd gone out twice more without her, including today.

Now, just inside the gate, the little cart they'd pulled with them to collect bigger pieces stood with its harness end resting on the broken pavement of the entrance lane. Aidan's father, Bob, lay in it, leaning against a rusted fender from what looked like a pickup truck, unconscious and ghastly pale. His shirt sopped with blood. Their healer, Elsie, crouched beside him, cutting his clothes open. Helen, Bob's wife, grabbed Aidan as he ran back and clamped him into a terrified embrace.

Diana saw all that as she sought a much more crucial sight. Then Buddy barked and ran forward, and Diana followed him, pushing through the tight crowd of worried people, until she saw Gus. He sat against the wood post that held up the fading arrow sign directing vacationers to the motel office. Blood ran over his face and dripped from his beard, and he held a bloody hand awkwardly over his shoulder, but he pushed Amy, Elsie's daughter and assistant, away.

"Help Vince and Bob. I can wait," he said to Amy as Diana landed hard on her knees at his side. "Hey, honey." He smiled a little; in his blood mask, the expression wasn't as reassuring as he'd probably intended.

"Hi!" She kissed his gruesome mouth, and his cheek, again and again, until he groaned.

"Ow, hon."

"Sorry. What happened?"

Gus's eyes left hers, and she followed their path, looking over her shoulder to the cart. Bob wasn't the only one in it. As she watched, Howard—blood-drenched like the rest of the team but seemingly strong as ever—lifted Vince out of the cart. He was obviously dead; his head hung slackly back, eyes staring emptily. And he was missing his left arm at the shoulder. The wound no longer bled.

"Ah, fuck," Gus moaned. "Fuck!"

Diana returned her attention to him. She brushed his hair back and saw a deep gash at his hairline, from his temple to his ear. "You're hurt. What happened?" She pulled his hand away from his shoulder and tore his tunic. He'd been stabbed with something dull or rough-hewn; the edges of the wound were frayed.

Fiends, Aidan had said. Well, that was obvious.

There was a group nearby of what the Shire called Fiends, which were what Gus had called Ferals, and maybe what she'd called monsters, though she'd called everyone monsters. The group wasn't so close that they were a constant presence, but close enough to be a constant threat. This was the first time since Diana had joined the Shire that they'd attacked.

She shrugged out of her flannel shirt, balled it up, and held it to his heavily bleeding forehead.

"You need stitches."

"I know. A few more scars for my impressive collection. Scars are sexy, right?"

"Very." She smiled and kissed him again, soundly, ignoring the taste of his blood.

"Are they coming?" Sarah asked, loudly, speaking to anyone who would answer.

Howard did. "They always come. We killed that whole group, so we have some time. But you know they'll come when their people don't come back. They always come."

Her hands on her hips and her mouth ironed grimly flat, Sarah squinted at the closed gate and nodded.

"Yeah. They always come."

Twenty-Five

Oh the sun is on the harbour, love,
And I wish that I could remain,
For I know that it will be a long, long time
Before I see you again.

The members of the Shire stood around two fresh graves in their little graveyard, their heads bowed as Helen sang. Her lovely, sweet, high voice rocked on the tears that ran down her cheeks.

Bob had died as well, his belly torn open by a Fiend blade, too much damage for Elsie and Amy to undo. His grave and Vince's were dug side by side, friends going to the next world together.

Diana was no longer sure there was a next world for them after this one, but she watched Helen and Aidan, and Vince's daughter, Linda, and his partner, Brendan, in their grief, and she remembered the comfort the belief in a god could bring. She'd felt it when she was a girl, when her Big Pa had died and then her Grammie, only weeks later; she remembered her father promising her that they were together again, that God had taken Grammie, too, so she wouldn't be lonely without the love of her life.

Standing at Gus's side, their fingers linked together, she hoped her father had been right.

Gus had never believed in any god. He'd believed in the beauty of creation and in the power of proof and reason. He was a musician because, he'd explained, it was the nexus of both—the science of sound and the aesthetics of art. In music, as in all art, for Gus, the world was explained.

It wasn't until Helen had begun singing the old ballad in her grieving soprano that Gus's composure had shaken. Now, as the last notes of her song drifted away and Aidan hugged her hard, Gus's jaw twitched and his hand clenched Diana's fingers with such force that their tips throbbed.

He was angry. In the year that she'd known him, she'd never seen him angry. But she recognized it at once: he was furious.

Howard leaned his immense shoulders in and gave Gus a hard look, one hanging at the edge of a threat. "You need to sit back now, Gus. Take a breather. Let somebody else talk."

"You agree with me, Howard. You know it's time."

"Gus, enough," Sarah cut in. "You've made your case. It's time for you to listen."

"Verily, 'tis time long past," Doug added, in his 'ye-olde' way of speaking. "Yet I would ask of him a question. Pray thee, brother Gus, wherefore should we follow thee, who dwells with us so short a time?"

Gus sighed and rubbed at his forehead, worrying the skin just under his stitched wound. Diana reached for his hand and held it. When he spoke, his impatience sliced off the edge of each word. "You're asking why you should listen to me because we just got here and I don't have standing?"

"Aye, so I am. 'Tis weeks only that you're with us."

Howard put his hand on his brother's shoulder. "It's not that you don't have a standing, Gus. We voted you and Diana in, and you have all the standing of any of us. You're both part of us, and I don't think there's anybody who's not glad of it. But most of the rest of us have been here for seven years. We've fought off the Fiends for seven years, and we've made this good place. You're saying we should put that all at risk. If we lose, we lose everything. This can't be something we decide because you yell louder than the rest of us."

"How many Rennies has that one group of Fiends killed in seven years?"

Sarah answered Gus. "In seven years? As of today, nineteen."

"How many have you lost to sickness or other kinds of hurt?"

"Fifteen."

Gus leaned forward again and clamped his hands together. "They're the greatest cause of death in a world full of ways to die, and you don't want to do anything about it. Sarah."

"We kill more of them," Danny cut in. "We hold our own."

"No, you don't." Diana had seen the foundation of Gus's new point, seen its basis in his whole view of this world, and understood that he was right. "The Fiends make more of themselves. However, they do it, they don't get fewer, right?" Heads nodded all around her. "Their losses don't last. Maybe we don't even do damage when we kill a few, because they just make more. We can't make more of ourselves. Can we?"

She looked around the circle. Fewer than eighty people lived in the Shire now, and only three had been born after the Sunstorm. Bethany, the only healthy little girl, slept on her mother's shoulder. The other two youngsters sat with their parents. Diana saw umbrage and defensiveness in their parents' eyes, but she also saw concession.

Gus gave her hand a grateful squeeze and picked up the thread she'd started. "Most of us are sterile, it's pretty clear. Not just here, but everywhere. We can't make more of us. Not enough to keep going. All we have is us. The Fiends do us much more damage than we do them. They'll kill us a few at a time, picking us off on the road, where we send our strongest out, until there's no one left strong enough to fight them off, and then they'll kill the rest."

"And your solution is to attack their hold." Sarah uttered the sentence flatly. "You say we're not strong enough to keep going, but you think we're strong enough to kill a hold full of Fiends."

"They'd never see it coming. We've got a group full of craftspeople, a full forge, and a goddamn catapult. We're strong enough to fight, but we're not fighting. I say we take it to them. Yes."

Sarah stared at Gus, and he stared back, while the rest of the Shire sat and watched, waiting. Then she sighed and addressed the group. "We've heard Gus's idea. If anyone has something to add or ask, do it now. Otherwise, we'll vote."

"Do you think I made a mistake?"

They'd voted to attack the Fiends, and then they'd discussed their strategy, talking deep into the night, while the fire waned to a red glow. In the end, the plan was simple—founded on years of defending themselves against their enemy—and bold, demanding a victory or ensuring a total defeat.

They meant to attack right away, leaving only a small contingent of fighters back to guard those who couldn't fight—the young, the old, the ill. Their greatest hope was to meet the Fiends on the road, wipe out the attack force, and continue on to attack a diminished hold.

A few times a year, the Shire sent out a team to the Fiends' hold, not to engage, but to try to judge the degree of the threat and make a strong defense. They knew their enemy. Now they would finish their own Seven Years' War.

Diana finished wrapping Gus's shoulder before she answered. "No. I think you're right. I also think the time for doubt is over. You made your case, and the Shire voted with you. You're a general now."

She'd said it with a smile, meant it lightheartedly, but Gus didn't share her humor. "That's not what I wanted. I was … damn, so angry. I'm tired of walking through the world waiting for somebody to kill me. I'm tired of burying people I care about." He caught her hand. "I want you safe."

She lifted his hand and kissed his fingers. "That's why I think you're right. Fighting back is right. Waiting to be attacked is waiting to be hurt." Setting the first aid supplies on the little stump table, and blowing out the candle, she scooted Buddy over and snugged in with Gus, laying her head on his healthy shoulder. "It's the right thing, to bring the fight to them."

"I hope so. If I'm responsible for ending this place …"

"Hush." She rose onto her elbow and hovered over him. "The time for doubt is over."

"I love you. I don't doubt that."

The Shire rose early that morning, and the few who would stay behind were tasked with completing the normal chores of the community. All the rest prepared for battle. Howard and Doug stoked the forge, and their hammers clanged throughout the day. Gus, Danny, Jerry, and Trevor worked on the catapult, readying it for the trip over the decaying asphalt of the main road and the pitted gravel outside the Fiend hold.

Diana worked with Doug, Howard, and Aidan, helping the others gear up. Armor and shields, axes, swords, bows and arrows, crossbows and bolts, flails, maces — the array of weapons Howard and Doug made dazzled her.

Sarah, Chloe, and Brendan, a leatherworker and former Army sergeant, ran training drills near the cold fire ring. Most of the people knew how to fight, but many of them had never met a Fiend on the road, and none of them had fought a real hand-to-hand war. Even the combat veterans among them, like Brendan, had fought modern wars, with guns and bombs. But Brendan was motivated by something more than expertise and a sense of mission. He'd lost his mate, and he wanted revenge.

They knew their enemy, and they knew the Fiends would attack the fence within a day or two. So the Shire took only this one day to prepare their war. When the moon rose, they rested.

When the sun rose, they moved.

The morning dawned crisply; each exhale puffed out into the air like an infant cloud. Summer was over, well and truly. But the sun shone in a clear sky and promised good weather. Autumn lasted longer here toward the foot of the mountain; Diana had forgotten that. Autumn was a real season here, full of color and fragrance, not merely a half-drawn breath between the warm ease of summer and the cold shock of winter.

As they walked away from the Shire, fifty sudden warriors in leather and mail armor, and plate helmets, carrying shields and broadswords and staves, few spoke, and no one louder than a murmur. The loudest sound among them was the level rumble of wooden wheels.

Drawing the partially disassembled catapult behind them, and a cart of weapons and catapult ammunition behind that, they moved more slowly than Diana liked. Tension twanged in her muscles and made her hairs stand at attention. She missed Buddy, though she was glad their cowardly protector was back at the Shire, probably distracting Eddie from his shepherding work.

Gus walked at her side, at the head of the group, his head swiveling to and fro, watching their perimeter, keeping an eye on their people. "You don't have to watch everything all at once," she said, tugging on his jacket. "Trust your back." Howard and Danny had the back.

"You once told me we had to remember to watch everything, everywhere, all the time."

"I was wrong. You were right."

He shook his head. "Was I? Is this crazy, what we're doing? Fiends ambush. We're walking straight at them."

"That's why it'll work—they won't expect us, and we're shielded at our flanks. We *want* them to attack from cover, right?" They'd decided that would be the best case. If Fiends saw them coming and split up to make an ambush, it would be easier to pick them off than if they made a solid front.

"I don't know why I thought I could lead this. Brendan should be up here. Sarah should have come."

"Sarah is leading the defense at home. She agreed with your plan. Brendan, too. They think this'll work."

"And I got your back, Gus." Brendan had moved up right behind them. "The man who makes the plan should lead the plan. My only advice is this: If you gotta think that bullshit, think it. But don't say it out. We're past the point of turning back, so only thing to say out loud is victory. We got a plan. We know our jobs. What we need to win is to know the guy we're following into battle thinks we're gonna kick some ass."

Gus studied Brendan over his shoulder for a moment. When he nodded, the old Army sergeant slapped his arm—the one attached to his wounded shoulder. Gus winced and then chuckled.

"All right then, let's kick some ass."

When the Fiends attacked, Diana's first thought, as she pulled her axe—the one she'd bought at the Tahoe Renaissance Faire to hang on her office wall in a world that had died, the one that her strange, kindhearted new friend Doug had made with his own hands—from its harness on her back, was that the people who'd attacked her on her mountain had not been Fiends or Ferals. Her monsters had been more human than this—and maybe more monstrous because of it.

These creatures—Were they still people? Had they ever been?—were so filthy and matted and scarred that she could hardly feel attacked as they leapt screaming from the tall trees that bookended the road. No more than she had when the mountain lion had pounced on her and Buddy.

They wore layers of tattered clothes and poorly tanned skins. Few of those who had hair on their heads had tended it; their heads were covered with dull mats. But as Diana leapt between a Fiend woman and Amy, she saw a faded tattoo on the Fiend's scrawny upper arm: a time-turner, from *Harry Potter*.

Once, this female had been, like Diana, a fan of *Harry Potter*. Once, she had been a woman who loved magic and fantasy and stories of good triumphing over evil.

The sight stopped her mind cold, but her axe continued its path, slicing at a downward slant through

446

the Fiend's shoulder, into her chest. Diana knew she'd opened the heart when a fat pop of blood spurted from the female's — the *woman's* — mouth, into Diana's face.

She yanked her axe free, and the body dropped. Amy lifted wide, shocked eyes, and Diana pushed her back. "If you can't fight, get back to the cart."

"I can fight," Amy brushed Diana's hands away and lifted her mace and shield. With a nod, Diana left her and found another Fiend to kill.

They outnumbered the Fiends, but the fight was intense even so. Fiends fought without apparent interest in life or death, with only the hunger to end the former and cause the latter, to inflict pain, to taste blood. In that way, Diana thought, her monsters and these were alike. Brutality aroused them; even their own pain, their own deaths, seemed to satisfy. Every one of them bore a maniacal grin while they fought.

Or maybe they were baring their teeth.

As she pulled her axe through the thick belly of an older male Fiend, Diana took a blow to the back that knocked her wind out. She turned, heaving in a painful gasp, and saw Gus, wielding his dripping katana like a samurai. Gore smeared his face and hung in viscous streams from his beard.

A headless body finished its drop between them. She'd been hit with its head.

Her eyes locked with Gus's—then his suddenly went wide. "DOWN!"

She dropped instantly into a crouch, tucking her head low, and Gus arced his sword over her head. A torrent of blood washed across her back, and a body thumped hard onto her, knocking her wind away again.

Gus's hand circled her arm; she knew his touch without looking—and he helped her to stand.

"You okay?"

"Yes," she gasped, filling her lungs.

"It's over."

Wiping blood from her eyes, Diana turned to survey the scene. Bodies mounded the road in gory drifts, and blood dyed the greying pavement to a murky puce, thick streaks of crimson making a macabre batik.

Every body she saw was matted and filthy. All Fiends. "Were we hurt?" she asked, offering the question to anyone.

"Brendan!" Gus called. "Who's hurt?"

"Danny, Eve, and Joe are hurt," Brendan answered. "Joe's hurt bad, but awake. Anybody else down?" Everyone looked. No one called out.

"I don't think we lost anyone," Gus marveled. He turned to Diana, and she saw in his eyes the need for a touchstone to prove it was real.

She grabbed his hand. "We need to keep going. To their hold."

Brendan walked up. "Joe's stabbed in the gut, but he says he can hold on. Danny's leg has a nasty gash, and Eve took a knock to the noggin. Amy can tend them on the roll if we put them in the cart. Your call, Gus."

Gus nodded, still clutching Diana's hand.

With a curt nod that was practically a salute, Brendan turned sharply and his heel and walked back through the blood-soaked Rennies. "Wounded in the cart," he called out. "Amy, too—first aid. We're moving out, people!"

The Fiend hold was a tiny strip mall of three storefronts. No wall defended it, but rusting debris and gutted old cars and trucks made a haphazard moat around the weedy gravel parking lot. The windows of the building had been broken out and were mostly replaced with scrap boards.

As the Rennies marched down the sloping gravel road toward the hold, the place seemed quiet, already dead. But there had been no more than thirty or so Fiends in the first attack. They'd estimated that twice that many had stayed back.

"They locked down," Brendan said, standing at the fore of the group with Gus and Diana. "They think they'll draw us into their lair."

"Plan B, then?" Howard asked; he'd pushed to the fore when they'd stopped.

Gus turned to Brendan and Diana, looking for support. Diana smiled, and Brendan nodded.

"Plan B. Let's get the catapult up."

The men in charge of the catapult had practiced all the previous day so that they could assemble it quickly. While they worked, the others prepared its ammunition. That little strip mall was a log-cabin-style build. Wood frame, and years past any maintenance.

When the catapult was in place and ready, they loaded a hefty, rag-wrapped rock into its bucket, poured precious, aging kerosene over it, and set it alight. Howard did the honors and fired the catapult, sending a fireball arcing toward the building.

It struck a roof kindling-dry after the summer, and the flames caught at once.

"Load up again!" Gus called; this time he didn't glance around for approval.

They fired four more flaming rocks, and struck the roof twice more, until it was made of flames, and fire dripped down the eaves and spouts like water, consuming all the wood it touched. Diana stood and watched, fascinated, letting the sight before her become her cabin, the one she'd lost, the one she'd never looked back on to see its destruction.

Then a boarded-up shop window broke out, and Fiends poured through, screaming, coughing, roaring, burning.

"NOW!" Gus yelled, and Diana and the other Rennies with melee weapons charged. Gus and five others armed with range weapons took up positions across the road and loosed their arrows and bolts at will.

The fire turned all the Fiends into black ghosts. Diana sighted on one and barreled forward, cocking her axe as she ran.

At dusk, the Rennies pushed through the gates of the Shire, limping, reeling, weary, bathed in blood—but whole. The cart swelled with wounded, and the catapult was broken, but they had lost not a single soul. Joe was hurt worst, with his belly open, but Amy had packed the wound tightly, and the blade that had caused it seemed to have missed his organs. Infection was still a worry, for all the wounded. But for now, they returned home as heroes, and none who waited for them would have to greet grief. Not yet, at least.

They'd won. Gus's plan had worked almost precisely as he'd laid out, and they'd cleaned out the Feral hold. They'd killed every one of them, even those who'd tried to run when they'd realized their defeat. Even those who'd died screaming in fear.

To those Fiends, they had become the monsters.

After all the Fiends were dead, they'd used water and dirt to put out the fire. The gravel lot around the building had served as a break as well. They stayed until the flames were dead and the embers were out.

That had been Diana's idea. Her demand. She did not want to wake to fire ever again, so she'd refused to leave while the one they'd made had burned. Gus had agreed, and even those eager to get the wounded home had obeyed.

Because they'd stayed, they'd seen the things that hadn't burned. The metal grates and bars, warped from the heat, and the charred bodies and bones at their bases.

Cells. Cages. The Fiends had kept captives.

That, Diana supposed, was how they'd made more of themselves. Torturing captives to madness.

When Buddy ran up to them, barking with glee, Diana dropped to her knees and forgot all that, wrapping her arms around his neck. Gus stood beside them, and she felt shielded, even in this place, their home. This was all that mattered, and they had made it safe.

Sarah met the warriors at the gate, her worried brow smoothing to relief as she scanned the group and realized that all were accounted for. Her attention fixed on the cart of wounded. "Elsie!"

"Right here. I got 'em." Elsie ran for Amy, her daughter, and Howard and Trevor pulled the cart toward the medical cabin.

"Gus did good, Sare," Howard said as he passed their leader. "We won. The Fiends are gone."

Sarah turned to Gus and Diana. Her cheeks swelling with a grin, she nodded. One bob of her head said everything.

As the tone of the homecoming became celebratory, Gus grabbed Diana's hand and pulled her up and into an embrace. She felt his exhaustion in the lean of his body against hers. "Let's go wash up and be alone," he murmured against her cheek. "I don't want to celebrate. I'm just tired."

When she nodded, he led her to their tiny cabin at the back of the Shire. Buddy trotted along beside them.

Book Six: Leader

Every light has its shadow,
and every shadow hath a succeeding morning.

~Nicolaus Copernicus

Twenty-Six

Gus groaned as Diana pulled his jacket off. His shoulder ached fiercely, and blood had soaked through the bandage and his rough cotton shirt. "I think I pulled a stitch or two."

"Let me see." She moved in front of him and worked his shirt off, taking care not to disturb his arm too much, then unwrapped the bandage. He'd barely felt his shoulder during the fights of the day, but on the walk back, each step had felt like he'd trodden directly on the wound.

Beyond the walls of their little hut, the Shire cheered. He heard laughter and manic chatter, and Dennis and Weezie had already taken up the pipe and the drum. An honest-to-god revel had started.

There was much to celebrate; the Shire had destroyed a whole camp of Ferals, or Fiends, whatever—

the greatest danger they faced. He should have felt festive, too, and he knew that he and Diana would be missed. He'd taken an array of risks to push a risky plan, and it had paid off. On the walk back, nearly everyone who'd fought with him had walked beside him for a while so that they could offer their gratitude. So they could call him a hero.

But he wasn't a hero. He'd had a crazy idea, and he'd pushed his point. He'd been angry and impatient, and he'd argued hard for a plan he hadn't even fully understood himself. If anything, he was a good talker.

He could just as easily have gotten them all killed.

He hadn't; they'd won—killed all the Fiends and suffered no deaths of their own. So he was a hero.

What did that mean?

"Not pulled, just stretched," Diana said, brushing her fingertips lightly over the skin near his wound. "The scar might be thick right there, but I don't think I need to poke you again."

He took hold of her fingers and brought them to his lips. The taste and smell of blood was strong, but whether it came from her hands or his beard was impossible to say. "You're not hurt?" He'd promised to protect her and then dragged her into a damn war.

She shook her head. "A few bruises, probably. But that's it. Gus, you did it. You saved everybody."

He let her go. "Don't. Not you." Crossing to their little stove, he checked the pot of water, decided it was warm enough, and soaked a cloth to wash his face.

Diana came over and dipped a cloth of her own. "Gus, talk to me."

He laughed; usually, it was him saying those words to her. "I don't know. I don't know what I'm doing any more than anybody else. I don't want to be anybody's hero."

"You're my hero. You saved me."

He stopped washing his beard and caught her chin, turning her face to his. She'd washed most of the blood from her skin, but her hair was still streaked. "I didn't. You'd made a good life all on your own."

"No. I wasn't living, I was just surviving. And I was going crazy. You know that. Having you and Buddy brought me back."

At his name, Buddy got up and pushed himself between them. They both obliged him with scratches and strokes.

"You saved me, too. You're my hero."

She beamed pleasure at him and wiped his cheek with her cloth. "See? It's not so bad to be a hero."

"What we did today—my plan—it doesn't feel heroic. I don't know why."

"Because we were the attackers. I feel it, too. Cutting people down while they ran away, while they were afraid — it was hard. I saw today that they were really people. My monsters, the Fiends, they were *people*. And those cages — I don't think everybody who becomes a Fiend wanted to be one. But killing them all was the only way to make the Shire safe. If you leave one enemy alive, then there is someone who still wants to hurt you."

"The Shire was different, though. They'd never attacked anyone. That wasn't who they were. What we just did — my plan — made them that way. Like everywhere else — kill first, ask questions later."

He thought of Erin, the case he'd made so long ago to save her life and welcome her into Carver's group. He'd judged them all harshly, himself included, for even having a discussion about whether or not to kill an innocent simply because she had more challenges than most. And now, he'd convinced a whole community to destroy another, to kill them all in their own interest.

He turned to the window and watched the warp and weave of long shadows dancing through firelight. "And they're celebrating it."

"Gus." Diana wrapped a towel around the now-steaming pot on the stove and set it on a stump table, then stood in front of him and held his hands. "Stop. You're forgetting how many times that camp of Fiends attacked the Shire, how many people here — *our* people now — they killed. You're forgetting that they attacked the scavenge party on the road three days ago and *killed Joe and Bob*.

You're forgetting that today, they attacked us on the road again. What we did today *was* self-defense. Every point you made to convince the people was right. They would have killed us all. They were already killing us."

She was right, of course, and he'd been right, too, arguing for the attack. It had made sense, everything he'd said, though each point had occurred to him as the words had formed on his tongue. And still, he felt terrible — tired and guilty and ... *disappointed*. He didn't understand it.

But he understood the woman at his side, her blue eyes shining at him with perfect trust, profound compassion, and deep love. She had saved him. She was still saving him.

"I love you, Diana."

"And I love you." She lifted his hand and kissed his fingers. "Let's finish washing up and go to bed. We can lie in the dark with Buddy and listen to the party. That sounds ... cozy to me. Like a way to enjoy their happiness and have mine, too."

"Me, too."

Gus lay in the dark long after the celebration around the fire had gone quiet. Diana rested in the nest of his body, her slow, soft, deep breaths telling the story of her ease. Buddy slept in Diana's arms, one paw twitching as he dreamed.

His whole family, fitted together like spoons.

They slept like this often, and it usually made him feel calm and serene, but tonight, his mind would not settle, and his thoughts stirred his blood so that lying still had become truly painful. The feeling in his heart was old and familiar, and it scared him badly.

The same feeling had driven him out of substakes and wandering groups, had driven him away from Carver's group, to trek through a Plains winter, into the Rockies, all alone. That crazy, angry, reckless, restless need to move on. That sense that where he was wasn't enough, that he needed to seek out more.

But what more? The Shire *was* enough. He loved it here — the people, the life they'd built, the way they lived it. If it had suddenly fallen short, *he'd* done it. He'd changed their principles. He'd made them killers, when before they'd been simply defenders. Protectors. He couldn't abandon them for becoming what he'd insisted they become.

And he certainly couldn't, he wouldn't, abandon Diana. In his sight, every good thing in this world was wrapped around her. His love for her ran deeper than any he'd felt before the storm or since. There was nothing he wanted without her.

Since the Sunstorm, the only time this restlessness hadn't overtaken him was on the mountain with Diana. There, he'd had everything—and she still carried the most important things inside her: love, peace, strength, purpose.

He would never leave her, and she'd found a new home here in the Shire. A better home, maybe. Here, she'd filled out to her true self, shedding her fears and suspicions, making friends and family, regaining her voice and self in every sense. To ask her to leave would be to tear out her tender new roots.

This restive gnawing in his muscles would lead him away, astray. The Shire was where they belonged.

But he couldn't be still.

He eased slowly out of the nested set of his family and stood up. He dressed quietly and stepped into his boots. As Gus crept to the door and grabbed his jacket off a hook, Buddy lifted his head, but the dog didn't follow. He settled back into Diana's embrace and let Gus go out into the world alone.

Gus hadn't had a plan for what he'd do once outside. The Shire was quiet, and the fire had been banked. A damp fall chill weighed down the air; Gus turned up the collar on his coat and closed the buttons. But a gibbous moon shone from a clear sky, and stars swirled and blinked. As he stared up at the lively midnight vista, framed by silhouetted leaves and branches, a meteor streaked, leaving an arcing contrail of light.

He grinned. If he were a more spiritual man, he might consider that a sign, and puzzle out its meaning. But he was not a spiritual man. He believed in the world of his senses, and of his emotions.

Everything that mattered in that world slept here in the Shire. There was nowhere else he wanted to be. As he stared at a sky that had never been so beautiful in the modern world, the restless itch went quiet. He inhaled fresh air fragrant with pine and eucalyptus, and felt calm.

His grin became a chuckle; that damn shooting star had brought on an epiphany after all.

He felt ready to go back to Diana and snuggle into their nest again, but he was out here, in the deep blue peace, and he decided to walk the compound and breathe that gorgeous air.

At the fire ring, he saw a shadow, sitting on a log. He could tell from the posture and shape that it was Sarah, alone in the dark chill. He went to her, slowly, so he didn't startle her.

"Sarah," he said when he'd gotten nearly to the ring and she hadn't yet seemed aware of him.

"Gus." She patted the log beside her. "Come sit. Can't sleep, either?"

He sat. "I was restless, but I feel better now. What about you? Too much reveling?"

An enigmatic smile greeted his question. In the moonlight, she seemed much younger. "Did you see the shooting star?"

"I did."

"I've always thought that a sight like that—random and unexpected—is more magical than a meteor shower like the Perseids."

"Do you think it's a sign?" Interesting how this unexpected conversation mirrored his earlier thoughts.

Her head swiveled back and forth—slowly, contemplatively. "I think it's a gift, something to be grateful to have seen." She put her hand over his. "What you did ... it's important, Gus. You changed everything."

Breath caught in his chest. Sarah hadn't called him a hero or said he'd saved them. She'd said the thing he'd truly believed: that he'd *changed* them. Her tone and her words had both been neutral and perfectly true.

"I know" were the only words he could say aloud. He held their complement—*I'm sorry*—back.

Her leathered fingers wrapped around his. "Do you know why I lead this place?"

He'd always assumed there'd been a vote. The Shire voted on everything. But he didn't actually know for sure, so he shook his head.

"It just sort of happened. I'm the oldest, as I'm sure you can see, and in the old world, I'd done the faire circuit far longer than most. I wasn't in charge; nobody was really in charge of anybody but themselves. We were all just vendors, dragging our trailers behind our beat-up old cars, camping rough, paying to put up our carts and tents at the faires. But I knew everybody, past and present, and I was ... well, I was like you. I'd been around. I'd seen things and done things the others hadn't. I was the lorekeeper. Really, I was just a busybody with some good stories. Having good stories worked to keep guests at my stand, too. Weaving isn't all that interesting to watch, but an old biddy who can tell a story is worth a listen, and maybe a browse through her wares."

Gus laughed quietly. He could imagine Sarah, dressed in costume, sitting at her loom and telling bawdy, but family-friendly, stories in the West Country accent he'd heard her affect. "I'd have stayed to listen."

She gave him an amiable tip of her head. "Well. When the Last Dance came, we panicked like everybody else at first we lived in the same world as everybody else most of the time. We all had smart phones and laptops, just like people. But so many of us had just come together a day or two before, all of us packed up for the faire. We sat together and commiserated while things went crazy around us, and then I said, just thinking out loud, trying to calm people down, that maybe we were about the best-prepared people alive to live in a world that had leapt back in time. We were all craftspeople, whose job it was to make things as they'd been made hundreds of years before electricity. We had trailers and wagons full of the supplies of our crafts, And we had merchandise—clothes and weapons, housewares, jewelry we could melt down for metal. Bob and Helen had their little petting zoo herd. We had everything, and we all knew our work."

Sarah looked up at the sky. She was quiet long enough that Gus had begun to think she'd lost her thought when she said, her head still tilted to the heavens, "I'm the leader because I said all that first. I saw it, and I said it, and then everybody looked to me." She let her gaze fall back to him. "I learned to lead by leading. But I'm a pacifist at heart. It never occurred to me to take the fight to the Fiends. Even when I cried tears over the graves of friends they'd killed, it didn't occur to me that we could, or should, fight. No one in all these years had ever said it out loud before. You're the one who saw it and said it. And you were right—we *could* take the fight to them. We *were* strong enough to beat them. We all know how strong we are now. And now, like my idea started the Shire and made it what it was, your idea has made it what it will be."

Gus pulled his hand from her grip as a shock of anxiety surged up his spine. "If you mean to finish this story by saying something about passing a torch, I'm leaving."

With a maternal chuckle, she took his hand back. "Nothing so much as that. Not yet, at least. But you *are* a leader among us now, Gus. Our people see that you saved them. You're their hero."

"I don't want that."

"And I just wanted to be a gossipy old biddy weaving cloth. It doesn't matter what you want. It matters what they need."

"I don't even know if what we did was right."

"Neither do I. There's never any way to be sure. That's not for us to decide. All we can do is our best. That's what you did, right?"

He nodded. That, at least, was true.

"Things are going to change now, my friend. I don't know how, but I know they will. I understand why you didn't stay for the celebration, but if you had, you'd have seen the thing that has me up tonight."

Gus let his head fall, waiting for the blow of her next words.

Sarah let go of his hand and rubbed his back instead. "They were happy. So relieved, like they'd been freed from a burden they'd forgotten the weight of—and that was beautiful. But there was bloodlust, too. They were proud to wear the blood of their enemies. They painted it on the people who'd stayed back. They held their weapons in the air. If they'd've had guns, they'd have shot them into the air. It was a kind of mania I'd never seen in our peaceful people. When they wake in the morning, on a new day, with the blood washed off, I'd like you to walk with me and see what world we live in now. Then we can decide what comes next."

"I'm sorry." The words finally would not be resisted. Gus dragged a despairing hand through his hair, tightening his fingers so that the strands strained at their roots. "Damn, Sarah, I didn't mean—"

She gave his back a sharp slap. "Stop. Regret is pointless except to shape what you do next. And we don't know if this change is a bad one. Personally, I think it could go either way. We *are* safer now. The Fiends were our greatest threat, and they're gone. You did that. But there are other threats, there will be new ones, and some might even come from within. It's up to us to shape what happens next. It's up to us to lead."

His woman and his dog were sitting on the porch of their cabin, waiting for him. Buddy jumped to the lane and trotted up, and Gus stopped to grab his ears and give his head a gentle, loving shake. The dog surged off his front paws and tagged him with a long, wet tongue.

Diana sat, watching, curled up in a knitted blanket. Her long hair was loose and spread over her back and shoulders. Just looking at her warmed his insides and calmed his mind. He dropped to his knees and laid his head in her lap, insinuating his arms into the blanket so he could wrap them around her body.

"You went away." She combed her fingers through his hair.

"Sorry. I needed to walk and think."

"Did it help?"

"I don't know. Sarah was at the fire ring. We talked for a long time." He wasn't at all sure whether the talk had made him feel better or worse. He'd had an epiphany moments before he'd seen her, one that had calmed him, but what she'd said had stirred up his worries and fears again.

But not, he realized, his restlessness. That compulsion to leave was gone. He snugged himself even closer to Diana and whispered, "I love you."

She curled forward, closing him within the fold of her body, and kissed his head. "And I love you," she murmured, her lips brushing lightly over his ear. "Come to bed and love me."

He nodded and stood, holding out his hand. Buddy trotted up to the door, tail wagging, and they all went back in to their tiny, ten-foot-square cabin.

Those walls, built with their own hands, held everything that mattered, in this world or any other.

As long as he had that, everything else would make sense.

The course of his life—the way of his travels, the people he'd known, the things he'd learned—had brought him to this moment. If he had made himself a leader, then he would lead.

But for now, he was only a man who loved a woman.

Twenty-Seven

"Carson City? That's safe?" Gus sat at a table under the new wooden canopy they'd erected near the fire ring. In years past, the Rennies had put up the largest of their canvas tents from the Faire days over the tables for the winter, preferring to eat out in the open during warm weather, but a storm in the early spring had torn the tent apart, so they'd built a sturdy shelter before the cold set in.

It was a beautiful structure. Most of the buildings they'd erected were made of deadfall as well as fresh cut, what they could scavenge from nearby the Shire. This wood was all fresh cut and matched in tone and grain. They'd been able to take their time and cut down their pick of trees, because they hadn't had to worry about being beset by Fiends. They'd even added Tudor details.

Howard sat across from him and dug into his venison stew. "It's Reno that's a cesspool. Carson City was just a town before, and it's a ghost town now. But about five miles out from it, there's a trading post. It's active most of the time, and just about every day at this time of year. It's good trading. We need that trip to get through the winter."

Gus soaked a piece of fry bread in his stew and thought about Howard's pronouncement. When he'd first wandered this way, he'd cut between Reno and Carson City, avoiding them both. He had only a vague memory of how far he and Buddy had walked after seeing signs for those towns. But more than a day, at least. "How far?"

"Say twenty-five miles to the trading post, maybe a mite less. Day there, day to trade, day back. Maybe two, depending on what we bring back."

"And if we get there and there's no trading?"

"There will be. But if not, I'd want to stay until there was. Normally, we could eke by without it if we had to, but the Fiends got in our way last year, so it's been two years since we've traded on that scale. We can't go longer than that. Winter is hard in these mountains, you know that. We got a lot of people to keep warm and fed. The autumn trading helps. Besides, it's our news. One day, things're gonna get better. Once a year is about the only time we see anybody who might know when it happens, and now it's been two. Heck, right now, we might be the only ones left thinking the world is over."

Gus doubted that wholeheartedly. In fact, he didn't really believe that things would get better. Not without children being born. Without a next generation, they were all simply living until their own ends. No legacy to be built, no history that mattered. Just trying to make what life they had as good as it could be until it ended.

Two weeks had passed since they'd wiped out the Fiends. Sarah had been wrong, at least so far, about a great change in the Shire. They'd all simply gone back to their routines, with the exception of building the shelter that Gus and Howard now sat under.

That wasn't entirely true; there had been a change, but a subtle one—and good, as far as Gus could tell. People moved through their days as if they were lighter. They were more confident. Happier. He would have said before that the people of the Shire were happy, but now, in these past two weeks, he understood that their previous lighthearted mood had been, in some part, as much a pretense as their old-fashioned clothes and broad, scattered accents. Without fear of the Fiends, the fantasy had become a bit more real. They'd made a world they could keep, as long as they needed it.

While Gus and Howard sat alone at a table, others trickled in under the shelter, now that the meal bell had rung. They seemed to understand that the men were talking seriously, and chose other seats for their own meal. Gus let his eyes roam around, seeking Diana and Buddy.

He hadn't seen them since breakfast. They were out with a few others, foraging for acorns and pine cones, among other things, enough for the cooks to grind for different flours. Days in which he didn't see her for hours passed more slowly than others.

Sarah had sent the foraging party out; she always managed assignments like that. She was still as much their leader as ever. Howard asking him about arranging a trading party was the first time since their fight with the Fiends that Gus had felt like he was now a leader here, too. He still didn't like it.

"What's Sarah say?" he asked now.

Howard cast a furtive glance over one shoulder, and then the other, and Gus sat up straight. "What's wrong?"

"I got two things to say right quick, and then we wait to talk more about it until we're on our own. One — the way Sarah wants it right now is you're in charge when it's outside the fence, and she's still in charge inside the fence. How I feel is that's fair. She's led us well for a long time, the Shire runs like it does because of her, but you made us safe. You know the world out there better than the rest of us. It makes sense that you'd share the lead."

"I don't want it at all."

Howard waved that off like it didn't matter. "This next thing, you can't tell anybody. Not even Diana. Sarah doesn't want anybody to know. She doesn't want *you* to know yet, and she's going to knock me upside the head when she finds out I told you. But you need to know."

"Jesus, Howard. *What?*"

The big man hunched his shoulders, and Gus leaned in, too. "She's sick. Something inside in her … her … she thinks she's got a woman's cancer somewhere."

Gus dropped his fry bread into his stew and pushed the bowl away. His appetite had shriveled and died in an instant. "Oh no." Not Sarah. "She has to tell somebody. Elsie, at least."

Howard shook his head. "She wants it quiet, and she's earned that. There's nothing one of Elsie's concoctions can do except make her hallucinate. You've said it yourself—this is how we'll die, if something else doesn't get us first."

"But not Sarah." The thought of that steely old woman wasting away in pain made him push his food even farther away.

"You're gonna lead us, Gus. That's gonna happen. Sarah sees it, I see it, you see it. We're going to need you to step up and help Sarah without letting on what you're doing."

"You should lead, not me. Sarah always looks to you first."

"Because I take orders real well. I don't have ideas or vision. Never did. Like I said, Doug's the artist at the forge. I do what people tell me, and I'm good at that. I'm good at getting other people to follow along with me. That's my role. Yours is to help Sarah and take over when it's time. So talk to her. Tell her that you know, I don't mind. Just let me know when I can help get the trading trip ready."

Sarah heaved a breath and slouched back in the chair, where she'd once sat to talk to Gus and Diana about becoming part of the Shire. Shit, that had been not much more than two months earlier.

"Well, I knew he'd tell you. I didn't think he'd run like a toddler with a stolen cookie right to you, but I knew he'd tell you."

"Why didn't *you* tell me?"

Sometimes, Sarah's smiles were absurdly wise. Like she had solved all the puzzles of the universe and waited patiently for the rest of the mortals to bumble their way along the path she'd forged. "Because I don't want to be subject to first reactions. I want to be selfish and not have to say, 'There, there, it's okay that I'm dying.'" She leaned forward, resting her arms on her knees. "In that spirit, I'm going to ask you, most sincerely, not to tell Diana. I like that girl very much. More than that. She's a tough little cookie, and I feel more maternal toward her than anyone else here. I don't want to lose her before I have to."

Diana hadn't said as much, but Gus knew that she'd come to think of Sarah as something of a mother as well. He was offended in her stead at the suggestion that she'd abandon Sarah in her need. "Diana would never turn from you."

"No. But she'd pull back. She has a lot of shields inside her, she's lost a whole lot in her life already, and I think she'd put those shields up to protect herself from pain she could see coming." This time Sarah's smile was rueful. "Like I said, I'm selfish about this. I know what I'm asking will make my death hurt her more, but I want to feel close to her as long as I can."

"Jesus, Sarah. I promised her I would protect her. I told her I wouldn't let her get hurt if I could help it." He'd been thinking of violence, but the promise stood whether the violence was physical or emotional. Keeping something like this from her — it would be a betrayal of her trust. "I can't keep it from her. I'm sorry."

With a nod and a sigh, Sarah gave up. "Okay. I understand. You're right, of course."

He'd make sure Diana didn't put up her shields; Sarah was right that she had many. "Sarah, how bad is it? How long have you felt bad?" She didn't look sick at all, not like the others, like Darlene, who had aged twenty years in the time Gus had known her. Sarah was strong and straight-backed, without that weary shade of illness around her eyes.

"I don't feel bad. There's just some bleeding, and I haven't bled for almost twenty years. And there's other signs. My mother died of cervical cancer. I know what it is."

Gus reached out and picked up her hands. Sun-darkened and spotted, they showed her age, and that she'd spent her years out of doors, but they were strong and graceful. "I'm so sorry."

She squeezed his hands and gave them a corrective shake. "Don't. I'm old, and maybe I'd've died of this in the old world, too. It's funny to say, but I've been happier in these years here than I ever was before. This life suits me, and I know that when I go, I'll be buried with friends in the most beautiful place in the world, and friends will stand over me and sing me to my rest. I'm not sorry to end my life like this. And to know I leave the Shire in good hands makes it all the easier."

Swallowing hard to loosen the knot in his throat, Gus sat back. "Tell me what you need from me."

"We need to start moving things around, from me to you, while I'm still strong, so there's no big change all of a sudden. I was a little worried, after you came back from the Fiends, that we'd given our people a taste for blood. But these are good people. The change in them is for the good. They believe in themselves now. We were cowering behind our fence before. Now we know that we can go out and try the world a little, and we'll be okay. You gave them that, and you'll lead them right."

"I still think it would be better if people voted for a leader."

She shook her head. "A vote will divide us. As long as the people are content to be led, then a vote will do more harm than good. If someone runs against you, that means that people will have to choose sides. Right now, everyone is on the side of the Shire. We all work together. No one's ever challenged me for my place. They trust my judgment. Now, they trust yours, too. And so do I. So use that power wisely. Keep our family strong. I'll help you while I can."

"I don't know why you think I can do this. You barely know me."

She crossed her arms and tightened her brow. "That's not true, and it's insulting. I knew your measure before I ever let you through our gates. I knew who you were when you ran from your own safety and saved strangers on the road. In this world, a stranger is always a threat, but you set your own interest aside and helped us fight the Fiends. When you came back with Diana, when you sought out our help, I knew you were meant to be with us. When you made warriors out of us and felt regret, I knew you were meant to lead us. That night, talking to you, was the first time I felt peace since I knew I was sick.

That you don't want it is the best reason I can think of that you should have it. You have vision and strength, and you don't seek power. You use your strength to help. So don't insult me by suggesting I'd hand over the well-being of my people to somebody I don't know."

"I'm sorry. Sarah, I'm scared." He really was. Maybe more than ever before since the end of the world.

She hit him with that damn wise smile. "Good."

Diana and Buddy met him on the lane as he walked stiffly back to the cabin, his body reeling along with his mind, trying to sort through everything he'd learned in the past couple of hours.

"Hey. Howard said you were with Sarah. Is everything okay?"

He reached her and grabbed her into his arms, holding her as tightly as he could, wishing he could be even closer. Tucking his face against her sweet-smelling neck, he held on and was quiet. Buddy bumped against them, his tail whacking the back of Gus's knees.

Diana held on just as tightly and stroked her hand over his hair, down his back. "What's wrong, Gus?"

With a lingering kiss to taste her skin, feel its warmth, its pulse, take in a deep breath of her scent, he leaned back. "Walk with me a while?"

She took his hand. "Sure."

They strolled into the woods, following a path that had been worn long before the end of the world, by vacationers leaving their rented cabins to enjoy the fresh mountain air and lush woods of the High Sierras. At this little motel, which would have been a short drive, maybe twenty minutes at most, from Lake Tahoe, the path had probably once been dense with people during peak months. Now, in a world without cars, they were almost a day's walk from that enormous lake and more than that from a main thoroughfare, and they were all but entirely insulated from the world. There were no substakes near the lake on this side but the Shire, and only the most intrepid wanderers went into the mountains when there were much easier paths west.

There had been Fiends, of course, who hunted the highways, but maybe not anymore. If that large hold had been the only Fiend settlement, maybe the highways were safe throughout the area.

At any rate, the Shire had been almost as insulated as Diana's cabin had been. Maybe that was why she'd been able to open up here and had learned to trust these people, to call this place home after a few weeks. It was enough like the world they'd lost for her to find purchase here.

Sarah had been a big part of that, knowing instinctively how to introduce her to the world of the Shire, letting her find her way, nudging her when she needed it, waiting for her to catch up. Just being there, minding her progress back into a world of people.

Hand in hand and quiet, they walked to the stream, running shallow at this time of year, at the end of a very dry summer and before the restorative snows of winter. The motel ran on a well, and they had the stream, so the Shire had the water they needed, but they were always careful with their usage nonetheless.

Buddy, lover of all things wet, rushed into the stream and splashed around, chasing the tiny fish that flickered in small pools, snapping at the water and snorting when he breathed in a snootful.

Gus led Diana to sit on a flat boulder that was often their perch when they took Buddy into the woods to play.

"Are you ready to tell me what's wrong?" she asked as he sat at her side.

He decided just to say it rather than let himself get bogged down in doubt. He folded his fingers around hers. "Sarah thinks she has cancer." When Diana gasped and put her other hand over her mouth, he added, "she doesn't want anyone to know, so we have to keep her secret." He knew Diana would; a gossip, she most definitely was not. "She didn't want you to know, because she loves you. But

I promised you that I'd protect you, and I don't want you to be blindsided when she gets really sick."

"She's sure?" The change in her tone was subtle, but in it, Gus heard the slightest of guards being raised—like a clench when you know you're about to be hit.

"Yes. Her mom died of it. She says she knows." He brushed a loose lock of hair back and tucked it behind her ear. "She needs you, honey. She doesn't want anything to change between you."

Buddy slipped on a slimy rock and landed face-first in a deeper pool. He got to his feet and barked at the rock.

Watching the dog's antics, Diana said, "I don't want it to change, either. Sarah ... I've never had a friend like her. She makes me feel like ... like I'm not missing something I always was before." She shrugged. "Even I don't know what that means. But I need her. I love her, too."

Gus thought he knew what she meant, but he didn't say it out loud. He'd known his woman for more than a year now, and she'd slowly let him deep inside. He knew her as well as he'd known anyone since his own sister. Sarah had said that she felt motherly toward Diana. Diana's own mother hadn't offered her that kind of connection. Now she had it, for the first time, and she would lose it.

He pulled her close. She let her head fall to his chest and wrapped her arms around his waist.

"Love her as long as you can." He kissed her head, brushing his beard through her hair.

"Nothing good stays," she murmured.

"I'm staying, Diana. I'm never letting you go."

She sighed and held him all the more tightly.

Twenty-Eight

Buddy had been agitated all morning, glued to their asses and whiny when Gus and Diana went in different directions and he couldn't keep them both in sight. He knew something big was up, and he knew he didn't like whatever it was.

When Gus looped the rope around his neck, the look the dog gave him tore him up: shock and betrayal, and a mountain of guilt.

He crouched down low, face to face with him, but Buddy turned his head away. Nearly two years they'd been a team, and it was the first time he'd turned away. It was the first time Gus had ever leashed him, too.

More importantly, it was about to be the first time they'd ever been apart overnight.

Gus and Diana had decided they couldn't bring him on the trading trip. Diana was at her wit's end already; she hadn't been around so many people, so many strangers, in years, and her trust only extended to the Shire gates. She didn't want Buddy with them, because she didn't trust he'd be safe.

Gus had thought she'd do better if she had Buddy with her. From the moment she'd first seen him, he'd been almost like a service dog for her, focusing her attention and grounding her in the moment whenever she got stressed. Gus owed his life to her devotion to the dog.

He'd made the case that Buddy should join them, that their people would keep him safe, and that he knew about trading centers, so he'd know what to be on the lookout for. Which wasn't *entirely* true. From the descriptions he'd heard of the Carson City trading post, it was much more like an actual business than anything he'd seen in this world before. Much bigger and more permanent than the crossroads bazaars that kept wanderers going. And likely, therefore, to be much more dangerous.

Diana had been close to frantic at the thought of losing Buddy, and the trip itself was enough of a stressor for her as it was. She wouldn't stay home, and, frankly, they needed her on the trip, her eye and her axe, so Buddy was getting left behind.

He seemed to know it, and he didn't like it.

"I'm sorry, Bud. You can't go, and you're acting too weird for me to trust you won't try. You're going to stay with Molly and Sarah and the others and keep them safe, and we'll be back in a few days."

He ruffled his fur and kissed his nose, and then stood and handed the rope to Molly, one of the younger of their people, who helped in the kitchen. One of the other Shire dogs, a little puff of a purse pup named Cupcake, was Molly's. Cupcake didn't play in the mud, but she didn't mind dogs who did.

Molly's two cats hated all the dogs, but they kept out of their way. Brutus and Caesar mainly lounged in the sun and gave contemptuous looks to passersby. And kept mice out of their supplies.

"He'll be okay," Molly assured Gus and Buddy both. "We'll have fun."

"Thanks, Moll." After one more pat of Buddy's head, Gus turned and walked away. He didn't turn back when Buddy did the barking whine that was his most strident complaint. He walked faster, trying to escape the sound and the guilt.

He couldn't escape either.

When he got back to their cabin, Diana was waiting for him on the porch, sitting on the step, fiddling with the fringe on the scarf she'd knitted. Of course, she'd turned out to be good at knitting, too. How this woman could have been a disappointment to her mother would forever be a mystery. Because she'd been heavy? Jesus, people had had their shit out of whack in the old world.

"You ready?"

When he'd come back for Buddy, most of the trading party had been making their way toward the gate. They wanted an early start. A party of twenty Rennies had been selected for the journey, but every craftsperson had heaped wares onto the carts. Those who weren't going trusted those who were to make good deals. All the trades would be made in the name of the Shire.

Here, no one person had any wealth. Personal possessions were few, but needs were none. They shared everything and claimed to own only the tiniest tokens of affection between each other—like the silver violin pendant that Gus wore on a leather thong around his neck, a gift from Eve, who'd made jewelry in the old world, to express her thanks for leading the attack on the Fiends. Or the braided leather and bead bracelet that Diana wore, which Gus had asked Eve to make for her.

Diana looked past his shoulder, back the way he'd come. Buddy's protest still filled the air, and Eddie and Cupcake and Duke were joining in now, too. She winced with every new bark.

"He'll be okay. And so will you. I bet there'll be books."

She'd accumulated a decent stack of books, and people borrowed them and returned them almost daily. She had a dream that they might have a true library in the Shire. Gus was glad she had a dream.

For his part, he was just trying to learn how to lead the Shire. He'd spent most of the apocalypse *leaving* places, not leading them. Sarah said he had vision, but if so, he needed to turn on some damn lights so he could see it.

Pulling two wooden-wheel carts of goods, they moved slowly and stayed on the main road, traveling northeast on Highway 50. Gus's wanderer's wariness creaked to life as they moved farther from the Shire, away from the remnants of the tiny town that had once bustled around the motel their home had been, into deeper and deeper woods. Eventually, as the afternoon waned, even the scattered enclaves of vacation homes disappeared, and they were surrounded by towering forest.

Highways were the hunting grounds of Fiends, and the farther they got from the Shire, the closer they got to Carson City, the more Gus worried that they'd encounter another group, one they hadn't destroyed.

Diana felt the worry, too. Though she walked steadily forward, her back straight and strong, she'd grown tense and quiet as the day had aged, and when he held out his hand for hers, she clutched it hard.

"Gus." Brendan strode up to walk beside him. "We're coming up on a group of hairpin turns. Takes about half an hour or so to walk it with the carts, and we'll be blind ahead and behind while we're in the middle."

"We need to stop for the night?" he asked. The sun wasn't down, but it was low, silhouetting the forest, and its color had taken on the deep, swollen hue that meant it would drop below the horizon soon. Still, he'd hoped to make it to the trading post before dark.

Brendan didn't answer. He walked along, his head canted slightly in Gus's direction, and waited. Because Gus had *asked*. He hadn't *told*. Brendan was another one with far more experience, who swore up and down that he wasn't a good leader. Brendan and Howard were pains in his ass sometimes.

He asked another question, one of fact rather than opinion. "How far from Carson City are we?" If there had been signs on the road, they'd been taken down, or had fallen on their own. He hadn't seen any sign at all, not even a snowplow guidepost, for the whole trip. He wondered if Howard and Doug had salvaged all that metal over the years.

"The trading post is about four miles closer than Carson. We're about six miles out from there."

They'd walked close to twenty miles, then. They could do the remaining six well before noon, if they got an early start in the morning. "Let's set up for the night." This time, he didn't make it a question.

About a mile from the trading post, according to Howard and Brendan, what had been a solitary journey became a traffic jam. Just as roads in the old world would mysteriously clog with cars and trucks, seemingly out of the blue, the road to the trading post filled with people heading in the same direction almost all at once — solitary wanders and small groups, larger groups from substakes, but no group as large as the Rennies. And no Fiends, that Gus could see. They tended to avoid places where normal people gathered in large groups.

All with the same destination, all carrying their goods for trade, no one bothered any other. A few friendly, or at least civil, greetings, but otherwise, just as in the world before, people pointed forward and continued their travel, minding their own business.

Howard was right — this trading center was already much bigger than any crossroads bazaar he'd seen, and he hadn't even seen it yet.

Diana walked right at Gus's side, her shoulders rigid, her eyes wide and unblinking. When her hand drifted up to close around the handle of her axe, he took hold of it and laced their fingers together.

"Stay close to me, honey. It'll be okay."

She nodded, but he knew she wasn't convinced.

By the time they were within sight of the tin roofs of the trading post, the road was as full as Bourbon Street on Fat Tuesday, and Diana had given up all pretense of being emotionally ready for this crush of strangers. She had both arms wound around his, and his fingers tingled from lack of circulation. But he was happy to have her hanging on him, if he could give her strength.

Like all marketplaces in this world, the Carson City Trading Post—there was an actual sign, made of scrap plywood and a bland rainbow of obviously scavenged paint—was guarded, because traders kept their weapons close. Usually, 'guard' meant a few big dudes with blunt instruments, companions to the traders, but these guards wore mismatched SWAT-style armor and carried assault rifles. With ammunition at a high premium, as far as Gus knew, those guns meant that somebody powerful ran this post. It wasn't like a crossroads, where people just found a place and laid their goods out on a blanket or a cart. Somebody somewhere was paying for this to happen, and that meant that somebody somewhere was getting paid. If not in currency, then in something of value.

In this world, that usually meant indenture or conscription. Goddammit. This was the kind of place he'd *avoided* all these years.

If Carson City was a ghost town, then he'd put his money on whoever ran Reno running this, too. Reno was a cesspool, Howard had said. Like ever other city Gus knew about. People with power were always bad news.

Which was why he didn't want any for himself.

Holding Diana close, he slowed, letting his group move forward around him until he was back with Howard, who pulled the heavier cart.

"Who runs this thing? Who pays for that security?"

Howard shrugged. "Never asked who runs it. There's a couple of places that serve meals here, and a saloon, and there's a place that trades for time with girls. They're permanent. Maybe they pay."

If Diana got any more tense, she'd rip his arm off, but she said nothing.

A place that traded for time with girls. People just would never change. And what were the odds that those girls were there voluntarily? "You ever been in the brothel?"

If Gus hadn't been worked halfway to rage, Howard's expression of affront, so completely encompassing of his face that it was caricature, might have made him laugh. "No, I have not!"

"Okay. Sorry." He wondered if any of the Rennies had, but it was a question to deal with later. They'd entered the center of the trading post. It was time to get their work done. Gus wanted to get done quickly and get the hell out. He was disgusted, and Diana seemed to have regressed entirely into the terrified, wild, silent specter she'd been when he'd first met her.

It was a mistake to have brought her. This was too much a world of monsters, too far from the world she'd made, on the mountain or in the Shire.

"I got you, Di. I'm sticking with you."

Her head jerked up and down as though on a sticky hinge. He thought she'd meant it to be a nod.

Howard grabbed his shoulder. Gus turned and saw that the huge man had gone pale. "It's different than it was, though. You're right. Can't put my finger on it, but it's different." He shook his head, and his face found some color. "We need to trade. Even if we didn't, it's too late to turn back."

"Buddy system!" Gus called, while the Rennies were still clustered together. "No women go off alone! Everybody with a partner, everybody armed, and no women without a man. Let's get done and get out."

He caught a couple of skeptical looks from the stronger among the women, but he sent a resolute gaze back. There was a brothel on the premises, and armored guards with automatic rifles patrolling the place. He was not about to risk women from the Shire getting snatched.

They went off in clusters of four and five, carrying bolts of cloth and baskets of sewn clothes, armloads of weapons and tools, pretties and knickknacks that were leftover from the Faire days, and pouches of hard breads, preserved fruits and vegetables, and cured meats.

Gus and Diana, neither of whom were artisans, stayed together, with Eve and Weezie, who had the pretties to trade. Eve and Weezie were both young and attractive, and Gus scanned the teeming crowd relentlessly, seeking someone who might make one or both of them disappear.

They both carried baskets of their offerings for trade, and they made good trades right away. Things like jewelry or pretty carvings had become rare in this world, because they had no practical use. But they made for decent trading at a place this big, which drew all kinds of people, including those in substakes who might have room in their life for a luxury or a token of affection.

Like his pendant and Diana's bracelet, sometimes the practical use was in the emotional expression.

They stopped to barter with a woman offering threads and yarns. While they did, Gus scanned the crowd, looking for trouble. He dropped his gaze low on one pass and saw an old man sitting cross-legged on a ragged Persian carpet, a few stalls down. His long, white hair was fixed back in a thin ponytail, and he had a pair of broken, wire-rimmed glasses perched on his nose. He read a book, and spread before him like arcs of playing cards were a few dozen more books. He didn't seem to be paying attention to his wares, and nobody paid him much mind, either. Traffic flowed by him without pause.

"Hey," he murmured against Diana's ear. She'd been watching the yarn deal with interest. "Look."

She looked, and her death grip on his arm eased at once. She even took a step away from him.

He held her fast. "Hold on. Stay with me. We'll go over there when Eve and Weezie are done."

"Okay." It was the first word she'd said since the road had begun to fill with people.

With Weezie's basket empty of carvings and full of yarn and thread—and two old plastic grocery bags filled with more yarn and thread—they moved on, and no one begrudged Diana the chance to crouch before the old man and see what books he had to offer.

She picked up a paperback without a front cover. The title page read 'The Mysterious Affair at Styles by Agatha Christie.'

"How much?" Diana asked, and Gus realized right there that she had never bartered. Of course she hadn't; he was an idiot.

He got down beside her. "Hon ..."

"Nothing at all, young lady," the old man said. "If you like it, it's yours. If you have a book to swap, I wouldn't mind that, but if you don't, that's just fine."

"We can't take without giving," Gus said, stopping Diana from shrugging her pack from her back.

"Words need to be read, son. Their lessons need to be learned. We've forgotten that, and God is making us pay for our neglect. When we remember, we'll heal. So this is my part to help us." He picked up a book and handed it to Gus. "Here. You take this one."

Walden, by Henry David Thoreau. Gus laughed. Thoreau had spent a couple of years hanging out in his friend Emerson's back yard and thought he'd had an epiphany about living simply. Gus hated this book. But he nodded and accepted the gift. "Thank you, sir."

As he wondered what he had to offer in exchange, Diana unzipped her pack. She handed the old man a slim book Gus hadn't known she'd brought, and a hard roll and a jar of preserved beans. It was a lot to swap for a couple of old paperbacks, but he understood.

The old man held both hands up high as if to thank the gods for the bounty. He read the cover of the book she'd handed him. "*Winesburg, Ohio*! Oh, this is a good one. And look at these beans! Nourishment for the mind and body. Thank you, sweet lady. Here." He picked up another book, a thick one with a plain hardbound cover. "This is one I think you'll like, too. It's very special."

Before the old man gave her the book, he opened it. "These are some of my favorite words ever written, in any language, at any time." Though he'd opened the book and Gus could see faded red ink underlining a passage on the open pages, the old man looked up to the sky and closed his eyes, reciting, "'What was any art but an effort to make a sheath, a mould in which to imprison for a moment the shining, elusive element which is life itself—life hurrying past us and running away, too strong to stop, too sweet to lose?'" He opened his eyes and lifted the book to Diana with a messianic smile.

Gus stood gaping, swamped suddenly with confused emotion. The words the old man had read had torn his chest wide open and grabbed his soul. Those few words, that single sentence—was what had made him a violinist. It was all he believed of the world, encapsulated.

Diana took the book from the old man's hands and opened the cover. *The Song of the Lark*, by Willa Cather. Gus had never read it, but it was all he could do not to snatch the book from her hands.

With a smile and a nod, seemingly oblivious to Gus's tumult, Diana thanked the old man, then held out her hand for *Walden* and put their new books in her pack.

The encounter with the Book Man, as they'd immediately started calling him, gave Diana a foundation on which to stand here at the trading post, and she relaxed enough that Gus could as well. Once they were beyond the reach of the old man's powerful presence, Gus felt normal himself. The place still gave him the creeps, and he could sense that things were happening around them they all needed to be cautious of, but now, Diana was strong at his side, using her keen eye, helping him stand watch.

In addition to thread and yarn, Eve and Weezie traded for empty jars for preserves, and sacks of dried plants not native to the Shire that they could use to make dyes. They found someone trading jars of honey, too, and that wiped them out of goods to barter.

"Oh! Look!" Weezie said just as they were about to head back to the carts. She gestured wildly and took off across the wide lane between the stalls, through the throng of people, and Gus, Diana, and Eve shot out after her.

Gus drew up short, hard and fast, when he saw where she was. A young man in a ratty beanie sat behind a long, rickety table. Arrayed over the table and hung from wire above it were musical instruments. Mostly ocarinas, recorders, and other kinds of pipes. But there were a few hand drums, and a dented and badly scratched Spanish-style guitar, and a ukulele — and a violin. It had no strings, and it was a cheap piece, but it was intact and in decent shape.

He had nothing to trade for it, but he had to ask. With the words the Book Man had read still echoing against his skull, he had no choice. "You got strings for the fiddle? A bow?"

The kid smiled and showed a mouth with more gaps than teeth. He rose from his folding chair and pulled a decaying cardboard box forward. From it, he pulled a bow, almost all of its hair intact, and two unopened packages of full strings.

"Jesus," Gus gasped. His heart literally hurt.

Diana grabbed the handle of her axe, and the kid jumped back as she pulled it free of its holster. "Whoa, lady!"

"Di, no!" Gus yelled at the same time.

But she held it out on her hands. "For the violin, the bow, the strings, and everything else you have for a violin. A case. We need a case, too."

Maybe she hadn't been oblivious to his reaction to Willa Cather's words. But she couldn't trade her axe, not for that, or anything else. "No, honey." He reached to pull her back, but she stepped out of his range.

She turned and smiled at him. "Doug will make me a new one. You miss playing, and I miss listening."

Still staring warily at the axe, the kid said, "Don't got a case for it. Got a gig bag for the uke. 'Bout the right size."

With a look, Diana asked if that was good enough, and Gus—his pulse pounding, his eyes burning—nodded. "That'll work. You got a rosin cake?"

"It's dried to shit, but yeah."

He could get it soft again. "Diana, are you sure?"

She pushed the axe toward the kid, and he took it from her hands. Hefting it, he grinned a triumphant grin, like he'd gotten over on them all.

But he hadn't. It was maybe the best trade they'd made all day.

Still, he wanted to get that grin off the kid's face. Weezie was fondling a daintily painted ocarina. Gus turned back to the dude in the beanie. "Throw in the ocarina, kid, and it's a trade."

"GUS? GUS!"

They'd been loading up the carts, preparing to get the hell out of the chaos and on their way home before the sun set. The trades had been good, and no one had gotten hurt. Gus's suspicions might not have been unfounded, but neither were they confirmed. They'd steered clear of the brothel, and they'd eaten their own food. They'd kept each other safe.

And on that cart, tucked safely in among soft goods, was a violin. Maybe this one, the universe would let him keep.

Howard had even suggested he could try to make strings for it, so he'd still be able to play when those he had broke.

Hearing his name called from a distance, when all of his people were close by, Gus felt his heart kick warily. Who knew him here? Was the voice familiar? He'd been too surprised to notice.

He turned, stepping in front of Diana with barely a thought, and saw Orion walking toward him. It had been two years since he'd walked away from the warehouse with Orion's katana on his back.

The katana that was on his back now.

"Hey, bruh!" Orion had a thick new scar across his face, from just under his left eye, across his nose, to just under his right ear. It was paler than his dark skin, and shiny. He held out his arms to Gus.

"Holy shit!" Gus welcomed the hug. "How are you? You still with Carver?"

"Carver and Talia, Alan, and me. We lost Loni the winter you left, and Jarod in Utah last summer. Mara and her kids split off from us on the coast, went north. But we picked up a few since you split, too."

"The coast?" Brendan stepped up. "The west coast?"

"Orion, this is Brendan." He caught Diana's hand. "And this is Diana." With a sweep of his arms, he indicated the rest. "These are all my friends."

"You in a sub, man?" Orion smiled. "*You?*"

He shrugged. "Found the right one. Miss you guys, though. I shouldn't've left like I did."

Orion's eyes took in the group around him, then settled on Diana. "Looks like it worked out for you. This world, that's what you gotta find."

"You've been to the west coast?" Brendan asked again. "San Francisco?"

"Yeah. We're coming back from there."

Gus let his mouth drop open. "You left? That was the destination." It was still a place he wondered about, when he was awake in the night. "It was supposed to be where things were better."

All the rumors had indicated that San Francisco, so close to Silicon Valley and a hotbed of innovation and engineering, was the cradle of the new world. For years, Gus had heard nothing else but that. Of course, he'd heard nothing at all for nearly two years.

Orion shook his head. "It's not what we thought. They took a hard hit of radiation from Asia, I guess. It's pretty bleak. And Sacramento's a hellscape. Wildfire took the whole valley out some time back. There's nothing west of the mountains worth shit."

"Shit."

"Yeah."

"So ... where are you headed?" Could he invite them to the Shire? Not without a vote, and it was a long trip back the way they'd come to have them turned away when they got there. Probably not a good idea.

"Back to Utah. There's a place, people say. Started out as a sub, but people are talking about it like Eden or something."

"That's how we talked about San Francisco, too." Rumors were obviously meaningless, and anyway, Adam and Eve got kicked out of Eden.

"I know. But it's a place to head toward." Orion grinned. "New Aurora, they call it."

"Aurora? Is there an Old Aurora?"

"Where've you been, bruh? Everybody's calling the Sunstorm Aurora Terminus these days. They say New Aurora started an information campaign, sending people out to spread the word—like they're trying to sort shit out, finally. I don't know what Aurora Terminus means, but there's a calendar and everything. There's people here passing them out."

"It's Latin," Diana said. "Terminus is 'edge'—or 'end,' I guess. Aurora is what those kind of lights are—aurora borealis, aurora australis. Aurora terminus—the lights at the end. I think that's what it means."

He gave her a cordial nod. "Well, that makes sense, then. Anyway, if you care about all that, they say we're living in the year 7 AAT. Anno Aurora Terminus."

"He's right, Gus," Howard said, coming up to stand between Gus and Brendan. "Lotta talk today about this New Aurora place." Howard's sour expression suggested some skepticism on his part.

Gus could only stare as his mind whirred and he tried to assimilate this knowledge. Well, Howard had said that they got their news here at the trading post. This news recalibrated the whole world.

"Hey," Orion said, casting a sidelong eye up at the mountain that was Howard, and then back at Gus. "You want to grab a drink or something? The moonshine tastes like otter piss, but it's free. We can catch up."

Half the Shire stood nearby, watching him and Orion converse. Diana held his hand. He wanted to spend more time with his old friend. He wanted to see Carver and Talia, and Alan.

But he was of the Shire now, and his path diverged from Orion and the others yet again. "I can't. We gotta get on the road. Long hike home. But damn, it's good to see you. Give my regards to the others."

Orion tilted his head, accepting his refusal. "Good to see you, too. You ever end up heading back eastward, look up this place. It's in the Utah mountains toward the south of the state. Supposed to be way above sea level, higher than almost anywhere else in the country."

Well, Gus could believe that a mountain retreat would rebirth the world. One had rebirthed his.

"I will." He remembered the sword on his back and shrugged the holster off. "Hey. This is yours. I thank you for its use. It kept me safe in a lot of scrapes."

Orion put up his hands. "Nah, bruh. It's yours. Just think of me when you use it." He grinned. "Don't think of me too much."

They embraced again, and Orion gave Diana a brisk nod of a bow. "You take care of him, pretty lady."

She smiled. "I try."

To the rest of the Rennies, Orion said, "I'm glad to know my friend's with good folks. Good travels to you." He turned and walked off.

Gus watched until Orion had folded into the still-thick crowd.

Diana circled her arms around his waist and, for the first time that day, she held him, offered him her strength. "I love you."

He lifted her chin on his fingertips and kissed her. "I love you, too. Let's go home."

Twenty-Nine

Gus set the shovel aside and kicked the snow off his boots before he went into the Shire office. Buddy bounded in without any concern for his snowy paws.

The dim after so much sun glinting off the snow rendered him blind for a few minutes. He stood in place with his eyes closed and let the pleasant warmth of the woodstove bring his fingers and toes back to life while the stars faded from his vision.

Laughter wafted on the warm air, and Gus smiled. "Having a good time here in the warm, ladies?" He opened his eyes. Sarah sat near the stove, swaddled in thick layers of blankets, with Buddy's head already in her lap. Diana sat beside her with a book in hers.

"I was just telling Sarah how sexy your pink earmuffs are."

In the eight weeks since their trip to the trading post, winter had come in hard, promising to erase the drought of the year before. And Sarah's illness had come in even harder. The time of her keeping it a secret had passed. It was obviously cancer, and it had obviously metastasized. She'd lost an extreme amount of weight, reduced to dry bones and leathery skin, and she struggled with deep pain.

She'd also lost her sight, as tumors had developed and swelled her eyes inside their sockets. She wore a bandage around her head, lightly infused with eucalyptus, offering her the tiny relief from pain that was available in this world.

But she was stalwart in her good humor. Gus and Diana, and Howard, were the only people she'd let see how weary and hurting, how sad and afraid, she truly was. And they all tried to help her keep up the front she wanted to show.

Gus came into the room and took off the earmuffs in question—fake fur things, holdovers from the old world. "I look *good* in pink."

"I don't doubt it," Sarah said, smiling her still wise and lovely smile.

"Whatcha readin'?" Gus pulled up a stool and sat near the stove, facing the women.

Diana lifted the cover. "*The Lion, the Witch, and the Wardrobe.*"

"Ah. A classic. I loved that when I was a kid. Read all the Chronicles."

"As did I," Sarah said. "It's nice to hear the story again, like the first time, when my mother read it to me."

Diana and Gus locked their eyes for a moment, and shared the melancholy they tried not to let Sarah hear.

But the old woman was no less perceptive without one of her senses. "Don't you two get maudlin. You know it hurts more when I'm sad, and you know I can't stand having to make other people feel better because *I'm* sick. Fuck that."

Gus and Diana barked out the same syllable of laughter. Sarah was a tough broad, but she didn't swear often.

"Sorry, ma'am. Only frivolity, I promise."

"Good. Speaking of which ..."

"Howard and Trevor got it up in the meeting house." They'd put walls around the shelter behind the office and installed a stove. In the spring, they could take the walls back down. "Everybody's putting up the decorations."

The people of the Shire had lost track of the calendar, just like everybody else. They hadn't celebrated a holiday or a birthday since the end of the world. But Amy had come back from Carson City with a perpetual calendar, marked with the symbol of New Aurora. There'd been people handing them out around the trading post.

Gus had been so intent on keeping Diana and Eve and Weezie safe, so busy seeking out the dangerous, that he'd missed many of the harmless or helpful things available.

Assuming, of course, that New Aurora was either harmless or helpful.

As Orion had said, New Aurora had started the calendar anew, but it had done so in an ancient way, using the cycles of the moon as their guide. This calendar had thirteen months of twenty-eight days each. They'd worked their way back to the day of the Aurora and begun the calendar there: Day 1, Year 1. Someone must have been keeping count.

This calendar wasn't based on any religion or history or belief except the movement of the celestial bodies: sun, moon, stars.

If anyone had cared to pay close enough attention, they could have pinpointed the winter solstice without the aid of a calendar. Civilizations had celebrated the longest night and the longest day well before anyone kept time so rigidly. But no one had cared enough to hone the world to that point again.

But knowing that other people, in other places, recognized the same time had somehow made the time worth celebrating. It was a connection to the world beyond their fence. A realization that there *was* a world beyond the fence — a world that deserved to exist.

Sarah wanted a last Christmas. They weren't exchanging gifts, but on this day of the winter solstice, according to the perpetual calendar that now sat on the cracked surface of the old motel desk, there was a tree festooned with decorations, a warm fire, a good feast, and family.

"I want to watch," Sarah said, and Gus and Diana caught a glance again. "You know what I mean!" she added, huffing her impatience. "I want to be part of it."

Diana stood. "You got it. Let's get you bundled up, and I'll finish this chapter later."

They helped her into her coat while she sat in her chair, and they wrapped her back up in blankets. When Diana helped her to her feet, she flinched and grunted with sharp pain. Gus swept her up in his arms and carried her out into the vivid bright of a mountain winter afternoon.

"Oh, it smells wonderful!" Sarah's grin beamed youth and health back into her wizened face. Gus squeezed her hand. It did smell good—the tree was fresh cut just hours before, and the balsam scent, deepened by the warmth of the room, curled around every head, settled into every corner. Soon, the scent of roast goose, the bounty of a recent hunt, and potatoes and bread and acorn honey cake and pumpkin pie would compete with the aroma of the tree, but that mélange was what the day should smell like. It made Gus's belly rumble and his heart ache with nostalgia.

Diana crouched at Sarah's side and described all that there was to see. Gus listened and followed along, seeing the room as Diana described it, as Sarah had to imagine it.

The tree was festooned with knitted garland and strings of berries and pinecones. Pine boughs were nailed to the rafters and scattered prettily over the tables. Each table had tallow candles in metal bowls. The sun would set soon, and the glow of those candles—not much different from the candle glow of every night, and yet entirely different, too—would add a reverential air to the space.

Gus remembered performing Christmas programs with the orchestra, the beautiful, sorrowful, spiritual music, the flicker of electric candles after the house lights went down, the doubly deep sense of awe among musicians and audience alike. He wasn't a believer, but at Christmas he'd always come close.

The Shire's only healthy post-Aurora girl, Bethany, now just old enough to toddle, laughed and clapped her hands as she stared up at the pretty tree. Sarah heard that joyful sound and clapped her hands as well.

She reached again for Gus's hand and caught his sleeve. Giving it a tug until he leaned close, she asked, "Do you have your fiddle close?"

"I do. I thought I'd play a little after dinner."

"Can you play something now?"

"For you? Anything."

He patted her hand and went to take his fiddle from its case, tested the tuning, and came right back.

"Anything special in mind?"

Sarah nodded. "Do you know 'The Coventry Carol'?"

It was one of the first pieces he'd ever performed, at a Christmas recital when he was a boy. He'd learned several more complicated arrangements since, but he began to play the simplest one.

By the second bar, a room that had bustled with people had gone quiet. Though there was no food yet served, people began to sit. It wasn't the first time he'd played for his people, but everything about this first holiday in the new world was, apparently to everyone, special.

Sarah began to sing. She didn't have a strong voice, it shifted back and forth from soprano to alto as she sought and missed her pitch, but it was beautiful anyway.

Lully, lullay, thou little tiny child,
Bye bye, lully, lullay.

O sisters too, how may we do
For to preserve this day
This poor youngling for whom we do sing,
'Bye bye, lully, lullay'?

More voices joined Sarah's with each word. By the second stanza, the whole Shire, sitting and standing around Gus and Sarah and their first Yule tree, sang.

It was a sad song, about Herod's dictum to kill all infants, and their mothers' grief, and it was about as deeply religious as Gus could imagine, and yet there was hope in it, too, and more than simply Christian faith. It was about the enduring love of mothers and the strength of family. Gus remembered learning, at Julliard, the history of the song, how it had become an anthem for the people of Coventry during World War II, after the Coventry Cathedral had been bombed. An assertion of their strength and unity. A statement that their world hadn't ended.

When the song was over and the voices went quiet, Gus played a few more notes to a graceful ending. He took his chin off the rest, and the people of the Shire were quiet and still.

Every face was turned to Sarah.

Gus let his forehead drop with a thump onto Diana's shoulder. Their heaving chests pushed against each other as they fought for breath. Her hands left his ass, and she lifted her arms and crossed them behind his head, twisting her fingers into his hair.

When he could take a full inhale, he flexed his hips, meaning to pull from her, but she clamped her legs around him. "Don't go. I'm not ready."

He kissed the slick, hot skin of her shoulder and let his body rest again on hers. "I love you."

"And I you." She brushed her cheek over his, caressing herself with his beard. "Do you feel better?"

"I always feel better with you."

But he knew why she'd asked. The solstice celebration had been beautiful and bittersweet, but when it was over, he'd realized something he hadn't seen coming: Sarah had passed her torch. Her insistence on the celebration had been more than a wistful desire for a last Christmas before she died. It was that, certainly. But it was also the first celebration of a world she was leaving. Today, the Shire had acknowledged that. Today, she had stopped leading them.

She'd said goodbye, in a way, tonight. And it fucking hurt.

He still didn't feel ready, but he knew it was time. That hurt, too.

It had made him needy and a little wild, once they'd been alone. But Diana had known what he needed and had given him everything. As always.

Rising onto his elbows, he brushed her golden hair back from her sea-blue eyes. Their cabin was dark, but he didn't need light to know her colors, her beauty, her sweetness, her steel. "I can't do this without you."

She shook her head. "You can, but you won't ever have to. I live with you."

"And I with you."

Lifting her head, she pressed her lips to his, then dropped back with a smile. "Sarah told me something today."

"Yeah?" He pulled from her and turned to his back, bringing her with him.

She settled in the crook of his arm, resting her head on Mudge. "We were talking about New Aurora and what it might be like."

"She thinks we should send a party out to find it."

Her head moved on his chest, nodding. "She said that to me, too. But that's for later. We can't do anything until spring, anyway. We can decide then if we care what's happening out there."

Gus smiled and kissed her head. He knew how she would vote. The woman who'd run from people on the very day of the apocalypse had no strong impulse to find more of them.

He felt much the same. But maybe they did need to. Contact with the world had brought them good things as well as bad. They'd had a holiday together because of that calendar, when in isolation they'd simply let celebrations like that fade away.

"No," Diana went on. "It wasn't about that. It was about the calendar. Anno Aurora Terminus. I said we were in the 'the seventh year after the lights at the end,' and she corrected me. She thinks I have the translation wrong — or that there's a better one, at least."

"What'd she say it means?"

She propped herself up on her elbow and smiled down at him. There was enough moonlight in the clear sky, through the bare window beside their bed, that he could see the lift of her cheeks.

"She said 'aurora' means 'dawn.' I'd forgotten that. Aurora Terminus means the Dawn at the End."

Thirty

Epilogue

Gus lifted his chin from the rest and lowered his fiddle and his bow, letting both dangle at his sides. The voices of the Shire, all around him, had already finished singing and gone silent. They stood and stared at the oblong mound of fresh dark earth, and no one made a sound.

All that was left of the deep winter snows were drifts against tree trunks, stretching long, wrinkled fingers, dotted with black dirt, brown pine needles, and grey leaves, out to the graves. The ground under their feet still gave gently under their weight, the sodden earth softening each step they'd made to this place.

Sarah's was the thirty-sixth grave in the Shire's little yard. She rested beside Darlene, whom they'd lost not long after the solstice. Each grave was marked with a carved post. Not a cross, not a stone. A carved post, showing the name of the soul who'd moved on. For Darlene, there was a date as well.

Howard stood at the head of the grave, a hammer and Sarah's marker in his hand. Hers was carved with a date, too.

According to the New Aurora calendar, this was the ninth day of the first month of the eighth year AAT.

Aurora Terminus. The Dawn at the End.

Beside him, Diana held out her hand. Gus moved his fiddle over, holding its neck with the same hand that gripped the bow. He hooked his fingers with hers and brought her close.

Still, the people of the Shire didn't move or speak. They circled Sarah's grave, clasped their hands, and bowed their heads. Howard held the marker and hammer and bowed his.

Gus knew that they waited for him to speak. He'd been expecting to; he'd tried to prepare words to say. But what words were sufficient to bid farewell to a woman who had been mother to them all and midwife to this place they loved?

No words. And Sarah would have been impatient with a long eulogy. She'd wanted to be sung off to her rest, and they had done so. They had said goodbye, and there was nothing more to say. Not here. This place deserved quiet.

Holding Diana's hand, with Buddy at his other side, Gus turned without another word and stepped away from Sarah's grave. The rest of the people of the Shire, Sarah's people, and now his, followed. They walked together back into the center of the Shire, back to their world and their routines.

He walked to the meeting house, still closed up against a receding winter, and went in, and his people followed. They sat together, facing him, waiting to hear what he would say.

He stood and took a deep breath. "We've all been quiet since Sarah passed because we all know there aren't words to say how much she meant, or how she'll be missed. She made this place a family. Those few of us who came later, she made the way wide so we could find our place here. She was a mother and a friend to everyone. And I think that says all that needs to be said or that she'd want to be said. But when she told me she was sick, she told me how she wanted to die — on her terms. She wanted to be laid down with her friends, and she wanted to be sung off to her rest. She died on her terms. We've done as she asked."

A gust of emotion blew at the back of his throat, and he paused, waiting for calm to settle back into place. Diana, sitting at his side, slid her hand around his. He felt her thumb brush over his skin, a soothing, strengthening touch.

Like a mother bird ready to push her chicks out of their nest, Sarah had wanted Gus to send a party out to see if New Aurora was what they'd heard it might be. Just to see if the end of the world was over.

Gus wasn't sure it was the right call. There'd been a time, not long ago, when he would have fought hard for the mission, insisted that they needed to know if the world was ready to move on. He would have argued that they couldn't risk being left behind.

But now, he wasn't so sure. All they knew of New Aurora was buzz from a trading post full of strangers. It was too much a rumor, too much a fantasy. A wooden calendar didn't change the truth of human nature, or the obstacles humanity faced. If there was truly a New Aurora, it was no more yet than an experiment. Maybe the Shire should wait until this 'new dawn' had become a true day.

They could stay inside their walls, in the world that Sarah had made strong and that Gus, leading the others, had made safe. If the modern world was, in fact, reborn, the people of the Shire could wait and let it come to them. Maybe they should.

Here in the Shire, they'd already had their dawn. Their apocalypse had already ended. The world they wanted was here. It was simple, and it was pure, uncorrupted by the artificial needs of a world that had died of its reliance on convenience.

Or maybe they should be a part of the rise of a new world. Maybe Aidan should take his light bulbs and his hand cranks and offer his invention to someone who could make more of it than a few minutes of golden glow. Maybe it was time.

Maybe it was time for someone else. Aidan was young. Weezie and Eve, and Chloe. Carl and Ellis. Sophia. None of them was yet twenty. Maybe *they* were the new generation that would build the foundation on which the world could rise. They had not lost so much in the Aurora that the loss had shaped them. They were growing to adulthood in this world. Maybe they needed to move through it and see it for what it was.

Those who'd lived fully in the old world, maybe they were too much of it yet to know what should rise from its end.

Diana's anxieties and suspicions of people had been entrenched even before the Aurora, and her experience of the world after had set them in stone. She wanted nothing that they didn't have within the Shire fence.

For Gus's part, he'd seen all he wanted to see of the world. He couldn't imagine what might compel him to wander in it again. He had all he'd ever searched for right here. The journey he'd taken had shown him that truth.

But what he wanted didn't factor in this decision. What was right for the Shire was the only factor, and that wasn't his call to make.

With another deep breath, he addressed his community, his family, again. "Winter is over. It's time to make a decision about New Aurora. We know what Sarah wanted. She thought it was time to leave the nest. She might be right, but I don't think we can make this call quickly. We need to think hard about why we'd go and who we'd send, we need to think about what we can risk, and what we have to keep safe. For the past few months, we've been talking about it like the Emerald City. It's time to shake off that fantastic thinking. Truth is, we don't know anything about it. What we know is us. We know each other, we know the Shire. We trust in that."

He looked around at all the people who followed him, who trusted him to keep them strong and well and safe, just as they'd trusted Sarah.

Together, they would make the right call.

He sat down. "So let's talk."

TERMINUS

About the Author

S.E. Fanetti is a native Midwesterner transplanted to
Northern California,
where she awaits the end of the world with her husband,
youngest son, and assorted cats.

Find her online at:

Website: https://sefanetti.wordpress.com/
Facebook: https://www.facebook.com/sefanetti/
Twitter: @authorsefanetti
Email: authorsusanfanetti@gmail.com

Made in the USA
Monee, IL
13 August 2022